Property of the
Sutten Mountain Book Exchange.

If found please return to

_____

Chase
OUR
FOREVER

KAT SINGLETON

ISBN: 978-1-958292-16-7

Cover Design by Ashlee O'Brien with Ashes & Vellichor

Cover Photograph by Melanie Napier

Developmental Edit by Salma R.

Edited by Sandra Dee with One Love Editing

Proofreading by Holly at Bird and Bear Editorial Services and Alexandra Cowell

Formatted by Kat Singleton

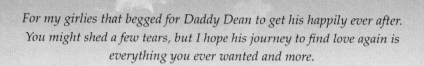

For my girlies that begged for Daddy Dean to get his happily ever after. You might shed a few tears, but I hope his journey to find love again is everything you ever wanted and more.

Playlist

Forever - Noah Kahan
Labyrinth - Taylor Swift
When The Stars Go Blue - Tim McGraw
Golden Hour - Kacey Musgraves
Grow as We Go - Ben Platt
Can't Help Falling in Love - Haley Reinhart
Porch Swing Angel - Muscadine Bloodline
Sun to Me - Zach Bryan
Guilty as Sin? - Taylor Swift
The Only Exception - Paramore
Forever And For Always - Shania Twain
You Are The Reason - Calum Scott
Apple Pie - Lizzy McAlpine
In Case You Didn't Know - Brett Young
The Way She Loves Me - Cody Johnson
If You Love Her - Forest Blakk

Author's Note

Chase Our Forever is a small-town, grumpy x sunshine, single dad x nanny romance. It is full of moments that'll make you swoon, cry, and blush. I hope that you love Dean and Liv as much as I do. This is the third and final book in a series of interconnected standalones set in the fictional town of Sutten Mountain.

Chase Our Forever contains mature content that may not be suitable for all audiences. Please go to <u>authorkatsingleton.-</u><u>com/content-warnings</u> for a list of content warnings for the book.

Prologue
DEAN

My eyes sting as I clutch my newborn daughter in my arms. Voices echo from all around me, but I can't make out anything anyone is saying. All I know is Selena is dead. The woman I fell in love with as a teenager is gone—taken far too soon by someone speeding and not paying attention to the road.

My entire body shakes with sobs as I hold our baby to my chest. Clara's barely two months old. She won't even remember her mother. She won't ever have the chance to know the incredible human who gave birth to her.

Selena won't get to see Clara on her first day of kindergarten. Or kiss her first scraped knee. Or watch her daughter graduate from the high school where we first met. She's going to miss out on so many things, and it's a devastating realization I can't come to terms with.

More words come from my family members who surround me, but I still can't make out a single thing they're saying. My mind is elsewhere, thinking of how I'm going to raise our daughter on my own.

Since the moment I met Selena at fourteen, I knew I was in love. I barely remember my life before her. We'd made so many plans together. Plans that have now been ripped away from us in a cruel twist of fate.

"I'm so sorry," I mumble, holding Clara to my chest. Her tiny little lips are pursed as she sleeps peacefully. She has no idea her entire world has changed from only a few hours ago when Selena kissed both of us goodbye before driving into the city to go shopping.

Someone places a hand on my back, but I don't even bother to check who it is. I can't bring myself to look at anyone but my daughter.

"It should've been me," I whisper. My throat feels raw from my earlier screams when I got the call. Or maybe it's from the sobs that have ricocheted through me since the moment I found out about the death of my wife. "God, why wasn't it me?" I croak.

Selena had asked me to go into the city to grab some things we needed for the house we'd just built together. I'd agreed to do it but then realized it might be good for her to get away for a few hours. Clara hasn't been sleeping well recently, and I just wanted to give my wife some time to herself. "It's all my fault." My words come out a jumbled mess with the sob that overtakes my body.

The choking sound of my cries, or the way my entire body trembles, wakes Clara up. She begins to wiggle in my grasp as her tiny eyes open and close.

I watch her, my entire world blurry except for the little girl in my arms. Selena is gone, and I don't know how I'm going to live without her. But I don't have a choice. I have to, for our daughter.

I close my eyes for a moment as grief washes over me. I don't want to face this life without Selena, but that isn't up to me anymore. From now until my very last breath, I will make sure Clara has the best life. I'll do everything I can to make sure her life is full of joy. I have to step up and be better. Become the best father I can possibly be to make up for the fact that Clara will never know her mother.

Taking a deep breath, I open my eyes and look down at Clara. It feels like my heart has been ripped from my body and discarded somewhere far away, but I have to find a way to keep going. Nothing matters besides my newborn daughter wiggling in my arms.

"I'll do my best, Selena," I promise in a whisper, hoping that maybe there is an afterlife where she can hear me.

Tears stream down my face. I'm not okay. I know it'll be a long time before I'm ever anything close to okay again, but I'll pretend for the little girl in my arms.

I take a deep breath, trying to stop my body from shaking. The adrenaline from the news is slowly wearing off, leaving nothing but a devastating numbness in its wake.

Maybe this is my mind's way of protecting me from grief completely overtaking me. It knows I can't break down. That I can't give in to the pain ripping me apart.

Clara coos in my arms, her tiny little body squirming. Her head moves back and forth, letting me know she's hungry. My mind flashes to every time Selena and I laughed over Clara's disgruntled protests and squirms when she felt like she hadn't been fed fast enough.

That small moment sends me into a spiral because Clara's been exclusively breastfed. We only have two bottles in the fridge that Selena left before she went shopping. That's all there is left. My daughter doesn't have her mother to feed her, the person who knew how to comfort her perfectly. My wife knew what our daughter needed just by the sounds she made.

But Selena's gone now.

I take another deep breath, forcing the grief to the furthest depths of my mind. When I'm alone, I can fall back to my knees and mourn the woman I thought I'd spend forever with.

Right now, my daughter needs me—and I need her.

I eventually bring myself to look at my surroundings and my eyes meet my mother's, who's standing next to me. Hers are red and swollen; I'm sure mine are the same.

I open my mouth to speak, but nothing comes out. I close my

eyes for a moment as I swallow, trying to bring moisture to my mouth so I can form words.

"Formula," I croak, my voice still coming out rough and gritty. "We need formula."

My mother nods, her shoulders shaking with an impending sob as if she's understanding the weight of my words. We need formula because Selena is gone.

And it's the cruelest fate that now all of us have to find a way to live with.

Chapter 1
LIV
three years later

THE SUN IS WARM ON MY FACE AS I GUIDE MY CAR DOWN THE winding mountain road, no other car in sight on the narrow lane. The wind blowing through my open windows rolls over me, and I adjust the baseball hat I'd picked up at a random gas station on my head. It does nothing to tame the long tendrils of my hair. They whip in every direction.

I smile to myself, loving the chill in the air. I'm used to humid heat and sticky air, so the coldness that whips against my cheeks is a welcome feeling.

For the first time in my life, I feel free. I've been on the road for days, and I don't know what's next for me or where I'm at, but none of that matters. The only thing that does is that I've escaped the clutches of my past. I get to start over, and I've never been more excited about having a blank slate.

The intense growling of my stomach pulls me from my thoughts, reminding me I didn't eat breakfast. I woke up this morning in a sketchy motel in a town I don't even remember the name of, and when I went to their vending machine to grab something to eat, the only thing they had were strawberry Pop-Tarts. I'd spent too much of my life living off stale strawberry Pop-Tarts because they were my father's favorite. I'd opted to go hungry instead.

I could've stopped at the small diner next to the motel, but I was too eager to get back on the road. I'd never seen any mountains before, and all I wanted today was to see the sunrise.

It didn't disappoint.

I grew up in Florida, and this trip is the first time I've ever left the state. I didn't have an end destination in mind when I left. Anywhere is better than what I left behind.

Watching the brilliant orange hues illuminating the road ahead of me, I'd never felt so free. I'd felt at peace for the first time in a long time—maybe in forever.

My stomach furiously growls again. I glance over at the passenger seat, where the snacks I've collected along the way sit. There isn't much left. There's a bag of beef jerky that I probably should've thrown away at my last stop because the only thing left in the bag are small crumbs that'll do nothing to curb my hunger. I could eat one of the granola bars I'd packed from home, but they were already expired and stale. I'd rather go hungry than stomach another one of those.

Thankfully, I only have to withstand a few more angry protests from my stomach before I see a sign for a town called Sutten Mountain. I'll be coming up on it in about ten minutes. Hopefully, the town is large enough that I can find some food. I'm starved and would love to stretch my legs a little bit before hitting the road again.

My mind wanders as I follow the signs to the small town. The road becomes a little wider and the trees a little more sparse as I get closer. I drive slowly down the cobblestone street, completely taken aback by how unexpectedly cute this town is. I let my gaze travel from one building to the next, thankful to have found it. I'll definitely be able to find food here and explore for a bit. I'm a little shocked by the number of people walking the sidewalks on either side of the street. It's fairly early in the morning for a weekday, even though I don't know exactly what time it is because the clock in my car is broken, and I forgot to charge my phone last night.

The moment my eyes land on a bright pink sign that reads

Wake and Bake Coffee and Cafe, I know exactly where I want to stop. I quickly slam on my brakes and yank the steering wheel to the right to snag a parking spot in front of a dark building right next to the cafe.

I roll up my windows and grab my purse, anxious to finally eat something today. I pretty much skip to the door of the cafe, already confident that I'm about to have *the* best baked good of my life just by the smell.

A bell chimes above me as I open the door and take in my surroundings. About half of the tables are filled with people enjoying a coffee or a treat, but I'm relieved to see some empty tables and booths. I'll be able to find somewhere to sit and hang out for a little bit. There's even a section on the other side of the space that has art on display, which I definitely want to check out while I'm here.

"Welcome to Wake and Bake!" a redhead says from behind the pink counter, pulling my attention from my perusing. She's got a wide smile on her face, seeming way more chipper than I expected for this early in the morning.

"Hi," I respond, stopping in front of the display case filled to the brim with assorted baked goods. My mouth salivates as my eyes roam over my options. I don't have enough money to buy much, but maybe I'll splurge and get a couple of pastries with a coffee and only get cheap gas station food for the rest of the day. I'll find a way to scrape enough pennies together so I can get whatever I want from here. It all looks too good not to.

I lick my lips, trying to decide if I want sweet or savory. Maybe I need to do both.

"First time here?" the girl behind the counter asks, the wide smile still on her lips.

"Is it that obvious that I'm an outsider?"

This makes her laugh. She shrugs apologetically. "I work almost every morning here. I could probably list off every person who lives in this town if you gave me enough time." She pauses for a moment, her eyes drifting over my body. "Also, tourists don't *typically* wear jean shorts and a tank top in the middle of fall. If anything, they come dressed a little too warm for the season. So, I'm guessing you're passing through?"

I think over her words for a minute, pulling my eyes from her and looking at the food again. "I'm not sure," I mutter. She seems a few years younger than me, but I don't feel like admitting to her how much of a mess my life is right now. Or that I have no idea what cities I'm passing through and where I'll choose to stay. For now, I'll just settle on making a decision on what food I want to eat.

"Well, glad you stopped by Wake and Bake. It's your lucky day. The owner, Pippa, has made some of her most popular recipes, even though, most of the time, she saves them for the weekend."

I smile, wondering which of these are the crowd favorites. My bet is that one of the most popular has to be the cinnamon roll that is bigger than my head. "What do you recommend I get?"

She claps her hands together enthusiastically as if she was just waiting for me to ask that. "I'm so happy you asked," she answers excitedly. "You can't go wrong with the pumpkin cinnamon roll. I know pumpkin in the fall is entirely cliché, but this one doesn't count. Trust me."

I nod, loving how easy it is to talk to her. I look at her name tag, finding out her name is Lexi. "Okay, I'm trusting you, Lexi."

"If you're hungry, I'd also recommend the parmesan and sausage croissant. It's delicious, and I have one almost every morning."

"I'll take one of those, too." I scan the cabinet full of food, trying to decide what else I want. Everything looks delicious. If I didn't have to save my money until I land somewhere and find a job, I think I'd buy one of everything so I could try it all. "And maybe one of the apple turnovers, and that's going to be it for right now."

Lexi nods, looking away from me to type some things on the iPad in front of her. "Would you like a coffee at all?"

I'm nervous about what the cost will be of the items I've already selected, but I'm exhausted from getting up so early. A coffee would be amazing, especially since I want to sit here and hang out for a bit. "I'd love a coffee."

"Perfect. What can I make you?"

I anxiously chew on my lips as I look at the bright pink board behind her. I have no idea the difference between a latte and a macchiato. I've drunk coffee since I was fifteen, but it was only because I needed to find a way to be able to handle going to school full-time and working until ten each night. Besides, the only option for coffee I had was instant coffee that tasted disgusting but got the job done.

"Ummm...surprise me?" A nervous laugh escapes me. I must look like such a mess to her. If only she knew just how much of a mess I *actually* was.

Luckily, Lexi doesn't seem thrown off by my lack of a go-to coffee order. If anything, she looks excited at the idea of surprising me. "I love surprises. Just tell me if you'd rather have hot or iced?"

I think about it for a moment. "Let's do hot."

"Is all of this for here or to go?"

"For here. Is it okay if I stay awhile?"

"Please do. Pippa should be in soon, and you *have* to meet her."

I give her a small nod and try not to flinch when Lexi tells me the price of my food and coffee. The total is close to what I used to spend on groceries for myself for the week, but I try not to dwell on it. Soon, I'll find where I want to start building a new life for myself, and I'll get a job. I've spent ages saving money to get by on my trip. This one little splurge isn't going to clear everything I've saved up, but my heart does race a little when I open my wallet and hand over the cash.

"You're all set. If you want to go find a spot to sit, I'll get you your food and coffee as soon as they're ready."

I give her a smile, tucking some of the extra bills she gave me into the tip jar before turning to look at the cafe. It's one of the most warm and inviting places I've ever been to. Everywhere you look, you see pink, but in a cute kind of way that makes you feel cheerful. The only other colors in the space are from the opposite side of the business where the art's on display.

There's a booth tucked into the corner of the space that catches my eye, and I walk over to it. It's the perfect spot for me to enjoy my food and coffee because it gives me a view of the entire cafe. I have no phone and only a book I found in a Little Free Library at one of my stops. It's a fantasy romance with tattered pages and a faded cover. The title is barely legible at this point, but it doesn't matter. I'm having the best time sneaking in more reading time any spare moment I can.

Sliding into the seat, I set my old and worn bag next to me and take a deep breath. My eyes scan the small little cafe as a realization settles over me.

I've been on the road for a few days now, and I've only wanted to stop long enough to eat or sleep. Nothing called to me that made me feel the urge to stay any longer than needed. But something about this town is different. I can't put my finger on what it is, but all I know is I think I might want to stay here longer than a few hours.

Chapter 2
LIV

I'M LOST IN BETWEEN THE PAGES OF MY BOOK WHEN A FLASH OF RED catches my attention. I look up, finding Lexi taking a seat in the booth across from me.

She wears a wide smile as she slides another coffee across the table in my direction. This is my third coffee of the day—well, it's probably about afternoon now—and each mug she's given me has been different. They look like they've been thrifted, which makes me love this little coffee shop and cafe even more. The one she's slid in front of me now has pink flowers all over it, and it even comes with a matching plate.

"I'm on my break," she explains. "Can I sit with you for a minute?" She lifts her mug to her lips, blowing on the steaming liquid before taking a hesitant sip. Her mug is a pale yellow. The color is so light it almost looks white.

I nod, excited to have some company. Although, not once have I felt lonely since I walked through the doors. Everyone has been so welcoming despite no one here knowing who I am. I don't know if I just scream that I'm a lost soul or if this town is really truly so small they all can spot a wayward traveler easily, but either way, many of them have smiled in my direction or struck up small conversations.

"I told Pippa—my boss—that if she gets a chance, she should come over and meet you. I thought she could when she first came in, but there was something else she had to attend to in the back before mingling. You two need to meet, though. Since you were a huge fan of the pumpkin cinnamon roll and all."

My eyelids flutter closed for a moment, thinking about that cinnamon roll. It might be the best thing I've ever put in my mouth. I'm already wondering if I should just buy another one to be able to experience the delicacy again. If I wasn't so full, I'd already have a second one in front of me.

"It was truly delicious. I'm going to be dreaming about that cinnamon roll for months."

Lexi laughs. "I could eat five a day. They're just *that* good." She reaches across the table and pats the book in front of me. "How's your book? You've been buried in it since you came in."

I shrug. "I've always liked escaping to other worlds, and the book is good. It's been really peaceful to sit here and read it."

Lexi takes a sip of her coffee, her eyes trained on me. Typically, I don't go out of my way to speak to strangers. Back home, talking with unfamiliar people led to nothing but trouble. I have to remind myself that not everyone is as terrible as I imagine them to be, and with this fresh start, I need to be more open to getting to know people. After all, even the best of friends or the most intimate of lovers start out as strangers. "Where are you headed to?" Lexi asks, setting her coffee back down.

I lean back in the booth, unsure how to answer the question. I decide to go for the truth, too tired to come up with a lie. "I don't know."

Her head tilts. "Like you don't remember, or you just don't know?"

"I just don't know," I answer honestly. "I just left home for the first time in my life. It was needed, and I'm enjoying the freedom of just not being *there*. As far as my final destination, I'm not sure where that'll be yet."

Lexi opens her mouth to respond, but her eyes go wide before she can get her words out. "Is that my Clara?" she asks enthusiastically, her eyes trained on the door. She slides out of the booth in an instant, closing the distance to the front door and scooping up a little girl with lopsided pigtails.

The little girl screeches, her arms closing around Lexi's neck. "Lexi!" she screams excitedly.

I miss whatever the little girl—apparently Clara—says to Lexi next because I'm distracted by the flustered, incredibly attractive man who runs through the door after her.

"*Clara!*" he gets out, his tone concerned. "You can't just run ahead of me, honey. I was worried."

The little girl looks between Lexi and the man with an apologetic smile. Her brown eyes focus on the man. "Sorry, Daddy. I wanted to see Lexi."

Lexi keeps ahold of the little girl but turns to face the man—who I've gathered is Clara's dad. "Good morning, Dean."

The man's chiseled cheeks hollow out for a moment before he lets out a rush of air. "Is it really still morning? Clara's been at work with me, and I could've sworn it was afternoon by now."

I shift awkwardly in the booth, wondering if I'm supposed to be eavesdropping on the conversation. They stand so close to the table it's kind of hard not to hear everything they're saying, but I also don't want to come off as creepy.

"You're right. It's afternoon," Lexi responds to Dean. "Have you been at work with your dad all morning?" Lexi wonders, looking at the little girl. She playfully tickles underneath her neck, earning the cutest giggle I've ever heard from the toddler. "How *boring* that must've been for you, Clara. Time to have fun with Lexi."

Lexi props her on her hip and looks back to Dean. "No Sally today?"

He frowns before running a hand over his mouth. "It didn't work out with *Callie*," he emphasizes the name to correct her. "She hasn't been Clara's nanny since last week."

I watch them carefully, wondering where Clara's mother might be. Lexi doesn't ask about her, but a brief glimpse at Dean's ring finger tells me he doesn't wear one.

"Did you find someone new?" Lexi asks, setting the girl down and watching her run to the display case of food.

Dean shakes his head. "I'm trying to. Mom's getting older now; I don't want to ask her to watch Clara every single day. But you know how it is, Lexi. It's hard to find someone I trust with my daughter."

Lexi nods as she sadly looks from Clara to Dean. "Well, Pippa and I can help out today if you have any important meetings to get to."

Dean lets out a breath of relief. I watch the interaction closely, feeling kind of sorry for him. He clearly seems stressed. He runs his hand through the longer hair at the top of his head. His eyes don't leave his daughter as she points to every sweet treat.

"I don't want to impose. She can come with me the rest of the day—I was coming in to get a few items to use to bribe her for the afternoon. You know Pippa's muffins and cupcakes are the key to her heart."

Lexi laughs. "Leave her with us." She looks at me as if she just remembered I was here. "It was slow anyway, so I was just getting to know…" She pauses, her bottom lip jutting out in a small pout as she thinks something over. "Oh my god, I'm terrible. I never got your name."

My eyes go wide as the little girl runs back over and pulls on her dad's pant leg until he picks her up. She mutters something to him, but I can't understand it.

"Oh, me?" I ask awkwardly, with both Lexi and Dean's eyes trained on me. I swallow, knowing Lexi wouldn't be asking anyone else. "My name's Liv."

"Just Liv?" Lexi asks.

I nod. "Just Liv."

"Well, Dean, this is Liv. Liv, this is Dean." Lexi focuses on Dean once again. "Liv and I were just talking about her road trip adventure. I have some time on my hands. Pippa's here, too. We'll watch Clara, and you can go to your meetings. Okay?"

Lexi's tone is matter-of-fact. She seems young, like she

couldn't have graduated high school too long ago, but the confident tone she uses makes her seem far older. Dean swallows, his
pronounced Adam's apple moving up and down his throat. "I
can't ask you to help again."

His answer makes me wonder if this is a normal occurrence.
It sounds like he often needs help with childcare. I also ask
myself if he and Lexi are friends? Maybe family? I want answers
to questions I have no right to know, but I can't help it. I'm naturally curious.

Lexi swats at the air, moving over to the counter. "It's already
been decided," she says, turning her attention to the little girl in
Dean's arms. "What kind of cupcake do you want today, Clara?"

Chapter 3
DEAN

My phone vibrates in the pocket of my jacket, but I ignore it, my attention moving between Clara and Lexi instead. Before I can protest, Pippa comes out from the kitchen. A wide smile breaks out over her face when she notices Clara in my arms.

"Clara!" she calls excitedly. Clara wriggles from my grasp and runs across the cafe to jump into Pippa's arms.

"We were just stopping by to grab some treats before I head to some meetings," I explain, keeping my voice firm to make it clear to Lexi that I'm not going to ask them to watch Clara for me. They've already stepped in far more in the last year than I'm comfortable with. I just have to find a reliable nanny, which has been far harder than I ever expected it to be.

Lexi lifts an eyebrow. "Actually, *wrong*. Dean was going to give us the honor of watching Clara for a little bit while he gets some work done. He's got some meetings to go to that poor Clara would be *so* bored at."

Clara nods as she clings to Pippa. "I be *so* bored, Daddy."

I fight a laugh at the sassy tone of her voice. She absolutely got that from her mother, and I'm already terrified of how it'll manifest in her teenage years.

"Clara, honey, Pippa and Lexi have to work. We'll get treats, and you'll come with me, remember?" I try to raise my voice an octave to convince her that coming to these meetings with me would be fun when, in reality, I know they'll be anything but. *I* don't even want to go to them, but as we're trying to expand the Livingston brand, these meetings are, unfortunately, important.

Pippa carefully sets Clara down. My daughter eagerly runs across the space again and skips right to the booth closest to us—the one with the stranger Lexi introduced us to.

"Are you working?" Clara asks the woman—I'm ashamed I've forgotten her name, even though Lexi just said it. I was too caught up in making sure my tornado of a daughter didn't wreak havoc moments after stepping into Wake and Bake.

The woman in the booth sits up straight, pieces of her blonde hair falling into her face. "Ummm…" she mutters, her eyes wide underneath the brim of her baseball hat as she looks over at Lexi. "No?" The word comes out more as a question instead of an answer.

This makes my daughter smile. Clara climbs into the booth, clearly not having any sort of stranger danger. It's something we'll have to talk about later, but I don't blame her. I know nothing about the woman in the booth, but her timid smile convinces me that, at least for the moment, I don't need to be concerned about my daughter crawling into the booth across from her.

"I sit here, Daddy," Clara announces, folding her chubby little hands in her lap and giving me a smile that tugs right at my heart. However, the way she says Daddy instead of Dada also breaks my heart a little. It's a sad sign she's growing up.

I tuck my hands into my pockets as I let out a deep breath. My phone vibrates again, but yet again, I ignore it, knowing I need to get things settled with Clara first.

"Clara, honey…" I begin, trying to keep my tone soft. My eyes wander over the table and the woman sitting at it. "You can't just sit here. She's busy."

Clara juts her lip out. She adjusts her position until she's on her knees before reaching up to put her elbows on the table and leaning over it. "You busy?" she asks, her focus solely on the woman at the table. I wonder what it is about the stranger that draws Clara to her, but she clearly is set on spending time with her. Maybe it's her calm demeanor or the soft smile that seems to stay on her face.

The woman's eyes go wide as she looks to Lexi for help.

Lexi smiles, clearly finding Clara's antics adorable. "Liv might want to read her book alone, Clara. You can come hang out with me, though."

I sigh, trying to be patient with my daughter but needing to leave to make it to the meeting on time. "Clara, she was enjoying reading her book. Why don't you go pick out a treat before we leave?"

Clara shakes her head, apparently not wanting to listen to Lexi either. "I love books."

The woman—Liv—laughs, the sound so soft I almost miss it. "I don't know if you'd like *this* book."

"I *love* books," Clara repeats. She's not lying. Bedtime drags on every night because of the number of books she wants to read. I could cut her off after two, but I'm a softie when it comes to my daughter, and I can't tell her no when she begs for just one more. Even when that *one* more turns into *three* more.

I take a step forward, holding my hand out for my daughter to take. I make eye contact with Liv and try to relax the muscles of my face a little in what I hope is a look of apology. "I'm sorry." I then focus on Clara. "Time to go pick out our treats."

Clara doesn't budge. If anything, she leans even further onto the table, practically climbing on top of it to get closer to Liv. "I stay right here, Daddy. I want banana bread today."

I sigh, pinching the bridge of my nose between my thumb and forefinger. Before I can say anything, Liv speaks up.

"She can sit here if she wants. I promise not to read her any of the book." She laughs again, and for some reason, the laugh eases the tension in my body ever so slightly. I have no idea who this woman is, or anything about her, but Clara instantly being drawn to her helps ease my mind.

"You're trying to relax," I tell the woman before turning to my daughter. "How about I let you stay here with Pippa and Lexi if you just promise to let Liv enjoy her peace and quiet?"

"Technically, I was already interrupting her quiet," Lexi pipes up, giving a casual shrug.

"I'm not much a fan of the quiet anyway," Liv offers, leaning forward to smile at Clara. She takes her attention from my daughter and directs it to me.

Her big blue eyes crinkle at the edges with her smile. Next to her smile are two of the deepest dimples I've ever seen, and it's hard to miss how beautiful she is. Maybe it's because that smile doesn't leave her face. She's still smiling as she looks from me to Clara. "As long as your dad is okay with it, I don't mind if you keep me company."

"We'll be here the entire time, too, Dean," Pippa interjects, walking up to the table and smiling at Liv. "I'm Pippa, by the way. Owner here at Wake and Bake."

Liv stretches her hand out. "Liv. It's so nice to meet you. If I lived here, I think I'd have to have one of those pumpkin cinnamon rolls every morning."

I anxiously rub my hand over my mouth, trying to figure out if I'm going to continue to attempt to persuade my daughter to leave this booth or if I'm just going to give in. If both Pippa and Lexi are going to be here, too, maybe I can try not to stress about leaving her in the company of a stranger.

I'm so deep in thought, wondering if this is a good idea or not, that I miss some of the conversation happening around me. I tune back in to hear Lexi talking.

"Well, maybe if you feel like it, you can pause here in Sutten for a bit before you keep traveling."

Liv sighs, making me wonder what was said between them when I wasn't paying close attention.

Pippa steps away from the conversation between Lexi and Liv and stops next to me. She smiles, reaching out to give my arm a reassuring pat. "Go to your meetings, Dean. I promise either Lexi or me will have eyes on Clara the entire time."

My cheeks puff out as I let out a rush of air. "Are my nerves that obvious?"

Her smile gets wider. "Your history of firing one nanny after the next shows how little you like the idea of Clara spending the afternoon in the company of a stranger."

I frown. The only reason I've gone through so many nannies is because none of them were suitable for Clara. Either Clara would complain about not liking them, or I'd find out that they weren't a good fit for our family. Clara is stuck with just having me as a parent, and while my family helps out as much as they can, she has to spend a lot of time with a nanny. I need to find the perfect one for her and won't settle for anything less.

My gaze focuses on Clara, who has already sweet-talked her way into sitting right next to Liv in the booth instead of across from her. Liv intently listens to something Clara is telling her, but before I can tune in to their conversation, Pippa starts talking again.

"Let us help you. You're the reason I still own Wake and Bake, so let me return the favor."

I meet her eyes. A year ago, Pippa almost lost the cafe to someone from New York who wanted to buy out the entire block. I only helped by pulling some strings and planting the seed that the business block should go up for auction instead. My family and I were ready to bid high to keep the ownership local, but Pippa's fiancé, Camden Hunter, came in and outbid everyone else.

I tighten my jaw. "I only helped a little."

Pippa rolls her eyes before swatting her apron at me. "You helped a *lot*. Now, let me help you. Let Clara hang out here and be a kid. She doesn't need to be in meetings all afternoon with you."

I nod, tucking my hands in my pockets. I look back at my daughter to find her giggling with both Liv and Lexi. Pippa's right. Clara's little. She doesn't deserve to be locked up in an office with me for hours when she could be having fun. "Okay. But please call me if anything comes up and you need me to come back. If you get busy or—"

Pippa lifts her hands to cut me off. "We aren't going to get too busy, and it's going to be *fine*. I'm not a paid nanny. You can't fire me."

"Want to be a nanny?" I tease, even though my tone is serious.

She shakes her head. "Camden already tells me I've been working too much."

I shrug. "It was worth a shot." There are only a few people I trust Clara with, and Pippa is one of them.

I know there's no way she would ever accept a nanny position or that I would let her, even if I desperately need one. This cafe is her baby, and she's spent the last year renovating the space and expanding. I walk over to the booth and attempt to tighten one of Clara's pigtails. I'm awful at doing her hair, even though I try my best every morning to get it right. I thought with years of practice I'd be getting better, but I'm not. If anything, the more hair she gets, the worse I am at doing it.

"I'm going to go work for a little while. I'll be back in a bit," I tell her, trying not to let the worry show in my tone.

Clara waves, clearly not upset with me leaving at all. "Bye, Daddy."

I pause for a moment, watching her laugh at something Liv whispers in her ear. When I look away, I find Pippa watching me with a knowing smile.

"Go," she says under her breath. "We've got it here."

I'm bad at trusting others. Even worse at asking for help. But still, I go, knowing Clara is in good hands.

Chapter 4
LIV

"So you really have no idea where you're going next?" Pippa asks, her eyes focused on me. Clara squirms in her lap, too busy coloring all over a paper menu to pay attention to our conversation.

"I really have no idea," I respond, folding my arms over my chest. "I do love the mountains here, though. So maybe somewhere like this with mountains." I've been talking on and off with Pippa and Lexi for almost two hours now. We've done different activities to keep Clara entertained, and I can't help but think this is the best afternoon I've had in a long time.

Pippa nods. I really like her. There's no judgment in her features as she mulls over my words. I know it'd be easy for her to tell me it's crazy for me to leave without knowing where I'm going. Or she could easily ask me a million questions about why I'd travel without any destination in mind, but she doesn't do either.

Clara slips off Pippa's lap and comes to my side. She climbs into the booth and right into my lap, making herself at home, even though we only just met. I haven't been around a lot of kids in my life. Mostly because before this trip, all I ever did was work. I waited tables, cleaned hotel rooms, and did anything possible to earn money for myself—and avoid being home.

There wasn't time to be around kids, not that I knew anyone with them anyway.

"Like my butterfly?" Clara asks, pointing to a couple of obscure lines that look nothing like a butterfly.

"I *love* your butterfly," I tell her, turning my head to see if maybe looking at it from a different angle will help me see it better. It doesn't.

Pippa lets out a dramatic sigh. "Hopefully you don't find this creepy, because I don't mean it that way at all, but I kind of wish you were staying in Sutten longer, Liv. I like you." The way she hurriedly gets out the last sentence makes me wonder if most of the time she *doesn't* like people.

"Have you always lived in Sutten?" I ask, changing the subject. The only things I know about this town are this cafe and the things I've learned from Lexi and Pippa.

Pippa smiles, her eyes wandering over to the register where Lexi helps the one other customer in here besides me. "Yes, basically. It's the best place to live. Wouldn't ever want to live anywhere else."

"Really? Have you ever gone anywhere else?" Hopefully she doesn't take my question wrong. I don't mean anything by it. I just can't imagine falling so in love with living somewhere that I'd live there my entire life. For as long as I can remember, all I dreamed about was getting out of Florida. I never wanted to stay —and I never want to go back.

Pippa shakes her head. "Oh, absolutely. I left for college, so I was away from Sutten for a bit. And after college, my best friend lived in Chicago for a long time, so I visited her a lot. My fiancé's from New York and still has work there, so we visit often. I enjoy the city and love going there but definitely couldn't live there. I love seeing what else the world has to offer, but at the end of the day, I can't imagine myself living anywhere but in Sutten. It's home."

I'm quiet for a moment as I let her words sink in. *What's it like to love home so much you'd never want to leave?* Pippa seems to have her life so together. It makes me a little sad, knowing she can't be much older than I am, and she seems to be so sure about the rest of her life. I, on the other hand, can't even answer where I plan to end up at the end of this journey.

"I wish I had more time to get to know Sutten," I mutter, realizing how much I mean the words.

"Why don't you?"

"Why don't I what?"

"Why don't you have more time? From what you've said, it sounds like you're in charge of when and where you're going."

Before I can respond, Clara turns around and pushes a loose strand from her face in the process. The stray hair falls right back in front of her eyes, making her let out an annoyed groan. "Fix my hair for me? Daddy sucks at it."

I try not to laugh. Something tells me she's probably not supposed to use the word *sucks*, but it isn't my place to correct her.

"He tried his best," I tell Clara, scooting back in the booth slightly so I can angle her in front of me well enough to do her hair. My mother wasn't around growing up, and I didn't have anyone to brush my hair or do cute hairstyles on me like the other girls in my class. I had to learn on my own, so although I don't have the most experience with kids, I can do hair.

"Daddy always tries his best. He still bad at it," Clara responds.

My eyes briefly meet Pippa's as we both fight a smile. Gently, I begin to undo the ponytails from Clara's head so I can fix Dean's attempt at pigtails.

"Your dad always tries his best," Pippa tells Clara as Lexi slides into the booth next to her after the other customer walks out the door.

"I know," Clara responds, her tone rather sassy. I brush through her hair with my fingertips. This would be easier if I had a brush, but I make do however I can.

Pippa stares at the toddler affectionately. It's clear she cares for her. So does Lexi. It makes me wonder how much they're in Clara's life and who is maybe missing from hers as well. "Maybe one of these days, your dad won't be so picky and find you a nanny that'll last longer than a week. Then *she* can learn all sorts of fun hairdos for you."

Clara lets out a knowing sigh. The drama seems to be high with her, and I can't imagine she's much older than two or three. "Daddy has trust issues."

This makes both Pippa and Lexi burst out in laughter.

"Where did you even learn that?" Lexi manages to get out.

"Mimi," Clara immediately responds.

I smile. The comment from Clara was incredibly cute, but I think that was because of the exasperated way she talked about her dad. It reminded me of a tiny teenager instead of a toddler.

"Do you want pigtails again?" I ask Clara, missing some of the conversation between Lexi and Pippa that seems to still be about Clara's dad.

"Can you braid? Poppy always has braids. I want braids." It makes my heart sting a little the sad way she talks about another little girl having braids when she doesn't. I remember the feeling all too well. My dad had no idea how to braid. He wouldn't have cared enough to do my hair even if he did know how.

I realize I'm so lost in my thoughts that I've forgotten to answer her. "Yes, I can do braids."

Clara giddily claps her hands, her body wiggling in excitement. "I want braids."

I comb through her hair more with my fingers in an attempt to untangle it enough to do braids. I work at beginning one braid while Pippa and Lexi watch closely.

"Lexi, have you also lived in Sutten your whole life?" I ask. As someone who hates sharing details about my past and personal life, I'm never one to pry into others' lives. But I am curious to know if most of the people who live here have been here since they were young.

Lexi nods. "I have. I used to dream about getting out, but now I'm not so sure."

"Why aren't you so sure?"

Lexi smiles, a wistful look coming over her face. "Because I like knowing everyone in the town. I love listening to the town gossip between all of the old ladies who come in a few times a week. I love that we have the pumpkin festival and the Christmas tree lighting. All the things I didn't like about living here when I was younger are the reasons that I now want to stay."

I secure the end of Clara's first braid and work on starting the next. "You have a festival for pumpkins?"

Pippa nods her head excitedly. "We do. And it's next weekend. I wish you could come to it. I make all kinds of pumpkin-flavored food for the event—including the pumpkin cinnamon rolls."

I want to drool just thinking about her cinnamon rolls. They were *so* good. I just know a whole feast of pumpkin-flavored things would be absolutely delicious. "I'm sad I'll miss it."

Lexi and Pippa share a look before looking at me. "You don't *have* to miss it," Pippa offers. "You could make an extended pit stop here in Sutten. You said you love the mountains and wanted to find a place like Sutten. Why not just choose Sutten?"

I think over her words for a moment. It's true I don't have a destination in mind or even a deadline on when I need to settle down somewhere. But I don't have the funds to stay here for almost two weeks. I have to take into account how expensive it'd be to stay somewhere. I have enough to give me time to travel to find the spot where I'll end up, but not much extra. As much as I love the thought of staying here longer, it just isn't in the cards for me.

I sigh, finishing the end of Clara's other braid. "I'd love to. There's something about this town that just feels…I don't know the right word, but…it feels *right*. But I only saved up so much for my trip. I have to get going fast so I can find a job at the end of this."

Before either of them can respond, the door to the cafe opens. There's a little chime as Clara's dad walks through the door.

"Daddy!" Clara calls, trying to slide out of my lap.

I laugh, trying to fasten the end of the ponytail on her hair as quickly as possible. "Let me finish this real fast," I tell her, trying not to pull on her hair.

She squirms in my lap, clearly wanting to get to her dad and not caring about the braids anymore.

"Done." I let out a sigh of relief before gently grabbing her sides so I can place her safely on the ground.

"Hi, sweetie," Dean says, crouching down and opening his arms wide for Clara. She runs into them immediately.

While Clara wraps her small arms around his neck, he looks over at us, his eyes connecting with mine for a brief moment before moving to Pippa and Lexi. "Did everything go okay?" The tightness in his voice makes his worry obvious.

All of us nod.

"It went great," Pippa offers, looking across the table to me. "I think Clara got Liv here to draw her probably twenty different variations of flowers. Clara also got her fill of sweet treats. I couldn't say no."

Dean shakes his head, lifting his daughter off the ground and standing to his full height.

"Like my braids, Daddy? Liv did them." Clara asks, pushing off his chest slightly as she grabs the end of her braids to show them off.

His nostrils flare as his eyes clash with mine for a brief moment. *Is he mad?* I was just doing what she asked. "I love the braids," he grits out. "But what was wrong with my pigtails?"

Clara looks back at me with a soft smile. She giggles, probably remembering how she'd just insulted her dad's hair skills. She's empathetic enough to not voice her displeasure with the way he does her hair out loud. She shrugs. "One fell out," she lies.

Even though I'm a little anxious that I overstepped by doing her hair, I can't help but smile at her words. I look from Clara to Dean, finding his eyes narrowed right at me.

He pauses for a moment, and I swallow, worried he really is upset that I did Clara's hair. I don't understand why he would be, but I also don't know these people, so maybe it was something I shouldn't have done. Both Lexi and Pippa mentioned he can't keep a nanny, but maybe the reason he seems upset with me over something as small as a hairdo is why he hasn't been able to keep one.

"Thank you," he finally gets out, his voice rougher than I was expecting. "As hard as I try, I can never get her hair just right. I'm sure you made her day by doing this."

I smile even wider, relief flooding over me that he isn't upset. I was just overthinking. "It was nothing."

Pippa leans forward, her palms slapping against the table. "Liv, did you know Dean is looking for a nanny?"

My head cocks to the side. "I think you guys mentioned it. Clara's great—I'm sure you'll find someone," I add awkwardly since I don't think there's much insight I can give into his search for a nanny.

"Liv was *great* with Clara," Lexi pipes up, a wide smile on her face. "And she's in need of a job."

My eyes go wide.

What are they up to?

Chapter 5
DEAN

My eyes travel over the women huddled around the table, wondering what I'm missing. By Liv's wide eyes and her mouth slightly hanging open, I'm guessing she wasn't prepared for Lexi and Pippa to meddle.

"Oh, I've never nannied before," Liv hurriedly gets out, her words jumbling together. "I've worked retail and restaurants. Not kids. Not looking to be a nanny at all."

Lexi narrows her eyes slightly while Pippa takes a deep breath.

Pippa is the one to speak up. "Well, it's clear that where you're lacking in the experience of being a nanny, you make up for with your natural instincts. For the last couple of hours, both Lexi and I saw how great you were with Clara."

Liv shakes her head, her eyes finding mine. Her cheeks get more flushed by the second. "I'm sorry. I promise I didn't put them up to this. I'm not staying in Sutten, and I don't need a job. I'm *so* sorry."

I'm quiet for a moment, trying to figure out why I feel a little let down that she isn't staying in Sutten. I'd have to look over her resume and do a background check before I'd ever consider hiring her as a nanny, but the natural way Clara was drawn to her isn't lost on me.

"No need to apologize. Pippa and Lexi just know how hard it's been for me to find reliable help with Clara."

Liv nods, her shoulders loosening just slightly with a breath of relief.

"You know, you could stay," Pippa pushes, her focus on Liv. "You might find out you really love Sutten, and you did say you didn't know where you'd end up."

Clara wiggles her legs, her way of telling me she wants out of my arms. I set her softly on the ground, wondering how quickly I can get out of here so I can stop being the reason for Pippa and Lexi clearly making Liv uncomfortable.

Liv adjusts the baseball hat on her head, staring at Pippa for a few moments as she thinks over her words. "Even if I became Clara's nanny, and it's a *big* if, considering I don't have the experience I'm sure he's wanting for the care of his child, I don't have a place to live here while working. And I don't really have enough saved up to stay in a hotel."

I can't help but wonder why she's in Sutten and what conversations she had with Pippa and Lexi to make them think she'd stay and take a nannying job. I don't waste time asking. Clara's had to deal with being juggled between one nanny and the next while I tried to find a perfect fit for our family. The last thing I want is to waste time discussing the position with someone who isn't interested in it.

Pippa smiles wide, looking right at me with a twinkle in her eye. "That's okay. Dean has a spare room in that big house of his for his nannies. The position is a live-in one."

A low growl of annoyance comes from my chest in response to Pippa's meddling.

Liv's mouth snaps shut. She's quiet for a moment, her eyes fixed on Pippa, and I wish Pippa hadn't decided to get involved. It's a very Pippa thing to do, so I can't be surprised, but it seems this stranger has no desire to become a nanny.

"Liv, you be my nanny?" Clara pipes up, walking over to Liv

and climbing into her lap as if she's known her for months and didn't just meet her earlier today.

Liv uneasily looks from Clara to me. She loosely puts her arms around Clara, who doesn't seem to notice Liv's stiffness whatsoever. "I'm not sure I'm staying here in Sutten, Clara. I don't know if I can."

I shift on my feet, unsure how to stop this conversation. I don't want Clara to get her hopes up when Liv is making becoming her nanny seem like the last thing she wants to do. I wish Lexi and Pippa hadn't gotten involved. Now I'm going to have to be the bad guy and break it to my daughter that having Liv isn't an option.

"Would you want to?" Lexi speaks up, her tone soft as she focuses on Liv. "If you could get a job and a place to stay, would you want to stay here?"

"I don't know," Liv answers honestly.

Her answer is respectable. I've found that most people lie when under pressure. Yet, she didn't do that, and for some reason, it makes me wish for my daughter's sake that she had plans to stay here longer.

I can't explain it, but I always felt like each of Clara's previous nannies had something about them that seemed off to me. Since I could never put my finger on it, I gave them a shot, only to be proven right later on.

But I'm not getting that from Liv, at least not yet.

"How about this..." I sigh as I reach into the pocket inside my suit jacket. "Clara's with my mother tomorrow morning, and I don't have any meetings set up. I'll be here at Wake and Bake around nine if you want to meet me to talk more about potentially being a nanny." I pull a business card from my wallet and set it down in front of her. "Here's my card if you want to email any references and your resume my way."

Liv hesitates for a moment, but she does end up taking the card from me. She sets it on the table in front of her, her eyes trained on it.

Clara climbs off Liv's lap and runs over to me. "Did she say yes, Daddy?" she asks, pulling on my pant leg. Her attempt to whisper is terrible. There's not a doubt in my mind that everyone heard her.

"Thank you for hanging out with us today, Clara," Pippa interjects, changing the subject.

I give her a curt nod, silently thanking her for doing so before I had to let Clara down, since Liv hasn't said anything.

Clara bounces on her feet, reaching for Pippa and hopping into her lap. "Thank you for the cupcakes. I play again tomorrow?"

"Cupcakes?" I ask with a small laugh.

"It really was only one and a half," Pippa explains, giving me an apologetic smile. "She's too cute, Dean," she continues. "I couldn't say no."

Clara nods triumphantly in Pippa's lap, a smug grin on her face. "Two cupcakes were *so* yummy, Daddy."

I stifle a laugh. I'm shocked she isn't bouncing off the walls from the excess sugar, but she looks happy, and she has me so tightly wrapped around her finger that I can't even scold her for eating two cupcakes before supper.

"We've got to get going, Clara. Daddy needs to get you home and make you dinner before dance class tonight."

"Can I wear my pretty braids to dance?" Clara asks with glee, her tiny hands clapping together.

"Of course you can," I answer, loving the pure joy all over her face. I've always felt guilty taking her to dance classes when I knew all the other girls had mothers who knew how to pull their hair back into buns or give them fancy braids. Clara doesn't have that, and it pains me that I can't do the same for her no matter how many video tutorials on the internet I watch.

It's in the small moments like these that I feel the void of Selena being gone the most. She was an amazing wife, but she was an even better mother, even if she didn't get to be one for long. She would've loved to do Clara's hair, and I hate that it's something I'm not good at.

Liv's been quiet throughout the end of our encounter. I don't know if that's a good or bad thing or why, all of a sudden, I'm wishing this stranger who Clara decided to become best friends with was a local.

I'm incredibly picky when it comes to who watches over my daughter, probably because none of them can even come close to being the mother figure Clara needs in her life. So, if Clara doesn't love who she spends her day with, I fire them.

It's unfortunate that the first person my daughter seems to really be excited about probably isn't an option.

"It was nice meeting you," I tell Liv, forcing a smile. "Thank you for helping out with my daughter. I know it probably wasn't what you were wanting to do when you stopped in here this morning."

She gives me a smile, showing off her dimples. "It was the *perfect* day. Thank you for trusting me."

I nod, not knowing what else to say to her. She has my card and knows where I'll be tomorrow. There's not much else to be said.

My eyes move from Liv to Pippa and Lexi. "As always, thank you to the both of you. It means the world to me that you help with Clara without any hesitation."

They both smile. "Anytime, Dean. She was a blast. Today, she even talked Ms. Rosemary into changing her coffee order. Ms. Rosemary's been ordering the same thing since I started."

I raise my eyebrows in surprise. "Did she now? Clara can be persuasive."

"What's pevasive mean?" Clara asks, completely butchering the word as she wraps her arm around my leg.

"It means you know how to sweet-talk. Now, c'mon. Let's let these girls have some kid-free time."

"But what does sweet-talk mean?" Clara asks, making the girls laugh. This kid is full of questions.

I run my hand over the top of her head before gently guiding her toward the front door. I want to make sure we have enough time before dance to feed her a nutritious meal since it seems like she might've eaten a lot of sugar with the girls. "Let's get home," I tell her, watching her skip in front of me to get the door.

"Bye!" Clara calls out, pressing her back to the door and holding it open as best as she can with her tiny body. "See you later," she adds.

I press my palm into the cold glass of the door, looking over my shoulder one last time. I have no idea if I'll see Liv again, but I can't help acknowledging that a large part of me wishes I will.

Something about her feels right.

Chapter 6
LIV

"PIPPA, YOU DON'T KNOW ME. I CAN'T JUST SLEEP ON YOUR COUCH tonight. What if I'm a serial killer?"

Pippa rolls her eyes as she cleans off a nearby table. I've managed to hang out at Wake and Bake all day, avoiding getting back on the road. When I first came into town early this morning, I thought it'd be a quick stop. I was starving, and it had food. But the longer I'm at Wake and Bake, chatting with various people who stopped by and getting to know Pippa and Lexi, the more I realize I don't want to leave.

Lexi left a while ago, having to go home to help her grandmother take care of her siblings. I've learned a lot about Pippa in the calm between lunch and dinner. I've learned so much about her that I now feel closer to her. I really think, in time, she could become a good friend. She was forthcoming with her entire story, something I should learn to be. Opening Wake and Bake was her dream for as long as she could remember.

I also learned that her family owns a ranch here in Sutten where they do trail rides—something I'd love to do if I end up spending some extra time here. She has a brother, whose name I forgot, but is the one taking over the ranch for her father.

She shared with me that her mother passed not too long ago, but it was touching to hear her speak about the amazing woman she was. I never met my mother; she left me with my father and chose not to be in my life.

Her brother is also engaged to *the* Marigold Evans, the author of *Rewrite Our Story*. I read the first book and fell absolutely in love. I've been waiting to read the second, and I still don't think I've fully wrapped my mind around the fact Pippa's her best friend. Or that her brother is the inspiration behind the book. The thought of getting back on the road makes me feel sad, but I've been planning to leave Florida for years. I thought I'd be on this long trip for weeks before I found somewhere I wanted to stay. But now, I'm only days into the trip and already considering staying—at least for a little while.

"You know, your dimples are far too cute for you to be a serial killer. I listen to true crime all the time. You're not giving me serial killer vibes."

I laugh as I pick at a stray thread on my shorts. "I think a lot of serial killers don't give off killer vibes. That's how they get away with it for years."

Pippa places her hands on her hips as she stares at me with a smirk. "Liv, are you a serial killer?"

I shake my head. "I'm far too squeamish. The sight of blood makes me want to pass out." A shiver runs through me at the memories flooding my brain. I try to push them away, wanting to leave all thoughts of busted lips and open cuts behind.

"Okay, then do you need a place to stay for the night?" For the last five minutes, Pippa's been trying to convince me to sleep in her guest room before my meeting with Dean tomorrow.

I was hesitant about the idea of speaking to him more, but Lexi and Pippa convinced me it was worth it to at least try. If it doesn't seem like a good fit, I can always hit the road again. Or if I decide I still want to stay in Sutten a little longer, I can see if there are any other job openings. But the idea of a job where I don't have to pay for housing is very tempting, even if I never expected to become a nanny.

"Liv?" Pippa prods, reminding me she'd asked me a question.

I blink, bringing my attention back to her. "What did you ask again?" I question, feeling guilty for my mind wandering.

"I asked if you needed a place to stay tonight."

I shake my head as I give her a smile that I hope conveys how thankful I am for her offer. "No, thank you," I begin, knowing I should probably be heading out soon. It's already dinner time, and as much as I've loved feasting on baked goods all day, I would like to find a meal somewhere. Something warm and filling, with maybe even a vegetable or two. "It's kind of you to offer, and I *really* appreciate it, but I'm fine with booking a room somewhere."

She nods her head as she lets out a sigh. "Are you sure? I really don't mind. I just want you to stay in Sutten."

"I'm positive. I really appreciate the offer and hope you don't mind me declining. I *will* be staying in Sutten, and you will be seeing me again, but tonight, I'd like to rent a room somewhere. Do you have anywhere you recommend?"

"My personal favorite is the Sutten Mountain Inn, and Carmen there is one of my favorite people in town."

I give her a smile, hoping she isn't upset with me for declining her offer. I'm not very good at asking people for help, and it turns out I'm even worse at accepting help from a stranger. If I'm going to stay in Sutten for a night, I'd like to pay to stay somewhere just like anyone else passing through would. "And where is Sutten Mountain Inn?"

Pippa lets me drop the conversation about staying with her. It's just another thing I like about her. She doesn't push for more information or explanation. "It's at the edge of town. About ten minutes from here. Since it isn't quite the busy season yet, you shouldn't have a problem getting a room."

I rub my lips together, hoping the stay for one night isn't too pricey. If I really do want to stay longer in Sutten, I'll have to find a job soon. Maybe I will with Dean. Or maybe I won't. Either way, staying one night at the inn while I figure things out shouldn't put me back too much. "Perfect. I might head there soon, then."

"I hope to see you again tomorrow morning. You won't just decide to leave in the middle of the night, will you?"

I shake my head with a soft laugh. "Like I said, I *promise* you'll see me tomorrow morning. I've got to meet with my potential future boss, remember? Besides, I don't love driving at night, and I wouldn't leave without saying goodbye."

Her smile is bright and wide. "How crazy would it be if you started working for Dean? It'd almost be like fate that you stopped here and got a job out of it. All because of my pumpkin cinnamon rolls. I *knew* there was a reason I wanted to make them on a Tuesday, even though I typically save them for the weekends."

This makes me laugh even louder as I shove my book back into my purse. "It really would be because of your cinnamon rolls. The moment I took a bite, I knew I needed to find a way to stay here longer."

It's quiet for a moment as Pippa stares at me. She continues to smile, but I have no idea what's going through her mind. Her shoulders fall with a small sigh. "I'm glad you came into my cafe today, Liv. I really want you to stay. Something about you just makes me feel like I'm supposed to know you. Like we were meant to be friends."

I blink, trying to figure out what I'm supposed to say back.

Are people in all small towns this nice? Or is it only just this one? Have I stepped into a small town straight out of a Hallmark movie?

I'm not used to people being nice. In fact, I'm used to the opposite. I grew up always having to have my guard up around others, so the smile I give her is probably awkward. It *feels* awkward. "Thank you," I manage to get out, feeling incredibly grateful to have met her today.

She lifts her hands, her smile not faltering at all. "I'm a hugger. Can I give you a hug?"

I'm not typically a hugger. Not because I don't enjoy them, but I just never get close enough with people to show affection like that. But she's just been so nice to me, and I'm ecstatic at the thought of possibly making a friend. A real, *true* friend. So even though I know I'm probably not very good at it and my body's probably stiff, I step into her arms and give her a hug.

It doesn't last long, but it feels nice. I'm the one to pull away first, but the smile I give her is genuine this time.

I feel hopeful that maybe this town has far more to offer me than I ever expected. And most of all, maybe it'll be the first place to bring me happiness.

Maybe, even if it's just for a short amount of time, it'll feel like home.

Chapter 7
LIV

I HAVE NOTHING TO WEAR FOR THIS JOB INTERVIEW. IF YOU CAN EVEN call my meeting with Dean a job interview.

I'm still undecided if I actually want to be a nanny or not. Clara was great in the little amount of time I spent with her, but kids have never been my thing. But as I lay awake last night at the cute little inn Pippa recommended, I thought about how it wasn't that I didn't like kids. I just never had the chance to spend time with them.

After yesterday, I actually do think I'd enjoy children and spending my days with a child. There was something about Clara that spoke to me. She was so excited about everything. The color of the pink crayon, the way the icing was spread on top of the cupcakes. She was just so happy, and I could use more happiness in my life.

Despite all that, I do have questions on why Dean needs a nanny in the first place and why he hasn't been able to keep one. Is it just him and Clara? Is there something I need to know about him that explains why no nanny has wanted to stay?

Even if I want the job—which I might, depending on how this meeting with Dean goes—I'm not sure I'll get it based on the clothes I have packed. My wardrobe in Florida consisted of jean shorts and T-shirts. Never did I think I'd choose somewhere cold to possibly settle down in, and now, as I try on my final outfit choice, I realize I'm going to look entirely unprofessional.

"Ugh." I fall face-first into the mattress, letting out a small yell of frustration.

"Everything okay in there, dear?" a voice calls from the other side of the door.

I fly off the mattress, embarrassed someone heard me. "Totally fine!" I call back, my cheeks heating as I nervously walk toward the sound of the voice.

"I'm here to drop off your breakfast," the voice on the other side of the door explains. It sounds like the same woman from the front desk last night—Carmen. She was an older woman with gray hair and a pair of glasses who was sweet as can be as I explained how I needed a place to stay for the night.

I pull the door open, giving her a warm smile. "I didn't know the stay came with free breakfast."

Carmen smiles, holding out a plate with a silver dish over the top of it. "It typically doesn't, but I felt like cooking for company. Although I'm afraid I forgot to ask you last night if you had any allergies."

I shake my head. "No allergies. But you didn't have to make food just for me."

Carmen's smile doesn't falter. She has the best energy. I don't have to know her well to know she's kind. But then again, it seems like everyone in this town is kind and welcoming. "I wanted to. The quiet season is always kind of hard for me, so I like things being busy. It was exciting to wake up and fix you some breakfast."

I take the plate of food from her and give her a shy smile. Her generous offer means more to me than I can even find words for.

Before I can thank her, Carmen looks over my shoulder at the absolute mess of the room and raises an eyebrow. "Quite the mess for one night."

A nervous laugh escapes me. "I have a job interview this morning, and it turns out I have nothing to wear."

This makes Carmen laugh. "What's the job?" Her eyes travel over my outfit—or, really, my *fifth* outfit, considering the amount I've tried on.

"A nanny," I answer, looking at the length of my denim shorts. I can't show up to an interview wearing a pair of cutoffs. Dean was practically in a suit yesterday.

Maybe I just shouldn't go to the interview at all.

Carmen chews on her lip for a moment. "We have a gift shop. There's got to be something in there better than this."

"Really?"

She nods. "Eat your breakfast, then meet me in there. It's right by the front desk. We'll find something that'll work for your interview, dear."

"Okay," I say, nodding my head in understanding.

She walks out the door and shuts it behind her, leaving me alone with the smell of bacon wafting throughout the room.

I can't get the food into my mouth fast enough. I'm happy there's no one to witness the way I shove the piece of bacon into it. It's delicious. It has the perfect crunch, and I revel in having a home-cooked breakfast made for me for the first time in forever.

The omelet might be even better than Pippa's pumpkin cinnamon roll—although I'd never tell her that. It's close between the two, that's for sure.

I pretty much inhale the food. Carmen cooked up an omelet loaded with veggies, the perfect bacon, and even included some breakfast potatoes that are to die for. I eat every last bite, pretty much clearing the entire plate.

The moment I'm done eating, I grab my bag and head to the gift shop. Since I woke up early, too nervous for the interview to sleep, I still have about an hour before I'm supposed to meet Dean. Even so, I want to make sure I get a new outfit and am ready well ahead of time so there's no chance of being late.

Carmen waits for me at the front desk, her body hunched over a book as I make my way to her. When she hears my footsteps, she looks up with a wide smile on her face. "That was quick."

I return her smile. "Yeah, well, I think that's the best breakfast I've ever had."

She swats at the air before sliding out of her chair. "You give me too high of praises."

"They're deserved. I'm not kidding. That was the best omelet of my life. And don't even get me started on the bacon."

She laughs as she leads the way to the gift shop. "You'll have to tell my husband that. He told me the bacon was overcooked today."

I gasp. "No, it was perfect."

Carmen winks over her shoulder as she walks to a rack of clothing. "I know it was. He's just trying to keep me humble. *Men*," she adds, exasperated.

I nod, even though my experience with men in any kind of romantic way is severely lacking. Basically nonexistent at this point. But I pretend like I have any idea of the bickering that comes with having a partner.

Carmen sighs, moving the hangers along the rack as she sorts through the clothing. "Our store is really geared toward the tourists, but I know there's got to be something in here that'll work."

I swallow, my eyes roaming the small corner of the shop that has clothes. She's right. There are definitely clothes here, but most of them have "Sutten Mountain" stitched across the front or have outlines of mountains embroidered on them. They might still work better than my thrifted T-shirt and cutoff shorts.

"What about this?" Carmen asks excitedly, pulling a tunic from the rack. It's a dark green plaid pattern. It buttons up the front, cinching slightly at the waist but not by a lot. There's a pocket on the front where, if you look close enough, you can see "Sutten Mountain, Colorado" stitched on the front, but it isn't too noticeable.

"I think this could work perfectly," I tell her, trying not to eye the price of it. It seems like nice, sturdy fabric. Add in the fact that the words seem hand-stitched to the front, and I'm a little nervous about how much it'll cost me. However, I don't have much of an option, so I grab it from her.

"Do you happen to have leggings or tights? Really anything I could wear underneath that'd work for the occasion."

Carmen purses her lips, deep in thought. Suddenly, her eyes light up. "We do have a pair of black leggings. There's a bear on the rear, but you'd never notice it with how long the shirt is."

"That's perfect," I say in relief. Somehow, I think I'll be able to show up in something somewhat professional for this interview.

Carmen points to where the leggings are, and I walk toward the table. I grab my size and hold them up, confirming that they'll be perfect for the outfit. We head over to the checkout counter as she rings up the two items.

"Is the nanny position for someone here in town?" Carmen asks as I hand her the cash for the clothes. They weren't as expensive as I thought they'd be, making me let out a small sigh of relief.

"His name is Dean. Dean Livingston," I add, remembering the name printed on the business card he'd handed me yesterday.

"Oh," Carmen gets out, seeming a little shocked.

"Is it that bad?" I ask nervously. I shift my weight from one foot to the other, wondering if something's wrong with him. I feared there might be, with everyone's mentions of how he seemed to fire nannies so frequently. I had brushed it off since, to me, he seemed pretty normal yesterday. He might've been a little quiet and standoffish, but maybe it just takes him time to warm up to people.

Both Pippa and Lexi gave him the green light of approval as a boss, but maybe I missed something.

"No, I'm sorry. Dean is great. He just hasn't quite been the same since his wife, Selena, passed tragically in a car accident a few years ago."

My chest constricts at her words. I wondered if Clara's mother was in the picture or not. But I kind of assumed it was the same situation as my own mother. "Oh my god," I whisper, feeling sorry for Dean and Clara.

Carmen nods as she puts my clothes in a red paper bag. "It rocked the entire town. We all watched their love story unfold from the time they were teenagers. He kept to himself for the longest time, and it took him a year to really even talk to anyone in town. I can't imagine what he went through." She pauses for a moment, as if her mind is going back to years ago. "He had to grieve his wife while taking care of a newborn. He was all alone in the house he and Selena had just finished building together."

I swallow past the lump in my throat. "I can't imagine," I mutter. I know I should probably say goodbye to Carmen and change before meeting Dean, but my feet stay planted because I want to know more.

"So Dean isn't a bad guy at all. In fact, he used to be the town's golden boy, but he changed after Selena passed. We all understood. It's hard to expect anything different. I just want you to know if he's grumpy or short with you, it isn't you, my dear. It's just the way he is now."

I nod. He wasn't the friendliest person I've ever met, but he didn't seem as bad as Carmen's warning is making him out to be. Maybe we just haven't spent enough time together. Either way, I can deal with a grumpy man. That's easy. I grew up with far worse. "Thank you for telling me all of this. It really helps me understand the situation more before potentially working for him."

Carmen smiles. The crinkles at the corner of her eyes get deeper with the movement. "Of course. Please still consider the job. We've only spent a short amount of time together, but I really like you, dear. It seems like you might be the perfect fit for

Dean and sweet Clara. That baby girl needs someone who will stay."

I swallow at her words. I hadn't thought much about if I got offered the nannying job and I accepted it, how long it'd be for. When Pippa first suggested I stay in town for a little while, it didn't seem like a bad idea. I could nanny for as long as I wanted to stay in Sutten and then leave.

But should I still be considering the job, knowing I probably won't be here for more than a few months? I guess it's something I'll have to discuss with Dean today.

"Thank you again for your help this morning, Carmen," I say, tucking my hair behind my ear and changing the subject. "It means a lot to me. I'm not used to strangers being so kind to me," I admit with a nervous smile.

Carmen reaches out and places her hand on top of mine. Her smile is so warm and comforting, putting my nerves at ease. "We don't believe in strangers here in Sutten."

Her answer makes me smile. Her words feel like a sign that being in this small little town tucked into the middle of the mountains is exactly where I'm supposed to be.

Chapter 8
DEAN

My fingers tap against the table as my eyes scan the coffee shop for what feels like the millionth time. Technically, there are still ten minutes until our scheduled meeting, so it's not like Liv's late. But still, I'm anxiously waiting to see if she'll show up or not.

If I'm being honest, I don't have high hopes. Many people have stood me up before as I've been on the hunt for the perfect nanny. Why would she be any different?

Although, she did send over her resume and two different references, so I might just be overthinking it for no reason.

Except I do have a reason—my daughter. Clara hasn't stopped talking about Liv since the moment we left Wake and Bake yesterday. She even told her whole dance class that she was going to have cute hair for every class now because she has a new nanny.

I take a deep breath, hoping this thing with Liv works out. Clara's obsessed with her, and because I've never seen my daughter this excited about someone, I have to do everything I can to get Liv on board. Even if I don't know or trust her yet.

Two more minutes tick by before the door opens, and Liv comes breezing in, the mountain wind blowing her hair around as she steps inside. She's not wearing a hat today, giving me a view of her entire face. Even from a distance, I can tell her cheeks are pink from the cold. At least today, she's dressed for the weather. I couldn't help thinking yesterday how cold she must have been.

It was a weird feeling for me to think that about her. To worry. I don't typically do that about anyone outside of my family. Even as I drove Clara home from dance and the temperature dropped drastically as it turned to night, I found myself wondering where Liv would be staying and if she had anything to keep her warm.

Standing up, I smooth out my suit jacket and step around the table to pull out her chair. "Morning," I greet her, watching her close the distance to the table.

"Morning," she responds, her voice a little breathless. Her hair sticks to the lip gloss coating her lips. She tries to fix it, but then the sticky hair sticks to her cheek instead. "I'm not late, am I?" she asks, her eyes moving to the chair I've pulled out for her.

I don't have to look at my watch to know she isn't late. "No, you aren't. Here, take a seat."

Liv nods, setting her large brown bag on the floor next to us and sitting down. "It's been quite the morning," she mutters under her breath. I don't know if I'm supposed to respond to her remark or not, but luckily, she decides for me by continuing on. "First, I realized I didn't pack any clothes for an interview. I had to go shopping at the inn, so don't mind me sporting the Sutten merch." She giggles uncomfortably as I take the seat across from her.

I look over her outfit, noticing the pocket of her shirt with "Sutten Mountain" stitched across it. Before I can tell her that I never would've noticed unless she told me about it, she continues to tell me about her morning. "And then I went to my car, and it wouldn't start. I kept trying and trying until, finally, I got it to turn on. Maybe it doesn't like the cold."

I make a mental note to check out the car if she does become Clara's nanny. "That *is* quite the morning."

Liv nods, taking a deep breath as she adjusts in her chair.

"Yes. And the clock on my dash doesn't work, so then I panicked that I was somehow late and you'd be gone and my hope for a job here would be lost."

I don't answer her, instead just watching her carefully as I take her in. She seemed a lot quieter yesterday than today. Maybe it's just that Pippa and Lexi were doing most of the talking, but now, her personality is shining through a little more.

As if she can read my mind, she winces a little as a smile spreads over her face. "Am I already talking too much? Sometimes I ramble and—"

I lift my hand to stop her from continuing. "It's fine." I leave out the part where I tell her I'd much rather listen to someone rambling than be left alone with my own thoughts.

Liv nods, but the smile doesn't leave her face. Is she always this smiley? Her personality is almost as bright as the sunshine color of her hair. "Okay," she finally gets out, her voice a little shaky with nerves.

It's quiet for a moment as we both stare at one another. But it's not an uncomfortable silence, even though it easily could be.

"Would you like a coffee?" I finally get out, trying to be polite.

She nods, still wearing a smile that softens something inside me. "I'd actually love one."

As if she can hear our conversation, Pippa walks up to the table with a relieved look on her face as she looks at Liv. "You're here."

Liv aims her smile in Pippa's direction. "I'm here. And *desperately* need caffeine."

"You've come to the right place. What would you like today?"

Liv thinks about the question for a moment. "Surprise me?"

This makes Pippa bounce on her feet in excitement. "I'd *love* to surprise you. Are you wanting the coffee hot or iced? And do you like sweet or unsweet?"

As if on cue, a shiver runs through Liv's body. It's pretty cold this morning for October, and even though her flannel shirt is long-sleeved, it doesn't look very thick. I can't help but wonder if she's cold.

Fuck. Why am I even thinking about this?

"I'll definitely take a hot coffee. And on the sweeter side, please," Liv answers.

Pippa nods and then looks over at me with a lifted brow. "Are you ready to order now that she's here?"

I clear my throat, wishing Pippa hadn't ratted me out for wanting to wait. I thought it'd be rude for me to order a coffee and not get her something, too, since I didn't know what she liked, I decided to wait. "Yes. I'll take my usual."

"Any food?" Pippa asks, her eyes finding Liv's once again. "We've got fresh pumpkin cinnamon rolls this morning just for you."

"As delicious as that sounds right now, Carmen actually surprised me by making me a huge breakfast this morning. I'm still full but will absolutely be getting the cinnamon roll at some point today."

Pippa's hand finds her chest. "That was so sweet of her. Did you love the inn? It's cute, isn't it?"

"Carmen was the sweetest. She got me quickly checked into a room last night and then made me breakfast this morning. Then, when I told her I didn't have an outfit for this interview, she even helped me pick something out."

I listen in on the conversation between Pippa and Liv for a moment before Pippa glances over at me, and her eyes go wide. "I totally forgot this is supposed to be an interview. I'll leave the two of you to talk for a moment, and I'll go get the coffees started."

She spins on the heel of her pink cowboy boots and dashes back to the counter. I stare at the boots as she walks away. For some reason, my mind flashes to the pair of bright red cowboy boots Selena got for her eighteenth birthday. She wore them until there were holes in them. They still sit in a box in our basement with the rest of her belongings I couldn't get rid of.

I sigh, trying to focus on the interview at hand. The best thing I can do in Selena's memory is hire the best person possible for Clara. Maybe Liv will be that. I sure hope so because of how much Clara seems to already love her. But I prepare myself to be okay with accepting she might not be a good fit either.

Now that Pippa's gone and I've attempted to clear my mind as much as possible, I look back to Liv. She's already watching me carefully, her teeth biting into her bottom lip.

She shifts in her chair and speaks up, clearly feeling like she needs to be the one to break the silence. "Thank you again for giving me the chance to talk more about the open nanny position. Although this is an unexpected turn of events, I'm excited to talk more with you to see if it would be a good fit."

I give her a curt nod. "No problem. Clara adores you. I'm really glad you didn't bail."

"Only thought about it for a moment," she teases, but I'm not sure if she's joking or not. I don't know her well enough yet to be able to tell.

"So, tell me about yourself. I've read over your resume, and it seems like you have quite the work history." I remember seeing her age when looking through her resume. I knew she looked young, but she's barely twenty-three, making her twelve years younger than me. What shocked me even more was the age she started working. She's been working almost half her life already, making me wonder about her past and why that is the case.

Liv shifts in her seat for a moment as she thinks through her answer. She sighs. "Money was a little tight growing up, so the moment I was old enough for someone to hire me, I started working."

My thumb dances over my jawline as I listen to her answer. I fight the urge to ask questions about why money was tight and wonder how she was able to work and graduate at the top of her class from high school, both details I found out while reviewing her resume. I decide to hold my tongue, knowing those are questions I don't need answers to for her to be hired on as a nanny.

"I haven't had a chance to call your references yet, but from your long work history, it seems like you're great at committing to a job."

She tucks a piece of her blonde hair behind her ear. "When you do call them, do you mind leaving out specific details about where I am?"

My head tilts to the side because her question came out a little uneasy. There might even be a little bit of fear in her tone with it. I want to ask her why, but it's not my place to do so.

She must take my silence as a refusal because she adds, "If it's too much to ask, I understand. I'm sorry to have even—"

"I won't tell anyone about your location," I say, interrupting her and not wanting her to feel like she has to explain herself any further.

"Thank you," she whispers, her shoulders sagging a little with relief.

I stare at her for a moment, wanting to know more about the woman sitting in front of me. I'd come up with a list of questions I wanted to ask her for this interview, but all of them seem to have vanished from my mind. The only questions I can think of are ones I don't need to know to hire her.

Pippa saves me by walking over with our coffees. She sets them down in front of us. "Here's your usual, Dean, and a pumpkin latte with a dash of nutmeg for you, Liv."

"Thank you," both Liv and I say in unison.

Pippa nods before clapping her hands together. "Okay, I'll leave the two of you to it."

She disappears as quickly as she showed up, leaving me and Liv alone in the corner of the cafe.

I clear my throat, now having had enough time to remember the biggest question I wanted to ask her this morning. "Maybe we could start this interview with you telling me why you want to be Clara's nanny and why you think you'd be the right person for the job."

Chapter 9
LIV

DEAN'S QUESTION MAKES ME SMILE BECAUSE IT'S ONE I THOUGHT A lot about last night. While I never envisioned myself becoming a nanny, I think it's something I'd be good at.

"As I'm sure you saw, I've never had a job in childcare, but I still think I'm more than qualified to do it. Not to divulge too much of my upbringing, but I pretty much raised myself." That's an understatement. I absolutely raised myself. If I hadn't depended on myself to even have my basic needs met, I don't know what would've happened to me. "I learned from a very early age how to take care of myself, and I think that's taught me a lot about how to care for someone else as well."

Dean nods, his eyes fixed intently on me. He doesn't take notes or look anywhere but *at* me. I don't know if it's something I like or if I wish he'd look anywhere else, but either way, I keep going, wishing I could get a better read on him. He gives me no clues about what he's thinking with his stiff posture and narrowed eyes. "I've worked many different jobs, but all of them have been in hospitality. I know how to take care of people. I'm a quick learner—I had to be—and I'm always open to constructive criticism."

He lets my words hang in the air for a moment. A crease appears between his eyebrows as whatever is going through his head shows on his face, and I swallow, anxious that my answers weren't as good as I thought they were. If he doesn't like them, then this won't be a good fit. While I'd rehearsed what I was going to say to him, everything I've said is completely honest.

"Ideally, I'd love to find someone for Clara that could be our nanny longer than for a few months. How likely is it that you'll stay in Sutten for an extended amount of time?"

I sit straighter in my chair as I think about his question. I take a sip of my coffee, using it as an opportunity to gather my thoughts. "Truthfully? Yesterday morning, I didn't even think I'd stay the night in Sutten. I'm at a place in my life where I could do anything with it, and I'm just trying to figure out what that anything will be. I can't sit here and promise you that I want to stay here. So far, I do love the town. Everyone has been so incredibly nice. I'm not used to that at all. I'm just not sure where life will lead me. I can promise, however, that if, or I guess when, I decide to leave, I'd give you ample time to find someone to replace me."

He frowns at my answer, making me unsure if I'll even be offered the position to begin with.

"That's if you offer me the position, of course. I wasn't trying to assume anything," I hurriedly get out.

"If I knew you were wanting to stay in Sutten longer, I think I'd offer you the job right now. Which I must admit is pretty out of character for me, but Clara loves you, and for some reason, offering you the job feels like the right thing to do. I'm just a little apprehensive to let you into my daughter's life if you don't have any intention of staying. She's lost a lot already, and I'm worried I'm a terrible father if I bring someone else into her life, knowing they won't be in it long."

His tone is a little sad, which stabs me right in the heart. He hasn't told me about his wife's passing yet, but I can read between the lines of his statement to know what he means. His daughter's had to go on without a mother, and that's something she'll have to live with for the rest of her life. I admire how much it seems he's trying to do right by his daughter.

I nod in understanding because he has a point. I remember when I was ten, a woman moved in next door to us. Her name was Sherrie, and she always spent time outside on her porch. She seemed lonely, which I later learned was because her husband had been deployed. I was lonely, too, so we quickly struck up an unlikely friendship. She'd make me a lemonade, and we'd sit on her porch together.

When she moved away without any warning, I was crushed. If I got close to Clara, I could never do that to her.

Dean gives me time to think of a response. He just sits there with his permanent scowl, sipping his coffee as I think about the right thing to say to him. I'm not sure if there is an exact right thing. All I can give is honesty. "I only got to spend a little bit of time with her yesterday, but I don't want to hurt her. If I start as a nanny and my journey with you guys comes to an end, I will make sure she's fallen even more in love with my replacement before leaving."

I don't know why I make the promise. I could end up hating the nanny position and wanting the first excuse out of the job, but something tells me that won't be the case. Even with Carmen's warning about Dean this morning, I'm realizing I want this job. Both Dean and his daughter have gone through a lot. Something neither one of them should ever have had to go through.

I feel a purpose at the prospect of becoming a small puzzle piece in their family.

Dean takes another sip of his coffee. I'm learning very quickly that he isn't afraid of the quiet. He doesn't needlessly blurt something out to just fill the silence and instead thinks deeply about his words before saying anything.

"This might be a terrible idea." He sighs, running his hands down his thighs as he adjusts his position in his seat. "But I can't move past how much Clara already loves you. How about I run through what a typical day looks like, and you can decide if the position is still something you're interested in?"

"That's perfect," I respond, cupping the coffee mug between my hands and blowing on the hot liquid.

"Clara typically wakes up between seven and eight in the morning. Most mornings, I'm still there to say goodbye to her after she wakes up, but sometimes I'll already be gone, depending on my meetings for the day. Whenever she gets up, you'll make her breakfast and get her ready for the day. I'll make sure my assistant gets a schedule printed out with her activities for the month and what her daily routine looks like. She's got dance some days, and horseback riding on others. I'd love for her to get the chance to do more playdates and just..." He lets out a sad sigh. "I want her to just be a kid. She's had to tag along with me or my parents a lot recently as I've searched for a new nanny. My goal is to get a little more stability in her life. The two of you would be able to choose whatever you wanted to do for the morning, and then you'd feed her some lunch. She still naps about an hour or two. During that time, you can have some time for yourself. I would love the house to stay tidy—I'll be honest, I'm pretty uptight about keeping the house clean."

His pause gives me a chance to laugh at his words. "Keep things clean. Got it. Lucky for both of us, I also like things neat and organized."

I was trying to make a joke and lighten the mood some, but it doesn't work. His face stays trained in a serious expression. "The hours might be longer than typical. I fully understand that. I try to be home for dinner with her every night, but some nights, it might just be the two of you, so you might have to cook."

I nod. "Of course. I happen to love cooking, so that's no problem. And I'm used to long hours, so there isn't an issue with that either."

The only acknowledgment that he heard me was a slight lift of his chin. "Housework isn't expected, other than tidying up after anything you and Clara do. After dinner, you're free to do whatever you choose. You'll be off until the next morning. I will put Clara to bed at night and wake her up in the morning—

unless something comes up. But I prefer to always make my schedule work where I see her at night and in the morning, so it shouldn't be often that I need your help at those times."

"Sounds good to me." My heart starts to race a little. He's talking as if I already have the job. Which makes me excited— hopeful even. Giving me exactly the answer I needed, despite my lack of experience as a nanny and spontaneously agreeing to live somewhere that was only supposed to be a pit stop...I want the job.

I want to stay in Sutten.

Chapter 10
DEAN

Liv shifts in her chair, clearly waiting for me to say something. Many different things run through my head. I still need to call her references and make sure her background check comes back clear. There are numerous reasons why I shouldn't offer her the job right here and now, yet I want to.

We've gone through our fair share of nannies recently, but part of the problem is none of them seemed to connect with Clara. Liv bonded with her effortlessly in one afternoon. I'm hard to impress, but Clara is even harder to impress.

And Liv's impressed us both.

There are so many reasons why I should wait, but I did all the right things with our previous nannies, and none of them lasted. Maybe it's time for me to go with my gut instead of with my head.

I sigh, sitting up in the chair. My fingers anxiously tap against the table as I give myself a few more moments to change my mind.

I don't.

"I'd like to offer you the job," I begin, my fingers still tapping against the table. "As long as your background check comes back clear and nothing comes up with your references, I think Clara would love spending her days with you. We can talk more about what your starting rate will be and time off, and if it's something you're really interested in, my assistant, Tonya, can draw up a contract and terms of employment. *If* you're wanting to accept, of course."

She tries to bite back her smile but fails miserably at it. "I'd love to talk more details. I understand since you'd also be giving me a place to live that it won't pay much additionally."

I frown at her comment. Just because she'll have a place to sleep doesn't mean I won't be also paying for the time she works. The days can be long, and she deserves to get paid accordingly. "You'll get paid just like any other job. You staying at the house is more for my own convenience than yours. I'll get Tonya to put everything together for you today. You should hear from her by tonight. If everything looks good to you, or if you want to negotiate anything, you can give me a call."

Liv nods. She fidgets with her hands in her lap. "I don't think I'll have many questions. I'm just grateful things have worked out the way they have."

"Make sure to read over everything carefully. And then read it over again. I want to make sure we're in a mutual under-standing before you agree. Like I've mentioned, I really want this to work out for Clara's sake." And maybe for mine, too, but I keep that thought to myself.

This makes her smile, and it's a genuine one, lighting up her entire face. It thaws my cold demeanor slightly. I think she'll be good for Clara, and that allows me to take a breath of relief. Finding good childcare for Clara has been a struggle. My daughter deserves the world, and I'm feeling pretty confident about the woman sitting across from me.

"I'll read it over. Multiple times," Liv agrees. She pulls the coffee mug to her lips and takes a drink, her eyes watching me carefully the entire time.

"Perfect," I respond, leaning forward in my chair. "Then it seems like this interview is done. Unless you have any more questions," I add, wondering if I'm cutting the interview too short. It doesn't seem like we have much more to talk about until she reads over her contract.

Liv shakes her head. "I don't think I have any more. Well, I guess maybe one. If everything looks good to me after reading over the terms, when do you think the start date would be?"

"I'll give you a couple of days to look it over and think about it. If everything looks good to you, maybe we could meet up Saturday morning? Tonya can send you my address if you sign. I'm off all weekend and can help you get settled before the week starts."

She appears to bite the inside of her cheek as she thinks about my words. Her hesitance takes me a little by surprise. Maybe she wasn't wanting to start so soon. Or maybe she's just having second thoughts.

"Something wrong with that?" I ask, watching her through narrowed lids to see her reaction.

She shakes her head, having to tuck her hair back behind her ear because of the movement. "No," she rushes to say, her eyes wide. "There's nothing wrong with that at all. I'm ready to start as soon as possible. I just went quiet for a moment, hoping the inn still had rooms available until Saturday. But she made it seem like they weren't very busy, so I don't think it'll be a problem."

I make a mental note to give Carmen a call over at Sutten Mountain Inn to make sure Liv is all good to stay there for a few more nights. "Yeah, we still have some time before it gets busy here. I'll make sure it isn't a problem for you to stay there until Saturday."

Her eyes go a little wide as she shakes her head. "Oh, you don't have to do that. I can handle it myself."

I watch her for a moment, wondering what's happened in her life. It's clear she's fiercely independent. She's panicking at the thought of me helping her by just making a simple phone call, which is incredibly telling.

Before I can ask the personal questions running through my

head, I take a final drink of my coffee before standing up. "I'll make sure Tonya gets you everything you need by the end of the day. Remember to really look it over before reaching out."

Liv stands up, her lips spreading into a hesitant smile. She anxiously runs her palms down the front of her pants. "Thank you again for taking a chance on me. I promise you won't regret it."

I tuck my hands into my pockets, wondering if I'm supposed to shake her hand or not. "You have a great work history and an already established rapport with Clara. It doesn't feel like too much of a chance."

She holds her hand out as she smiles even wider. "Well, thank you anyway. I'm excited about the opportunity. I already adore Clara so much."

My hand engulfs hers as I shake it once. It feels weird to shake her hand, but I'm trying not to be rude. Pippa lectured me before Liv ever showed up this morning to be a little less grumpy—her words and not mine. I'm just trying to make sure I don't ruin this for Clara before it's even started.

"The contract will be fine, I'm sure. See you Saturday, Mr. Livingston." She doesn't pull her hand from mine, so I don't pull away either. Instead, I look into her warm, blue eyes and hope she's the perfect fit.

I shake my head, hating the formality. "Call me Dean. And you don't know that. Maybe you'll find something you don't agree with."

She slowly nods her head as she mulls my words over. "I've got a pretty good idea everything will be perfect. Looking forward to Saturday, *Dean*." She emphasizes my name, and I don't know why the sound of my name coming from her mouth does something to me. It's like hearing my name woke up something inside me that's been dormant for years.

I clear my throat, trying to shake the weird feeling. "Perfect." I let go of her hand and let it fall to her side.

Without even saying goodbye, I rush out of Wake and Bake and hustle to my truck.

The moment I slam the door of my truck shut, I let out a long breath.

What the hell is wrong with me? I was just a total dick to, hopefully, my new nanny without any explanation—or good reason.

I let out a low whistle as I start the truck. Pippa will be very disappointed in me.

Chapter 11
LIV

My heart feels like it might beat right out of my chest as I slow down before turning into the long, narrow driveway that leads to my new home. I don't know if I would've ever found the driveway if it weren't for the freshly painted black mailbox sitting in the clearing with "Livingston" painted neatly on the side.

When Dean mentioned his house was tucked into the mountains when we talked after agreeing to the terms of employment, I didn't realize he meant it was literally on the side of the mountain with nothing around.

I guide the car down the driveway, shocked by how nicely paved it is. It's a lot smoother of a ride than the road it took to get out here. I thought the drive into Sutten Mountain was one of the most scenic views I've ever seen, but the view panning out in front of me is breathtaking. I press on the brake for a minute, sitting in the middle of the driveway as I take in the scene before me.

The trees have gone from dense and close together, the brilliant hues of oranges and reds painting the most beautiful painting, to further apart the closer the tree line gets to the house.

"Oh my god," I mutter under my breath, wondering for a moment if I'm in the right place. I know I'm where I'm supposed to be. His last name on the side of the mailbox gave it away. I just didn't realize the house he built with his late wife would look like *this*.

I don't think I can even call it a house—it's a mansion on the side of a mountain.

Dean's *rich* rich. I should've known when I saw what my salary was.

It's the prettiest place I've ever seen. It looks like it's been picked right out of a home magazine and placed here.

And then the view around it is even more breathtaking. It's tucked into a valley of the mountain, giving way to the most stunning rolling hills all around it. I know I should press the gas and close the distance to the house, but I can't. I'm too stunned. I'd seen episodes of *Yellowstone* over my dad's shoulder occasionally, and the house in front of me looks almost exactly like the one from the show.

It's rustic but classy. There's a classic look to it with the light color of the wood. A porch wraps around the front, and might even wrap around the back, too. At least, it looks like it does from here.

"What is even happening right now?" I whisper, lightly tapping the gas to continue down the driveway. I must be dreaming. There's no way I stumbled upon a live-in nanny position and this is where I'll be spending my days.

It seems too good to be true—and nothing good ever happens to me.

The driveway gets wider, opening up to a space to the side of the house for what I assume is parking. I park my car there, my gaze traveling over the house up close.

I don't know what to say as I step out of my car and look up at the beautiful house in front of me. My old car looks so out of place sitting in front of it, nowhere near new enough to sit by something this pretty.

Before I can gather my thoughts, the front door of the house opens, and a flash of dark hair comes racing toward me.

"Livvy!" Clara shouts, a giggle erupting from her small body as she launches herself right at me. I drop my duffle bag and wrap my arms around her, pulling her body to mine.

"Hi, Clara." I squeeze her tight, a sense of joy taking over me at seeing her again. Her smile and happiness are infectious. I think being around her every day is really going to be great for me.

"You coming to stay with me?" Clara asks, pulling away to look me in the eyes. Now that I've sat across from Dean and got a better look at him, I realize how much she looks like her father, and I can't help but think about what her mother looked like and what features she has from her.

I nod. "If that's okay with you?"

Her smile gets even wider. "Yes. You can sleep in my bed if you want."

I laugh as I notice Dean approaching us. I hadn't even seen him come through the front door. I'd been so focused on greeting Clara that I hadn't really been paying any attention.

"Honey, Liv has her own room and bed."

Clara juts her bottom lip out. She crosses her arms over her chest as her eyes narrow on me. "I want a sleepover," she states matter-of-factly, her eyes bouncing between me and Dean.

"Oh, I promise you don't want to sleep with me. I'd wake you up all night."

Clara reaches up and presses her tiny palm to my cheek. The gesture is adorable, stealing a little piece of my heart. "Do you have bad dreams like Daddy?"

I can't help it—my eyes immediately travel to Dean. He must have nightmares often if Clara knows about them, but I try to pretend I didn't hear her. It seems like her comment isn't something I'm supposed to know about by the hard set of Dean's jaw and the vacant look in his eyes as he looks back at me.

"No nightmares for me," I tell her, trying to lighten the mood. "I just snore *so* loud," I lie. I reach out and tickle her sides a little, making her double over in a fit of laughter.

"Ah!" she screams, trying to wrestle out of my grasp. "Daddy snores, too!" she gets out through more laughs.

I laugh with her, unable to resist with how cute her giggles are. "Oh, so then you know you definitely don't want me to share a room with you. My snores would keep you up all night."

"*Fine*," she agrees with a sigh, finally breaking free from my grasp and backing away. "I want to show you my room."

"How about we let her step foot inside before we start making demands?" Dean interjects, his eyebrow raised as he stares at his daughter.

"Step foot inside, Livvy?"

I smile at the nickname, playing with the end of her messy ponytail. "Let me get my bags first, and then you can show me inside. Your house is pretty."

"My daddy built it with my mommy," Clara declares, looking proudly over at her father. "Mommy doesn't live here, though. She lives in Heaven."

Dean clears his throat, his jaw tightening as he takes a step forward, picking up my duffle bag off the pavement. "Let me help you with your bags. Are there more?" He completely ignores what Clara just said, and I let him. I don't know if the tragic passing of his wife was something I'm supposed to know about yet.

I nod as I open the door to my back seat. Heat floods my cheeks as I look in the back. Suddenly, I'm a little embarrassed for him to see it. It's clear I've been partially living in my car with a pillow and blanket folded nicely in the seat and my small, dwindling stash of food. I'd kept it clean for the most part, getting rid of trash when I had it, but I still can't hide how all of my possessions fit inside the back seat of this car.

"Uh," I begin, trying to fake a smile as Clara skips across the driveway. "Just these two additional bags. I pack light," I add at the last minute, trying to laugh at the uncomfortableness of the situation.

Dean doesn't say anything. He simply takes my purse, as

well as the other bag from the back seat, and closes the door with his free hand. His eyes meet mine, and I hate the look of pity etched across his face. He's sorry for me, and I *hate* it. I don't need anyone's pity. Getting out of Florida was the best thing that could've happened to me. I'm exactly where I need to be, even if I don't have many belongings to my name.

"Let's show Liv inside, Clara," Dean calls over his shoulder, walking to the front door. Only when his footsteps hit the wood porch do I notice he's wearing a pair of cowboy boots. I don't know why the sight of them makes me smile, erasing some of the embarrassment from my system. The two times I've seen Dean in the past, he wore a suit that screamed business. It feels almost wrong to see him dressed down in a pair of worn jeans and a flannel—the look complete with a pair of cowboy boots.

I hate to admit that I love it. I remind myself that he's my boss and I can't be attracted to him. The last thing I need to be doing is studying the way his old pair of jeans expertly cling to his thick thighs, yet here I am, watching him walk to the house in a pair of cowboy boots and worn jeans that only fuel my attraction to him.

My boss is a whole lot more interesting than I was expecting.

I push the thought to the back of my mind, and with a deep breath, I follow Clara and Dean up the porch, excited to see my home for the foreseeable future.

Chapter 12
DEAN

LIV'S EYES ARE WIDE AS SHE TAKES IN THE SPACE. SHE STANDS IN THE opening of the front door, her gaze raking across the great room.

"This is…" Her words fall off as she continues to look around. "I don't even have a word for what this is."

I swallow, trying to look around the space through her eyes. It's stunning. Every single detail of this room Selena pored over in the planning of the house. It was her baby. She spent every day huddled over wood samples and paint swatches, wanting to make sure she got everything perfect.

It did end up perfect. I just hate that she didn't get to see it through.

The house is still missing the finishing touches. Selena hadn't finished doing the interior design. She was still picking out the pieces that made this house a home. Years later, I look at the empty walls and the lack of decorations and wish she was still here to finish out the planning of our dream house.

As I look at the house through the eyes of a stranger, a knife twists in my heart. If Selena was still here, this house would seem so much more full of life. But it's hard to recognize life's fullness after losing someone like her. It's hard to accept she won't ever be here to finish the house, but I need to for my daughter—and for me.

Maybe getting Clara's help to finish decorating the space will allow me to do that.

I focus back on Liv as her eyes drift from place to place, wondering if she's looking around and thinking I'm pathetic for not bringing any personal touches to the home.

"Here's where I keep some of my toys!" Clara calls, breaking me from my thoughts. She runs to a wall of built-in shelving. The bottom portion is cabinets, giving us room to store her toys and art supplies without them being on display when people first walk into the house.

Clara opens up one of the cabinets and pulls out a box of Barbies. "See?" she yells, her voice echoing off the walls across the space from us. "Toys!"

Liv nods, her eyes still wide with shock as she takes in the house. "I love it," she manages to get out, her eyes finally stopping on the kitchen. "This is the most beautiful house I've ever seen." Her voice is full of wonder as she follows me into the kitchen. I cock my head to the side as my eyes track her face. *Is she telling the truth?* I can't tell. "Surely not. It's big but simple. I haven't finished decorating."

I shift her bags in my grip, wondering if she's judging the lack of decorations in the house. *Does it feel cold? Is she judging me for not making it homier for Clara?* The things that make it more of a home than a house are things my mom has brought over.

"It's still beautiful," she notes, running her fingers along the wood slab of the kitchen island.

I clear my throat, not knowing how to respond. I wish Clara would interrupt with something random to ease the awkward energy around us, but instead, she chooses this *one* time to be perfectly entertained with her Barbies.

At least it feels awkward to me, but the wide-eyed amazement of Liv tells me maybe the awkwardness is only one-sided.

"So, this is obviously the kitchen," I point out. "The pantry is behind those wood doors. Add any food you want to the grocery list on the fridge. Tonya runs out and grabs groceries on Mondays."

Liv chews on her lip as she nods. "I'm not picky. Whatever you normally get is fine."

I bite back the urge to argue with her. I want her to feel comfortable enough to stock anything she could want in the house. But that'll be a discussion for another day. Right now, I want to continue to give her the tour and let her get settled.

"To our right is the living room. The stairs go up to the second floor, where most of the bedrooms are. The only bedroom down here is the primary one. The basement has a playroom for Clara, as well as a theater room. She'll beg you to watch *Frozen* in there every morning."

This makes Liv laugh, her eyes finding mine. "I guess it's a good thing I've never seen *Frozen*."

My jaw opens. "You've never seen *Frozen*?" I can't hide the shock from my face. I've seen both *Frozen* movies—and all the spin-offs—countless times. I could probably quote many of the scenes if I needed to.

Liv shakes her head. "I haven't seen any of the newer movies. Maybe Clara will fix that for me."

I let out a low whistle. "Oh, she will. Trust me on that. She's begging to be Elsa for Halloween this year—for a second time. Want to follow me to your room? We can set your things down before continuing with the rest of the tour."

"That sounds perfect."

I nod, not feeling the need to make small talk as I lead her up the stairs. She follows behind me quietly as Clara trails behind us, still playing make-believe with her dolls.

I walk us down the long upstairs hallway. "This room is a guest bedroom. It's got bunk beds for when Clara's cousins stay the night with us. The next room is Clara's—"

"This is my room!" Clara excitedly interrupts. She jumps up and down in excitement. "Want to see it?" she asks, her focus on Liv.

Liv looks at me, letting me be the one to answer my daughter's question.

"How about we show Liv her room first? Daddy's getting old, and these bags are heavy. Let me put them down, and then you can show Liv your room."

Clara nods her head before lifting her shoulder in a small shrug. "Okay." She looks to Liv. She cups her mouth with her hand, leaning a little closer to Liv. "Daddy *is* getting old. He has gray hair."

Liv raises her eyebrows in amusement, her focus on my daughter. "Does he?" she asks, pretending to be shocked.

I roll my eyes. "Clara was with us when my mother pointed out that I have a few gray hairs. Nothing crazy. Be nice to your dad," I tell Clara, playfully narrowing my eyebrows at my daughter.

It doesn't faze her at all. She skips ahead of us and heads right to Liv's room.

"The study is right here, as well as a guest bathroom." I gesture to each room as I point them out to Liv before we make it to the end of the hallway where her room is.

"And this is your room!" Clara pushes the door open, immediately running into Liv's room. When I walk into it, I find my daughter already sprawled out on the mattress, making a pretend snow angel on the bed.

"This is yours." I carefully set her bags down on top of the dresser before crossing my arms over my chest. "Will it work?"

Liv snorts, her head shaking. "Will this work?" she mimics, her voice filled with disbelief. "This room is almost as big as the entire first floor of the house I grew up in. I've never slept in a bed this large."

She steps forward, her fingers running along the off-white comforter.

"So...it'll work?" I repeat, needing the peace of mind of knowing she'll be happy here. "You have your own bathroom and closet."

Liv's eyes meet mine. She's quiet for a moment as she stares at me. I get an overwhelming urge of longing to know exactly what's going through her head. I want to know how this room—this house—looks through her eyes.

I want her to stay on as Clara's nanny for as long as possible. The cards have aligned, and I just know Selena would've loved her for Clara. I can feel it in my bones.

So I want this to work. For Liv to be comfortable here.

"It'll more than work. It's perfect. I'm sorry—typically, I'm great with words. I've always been a little on the chattier side." She sighs, her eyes roaming the room once before she looks at me again. "I just can't quite find the right words now other than this room is *more* than enough."

I give her a curt nod. I don't know how to respond to her, having the same problem as she does. Except, unlike her, I can *never* find the right words. I'd much rather say nothing at all. "It's nothing."

She rolls her eyes, choosing not to say anything. Instead, she walks up to Clara, who is still gleefully making snow angels on the bed. "Show me your room now?" she asks, playfully grabbing Clara's foot and pulling her across the mattress.

"Finally!" Clara shouts, her tone full of drama, as if she's been waiting hours instead of minutes to show Liv her room. She drops her Barbies to the ground, no longer interested in them.

"Then let's do it," Liv demands, letting Clara jump onto her back for a piggyback ride.

Chapter 13
LIV

"I CAN'T BELIEVE YOU WAKE UP TO THIS VIEW EVERY MORNING," I marvel, leaning over the banister of the back porch of the house. In front of us is a beautiful watercolor painting of reds, yellows, oranges, and even touches of green. Calling this a backyard seems like an insult.

There are rolling hills you can see for miles, the mountain-tops reflecting on the pond that sits not too far from the back of the house. There's even a barn to our right with a wood fence right next to it.

Dean's quiet next to me for a few moments, his eyes tracing over the same view as mine as he thinks over my words. He and Clara spent the morning walking me through the house and showing me where everything is. I had time to unpack my things and ask any questions I had before Clara went down for a nap twenty minutes ago. She fought it hard, wanting to stay up to show me around more before Dean finally convinced her to give in. "It really is a beautiful view, isn't it?" he finally responds, his voice a little rough.

"The most breathtaking one I've ever seen. I don't know if I'd ever leave the house if this is what I had to leave."

This makes him laugh, the sound coming from deep in his chest. It's the first time I've heard him laugh. It seems like a monumental moment that I got him to do it. It was the smallest laugh imaginable. Barely a laugh by some standards, probably, but I'm going to count it. He's been short and closed-off since we met, which I understand, but it's nice to see him let his guard down slightly, even if just for a brief moment.

His hands wrap around a red mug as he brings it to his lips. I hold a similar one, enjoying the coffee he made me. "Spend enough time in this town and the people here will comment how I don't like to leave the house often."

I nod, holding my tongue to tell him I've already been made aware of his tendencies to stay home. "I don't blame you. This view just doesn't seem real."

He lets out a long sigh, his shoulders sagging a little as he places his forearms on the railing. "The view does make you seem small, doesn't it?"

I watch him for a moment. I don't know what I was expecting him to say, but it wasn't that. He's been so quiet, keeping his thoughts to himself. He took me by surprise, but before I can respond, he stands back up and clears his throat. "Do you have any questions on where anything is? I know I showed you a lot."

I shake my head. I know I won't remember everything he told me today, but I know the important things—where I'm sleeping and the gist of where things are to take care of Clara. I'll spend the rest of today and all day tomorrow getting the hang of their routine before being with her fully on Monday. I'll definitely be able to figure things out.

"I think I'm good for the most part. I appreciate you taking the time to show me around. Everyone in the town has mentioned how busy you are, so I appreciate you taking time out of your day to help me get comfortable."

His jaw clenches, almost as if he's annoyed by my words. I shift on my feet awkwardly, wondering if I said something wrong. I just wanted to thank him, to let him know I appreciate his generosity today. Maybe I shouldn't have mentioned the fact I spoke with others in town about him.

"You'll be living here. Of course I needed to show you around and make sure you're comfortable finding things on your own." His voice is gruff. We haven't spent a ton of time together, but I'm learning very quickly how he often gets straight to the point.

I nod in understanding. He has a point. I'm just not used to people being thoughtful, even if there's a reason for it. I swallow, thinking about another nice thing he did for me that we haven't discussed yet.

I shift on my feet, not knowing how to broach the subject but knowing I have to. Even though I'm not used to people doing nice things for me, it doesn't mean I don't appreciate it.

"Thank you for offering a salary that I feel is far more than what I'm qualified for. And on top of that, thank you for paying for my stay at Sutten Inn," I manage to get out, my words a little rushed from nerves. "That wasn't necessary at all."

Dean turns, his body now fully facing me. He leans his elbow against the wood railing, his eyebrows drawn as he takes me in. I don't know if I want to know what's going through his head or if I'm relieved I don't know. Either way, I wait with bated breath for whatever he's going to say next.

It seems like he takes forever to answer me. I want to fold underneath his intense gaze. I try to look away from him as I wait for him to say something, but my eyes only get as far as staring at his chiseled jaw. A muscle in it ticks against his jawline, and for some reason, I can't look away from it.

What would it feel like under my touch?

I brush off the fleeting thought and straighten my spine, ripping my eyes from his jaw and looking at the mountains in front of us.

Finally, he speaks up, taking me by surprise again with another question I wasn't expecting. "Have you never had anyone do the right thing when it comes to you?"

I frown. "What do you mean?"

He lets out a sigh, as if he's annoyed at having to repeat himself. Not that he's necessarily irritated with me, but more that he doesn't strike me as someone who likes to repeat or explain his reasoning. "I mean, *I* asked you to wait until today to start. The whole reason you were staying there was because of me. It was the right thing to do, to pay for your stay."

I tilt my head to the side, thinking his words through. I guess I understand his logic, but I don't necessarily agree with him. It wasn't his responsibility to pay for my lodging. It's not like I traveled to Sutten for a job interview with him. The job stumbled into my lap in a twist of fate actually going my way for once. Never once did I expect him to pay for my stay at the inn, even after he asked for me to wait a couple of days before starting the job.

"I don't know you well, but your face pinching together in a scowl tells me you don't like what I just told you."

I hadn't realized I'd been scowling at him—more at his words than at him. I relax my facial muscles at his comment. All he ever does is scowl, so I'm shocked he's calling me out for it the one time I might've been doing it. "We'll just agree to disagree." I look at him, brave enough to let my eyes travel over him as I try to figure out the man standing in front of me.

He's more blunt than I was expecting. The times we met at Wake and Bake, he seemed so quiet. He's still not the most talkative man I've ever met, but he's got more to say than I was expecting. "It's not that I don't like it. Have you not had anyone vocally appreciate you doing something nice for them?" I throw his sarcasm back at him, loving how it's *his* turn to scowl at my words. Although, I don't know if getting him to scowl is considered a win. His face almost seems to be forever plastered in a permanent scowl. It just got deeper this time.

Dean whistles, and I *swear* my words earn the smallest whisper of a grin on his lips. "I see what you're doing."

I shrug, letting a smile take over my face, feeling triumphant.

"I wasn't trying to hide anything. If you're going to call me out, I'll do it right back. So, *Dean*," I emphasize his name, remembering the hard set of his jaw when I'd called him Mr. Livingston. "Thank you again for covering the bill at the inn. I really appreciate it."

"You're welcome," he grits out, clearly wanting to say more but holding back.

I rub my lips together, fighting the urge to smile even wider, feeling satisfied by him accepting my gratitude instead of arguing over it. "Since you're already clearly uncomfortable with accepting my appreciation, I might as well say everything else I want to as well."

He lets out a slow groan of displeasure. "I understand you're thankful. We don't have to keep making this awkward."

I cock my head to the side, watching him carefully. He refuses to look at me, instead choosing to look out at the mountain view in front of us. It doesn't bother me that he won't look my way. I still want to get the words out regardless. "I want— more like *need*—to just express how thankful I am for you taking a chance on me and giving me the job. After seeing the house and spending more time with Clara, I'm just incredibly grateful to start this job. I just know I'm going to love it."

"Even if your boss is kind of an asshole?"

He looks over at me with a quirked eyebrow and the shadow of another grin. I don't know if it's his words or the mischievous tilt of his lips that catches me off guard more. A small laugh escapes me as I shake my head.

"Hey, those were your words, not mine. I was busy being professional and saying thank you."

He holds the mug to his lips, the grin disappearing as quickly as it appeared. "I know you were thinking it."

I stay quiet, not wanting to tell him I was thinking that I think the town he grew up in might not understand him fully. Yes, he clearly has his walls up high. Could we really blame him? But there's still some of the old Dean in there they all talk about.

He's got a grumpy exterior, but I've already seen it slip a little.

And even though it's only my first day with him as my boss, I know having him as one won't be as bad as people made it out to be.

Chapter 14
DEAN

Yesterday was a busy day of getting Liv settled and introduced to as much of Clara's routine as possible. The day flew by quickly, and I was impressed by how easily she seemed to settle in. I haven't seen Liv since last night. It was a few hours after Clara went to bed for the night when Liv snuck up the stairs and told me good night as she hung over the banister.

We hadn't talked a lot. I'd gone to my office to get some work done, and she'd sat on the back deck even after the sun disappeared and the temperature dropped. I kept finding excuses to go to the kitchen to see if she was still sitting by the fireplace. She always was, despite it being cold. It was almost ten o'clock when she finally came inside.

I'd been sitting at my desk reviewing some work when I finally heard the door shut. Her footsteps were quiet as she tiptoed her way to the stairs, but the moment she'd looked into my office and found me still awake, she'd given me a timid smile.

I'd waited to say good night to her until she made it to the stairs, not expecting her to say anything back. But she'd leaned over and whispered good night, and for some reason, I'd wanted to know if she'd had a good day.

Had I done a good job of walking her through Clara's day? Did she feel prepared? Did she think she could be happy here? Did she think she'd stay awhile?

Those questions kept me up all night, but I embraced them overtaking my mind. These days, I much preferred being kept from sleep with my mind wandering than succumbing to my exhaustion and letting my dreams take over. My dreams were never good. They were filled with loss and devastation. Worrying about whether Liv will finally be the nanny that sticks for a bit was a very welcomed distraction.

I'd expected her to come downstairs for breakfast this morning, but she stayed in her room. Clara and I had gone to church, and for some reason, the entire service, all I could wonder was what she was up to at the house. It seemed logical. She's still a stranger alone in my house. But I wasn't worried because I didn't trust her; I worried because I hoped she wasn't upset that we left.

I tell myself the reason I'm going out of the way to the house before going to my parents' is because my mom won't stop pestering me about bringing Clara's new nanny to Sunday brunch. My mom had a point about inviting Liv. It was rude for me not to tell her about our family tradition. It only makes sense for me to run by the house before spending the rest of the afternoon there.

I'm just being polite.

I repeat that to myself over and over as I park my truck in the driveway, letting out a small sigh of relief when I see Liv's old car still parked there. My mom offered to take Clara straight to their house after church since my daughter was distraught at the thought of missing any play time with her cousins.

Which leaves me alone to stop by the house and invite Liv.

Since it shouldn't take long for me to tell Liv where we'll be for the rest of the day, I leave the truck on. I open the garage and head inside, finding the house eerily quiet. Liv isn't anywhere on the main floor or out on the back deck, so I climb the stairs to see if she's in her room.

I'm busy reminding myself that if her door is shut, I'll just leave her alone and leave a note downstairs telling her where we are when she steps out of her room.

"Shit!" she shrieks, her hand flying to her chest.

"I'm sorry," I rush out, seeing the fear in her eyes. "I should've probably called out or something, but I was worried you were maybe sleeping, so I came upstairs quietly and—"

Liv shakes her head, holding her hand up to stop me from talking. Her chest still rises and falls in quick succession as she tries to regain her composure. "It's fine. It's your house. I was just downstairs five minutes ago getting water and knew the house was empty, so you just surprised me, that's all."

She takes a deep breath, trying to even out her erratic breathing.

"We were at church, and when I mentioned you were still back at the house, my mom wouldn't stop bugging me about inviting you back to their house for Sunday brunch. It's kind of a big deal in our family. All my brothers go, too, and I think she contemplated disowning me as her oldest son when I'd told her I hadn't invited you."

"That's so nice of her," she notes, a soft smile playing on her lips. "I'm okay with staying here so you guys can have family time. "

I don't bother to hide my growl of displeasure. "You've been alone all day."

"I'm used to being alone," she quickly responds. I don't know why, but her words create a dull ache in my chest. I typically prefer being alone—aside from being with Clara. But now, I'm wondering if those around me feel that same ache in their chest when I tell them I'd rather be on my own. I take too long to say anything, so she clears her throat and rushes to get her next words out. "It's a family thing, like you mentioned. I don't want to intrude. But do tell your mom I appreciate her thinking of me." She plasters a smile on her face to try and convince me she's fine here.

I return her smile with a frown of my own, not liking her answer. "What if I said *I* want you there?" My voice is low and gravelly as I second-guess if it was the right thing to say. It's the truth, but the way she stares wide-eyed back at me makes me wonder if I should've kept the thought to myself. I sigh, trying to think of a way to not sound unprofessional. "It'd be nice for you to get familiar with my family," I rush to get out. "Plus, Clara would love to show you around the family property."

She purses her lips as she mulls over my offer. It's only in the silence between us that I realize she's wearing a familiar sweatshirt,

"Find some warmer clothes?" I ask, the slightest hint of humor in my tone.

Liv's eyes go wide as she looks down at the sweatshirt that is far too big on her. She immediately pulls at the bottom and begins to pull it up to take it off.

I reach out, grabbing her arm to stop her. "Don't. Keep it on. It's cold, and you need warmer clothes. I was just teasing you."

Liv freezes as she watches me carefully. "I don't want you to think I was trying to take it. I was just reading outside, and it was colder than I was expecting. The hoodie was hanging by the door, and I just...well, I took it." She lets out a nervous laugh, one that makes a corner of my lip turn up.

"We have countless Livingston Real Estate hoodies at the office. Keep this on. It's cold—plus, you'll become my dad's favorite if you wear it. I don't typically wear mine unless it's around the house."

"I didn't say I was going," she counters, her cheeks a little pink from me calling out the sweatshirt.

"Don't spend today alone, Liv. You don't have to be alone anymore."

I don't know why it's so important to me to convince her to come to Sunday brunch. Sometimes *I* barely want to go to Sunday brunch, but it's important to my mom. I missed two after Selena's death before my mom drove over here herself and forced me to attend the tradition. As much as I thought I wanted to be alone at that time, I didn't.

Maybe that's why I'm still standing here trying to convince Liv to attend as well. I don't know her backstory, but without her telling me, I know it seems like life hasn't always been kind to her.

I want her to see kindness here in Sutten. With this job. And with my family.

She sighs. "Is this *you* inviting me or just your mom?"

I can't help but smile. She's wittier than I was expecting. "Both."

"Fine. But are you sure the sweatshirt is okay? If it's yours, I can change real quick. The flannel Carmen picked out is fi—"

"If I didn't want you wearing it, I would've said something. I'm blunt—sometimes to a fault. It looks better on you than it does me anyway."

We're both quiet for a moment as my last words hang in the air. I didn't mean anything weird by it. It slipped out before I could think better of it.

My ears feel hot as I try to figure out if I should apologize or not. The last thing I need is for her to think I'm a creep. "I didn't mean that in any weird way. All I meant was I wear it and look like I—"

"It's fine." She laughs, and it seems genuine. The softness of her eyes and the smile on her lips tells me I might be worrying for nothing. "I'll accept the compliment. Let me get my purse, and we'll go."

She turns around and heads back to her room as I let out a sigh of relief. I'm going to have to get used to sharing my space with someone. I've had plenty of nannies stay here with me and Clara, but none of them lasted long. I never really cared about establishing a professional relationship with them because they were gone as quickly as they started.

But with Liv it feels different.

I already want her to stay awhile. There's something about

her. She radiates light, even with the knowledge she seems to have gone through a lot. And I want Clara to have that in her life.

When she walks back out with a smile plastered on her face and her purse swung over her shoulder, I accept that I might need a little of that light in my life, too.

Chapter 15
LIV

"HOUSES IN COLORADO ARE WAY DIFFERENT THAN HOUSES IN Florida," I mutter as Dean takes us down a long, winding driveway toward his childhood home.

"I've been to Florida before. There's definitely beautiful real estate there," Dean remarks as he parks his truck right next to another one that almost looks identical to his.

"I wouldn't know. There was nothing beautiful about where I lived."

He frowns but doesn't respond to my comment. I like that he doesn't ask a lot of questions. I wouldn't answer him even if he did.

"Sounds like you need to see better parts of Florida."

I laugh. "I never want to go back to Florida. I'll stick to different views. Like this one right here." I lean forward in my seat and rest my elbows on the dashboard.

In front of me is another breathtaking landscape. While Dean's house is more nestled in a valley between mountains, his family's home is right on the side of a mountain. There are trees everywhere, but they're spread out enough that you can still see their neighbors. At Dean's house, all you can see are trees, mountains, and the little pond behind his house. There isn't a neighbor in sight.

"What do you think?" Dean asks. I can feel his eyes on me even as I look ahead at the beautiful house in front of us.

Where Dean's house had modern accents that show it was recently built, his childhood home is the complete opposite. It looks like a house you'd find in Colorado. It's a cherrywood-colored cabin, but still larger than the typical size I was expecting of cabins. As someone who grew up in Florida, maybe my perceptions of the size of what a cabin should be are just wrong.

"I think that the house is beautiful. I haven't been inside yet, but I can just feel that you had a good childhood here. That it was a great place to grow up."

There's an old tire attached to a huge tree not too far from us. The rope has been weathered by the sun over the years, but it still hangs like someone could use it even today. I try to imagine a small Dean swinging from it. Even though he seems calm and reserved, I get the feeling he was still a daredevil in his younger years.

The thought makes me smile. Clara seems like him in that regard. I've spent one full day with her at this point and have quickly learned she has no fear.

I keep looking around, taking in the sights. There are more cars here than I was expecting, making me wonder how many siblings he has.

He hums but he doesn't take his eyes off me. I don't know why, but my cheeks heat under his gaze. I both want him to keep looking at me and for him to look away. "It was the best place to grow up. This house, this town, I could never imagine leaving."

"Pippa said the same thing," I respond, my eyes catching on a giant yellow dog running along the fence line.

"You'll see. This place is hard to leave. We do need to get out to Jennings Ranch before it gets too cold. Going on one of their trail rides will guarantee you the best view of all time."

I finally look at him, finding his brown eyes still on me. I can't help but smile at the thought of seeing views more beautiful than what I've already seen of Sutten. "I'd love that. Although, I've never even ridden a horse before…"

This makes him raise a dark eyebrow. "Don't worry. I'll show you the ropes."

The husky tone to his voice sends a shiver down my spine. I can't explain why. I know his innocent sentence shouldn't have any kind of effect on me, but I can't help that it does. I shake my head, trying to get rid of the weird sensation as quickly as it appeared.

Luckily, Dean doesn't seem to notice my weird reaction. He grabs an old baseball hat from his side of the dash and places it on his head. When he looks over at me, that mischievous tilt of his lip is back. "Let's see how long it takes my mom to lecture me on wearing a hat at the dinner table."

A squeak of panic falls from my lips when I look at my outfit. I'm wearing leggings and a hoodie to their family function. "Was I supposed to dress up?"

"No. My mom just has a rule about hats at the table no matter the time of day."

I chew on my lip for a moment, wondering if this is a good idea. I do want to get to know his family in case something happens and I can't get ahold of Dean, but I'm wondering if I should've waited a little bit longer. I technically haven't even started the job yet. "Ready?" Dean asks. "I bet Clara has asked when you'd be here five thousand times by now."

I sigh, trying to calm the nerves racing through me. I don't know why I'm nervous. All that I know is that I *am* nervous. Maybe it's because I've never had a family. Nothing about my upbringing is normal. What if I say something wrong and his mom hates me? What if one of them thinks I'm not qualified to be Clara's nanny?

"Liv?" Dean prods. He reaches across the center console of the truck before he lets his hand drop between us. The sound of it hitting the leather has me looking at him, my heart still racing with nerves.

"I'm nervous your family might hate me and tell you to fire me," I blurt. The words come from my mouth before I can think better of them. I wish I knew why I was suddenly so nervous. I'm normally a look-on-the-bright-side kind of person. Thinking in worst-case scenarios was something I grew tired of. My life could be sad enough at times. The least I could do for my own mental health was try to be more positive.

But for some reason, as I sit in Dean's pristine truck, I'm realizing that for the first time in a long time, I have something I want. And the thought of losing it just days after getting it is making me incredibly nervous.

Dean's silence doesn't help in the slightest. Neither do the two deep lines between his eyebrows that help make up his deep scowl.

"Here's where you give me some kind of words of encouragement," I add, trying to lighten the mood but also trying to have him talk some sense into me.

"There's no way they're going to hate you. How could they? Clara loves you, and she's got every single one of us wrapped around her finger." He jerks his head toward the door. "Now, let's go inside so I can prove to you how ridiculous it is for you to think they'd ever hate you."

I take a deep breath and nod. He understands the cue. Immediately, he opens his door, and before he can even step out of the truck, the giant yellow dog I saw earlier is jumping all over him.

"Hi, Missy," he says, gently running his hand down her back. His door shuts, and before I can open my own door, he's pulling it open. The massive golden retriever comes with him, her tail wagging enthusiastically as Dean holds out his hand to help me down.

"I know she's huge, but she's like a giant teddy bear. You have to watch out for—"

"Oh, hi." I laugh as two massive paws land on my shoulders the moment I step out of the truck. The dog's tongue swipes along my cheek. Before she can lick me again, Dean reaches out, grabs her collar, and pulls her off me.

"Sorry," he apologizes, holding tight to her collar even as she tries to jump on me all over again. "She's still learning her manners."

"Is she a puppy?" I ask, squatting down to scratch the dog's ears. She's adorable. Her tail thrashes in the air excitedly as I move to scratch her chin.

This makes Dean chuckle. It's a low rumble from deep inside his chest, but I love the sound of it. It's nice to know that he can laugh and find humor in the world, even after the devastating things that have happened to him. "No, she's not a puppy. In fact, she's a mommy of four adorable puppies inside. Mom and Dad have just been soft with her training now that they're empty nesters. They spoil you, don't they, Missy?" He uses a slight baby voice when talking to the dog. She revels in it. Her tongue peeks out from the side of her mouth as she basks in the attention from both of us. She rolls over, placing herself right over the toes of his cowboy boots—the same boots I find far too attractive.

"So, there are puppies inside?" I ask, probably more excited than I should be.

Dean picks up a nearby stick and throws it for Missy. She runs after it without any second thought of us. "There are. I know some have homes lined up, but it'll still be a few weeks until then. Do you love puppies?"

I nod. "Doesn't everyone love puppies?"

"Fair point. Let's get you inside then, so you can get your puppy fix in. I'm sure that's where we'll find Clara," he adds.

I follow him, suddenly forgetting I was ever nervous about meeting his family in the first place.

Chapter 16
DEAN

OF COURSE, THE MOMENT WE WALK THROUGH THE FRONT DOORS OF the house I grew up in, everything goes quiet. My family's close-knit—and incredibly nosy—so the moment I opened the door, I should've known they'd all go quiet in their excitement to meet Liv.

"We're here," I call out, knowing full well they all know we've walked in the door. I wouldn't put it past my youngest brother, Reed, or even my mother to have been watching us through the blinds. I'd never brought any of the past nannies to Sunday brunch. I saw no reason to. I knew they weren't going to last right when they started, just like I know now that I won't be the reason Liv stops being Clara's nanny. It'll be because she's ready to move on.

"Dean!" My mom rushes out from the living room, a wide smile on her face. I'll hand it to her; she's great at pretending not to know we were here until just now. "This must be the Livvy we've heard all about."

Mom doesn't even reach out to give me a hug. I guess she had just seen me, but it does take me a little by surprise that she immediately pulls Liv into a hug without asking first. "I'm Shirley, Clara's mimi."

"And my mom," I add, pretending to be hurt that she just forgot all about me.

Despite just meeting her, Liv still wraps her arms around my mom's shoulders and hugs her back. She's a little stiff, making me wonder if Mom's hug makes her uncomfortable. I bite my tongue, wanting to tell my mother to let Liv breathe. Mom looks at me from over Liv's shoulder. "Oh, you know what I mean, honey. Don't be jealous. I only said it because she's Clara's nanny."

I shake my head, knowing she didn't mean anything by it. She's the best mom in the world. We couldn't have asked for anyone better growing up. I still like to give her shit when I can, though.

Mom pulls away from the hug first, but she still doesn't give Liv very much personal space. Her hands rest on her shoulders as she looks at Liv like she hung the moon. "Welcome to the family, darling," she says fondly.

"Oh, uh, thank you," Liv responds. She shifts on her feet, but other than that, only the slight uneasiness of her tone shows that Mom's words took her off guard.

"Maybe let her work a week before freaking her out?" my dad chimes in as he plants his feet next to Mom.

I try not to laugh at the glare my mom aims in his direction. Behind Dad, the rest of my family files into the wide entryway to meet Liv.

"I'm Marshall." Dad holds his hand out.

Liv takes it immediately. "Liv," she responds, her eyes roaming over the group of people forming in the entryway.

"Nice sweatshirt," Dad gets out, a look of approval on his face as he looks at the emblem printed on the front.

Liv's cheeks get a little pink as she looks at what she's wearing. "Don't mind my outfit." She looks at my mom with an apologetic look. "I'm still working on getting weather-appropriate clothing."

Mom swats at the air dismissively. "Oh, don't worry about it. There's no dress code for Sunday brunch, darling."

Liv's eyes instantly find mine as we share a knowing look. I try to fight the smile but can't resist when Liv's entire face breaks into a beaming grin. It feels nice to smile casually. Something about her sunshine personality makes me want to break through the darkness that's constantly pulling me in. I playfully grab at the ball cap on my head, knowing it won't be long before Mom will comment on me wearing the hat.

I turn my focus to my mom, finding her already looking at me with raised eyebrows and a wide smile.

"Where are all the kids?" I ask, despite knowing they're probably on the screened-in back porch with the puppies. I ask before having to explain to my mom how I've known Liv for such a short amount of time, and yet she's been able to get me to crack a smile. If only Mom knew it was because I'd told Liv about Mom's hat rule—and how I was sure to get in trouble for breaking it.

"With the dogs," Jace cuts in, stepping around Dad to shake Liv's hand.

"I'm Jace," he introduces himself before hooking a thumb over his shoulder. "And that beautiful woman over there feeding the baby is my wife, Hattie. The darling baby girl is Ruthie—although she's not as cute today after being up all night. We also have a five-year-old running around somewhere named Miles."

"So nice to meet you guys." The smile on Liv's face never falters.

"I'm going to give you a run-through of everyone," I begin, closing the distance until I stand right next to her. "Don't worry if you can't remember everyone's names—it's a lot. So obviously, you met Mom and Dad—Shirley and Marshall." I point to everyone as I rattle off their names. "Then you met Jace, who is married to Hattie, and their kids are Miles and Ruthie. Then we have Finn and his wife, Ashton. They have three boys who are probably teaching Clara all the things they shouldn't be. The boys' names are Jack, Clark, and Max. And then we have Reed, who is, well…it's just Reed."

My youngest brother pretends to be hurt by my words. "Way to cut deep, Dean," he jokes, wrapping his arm around me.

"Is it cutting deep when it's just pointing out the obvious?"

Reed is twenty-three and the baby of the family. He still has a lot of life to live; we just like to give him shit because everyone else got married and has kids while he's still living life, enjoying being young and not settling down.

His carefree personality reminds me a lot of Selena. She and Reed got along great despite their age difference. They both always loved to give me trouble, and I know if she were here right now, she'd be ganging up on me with Reed. He brings out the more playful, carefree side of me, just like she did.

He wags his eyebrows at me and smiles. "It's good to meet you, Liv." Reed completely ignores my words and instead wraps his other arm around her.

Seeing his arm wrapped around her shoulder makes me realize they're the same age.

Liv doesn't seem too bothered by his carefree demeanor. She allows his arm to stay in place, even if, for some reason, I hate seeing him have any kind of contact with her at all.

"Nice to meet you, Reed." She doesn't seem overwhelmed by the number of introductions. If anything, she seems excited to strike up small conversations with my family, who are all anxious to meet her.

I love how they all instantly want to get to know her. I'm biased, but I truly have the best family in the world. I wouldn't have survived the last few years if it wasn't for them. They've pulled me out of some really dark times, and it feels like a breath of relief to see them naturally gravitate toward Liv in the same way Clara and I have.

So many questions are fired off in her direction at once.

"How was your first night?"

"Do you have any allergies?"

"Have you thought about quitting yet?"

Reed's question makes me narrow my eyes at him. I playfully push him away.

"*Reed.*" Mom beats me to scolding my younger brother. She pinches her face together while looking at him, aiming her pointer finger in his direction. "Be nice to your brother."

Reed lifts his shoulders defensively. "I didn't say anything about Dean."

I walk over to him and wrap my arm around him to put him in a headlock. It isn't tight. He's the athlete, not me. If he wanted out, he could get out. He doesn't. "Insinuating that Liv should quit before her first full day *is* saying something about me."

He shoves at my side with a cocky laugh and pulls himself free. "Listen, everyone here knows your track record. I'm shocked she didn't run for the hills after one night."

Liv looks at me with a raised eyebrow. "Are you really *that* bad?"

"Yes."

"No."

I glare at Reed as we both get the words out at the same time.

Thankfully, Ashton steps in and loops her arm through Liv's. "Dean really isn't bad. Reed just likes to annoy his older brother."

"What are younger brothers for?" Reed asks with a smug grin.

"Annoying the shit out of me," I fire back, watching carefully as Ashton leads Liv down the hallway.

The family disperses in different directions. I decide to follow Ashton and Liv, wanting to know where my sister-in-law is taking my new nanny.

As if she can read my mind, Ashton looks over her shoulder with a smile on her face. "You don't have to supervise us, Dean. I was just going to give Liv a tour."

I frown, crossing my arms over my chest, unsure if I like the idea or not.

"I want to join!" Hattie calls from the living room. She rushes over to Ashton and Liv, handing Ruthie over to Jace. "Take your daughter for a minute. My boobs shouldn't be needed for at *least* an hour, which means you're on Ruthie duty."

Jace carefully adjusts the newborn in his arms. He meets his wife's eyes with a cautious smile. "Just don't scare away the nanny, okay? You and Ashton can be a...lot. It'd be nice for Dean to actually keep a nanny for once."

Reed busts out laughing from my side.

I let out a frustrated growl. "For fuck's sake, everyone. Do you think we could lay off the nanny jabs?"

"Language," Mom scolds.

Hattie takes her spot on the other side of Liv. "This family is always fun. Promise."

To her credit, Liv doesn't look bothered by our bickering at all. If anything, she looks like she might actually be enjoying watching the show. I'm sure we are entertaining from an outsider's perspective.

"So, where to first?" Ashton asks, leaning forward to meet Hattie's eyes.

Liv looks between my two sisters-in-law with a growing smile. "I vote we go see the puppies first."

Chapter 17
LIV

"I'M IN LOVE," I DECLARE FOR PROBABLY THE TENTH TIME. The puppy burrows deeper into the crease of my neck as I clutch it to my chest, never wanting to let it go.

"She does look cozy." Hattie laughs as the puppy she holds tries to lick her cheek.

"Why won't my puppy chill out?" Ashton asks, trying her hardest to keep the energetic golden retriever in her lap. It keeps trying to leap out of her lap and nibble at the bow in Clara's hair.

"Yours my favorite," Clara tells me, leaning over to gently pet the puppy snoring against my chest.

I smile, finding it absolutely adorable how obsessed Clara is with the puppy taking a snooze on me. "She's my favorite, too," I whisper, gently scratching the puppy's ear. "She's just too sweet. I'm in love."

Ashton hands her wild puppy over to her son Jack, who begins to run around the back porch as the puppy chases after him. "Maybe you can talk Dean into letting Clara get a puppy."

"Yes. I *need*." The way Clara emphasizes need is the cutest thing ever. She even juts her bottom lip out.

"If it were up to me, you'd absolutely get the puppy," I tell Clara, wishing Dean would agree to it so I could get snuggles like this all the time.

"Want to hold her?" I ask Clara. I could sit here forever with the puppy nestled into my chest, but I know Ashton and Hattie are wanting to continue to give me the tour of the Livingston home.

Clara excitedly nods her head. She sits back in the chair with her arms held out. I slowly place the dog on her chest as it stays fast asleep. The smile on Clara's face is giant as she holds still as a statue, letting the pup sleep soundly in her lap.

"I'm ready for the rest of the tour when you guys are," I tell Ashton and Hattie. I don't know if they were as excited to see the puppies as I was, but they humored me, and we spent what's got to be at least fifteen minutes on the back porch with them.

"Jack and Miles, you're in charge of watching the others. Please make sure everyone makes good choices, okay?" Ashton lovingly ruffles the hair of her oldest son, Jack. He nods his head before going right back to running around with the wild puppy.

"While we're here, let's show her outside," Hattie offers, already holding the door open that leads outside from the back porch.

"You're just trying to get as far away as possible from Jace in case Ruthie starts crying," Ashton teases while walking through the back door.

Hattie laughs. "He's fine manning the children. Plus, we all know that if Ruthie starts crying, Shirley is going to jump in to help immediately."

I'm quiet as I follow the two of them down the stairs. My attention is drawn to the sheer beauty of the backyard. There are trees for miles, and with it being fall, it creates the most beautiful picture of brilliant oranges and reds.

"It's really stunning, isn't it?" Hattie asks quietly.

I nod. "I don't know if it's just because I hadn't seen mountains before this, but I'm still just taken aback by how beautiful it is. I didn't know leaves could be so pretty. Which sounds very poetic of me, and I'm not normally this cheesy, but wow…"

"I get it. I'm from Kansas. You just can't understand the beauty of this state—really, this town—until you're here. Give it one more week when there's barely any green left on the trees, and you're going to be in for a treat." Hattie has a whisper of a smile on her lips with her words.

"You're not from here?" I ask. I don't know why I assumed everyone in his family, including the wives, were from Sutten.

Hattie shakes her head. "Not really. I moved to Sutten my junior year of high school, so I've been here a while. But I still remember the first sunset I saw here. Selena couldn't stop laughing at me because I cried."

My ears perk up at the mention of Clara's mom. Dean still hasn't mentioned the passing of his wife, not that he owes me any explanation of her life or death. But I do want to know about her. She gave birth to the most beautiful daughter, and I'd love to be able to remind Clara of her mom when I can. Getting stories about her from the people who knew her—even if they're not from Dean—is a way I can do that.

"God, she didn't let you forget about that for years," Ashton adds, her arms crossing over her chest.

I stay quiet, wondering if I should say something or not. I guess I should've known that Selena wouldn't have just meant something to Dean and Clara but to the rest of his family as well. Carmen mentioned how long he and Selena had been together. It only makes sense that her death is felt by everyone in the Livingston family.

Hattie lets out a slow breath before plastering a smile on her face. Unshed tears make her eyes glossy, but she quickly blinks to try and hide them. "I'm *so* sorry," she begins. "I'm not trying to make this sad at all. Her birthday is next month, and she was my best friend since high school. Sometimes it just hits hard, you know?"

I nod. "Please don't apologize to me. I can't imagine losing a family member like all of you did so tragically. I only know small tidbits from people in town, but she seemed like a really great person."

"Dean hasn't told you about her yet?" Hattie asks, her voice quiet but rough with emotion.

I shake my head, wondering if I should've told them that or not. "I'm still new. I haven't expected him to share anything."

Hattie sighs. "It's still hard for him to talk about her. He really loved her, and instead of talking about how incredible she was, he keeps everything bottled up inside. Just know he isn't neglecting to tell you about her because he doesn't trust you or doesn't want to tell you. He doesn't really speak about her with any of us."

"I get it. I don't blame him for it. It makes sense she was so great, though. Clara's the best, and I'm sure she gets that not only from Dean but from her mom, too."

Both Hattie and Ashton nod, but Ashton's the one to speak up. "She was incredible and loved by all of us. We miss her every day."

"Anyway..." Hattie begins, wiping underneath her eyes. "Sorry. It's the postpartum hormones hitting me. Back to it. Yes, this view is stunning, and no, it never gets old, even if you've lived here for years."

"Is this where all the boys grew up?" I ask, hoping a change of subject is what they want.

They both nod.

Ashton laughs. "Yes. Marshall built this house before Dean was ever born. He loves to tell the story of how his dad was pissed at him for building so far from the town. The house closer in town was renovated into an office space for the realty group. Marshall will *surely* tell you how his dad ended up falling in love with this property and would come visit any chance he could, before he passed, because of the views."

The comment makes me smile. "I love that. Marshall was onto something. It's really beautiful here."

"Wait until it snows. Having this view for Christmas is even more spectacular," Hattie chimes in. Our steps fall in unison as we walk along the property. The tire swing is in the distance to the right. To our left is a doghouse with at least ten tennis balls sitting in front of it.

"Is it possible to have a white Christmas?" I ask excitedly, dreaming of actually seeing snow on Christmas Day for the first time.

Hattie and Ashton look at each other with wide smiles. "It's almost always a white Christmas since we're in the mountains," Ashton responds.

Hattie excitedly grabs my arm and pulls me toward a door on the side of the house. "I've always been someone who loves Christmas, but oh my god, Liv, you just made me even more excited for you to have your first Sutten Christmas. It's magic and will be here before we know it."

I hadn't thought about spending the holidays in Sutten. I knew I'd be here for Halloween because it's only a couple of weeks away, but I hadn't thought too far past that. I guess I hope I'll still be here and things will still be running smoothly with Clara and Dean.

"You do plan on being here for the holidays, right?" Ashton asks, as if she can read my mind.

I shrug as we walk through a side door into the house. "I guess."

I don't really know how I feel. Now that they've asked, I would love to be here for Christmas, but that realization terrifies me. If I'm here until Christmas, it's because I've fallen in love with the job and this town—and the people in it. It means I'm happy here, and being happy means I have something to lose.

I've never been truly happy somewhere. My life hasn't always been good, and now with things lining up, I'm scared of how quickly that can change.

But I do still really want to be here. I want things to work out for me to see a white Christmas. To spend the holidays with this family. I'll just have to deal with the uneasiness of finally having the potential of something I wouldn't want to lose. Right now, I'll try and focus on the good.

We walk into a laundry room. The array of different shoes lining the floor makes me smile. There are ones of all different sizes, showing that even though Shirley and Marshall's kids are all grown up, this house is still full of love. I realize both Hattie and Ashton are still quiet, probably waiting for me to say more about Christmas. "I've never really done anything big for Christmas, so it'd be fun to be here for it."

"So it's settled. You won't quit before the holidays, and you'll get to experience the most magical time of year in the most magical place to live." Hattie winks at me as she playfully lifts her shoulder in a shrug. "Not that I'm biased or anything."

"People really seem to think I'll quit. I don't get it. Dean doesn't seem *that* bad."

Hattie and Ashton share a look. They both smile, but there's also sadness in their eyes. I don't know if it's at the mention of Dean or if they're still thinking about Selena. "Dean isn't bad. He's just…"

"Dean," Ashton finishes Hattie's thought. "The thing about him is you just have to give him grace. Every now and then, we get glimpses of the man he was before we lost Selena. He was carefree and happy with her around. Always a little quiet, but there was light in his eyes. After losing her, the light disappeared. It comes back every now and then, but a lot of the time, it's hard for him to be even a shell of the person he used to be. He can seem cold and closed off at times, but I think it's just because he's terrified of ever allowing himself to be happy again."

Her words make me stop in the middle of the laundry room. They both wait for me in the opening to a hallway, but I'm too busy still letting her words sink in to move. They make me sad. For Dean, for Clara, for everyone.

I give them both an encouraging smile, wanting to ease their minds that I have no plans of quitting anytime soon. "He's been fine. I understand he's been through a lot. Maybe he hasn't always gone about it the right way with people, but after knowing Clara for only a short amount of time, I know she's special. He's just doing his best to give her what she deserves."

Ashton nods. "Some of the nannies did suck. Or were weird, so I couldn't blame him for some of the firings."

This makes me laugh as I follow them down the hallway. There are pictures lining both walls. It seems busy but in the best possible way. Years of memories line each side, and if Hattie and Ashton weren't busy leading me to other places in the house, I'd take a minute to stop and look at all the photos to get a glimpse of the Livingston family over the years.

"Okay, let's continue the tour. I have so many questions I want to ask you to get to know you better," Hattie states excitedly, grabbing my arm and pulling me down the hallway.

They spend the next hour showing me around, and even though it's something as simple as a house tour, it's so great to spend time with them. They asked questions, but they never seemed intrusive. Both Hattie and Ashton just seem genuinely interested in getting to know me.

I'm not used to people wanting to know anything about me. I thought I'd be uncomfortable sharing things about myself with people I only met today, but I actually enjoyed it. It's refreshing to have people interested in the little nuances of my life.

By the time we meet up with the rest of the Livingston crew, Hattie and Ashton are already demanding we have a girls' night one weekend soon.

It feels like for the first time in my life, I might be on the verge of having real friends. Between Hattie and Ashton and then Lexi and Pippa, I'm thrilled at the idea of Sutten not only bringing me a job and a safe place to live but real friends, too.

I didn't used to want friends—now, I'm cautiously excited about making them.

Chapter 18
DEAN

CLARA SLEEPS PEACEFULLY IN THE BACK SEAT AS I PUT THE TRUCK IN park in the driveway.

Liv sits quietly in the passenger seat. She leans against the window, her eyelids a little heavy as she gazes outside.

"So did my family scare you away from the job, or are you ready for tomorrow?"

Her laugh is quiet, just a small little breath of air, but for some reason, it calms my nerves. My family can be a lot. Especially since she hasn't even officially started her first day, I was nervous to take her to meet all of them.

But she seemed to have handled it perfectly, something that makes me happier than it should. Not just for my family's sake, or even Clara's sake, but for mine, too. I try not to think too deeply about what that means.

If I don't analyze it, I can tell myself it's for professional reasons only.

The smile on her face as she thinks over an answer to my question tells me what I need to know. "I don't scare easily. I loved your family. They were..."

"A lot?" I finish for her, trying to keep my voice quiet so as not to wake Clara.

She nods as she unbuckles her seat belt and pulls her knees to her chest. Her eyes focus on me as she opens her mouth to answer. "They're a lot, but in a good way. You can feel the love in the room, even when people are bickering or teasing each other."

"They drive me crazy. Absolutely up the wall more often than not—especially Reed—but they're the best. They've been there for me, even when I was at such a low place I kept trying to push them away. They're everything to me. I'm glad you enjoyed them. When you snuck away with Ashton and Hattie, I got a little nervous that you'd spend five minutes with them and decide you weren't interested in the job anymore." It might be the most I've admitted to Liv. I should feel uneasy about being so free with my words to her, but I'm not. If anything, it feels good to recognize how much my family have been there for me and how much I appreciate them for it.

A little snore comes from Clara in the back seat. We both turn to look at her. Her head is tilted all the way back in what can't be a comfortable position. She's got her hands folded adorably in her lap as her eyelids flutter with whatever she's dreaming about.

When I look back at Liv, I find her eyes already back on me. "I'm still very much interested in the job. I haven't even been in Sutten for a week, and I can't imagine leaving yet. You're kind of stuck with me for a bit."

I smirk at her words, fighting the urge to tell her it doesn't sound so bad to be stuck with her. Not when she's not only great with Clara but with my crazy family as well. I love the thought of having some consistency in our life. And there's something about Liv that makes me feel like—and maybe even hope—she'll be in our lives for a little while.

"Clara's lucky to be stuck with you," I finally get out, taking a deep breath. "We both are," I admit under my breath. My heart slams against my chest at being so open with her. Even with the rush of adrenaline, I don't regret it.

She makes me want to be a little more open.

I let my words hang between us. In the past, I'd dreaded going to work in the days after I'd hired a new nanny. There was always something in the back of my head telling me why I didn't think they'd be a good fit. With Liv, I don't feel that pit in my stomach about work tomorrow. If anything, I'm excited for Clara to have the day with Liv. I know she'll have the best day ever, and I'm going to love getting home at the end of the day and hearing about every second of it.

"I feel lucky, too," Liv admits. "I know you took a huge chance on me since I don't have any experience. I'm ready to show you that you didn't make a mistake."

I nod as I fight the urge to tell her I already have the feeling I didn't make a mistake. Although I'm sure she'd be relieved to hear me say it aloud, I keep it to myself. No matter how good I feel about her—which I do—I know there's still a chance this could not work out. I want to make sure I don't get too hopeful in case that were to happen. I've already been more open with her than I should; the least I can do is keep my hopefulness at a minimum.

"We should probably get inside," I say, rubbing the back of my neck. All I want to do is take a nice, hot shower and get into bed. I'd been afraid of falling asleep last night, worried Liv might hear my nightmares even from a different floor of the house. Hopefully tonight, I'll be too exhausted for the nightmares to even reach me.

"Do you need any help getting Clara inside?" Liv asks, her voice soft. She looks back at Clara with an adoring look in her eyes.

It does something to me, seeing her look at my sleeping daughter with so much affection. It's bittersweet. I love that someone new in Clara's life looks at her like that, but it also hurts knowing Selena never got to see her toddler doze off in the back seat after a long day of playing.

I shake my head, trying to clear my mind. "I've got it. I'm used to having to carry her to her bed. Thank you for offering, though."

Liv gives me a smile before slowly turning to open her door.

Even though I told her I could manage, she helps by opening all the doors for me as I carry Clara to her room.

I'm busy helping a sleepy Clara into her pajamas when I turn to find Liv waiting in the doorway. She leans against the doorframe, the softest of smiles on her lips.

'"Good night," she whispers, keeping her voice nice and low so as not to disturb Clara.

I give her one curt nod of my head before mouthing, *"Night."*

She leaves and softly closes the door behind her, leaving me and Clara alone.

I thought my daughter was pretty much asleep, but when I turn to her, I find her eyes open and watching me. She burrows into the blankets on her bed, pulling her favorite stuffed animal close to her cheek.

"Livvy be here in the morning?" she asks, her voice incredibly groggy and adorable.

I nod. "Yes, honey, she'll be here in the morning."

Clara's face breaks out into the cutest smile. "That makes me happy, Daddy."

I swallow, my emotions getting the better of me in the moment. My throat feels clogged with them threatening to spill out. I take a deep breath, not wanting to lose my composure in front of my half-asleep daughter. "If you're happy, then I'm happy."

"I'm happy, Daddy. With you. And I think Livvy, too."

I lean forward and press my lips to my daughter's forehead. My shoulders shake a little as I let out a long sigh of relief. This is the first time Clara's voiced excitement about spending the day with a nanny. It's like I can finally take a deep breath after waiting ages for someone that both Clara and I are comfortable with.

"Night, honey," I croak, the weight of being the only person responsible for how her life turns out weighing heavy on me.

So many of these decisions I thought I'd have Selena to help me with. If she were here, we wouldn't need a nanny at all. She was thrilled at the thought of staying home and raising our children. With her gone, I'm terrified I'm making the wrong choices.

Clara dozes off as I brush the stray pieces of hair from her face. I look at her, picking out the features on her little face that remind me of Selena. Something suddenly overcomes me. I don't know exactly what it is, but it's an overwhelming sense of peace. I can question many of my decisions as a single father and if I'm making the same ones Selena would've made if she were here.

But one decision I don't have to question is hiring Liv.

I clutch my daughter tight, knowing that Selena would've loved Liv. For the first time in a long time, I feel like maybe I'm finally doing something right when it comes to our daughter.

Chapter 19
LIV

Clara is busy coloring a picture at the table when Dean walks into the kitchen, ready for work.

"It smells amazing in here," he notes, setting his briefcase down on the island and stepping closer.

I smile as I focus on flipping the pancakes. "Clara *insisted* on pancakes this morning."

"With cimamim!" Clara calls from her spot, not even bothering to look up from what she's coloring. The way she's been saying cinnamon all morning has killed me. It's adorable, and I hope she never grows out of it.

"With cinnamon," I confirm.

The smell of Dean's cologne—or maybe it's his aftershave—overpowers the smell of the cinnamon pancakes as he stands right next to me, watching closely as I begin to place the pancakes that are done on a plate next to the stove.

"I've got a couple of meetings this morning," Dean explains, reaching into the cabinet next to me. He pulls out a coffee thermos and places it on the counter. "I won't always be able to check my phone if you need anything, but please, if anything happens or you have any questions, call my assistant, and she'll alert me immediately."

I try not to smile at the nervousness in his tone. It's kind of cute, and I shouldn't find my widowed boss cute whatsoever.

His smell is more overpowering than I thought. It's going to my head. The way his scent surrounds me, fogging my brain with thoughts of wanting to get even closer to smell him.

"We should be perfect. We're going to have the best first day together, aren't we, Clara?"

Clara pushes her dark hair out of her face as she looks up at both of us. She wears a wide smile as she meets my eyes. "The *best* day, Livvy." Her eyes move to Dean. "Bye, Daddy."

Dean pauses while pouring steaming hot coffee into his mug. He looks at his daughter with raised eyebrows. "Are you already ready to get rid of me?" There's a hint of a teasing tone in his voice.

I'd smile, but I'm too caught up in how he looks this morning.

Maybe it's the way that the ends of his hair are wet and he stands close enough to me that I can see the little droplets hitting the pressed white collar of his shirt.

"Do you want some?" Dean asks, his tone hesitant as he holds up the coffeepot.

I jump, realizing he mistook me staring at him for wanting some coffee. I shake my head. "No, I'm fine. I had a cup already." I turn to the pancakes, wincing when I realize the two still on the pan are a little more brown than I intended.

Get it together, Liv.

I blame the fact that I can't stop looking at Dean on my lack of sleep last night. Nerves for my first day alone with Clara got the better of me. I want to do a good job, and meeting Dean's family and feeling like I fit in with a group of people for the first time in my life made me realize how good I already have it here in Sutten.

The fear of losing it had me spending all night with my brain spinning over all the different things Clara and I could do to have fun. I repeated Clara's schedule to myself so many times that I could recite it in my sleep. All I wanted to do was be prepared for today, but apparently, my desire to feel confident going in made it so my exhaustion is making me daydream about my boss.

My *very* off-limits boss.

The boss I'm still staring at as I watch his lips turn down in a frown. "Are you feeling okay this morning, Liv?" His voice is tight.

I nod as I plaster a smile on my face. "Totally fine. Want any pancakes before you go?"

I make sure to keep eye contact. All I want to do is take a moment to really appreciate the suit he's wearing this morning, but I know better. I don't want to make this weird, and I'm really only even giving him a second glance because I'm tired and he smells good.

That's got to be the reason.

Dean stares at me for a few moments with narrowed lids. Slowly, he shakes his head. "No, I'm okay." He leaves it at that as a blush creeps onto my cheeks.

I've weirded him out.

Or maybe he's just in a rush. I try to comfort myself into thinking I'm not being creepy as he walks over to the breakfast nook. Clara barely looks up from her coloring sheet as he presses his lips to her hairline.

"You have a good day today. I'll miss you." He strokes the hair from her face as he looks down at her lovingly. I can tell he's nervous about leaving her today, and I'm sure me acting weird this morning isn't helping at all.

"You don't have to miss me, Daddy. Livvy and I have fun."

Her comment makes me smile as I finish cutting some strawberries to go with her pancakes. Hopefully, her excitement about our day together will help ease some of Dean's nerves.

"You're right. You'll have the best day. Just don't have too much fun without me." He presses one more kiss to her forehead before backing up.

When his eyes meet mine, I can see the hesitation in his face. He doesn't want to leave, and I get it. I clearly have no idea what it feels like to be a parent, but I can imagine it's hard to trust them with someone else.

"I'll call you if anything happens. We'll have a great day, and she'll be so excited to tell you all about it later." I know it probably won't help, but I try to ease his mind anyway.

He gives one curt nod of his head. He walked into the kitchen this morning seemingly in a good mood, but things have shifted a little. Maybe this is normal for him. His family seemed to think so yesterday when they kept warning me of his shifting moods. Or maybe he's creeped out by the fact I couldn't stop staring at him after he strolled in freshly showered and ready for work in a nice suit, smelling woodsy and rich all at once.

"Goodbye," he calls while screwing on the lid of the coffee thermos. "Have a good day."

"You too," I respond, walking Clara's breakfast over to her. The pancakes get her attention. She pushes the paper she was coloring to the side and gets right to shoveling almost an entire pancake into her mouth.

I thought Dean would be gone, but when I turn around to make myself a plate, I find him watching us from the entry to the kitchen. His lips turn down in a frown as he anxiously taps his fingers on the thermos he holds.

"I'll take good care of her," I promise, hating how uneasy he looks. I understand and don't take it personally. I just wish there was a way for me to calm his nerves. "Clara and I are going to have a great day, and I'm going to make sure she stays safe."

He sighs, his broad shoulders sagging slightly with the rush of air. "Are my nerves that obvious?"

I shrug, giving him what I hope is a comforting smile. "They're a little obvious, but I understand."

His cheeks puff out. "Okay. I'm leaving now. It'll be fine." I think the last part is said more to reassure himself more than to reassure me.

Clara is completely unaware of the stress her dad is going

through at leaving her with me. She continues to shove pancakes into her mouth like she's never eaten.

"Goodbye, Dean," I say, looking back to find him still frozen in place.

He doesn't respond. We just stare at each other for a few moments before his eyes flick to Clara. He watches her for a moment, and then he turns around and disappears.

I stare at the space he just left for a few moments before Clara's dramatic sigh behind me catches my attention.

"Livvy, I thought Daddy never leave."

I laugh, completely agreeing with her.

Chapter 20
DEAN

My heart races as I pull into the driveway of the house. I come down the driveway a little faster than I normally do, but it's only because it's been a few hours since Liv sent an update, and I'm a little worried about not hearing from her since.

She'd sent me photos of their day together, which I appreciated. They'd gotten out of the house and went to Wake and Bake, hanging out with Pippa and Lexi. Liv had fought me when I told her to drive the second car I own around town for their activities, but she finally relented when I insisted that every nanny drove it. It was kind of true; some of the nannies did, but I really only said that because Liv's old car was not something I'd wanted my daughter to be in. If I thought about it too long, I didn't like the idea of Liv in it either.

The car parked perfectly back in its place in the garage tells me they're home. Liv just maybe hasn't checked her phone in a while. I allow myself to let out the smallest sigh of relief. They're safe inside.

I pull my truck into the garage next to the SUV and don't even bother to gather my old coffee or bring in my briefcase. I'm out of the driver's seat as quickly as possible and practically running to get inside and see my daughter.

The moment I open the door, I'm hit with the aroma of basil

and garlic. It smells incredible, and I've barely stepped foot inside.

The sound of Clara giggling in the kitchen makes my chest feel a little less tight. She's here, and she's fine—the infectious laugh of hers showing she's *more* than fine.

I step into the kitchen to find the most adorable scene ever. Clara sits on the counter, flour all over her hands and face, as she looks at Liv with the widest smile. Liv stands next to her, busy kneading dough and making funny faces at Clara every time she flips it over.

Two pizzas sit on top of the oven, presumably cooling. There's a large salad bowl already on the table, as well as what looks to be a spread of fruit and vegetables to snack on.

"Okay, last one. Are you ready?" Liv asks Clara, handing her the ball of dough.

Clara excitedly nods her head as she takes the dough. She holds it to her chest for a moment with a mischievous grin on her face.

Liv nods. "One last time. Do it."

They both smile so wide I'm wondering what the backstory is of whatever they're doing. I don't have to wonder for long. Clara chucks the ball of dough onto the counter and lets out the loudest scream of delight.

"Perfect!" Liv tells her, sprinkling some flour in front of her. She spreads the ball of dough Clara just threw onto the counter, while Clara laughs with excitement over getting to toss the dough around like that.

I clear my throat, letting them know I'm home. Liv looks up, her smile faltering slightly when her eyes meet mine.

Before we can exchange any words, Clara's excitedly yelling my name. "Daddy! We throwing pizza."

"Well, just the dough," Liv corrects, letting out a nervous laugh. Her hands continue to spread the dough into a circle.

"You want to throw one, Daddy?" Clara asks, excitedly putting her flour-covered hands on her cheeks.

I shake my head, loving the bright smile on my daughter's face. I don't even have to ask her. She had a good day with Liv, and it's so refreshing to know that. "I'm okay. You have fun today?"

The little giggle from Clara melts my heart. "We had best day without you, Daddy."

I raise my eyebrows. "Oh, did you?"

Liv shakes her head as she begins to spoon what looks like homemade pizza sauce onto the pizza dough. "We had a good day, but she did ask about you a lot."

Clara's face pinches together in confusion. "No, I didn't."

Liv gives me an apologetic look, but the apology isn't needed. My feelings aren't hurt in the slightest. In fact, it feels like a weight has been lifted off my shoulders to know Clara enjoyed herself so much.

"So, what did you do today?" I ask, taking a seat on one of the barstools at the counter.

The smell of the finished pizzas sitting on top of the oven makes my mouth water. I must admit, although I don't mind cooking, often Clara and I will eat carryout, or I'll throw together the simplest of meals. It isn't often we eat home-cooked meals in this kitchen—unless my mom's dropped them off for us.

Clara throws her hands in the air dramatically as she shakes her head. "I can't tell you everything…we did *a lot*."

I smile at the way she emphasizes a lot. Or maybe I smile because of the way Liv stares right at me with a light in her eyes so bright that it makes it hard to fight a smile when sunshine bottled up into a person is beaming at you.

"What if I want to know everything?" I counter, my ears burning with having Liv's eyes still trained on me.

Clara lets out an exasperated sigh. She rolls her brown eyes at me. "We saw Pippa and Lexi." She looks over at Liv with a mischievous grin before looking back at me and covering her mouth with her hand like she's telling a secret. "And Pippa let me try one of her new cake pops."

"Oh, yummy," I respond. "Do you need help?" I ask Liv as she picks up a bowl of freshly grated cheese.

She shakes her head as she begins to sprinkle it on the top. "Nope. I told you I'd make dinner. Just sit and take a breath for a moment."

Clara reaches into the bowl and helps her sprinkle cheese over the top. "We called Mimi to find out your favorite pizza. Sausage and pepperoni, right, Daddy?"

My eyes immediately find Liv's. She stares down at the pizza, avoiding eye contact with me as she carefully places slices of pepperoni on the pizza. "Yeah, that's right," I get out, wondering why the fact that she called my mom to ask means something to me. When I'd asked her to prepare meals during the week, I'd meant more that she can make something that Clara will like, and I'll just eat it as well. I hadn't expected her to go out of her way to make my favorite as well.

But she had. I want to thank her, but I keep my gratitude to myself, unsure if I want her to know how much it means to me that she did that.

"How was your day?" Liv asks.

I sigh, thinking of how busy today was. It felt like I was putting out one fire after another, but this time of year is always busy. People decide right before ski season that they want to buy properties here in Sutten. We also help manage a lot of the rental properties here in town, and today I was dealing with a lot of that. "My day is much better now," I finally get out, meaning every word.

Liv smiles at me, and fuck, why do I like it when she smiles at me like that? Why does it make me want to smile back? Why am I wanting to say more to get my daughter's nanny to smile at me? It isn't professional—it's far from it. Maybe I can just blame the long day for my lapse in professionalism.

She nods, letting me get away with the confession that my day is far better now that I'm back home with Clara—and her. "I wasn't sure exactly what time you'd be home, so I wanted to make your pizza last. It'll go into the oven now, so it stays warm, but there are other pizzas if you're hungry now, plus a salad and some snacks."

"I want my cheese pizza!" Clara declares, stepping off her step stool and running toward the set table.

"Let's wash your hands first," Liv offers, sliding the pizza into the oven. She wipes her hands on an old pair of jeans that have so many holes in them they might as well be shorts.

Clara surprisingly listens to her. She turns around and heads to the sink as Liv assists her in washing her hands.

"Wow," I remark, sliding off the barstool. "It seems when I ask you to wash your hands, you have nothing but protests."

"What's protest mean?" Clara asks as Liv helps rub soap all over her hands.

"It means when I ask you to wash your hands, you tell me you can't do it, but when Liv asks you, you listen right away. What's up with that?"

Clara shrugs, a wide smile on her face as she looks at Liv. "Livvy ask nicer."

This makes Liv let out a snort of a laugh.

A low growl comes from me as I raise my eyebrows. "I ask nicely, too."

Clara finishes washing her hands before wiping them off on a towel. "Sure, Daddy." She laughs at me and shakes her head as if my comment is the most ridiculous thing ever. "You're the best, Daddy. But you are a little grumpy." She holds up her thumb and index finger to really hit home with her words before she skips over to the dinner table.

"She's so sassy," Liv comments as she fills up a pitcher with water.

I let out an amused sigh. "Yeah, she got that from her mother."

Liv stops, her eyes trained on me as a soft smile passes on her lips. I realize this might be the first time I've openly talked about Selena with her. It felt good to be able to share the small nuances of my daughter that she got from her beautiful mother. I make a mental note to do it more.

We just stare at each other for a moment. It's one of those moments that feels both heavy and light all at once. Light, because even though today was only her first official day, having Liv here feels like she's this light at the end of the tunnel for both Clara and me. That maybe with Liv's help, we'll finally find the consistency and routine we've been looking for.

It also feels heavy, because despite knowing I absolutely shouldn't, I'm fond of Liv. Not because she's Clara's nanny...but because she's just Liv. And I know if she stays around long enough—which I really hope she does—that she has the potential to mean a lot to me.

More than she should.

And that realization is absolutely terrifying.

Chapter 21
LIV

"PUMPKINS!" CLARA YELLS EXCITEDLY AS SHE JUMPS OUT OF DEAN'S truck the moment he unbuckles her from her car seat.

She takes off ahead of us, running toward the large entrance to the pumpkin festival.

"Wait!" Dean calls, his eyes pinned on his daughter. "Clara, you have to stay with me and Liv, okay?" he tells her as he catches up with her and grabs her hand.

Clara bounces on her feet, clearly unamused with the pace at which Dean and I walk into Sutten Mountain's famous pumpkin festival. "I want to climb the giant pumpkin," Clara whines, holding her hand out for me to take.

I gladly take it as the three of us join the group of people walking toward the front entrance. Clara's quickly become my tiny best friend over the last week, so it was a no-brainer when Dean mentioned he and Clara were going to visit the festival this afternoon and invited me to come along.

Plus, I'd told Pippa I'd see her there. This pumpkin festival is what gave me the idea of staying in Sutten in the first place, and I wasn't going to miss it.

Clara rattles off everything she wants to do while we're here as we make our way through the entrance. Someone hands me a map of all the different activities going on today, and I open it to find where Pippa's pop-up will be. I have to say hi to her and get a pumpkin cinnamon roll, of course.

"This way to the giant pumpkin!" Clara demands, pulling both me and Dean forward toward a bunch of hay bales stacked on top of one another to make the shape of a jack-o'-lantern.

"It really is a giant pumpkin," I note as we get closer. All week, Clara had been begging to come to the festival for this thing alone. Now that she's here, she barely spares either one of us a backward glance as she runs toward it.

Dean stands next to me. His elbow brushes against mine as he folds his arms across his chest and looks at me. "You can go," he states, his voice deep and gravelly. I've learned in the last week of living with him how much I love the deep tenor of his voice. It's sexy, and I know I shouldn't find my boss's voice sexy...but I can't help it. Something about it sends shivers down my spine.

"Are you trying to get rid of me?" I tease, my lips twitching as I try to fight a smile. It's officially been a week since I first showed up at his house, ready to move in. The week flew by so quickly, something that makes me a little sad because I'm enjoying it so much.

I love Clara. Spending my days with her is the best. I never saw myself being a nanny, but I've felt more purpose in this week alone than I ever have before.

I know I shouldn't admit it, but I like being around Dean, too. I look forward to seeing him walk through the door after work. Eating dinner together, the three of us, has become the highlight of my day, and I'm slowly getting attached to not only Clara but her annoyingly attractive father as well.

Dean's low growl pulls me from my thoughts. "I didn't mean it harshly," he begins, shifting on his feet. There's a hard set to his jaw as he keeps his eyes pinned on Clara, who's already made it to the top of the pumpkin. "What I meant was, you only get two days off a week. You don't have to spend them with us."

I keep my eyes on him, even though I know he won't take his

eyes off his daughter. I like his protectiveness of her—maybe I like it a little too much. "What if I want to spend time with you both?" I counter, watching him closely for his reaction.

Am I flirting with him? Maybe.

Is that dangerous? Absolutely.

Do I regret it? That's to be determined.

The muscle on his jaw ticks away as he thinks through my question. It was rhetorical; I don't really need an answer from him. I really just wanted to see how he'd react if I admitted that spending the day with him and Clara at the pumpkin festival was exactly how I wanted to spend my Saturday. I'll say yes to going to Sunday brunch with him and his family tomorrow, too, if he asks me.

"That's a lie," Dean finally gets out through gritted teeth.

Everyone's warnings about Dean have been true. He is grumpy and moody and has his guard up almost all of the time, but it doesn't deter me at all. Because when he does let his guard down, even for a fraction of a second, it's special. It's happened sparingly in the week I've been living with him and Clara, but it's happened enough for me to realize I'm attracted to him.

"It isn't a lie," I respond, letting my eyes wander to Clara for just a moment. She's at the top of the pumpkin, her hand waving vigorously in the air at us.

I lift my arm and wave back to her, waiting for Dean to say something else.

He finally does—but not before letting out a grunt of disapproval. "My family should be here any minute. They'll help me keep Clara entertained while you can finally spend some time alone without us bothering you."

I ignore him, deciding to also keep my focus on Clara as she makes quick friends with someone else at the top with her. They both take a seat on the hay bale and let their feet dangle off the side.

With Clara seemingly staying put in one spot for a moment, Dean finally looks my way. I can feel his gaze hot against my cheek as I continue to stay put. "Liv?" My name comes out like a question. A deep, gravelly question where I enjoyed hearing my name from his mouth a little too much.

I pull my eyes from Clara and look at him. "You know, scowling at me isn't going to change my mind. I want to spend my day at the pumpkin festival, and whether you want to believe me or not, I was looking forward to having you and Clara show me around."

Dean's lips press together in a thin line. It looks like he wants to say something, but before he can, a voice calls his name from behind me.

"Dean! There's my favorite oldest brother."

I turn to find Reed and Dean's parents heading right for us.

"Mimi! Papa! Uncle Reed! Look at me!" Clara triumphantly shouts from the top of the jack-o'-lantern. She still sits there with the little friend she made. Her dark hair and the two orange bows I put in it this morning make her hard to miss amidst all the other kids.

"Look at you," Shirley yells back, coming to a stop next to Dean.

"See me, Livvy?" Clara shouts.

"I see you, Clare Bear," I respond, smiling at how cute she is.

"Clare Bear," Reed remarks from my side. "I like it. I might have to steal it."

I look over at him with a smile. "Come up with your own nickname," I tease. This is only the second time I've met Reed, but his easygoing personality makes it impossible to not mess with him.

Reed puts his hands to his chest as if I've hurt him. I shake my head before stepping around Dean to give Shirley a hug.

"It's so good to see you again," I tell her, welcoming the feeling of her arms wrapped around me. Yesterday, Clara and I spent the morning at Dean's childhood home, spending time with Shirley. We'd baked cookies, walked around the property, and got our share of puppy snuggles.

Shirley squeezes me tight before pulling away. "What have you guys been up to? Have you been here long?"

I shake my head. "We just got here. Clara immediately ran to climb this. Which makes sense because it's all she talked about this week."

Dean clears his throat. "I was just telling Liv how she should enjoy her day off and go wander the festival without me and Clara as deadweight."

I roll my eyes. "And I was telling Dean that—"

"I can show you around the festival," Reed offers, cutting me off with a polite smile.

I tuck my hands into the pockets of my new jeans. I'd used the little bit of money I had left for my travels to get a few new pieces of clothing from the local boutique in town called the Chic Peak. I plan on finding some local thrift stores when I get paid at the end of next week, but until then, these were quick and easy to find while Clara and I were out the other day.

Reed must take my silence for hesitation because he lifts one of his shoulders in a small shrug. "You don't have to. But I do know where the best stands are with the best food. I practically eat my way through this festival every year."

I think about his offer. I don't know him very well, but he's got a charming smile and calming demeanor that makes me feel safe with him. I really would love to go visit Pippa. Clara and I visited Wake and Bake a few times this week, but Pippa told me her fiancé was going to be at the festival with her, and I'd love to meet him. Plus, she mentioned that her brother and his fiancée might hang out at the booth with them for a bit. I might get nervous and make a fool of myself, but I'd love to meet Marigold Evans. She wrote my favorite book and meeting her would be unreal.

"Only if we can stop by Pippa's booth," I counter, focusing on Reed even though I can feel Dean's eyes on me. He'd made it seem like he wanted me to leave him and Clara alone anyway. Maybe having Reed show me around is a good idea.

Reed's smile gets even bigger. "Of course we're stopping by her booth first. The pumpkin cinnamon roll is the reason I don't leave Sutten."

"You're in Sutten because you're working here," Dean deadpans.

Reed rolls his eyes at his brother. "There's plenty of places one could ski-patrol for. I just happen to live on the best mountain with the best pumpkin cinnamon rolls out there."

His words make me smile. I like him. I never had a brother, but he's exactly what I imagined a brother to be. He's goofy and charismatic, and if Dean would rather spend some alone time with Clara and his family, I'll take up Reed on his offer.

"Let's go, then," I tell Reed, not having the courage to look Dean in the eyes.

"That okay with you?" Reed asks, looking at his brother with a lifted brow. The two of them stare at one another for a moment. It's as if they talk without saying a word at all.

Finally, Dean rips his eyes from his brother and does one small pass over me with a fire in his eyes before he focuses on Clara once again. "It's Liv's day off. She's free to spend it how she chooses," he all but growls.

His posture is stiff as he crosses his toned arms over his chest and stares ahead of him. His jaw is clamped so hard it must hurt, but I don't comment on it at all. If he wanted me to stay with Clara and him, he had the chance to say so.

Reed nods. There's a small smirk on his lips as he looks from his brother to me. "Let's go get the world's best cinnamon roll." He holds his arm out for me to take, and I gladly do so, excited for him to take me to Pippa.

"I'm ready." I laugh, letting him take the lead.

Before we get too far, I look back once, unable to resist. I find Dean staring daggers at Reed's back. Before I can think too deeply about this new heated scowl on Dean's face, I turn around and let Reed lead me deeper into the festival.

Chapter 22
DEAN

"YOU'RE QUIETER THAN USUAL," MOM NOTES AS WE WAIT IN LINE for the hayride to take us to the pumpkin patch.

Clara plays with her cousins, who showed up a little after Liv and Reed left. They all compare the face paint they got at one of the booths. Clara had to get a butterfly—even though her boy cousins all opted for the creepy spiders.

"Dean?" my mom prods, bumping her hip against mine to get my attention.

"Hm?" I ask, pulling my eyes from searching the faces in the crowd around us.

"I said you're quiet. More than you typically are." Mom watches me with that look of hers that tells me she isn't saying everything she wants to say.

"Didn't sleep a lot last night," I lie, because I surprisingly slept well last night. Liv and I sat on the porch swing out front for what felt like hours. For some of it, we each read our books, but for the majority of the time, we talked about little things. About the gossip she'd already heard from the people here in Sutten and how she walked into a few of the small shops on Main Street and discovered we had a bookstore right in town.

It was a refreshing night full of small talk, and somehow, it left me at peace. So at peace that when sleep finally found me last night, no dreams plagued my mind.

Mom reaches out and runs her thumb under my eye. "You know, even though you're thirty-five, I still know you. You came out of me. When you're tired, your under eyes get dark and baggy. They're not dark or baggy right now. Now, stop lying to your old mother and tell me why you're quiet."

I grunt, my eyes scanning the crowd once again. "You're not old. You're in your prime."

This makes my mom laugh. "You know, if you had a problem with Liv going off on her own with Reed, you should've said something."

My eyes whip to my mom. I anxiously look around, hoping none of the rest of my family heard her. Luckily, Dad has joined in on checking out the face paint, and both Jace and Finn are too busy locked in conversation with their wives to pay attention to my conversation with Mom. "I don't have a problem with her going off with Reed at all. Like I said, she's free to do what she wants on her day off."

"Then why have you said almost nothing since the moment she left with your brother?"

I rub at the back of my neck. "I'm always quiet. I'm your closed-off, tortured son, remember?"

My own mother rolls her eyes at me. "Whatever you say, dear. I won't make you admit that watching Liv leave with your brother bothered you. But you're being a *little* obvious that you keep looking around for her."

I run my hand over my mouth as I try to hide my frown. I thought I'd been more inconspicuous about my search for Liv in the crowd, but apparently, I hadn't. Nothing gets past Mom. "Only because Clara so badly wants Liv to help her pick out a pumpkin."

Mom nods, but I can tell she doesn't believe me in the slightest. "Weird. All I've heard is how excited Clara is to pick out a pumpkin bigger than her cousins'."

I clench my jaw at her words. Technically, Clara hasn't mentioned looking for Liv yet, but it's only because we're still waiting in line. I know by how much the two of them talked about picking out and carving pumpkins this week that Clara will be disappointed if Liv is too busy with Reed to make it to the pumpkin patch.

Mom opens her mouth to respond, but something catches her attention over my shoulder. She smiles, her eyes finding mine once again. "I guess Clara will be relieved."

Her words pique my interest. I turn around and find Liv heading in our direction.

My nostrils flare when I see the way her arm is looped through Reed's. Or maybe it's the carefree way she throws her head back at something he says to her as they get closer to us. It seems that somewhere along the way, they collected more people to go pick out pumpkins with us. Pippa, Camden, Cade, and Marigold—Pippa's brother and his fiancée—join us in line for the hayride.

"Have fun?" Mom asks, looking between Reed and Liv.

Liv cradles a giant stuffed pumpkin to her chest. She nods, looking at Reed for a moment before meeting my eyes. "We had a lot of fun. Reed even won me this pumpkin. I thought Clara would love it."

My only answer is a small growl. Am I jealous of my brother winning a fucking stuffed pumpkin? Surely not.

"How've you been, Livingston?" Camden asks, stepping forward to shake my hand. He's been in Manhattan for work recently, and before that, things had been so hectic I hadn't seen him in a few weeks. We try to get together once a month or once every other month at Slopes to have a beer, but it's been longer than normal due to both our schedules.

"Staying busy," I answer, trying to avoid looking at Liv when that's all I want to do. From the corner of my eye, I see her and Reed have some side conversation I can't make out.

Camden nods, clearly understanding I'm not much in the mood for conversation right now. I sigh, realizing I need to say hi to everyone before my daughter comes barreling right at us.

"Livvy! That giant pumpkin for me?" She bounces up and down in front of Liv, barely able to contain her excitement as she looks at the stuffed pumpkin in Liv's hands.

"It is for you, Clare Bear. Your Uncle Reed won it for you."

Reed smirks and tilts his head. "I won it for Livvy, but I love that she wants you to have it."

I can't help but let out a disgruntled sigh at his use of the nickname. That's Clara's nickname for Liv and should be off-limits to him.

"I love it!" Clara cheers, taking the stuffed toy from Liv and holding it tight to her chest.

"Have you guys been having fun?" Liv asks, her eyes trained on me and only me.

I stare right back at her, hating that I missed the warmth of her gaze on me the two hours she'd been off doing who knows what with Reed. Hating that I know I shouldn't give a damn who my nanny spends time with during her free time but knowing I've obsessively thought about her and Reed from the moment they left.

"A blast," I answer sarcastically, needing to look away from her before admitting to her—and the rest of my family—I hated every second of knowing she was enjoying the festival alone with my brother.

Liv doesn't let my sour answer dull her mood. Her smile only falters for a fraction of a second before her eyes move to Clara, who dances around with the stuffed pumpkin. She taunts her cousins with it, clearly thrilled she got something. "Good," Liv gets out, her voice quiet.

I don't say anything else. I hate myself for making her smile falter, even if it was momentarily. She should be able to have a fun time at the festival—even if it's with my brother. I stuff my hands into my pockets and wait for our turn to get on the hayride while conversation breaks out between everyone around me.

When it's time for us to board the large trailer hooked onto the back of the tractor, I make sure to grab Clara and go to the opposite side of the ride from the one Reed chooses. Before Liv can pick a path, I sit Clara on one side of me and pat the other side.

"Liv!" Her name comes out more like a command than I meant it to. "Come sit by me. Clara wants you to ride with us."

Liv looks at Reed once before walking toward us. I let out a small sigh of relief when she walks in our direction. For some reason, the thought of being trapped on this trailer for the next five minutes while having to watch her and Reed talk more sounded like hell.

"I didn't say that, Daddy," Clara whispers.

My eyes dart to my daughter. "Pretend you did."

She lets out a dramatic sigh. "*Okay*," she responds with all the sass she can muster. Thankfully, she doesn't say anything else as Liv takes the seat next to me.

Chapter 23
LIV

Every time the tractor hits a bump, my thigh bounces against Dean's. I try to scoot over a little, but if I were to scoot any further, I'd fall off the hay bale they'd made into a makeshift bench for the ride.

We hit another bump, making me fly forward. Dean reaches out and steadies me by pressing his large hand to my thigh. There's a layer of denim between our skin, but I can still feel the heat of his hand through the fabric. His fingertips dig into my thigh slightly as he keeps his hand pressed to me.

"You good?" he asks, his voice rough. He's been grumpy since the moment we got in line for the ride. He's barely said a word to me, even as his family chatted away. I know he's typically quiet and broody, but he's been grumpier than normal for the last twenty minutes.

I nod, focusing on where he keeps his hand pressed to my thigh. We hit another bump, but my body doesn't jolt as much, thanks to him keeping me pinned to the hay bale. I want to tell him it isn't necessary, that I don't mind getting thrown around a little as we make our way to the field of pumpkins.

But I can't deny that I like the feel of his hand where it is. The weight of it feels nice. I almost wish I was wearing my old pair of jeans instead of the new ones I'd just purchased. If I were wearing the ones I'd brought with me from Florida, I'd have a hole on my thigh right where his hand is. Instead of a layer of denim between us, I'd be able to feel his skin against mine.

And I want that, even though I know I shouldn't.

We hit another bump, and just like with the other, Dean's hand stays firmly against my thigh.

"You don't have to do that," I mutter. My heart races at the closeness of him.

He grunts. "Yes, I do."

"Livvy, we pick out a big pumpkin?" Clara asks, her voice full of excitement as she leans forward to see around her dad.

"The bigger, the better," I tell her with a laugh. I've never carved a pumpkin before, but yesterday during Clara's nap time, I spent my break looking up different videos on how to do it. She insists she wants a pumpkin with Olaf carved on it, which makes me a little nervous, but I'm willing to give it a try.

"Real big," Clara demands, holding her hands out wide to prove just how big of a pumpkin she wants.

"Perfect." Without even thinking about it, I place my hand over the top of Dean's. "We'll pick out the biggest pumpkin the patch has to offer and make your dad carry it for us." My hand shoots off his as quick as it landed. I only placed mine over his to hit home the fact that he'd be carrying the pumpkin, but now I'm wondering if he found it weird.

Dean removes his hand from my thigh seconds before the tractor stops. The trailer comes to a halt while my cheeks heat. I miss the loss of his touch, even though I can still feel the press of his thigh against mine.

I look forward, unable to look at Dean as I wonder if I just made things weird. He'd just been trying to be a good guy by helping to steady me on the ride. I'd gone and taken things too far when I'd placed my hand over his, even if it was only for a brief moment.

He's your boss, I remind myself. *Not only is he your boss, but he tragically lost the love of his life in a horrible accident. The last thing he probably wants is for his daughter's nanny to develop a crush on him.*

But that's the thing. I think I already do have one.

I take a breath as my eyes immediately meet Pippa's. She stares at me with a soft smile. Her eyes ping-pong between Dean and me, making it clear that she saw everything that just went down.

My heart was already racing from Dean's touch, but it gets even faster the wider her grin gets. This isn't happening. She did not just witness me make things incredibly awkward by trying to hold my boss's hand. It's not that I was even trying to hold his hand. I was just trying to make a joke.

And now he's standing up and climbing off the back of the trailer without even looking at me.

"Perfect." I groan, letting my eyes flutter shut for a moment as embarrassment washes over me. Is he going to fire me? Did any of his other nannies develop crushes on him and then make it weird when he was just trying to be nice? Maybe that's why he's fired so many of them.

I wouldn't be shocked.

I knew he was attractive from the moment he ran after Clara inside Wake and Bake. He's so handsome it's hard to miss it. With his dark hair, which is messier on the weekends than it is during the week. He's got brown, whiskey-colored eyes that I could get lost in. They're framed by a set of dark, thick eyelashes that make it hard to look away from him when he's looking at you. There's a quiet confidence about him, too, that just draws you in.

I've heard from multiple people this week how wealthy the Livingston family is and how Dean especially has made some huge investments recently with major payouts. He carries himself as someone who grew up with money, but not in a cocky or pretentious way. Never once has he bragged about how deep his pockets may be, and I find that incredibly attractive.

Unfortunately, the more time I spend with him, the more things I find attractive. I like the way he growls instead of giving a verbal answer. Or how he has a specific smile that's reserved only for Clara. I've only lived with the man for a week, but it was long enough to develop a crush on him, and I wonder if others before me noticed the same things as me and fell into the same problem.

A pair of fingers snapping in front of my face pull me from my thoughts. Pippa stands in front of me with the same grin she was wearing earlier. "What are you daydreaming about, Liv?" Her accusing tone is filled with amusement.

"I was just thinking about how to pick the best pumpkin," I lie. I look around the trailer, finding almost everyone off it besides me and Pippa.

Pippa nods her head, but the look in her eyes tells me she doesn't believe me at all. "Mm-hm, sure you were." She claps her hands together. "Come along, then. Put all your daydreams about pumpkins to good use and pick out the world's best pumpkin."

Chapter 24
DEAN

I COME DOWNSTAIRS AFTER PUTTING CLARA TO BED TO FIND THE house quiet. Liv's bedroom lights were off, and her door was open, so I don't think she's gone to bed yet. There's no sign of her in the kitchen or living room, but one glimpse out the front window tells me she's right where I should've known she would be.

Pulling my coat off the hook by the front door, I open the door and step out to the front porch. Liv sits on the porch swing, a thick blanket covering her lap as she focuses on the book in her lap.

"I should've known I'd find you out here," I note. For it nearing the end of October, it isn't too cold outside, but it still bothers me that she's out here in only a sweatshirt with no coat. If she's cold, she doesn't show any indication of it as I take a seat next to her.

"Yeah," she whispers as she closes her book and looks in my direction. "I couldn't resist sitting out here and taking in the ambience of our carved pumpkins."

My gaze travels to the three pumpkins sitting on the front porch steps. Liv was surprisingly good at carving pumpkins, even though she swore she'd never done it before. Clara kept her promise when she said she wanted the biggest pumpkin. It took her almost an hour to find the biggest one in the patch, and somehow, Liv managed to carve an impressive Olaf onto the front of it. Liv carved a mountain scene into her pumpkin while I'd settled on the classic jack-o'-lantern.

I stare at the group of pumpkins as I begin to rock the swing forward. Out of the pumpkins, mine is definitely the least impressive, thanks to Liv's surprise pumpkin-carving skills.

It's quiet between Liv and me for a few moments as I try to think of what to say. I know I was a bit of a dick to her earlier for no reason. Well, I had a reason—I hated seeing her with my brother for reasons I don't want to look into. But it isn't a good reason, and because of that, I know I owe her an apology. I just don't know how to get it out.

"Thank you for letting me tag along today," Liv finally gets out. She anxiously chews her lip as her eyes dart around the space. I have to look away, finding myself too drawn to her. I can't help it—there's some kind of magnetic force to her that pulls me in and makes me never want to look away.

I blink a few times, my focus on my lap for a moment as I wonder why she seems so anxious about saying that. She must take my silence for indifference because she begins to speak again before I can get my thoughts together enough to respond.

"I understand maybe you want the weekends for just time with Clara and your family, and I'm sorry that I intrude—"

"Stop." My tone comes out harsher than I want it to, but I can't help it. She clearly thinks the reason I was acting up today was because I didn't want her to come. That couldn't be further from the truth. The problem is I *wanted* her to be there a little too much. I wanted her with me the entire time and hated when she left with Reed.

I was jealous because, despite knowing I shouldn't be, I'm attracted to her.

"Sorry," she whispers. She shifts on the swing, pulling the blanket tighter around her body.

I shake my head, pinching the bridge of my nose as I try to think of how to explain to her that my mood today wasn't her fault. If I tell her the truth, she'll probably think I'm some creepy boss and quit immediately. She doesn't need to know the electricity I felt with my hand on her thigh or the jealousy that thrummed in my veins seeing her smile at my brother. It's completely inappropriate, and I need her to stay for Clara.

With a sigh, I try to pull together a response that won't make her want to quit immediately. "I wanted you there, and I know Clara did, too. I was an asshole today for no reason, and I'm sorry."

I owe her not just the apology but an explanation as well. The problem is I'm blanking on any sort of explanation that won't send her running for the hills.

"It's fine. I just wanted to make sure you weren't upset with me for coming. I'd just never been to a pumpkin patch, and Clara'd been so excited about it all week, so I—"

"Liv," I manage to get out through gritted teeth. My eyes meet hers. The blues of them seem darker under the dull porch lights. "You can come to any family thing you want. You're always wanted there."

"Even to Sunday brunch tomorrow? I want to snuggle Honey before she gets adopted." She smiles, and those damn dimples pop up on either side of the corners of her lips. *I wonder what they taste like.*

I shake my head from the sudden thought and tilt my head to the side. "*Honey?*"

She nods, pulling her knees to her chest and wrapping her arms around them. "Yes. Clara and I named her Honey. She's our favorite. Clare Bear and Honey Bear. The perfect pair."

I can't help but laugh. "I wasn't aware you named the dog."

She tucks her chin over her knees. "I know naming her was a bad idea because it means we're attached, but we couldn't help it. She's so chill and sweet. Clara and I just fell in love and thought she needed the perfect name before getting adopted."

"She's been begging me to bring home that damn puppy," I

remark. The porch swing squeaks as I continue to use my foot to swing us back and forth.

"Does begging help? I'll start begging, too, if that'll get the job done. Clara would love to have a friend here."

"Funny, she told me tonight you were her best friend."

Liv rolls her eyes. "I meant a furry friend. I'm glad she told you that, though. I've had the best week with her."

I sigh before looking ahead of us. I need a moment from looking into her blue eyes. I'm scared that she'll see the things I don't want to admit if I stare into them too long.

"She had the best week with you, too. Every night I tuck her in, she asks if you'll still be here in the morning."

Liv's quiet for a moment before she clears her throat. "That's really sweet." Her voice sounds heavy with emotion.

I let the silence hang between us for I don't know how long. I love the sound of her voice, but I also appreciate the silence with her, too. We've had a lot of silent moments together here on this front porch swing. They mean more to me than I care to admit.

"Can I tell you something?" I ask, my voice rough. I don't have the nerve to look at Liv, so I keep my eyes pinned forward.

"You can tell me anything," she whispers.

"Today was the first time I'd gone to the pumpkin festival since Selena passed. It was always her favorite event of the year. She'd dreamed about taking Clara...but she never got to." My words trail off. They feel heavy as I remember all the times Selena and I roamed that same pumpkin patch. During our first year of dating, I'd tried to impress her while carving the pumpkin we'd picked out and ended up almost slicing the top of my thumb off. I have so many memories with her there, and the festival was something that broke me to go to with Clara but *without* Selena. "Clara's gone with my family the last two years. I haven't been able to until today."

"I bet today was hard," Liv responds. Her voice is soft and comforting, soothing the dull ache in my chest at admitting this was the first time I was brave enough to actually go to the festival.

"I wanted to turn around the whole way there. But then I looked over at you, and you were excited to go, and Clara was so excited to go, too, and suddenly I knew I wanted to as well. No matter how hard it was going to be."

"I never would've pressured you to go if I knew how hard it was. I'm sorry for—"

"Don't apologize," I demand, finally mustering up the courage to look at her. "I didn't tell you this to make you feel bad. I'm telling you this because I thought today was going to be gray and cloudy. And while it stung, and I know I was an asshole for the majority of the day, you were sunshine on a cloudy day. Even when I probably didn't deserve it, you were kind and warm. It meant a lot to me."

"I shouldn't have left with Reed."

I sigh as my head falls backward. I can tell myself I didn't want her going off with Reed because I wanted her company due to the toughness of the day, but I know it wasn't really that. I was jealous because of my attraction to her. Simple as that. "Don't say that. You're free to do what you want, Liv. I just wanted to explain myself a little."

I can't admit to her that I was jealous, but it does feel a little freeing to tell her today was my first day back at the festival. It's always been hard to talk about Selena, and I know it'll always hurt to talk about her. But for some reason with Liv, I want to talk about Selena more. Maybe it's because Liv never met her. Or maybe because Liv will be spending so much time with Clara that I want Liv to know about the woman that makes up half of my beautiful daughter.

Or maybe there's something about Liv that makes me want to open up. To not carry the weight of my hurt alone.

"Hey, Dean?" Her words break me from my thoughts. I love the sound of my name coming from her lips. It's only now that I realize I haven't heard her say it a lot, but I want to hear her say it again.

My eyes roam her face. She's so beautiful with her heart-shaped face and big blue eyes. "Hm?"

Her eyes scan my features cautiously, as if she doesn't know if she's allowed to say what she's about to say. She takes me by surprise by reaching out and placing her hand over mine. "You don't have to...but if you want to talk about Selena, you can. I know it might be hard to talk about her with people who knew her because their grief tangles with your grief. If you just want to talk about her life without being reminded of her death, I'm here. I'd love to hear about her."

I swallow past the thickness in my throat. My emotions threaten to spill out at her offer. I welcome the feeling of her hand over mine. Just the small amount of contact soothes something deep inside me.

Selena was incredible. I loved her with every fiber of my being, and I thought she'd be my forever. Liv's words make me realize that maybe all this time, I've been avoiding talking about Selena with anyone because I didn't want to talk about her death. She was so much more than the tragedy that ended her life far too soon.

But maybe Liv has a point. Maybe I should be talking about her but instead focus on the countless amazing memories. She deserves that.

"You wouldn't mind?"

Liv smiles, showing off those deep dimples of hers I suddenly have a fascination with. "Not at all. Whenever you're ready, I'd love to know more about her."

I stare at her, wondering how of all the small towns she could've decided to stop in, we were lucky enough for her to stop in ours. "That'd mean a lot to me," I manage to get out through the thickness in my throat.

She takes her hand off mine and leans back in the swing. She keeps her knees tucked to her chest as she gets comfortable. Her eyes don't move from me once as she patiently waits for me to start talking.

I want to say something, but I can't. I'm too lost in the heaviness of the moment. The way she's staring at me right now wakes up something deep in my chest. I try to take a deep breath in to stop the hammer of my heartbeat.

She cares so much. Enough to sit here and listen to me talk about the wife I lost, even though I was an ass to her today. I stare into her blue eyes and realize that something I never thought would happen is happening.

I care about Liv.

And because I care about her and trust her, even though there's so much about her I don't know, I begin to share with her things about Selena that I haven't brought myself to talk about in a long time.

Chapter 25
LIV

CLARA'S BUSY PLAYING WITH HER DOLLS ON THE COUCH AS I SET THE table for the evening. It's my second full week here, and we've easily fallen into a routine. Dean texted me he's running a little late, which doesn't surprise me. It's Friday night, and it's been a crazy busy week for him.

Halloween is on Monday, and he's already told me he wants to get off a few hours earlier than normal to help Clara get ready for the holiday. We're going to his parents' house to take pictures with the cousins and have dinner before trick-or-treating at all of the shops on Main Street.

I'm so excited.

I've never been someone who loves Halloween. It's been just another holiday for me that I didn't really care about, but I'm looking forward to this one. Clara's changed her mind about what she wanted to be about ten times but has finally settled back on being Elsa.

The timer for the oven goes off, reminding me to check the lasagna I'd made when Dean walks through the door. I pull out the lasagna and set it on top of the oven to rest before turning around to look at him.

"Evenin'," he drawls, taking me by surprise by wearing a smile on his face.

"Hi," I respond cautiously, wondering why he's got his

hands tucked behind his back.

"So, I did a thing…" he begins, stepping into the kitchen. He makes sure to keep his hands pinned behind him, holding on to something I can't quite see.

I pull the oven mitt from my hand and toss it onto the counter. "What kind of thing?" I press. He's been smiling at me more than normal in the last week. Something changed after the day we went to the pumpkin festival. It was as if hearing he can talk about Selena helped him become a little more free and realize he doesn't have to hang onto all of his pain alone.

"Clara." The way Dean says his daughter's name is adorable. It's filled with excitement—and happiness. We've turned a new leaf, and this Dean who smiles more freely and calls his daughter's name in a high-pitched tone makes it hard to not develop more feelings for him.

"Daddy!" she cheers, throwing her dolls to the side and running toward us. She was so content playing she hadn't even noticed he'd gotten home.

"I have a surprise," Dean tells us both, his lips still upturned in a grin.

"Let me see!" Clara demands. She tries to see what he holds behind his back, but he turns his body from her before she can get a peek.

The surprise rats herself out before he can. A tiny little bark comes from behind his back before he holds a box with the puppy out in front of him.

"Honey!" Clara screams, closing the distance to her dad and grabbing the puppy from the box. The dog eagerly licks Clara's cheeks, excited for the attention.

Dean stares at his daughter. I love that for even a brief moment, there isn't any sadness in his eyes. He stares at his daughter so lovingly and happily as she plops to the hardwood floor and cradles the puppy in her lap.

When his eyes move from Clara to me, I suck in a breath.

Happy looks good on Dean. *Too good.*

"Mom said someone was going to adopt Honey, and I couldn't let it happen," he explains with a casual shrug of his shoulder. He tucks his hands into his pockets while his eyes stay trained on me.

"So Honey's mine now?" Clara asks from the floor.

I want to look at her, but I can't pull away from Dean's intense stare. I can't look at anything but him. Not when his whiskey-colored eyes are locked on me. "She's ours," he responds, his voice thick.

My mouth feels dry. I swallow, wondering why those two words send a shiver down my spine.

"You hear that, Livvy?" Clara asks.

Dean rips his gaze from mine and looks at Clara. I follow suit.

"Hear what, Clare Bear?" I ask, still feeling the aftermath of the way Dean said "ours."

"We get to keep her."

I crouch down to the floor and scratch the puppy's ears. Her tongue hangs out the side of her mouth as she welcomes the attention from both Clara and me. "Welcome home, Honey."

"This is going to be a lot of responsibility," Dean begins, joining us on the floor. "Are you up for it, Clara?"

Clara nods her head immediately. Her face is completely serious as she looks up at her dad. "Yes, Daddy."

Dean's eyes find mine again. "I figured now was a better time than ever to finally give in to both of you begging for the puppy. With your help here, and you hopefully staying awhile, I think we can actually handle taking care of a puppy."

I bite my lip in an attempt to hide my smile. It doesn't work. Him mentioning he wants me to stay awhile sends butterflies fluttering in my stomach, even though I know he meant it for help with the dog and nothing deeper. "I don't plan on going anywhere," I admit, putting it out there that I can't see myself leaving anytime soon. I've never been happier, the pay is great, and

I grow more attached to Clara and Dean each day. I started this job thinking I'd only be here a couple of months, but now I know I want it to be longer if possible. "We'll take perfect care of her."

Honey climbs out of Clara's lap and runs right for Dean. She playfully bites at the sleeve of his suit jacket. "No, no, puppy," he scolds, gently prying his sleeve from her mouth. "Isn't this supposed to be the chill one?"

"Her name's Honey," I point out, picking the dog up and cradling her against my chest. "And she *is* chill, but she's still a puppy."

The smallest hint of a laugh comes from him as he stands to his full height. "It smells delicious in here."

I hand Honey over to Clara and stand up as well. Dean stands in front of the oven, looking closely at the lasagna sitting out.

"Does it look up to your standard?" I tease, turning the sink on and washing my hands after holding Honey.

He turns to face me, one corner of his mouth lifted. "I'll have to taste it to find out."

Blood rushes to my cheeks because, for some reason, the innocent words sound dirty to me. Instead of thinking about him tasting the lasagna, I think about him tasting *me*.

I close my eyes, trying to rid myself of the mental picture of his lips against me. This isn't appropriate. I can't think about my boss kissing me.

It doesn't help that when I open my eyes, he still stares at me. It suddenly feels hot in this kitchen, and it isn't because the oven was on. When his tongue peeks out to wet his lips, I stifle the smallest moan.

What is wrong with me?

"Liv?"

"Yes?" I squeak, terrified he can somehow read my mind.

He cocks his head to the side. "The water."

I jump. "Oh." I rush to turn the sink off. I'd been too lost in picturing Dean's lips against mine to turn it off once I'd been done washing my hands.

Dean doesn't say anything as I dry off my hands and walk over to the oven. I expect him to move as I get closer, but he keeps his feet planted as I step around him to check the lasagna. It's sat long enough that it no longer bubbles. He's right about the smell; it smells incredible in the kitchen.

"I can't believe Clara actually talked you into getting Honey," I say to Dean as I walk over to grab the plates from the table. I can't help but notice the shakiness to my voice from nerves. I hope my attempt at changing the subject will help me regain my composure—and that he isn't weirded out about how I'm acting.

He crosses one ankle over the other, clearly getting comfortable as I step closer to the oven. My elbow brushes the front of his dress shirt as I grab a serving spoon.

His cologne overpowers the smell of the lasagna. Or maybe it's just that I'm obsessed with the way he smells. I want to plead with him to move so I'm not plagued with unprofessional thoughts about him just because he's standing close to me.

"It wasn't just Clara who talked me into it," Dean begins, reminding me that I'd even said something to begin with. "It was you, too."

I let out a nervous laugh. *Why is he standing so close?*

I cut out a little square of the lasagna and scoop it onto a plate, all while Dean intently watches me do the whole thing. He brought home the puppy, and suddenly, the air between us seems thicker. I know it's got to be all in my head.

"Since I got paid this morning, I was going to go into town tomorrow morning to get some more clothes. Pippa told me there's a thrift store in town where I might be able to score some good finds. I can grab supplies for Honey while I'm out if needed," I offer.

Dean lets out a low growl of disapproval. My eyes whip to him, wondering if I'd overstepped by offering to get things for the dog. I didn't mean to suddenly shift his mood.

"I don't have to," I hurry to get out, placing the second plate of lasagna on the counter and pausing for a moment. "I didn't know what you and Clara had planned for the day, and I figured since I was already ou—"

"If you want new clothes, I'll buy you some." His voice is firm as he talks over me.

My mouth hangs open. I thought he was upset about the dog supplies. Never would I have guessed it was the comment of me shopping for myself. "Um," I begin, not knowing what to say. "That isn't necessary," I manage to get out.

"You need warmer clothes to take care of Clara, yes?"

His eyes never leave mine as he waits for my answer. Our closeness becomes even more apparent as he crosses his arms over his chest, his knuckles brushing over my ribs with the movement. "I guess," I answer.

"Then I can buy you the clothes. We'll go to the Chic Peak tomorrow, and you can buy whatever you want on me. Just include a coat."

I open and close my mouth as I try to think of what to say. His gesture is nice—incredibly kind, even—but it isn't necessary. I don't want him to look at me as a charity case, someone he needs to buy clothes for. "Thank you for offering, really, but I'm okay with getting my own. I've always thrifted my clothes, and while I bought a few new items at the Chic Peak to tide me over, I'm still more comfortable getting my items from the thrift store since I plan on getting a lot. Pippa said there was a little store right in town. Sutten Mountain Treasures or something like that."

"There is. But I don't understand why you wouldn't let me buy you whatever you need somewhere else. We can even drive into the city if you're not wanting anything from in town."

I smile, really appreciating how insistent he is on buying me new clothes. It's too much. He's already done far more for me than I ever expected when accepting the job. I won't let him buy me a new wardrobe, too. "I want to buy clothes right here in Sutten. At the thrift store. With money *I* earned."

Dean stares at me. I stare right back. This isn't a battle he's going to win. I thought the electricity between us might die down with my insistence on purchasing my own clothes and his shocking determination to buy them for me instead. It doesn't. If anything, it seems like there's even more tension between us.

I swear his gaze flicks to my lips for a fraction of a second before he lets out a long sigh and takes a step back. "Fine. But I'm coming with you."

Before I can protest, he's clapping his hands together and aiming his focus on Clara. "Time to eat this delicious meal Liv made us," he calls, leaving no more room for discussion.

Chapter 26
LIV

"You driving me really isn't necessary," I tell Dean, not for the first time this car ride. "I'm more than capable of going to the store alone."

Dean doesn't look at me. His eyes stay focused on the road, and his hands firmly hold on to either side of the steering wheel. We just dropped off Clara and Honey with Dean's parents for the day when it started pouring rain outside.

"You're not driving in this," he responds, his voice rough and straight to the point.

Too bad I'm used to his grumpiness and won't let his attitude deter me. "I can drive in this. I'm from Florida. I'm used to rain. There'd be torrential downpours during hurricane season, and I'd still have to drive."

He sighs, his eyes still staying trained on the road. His knuckles turn white with how hard he grips the steering wheel. "I'm not discussing this with you, Liv. Just let me drive you to get the clothes, okay?" His voice cracks a little, and the sound of it chips away at my resolve. If he wants to drive me into town to go shopping, I'm not going to stop him. Not when the panic in his voice was clear as day at the thought of me driving right now.

"Okay," I whisper. "But just because you're insistent on chaperoning me doesn't mean I'm going to let you buy me clothes. I'm buying. You got it?" I keep my tone upbeat, hating the distraught tone he used moments ago.

It seems like my attempt at lightening the mood works. The corners of his lips turn up in the hint of a smile. "If you say so, sunshine."

Sunshine.

It's the first time he's ever called me that. I love it. I want him to say it again and decipher what it means. Does he feel the same pull I do? Or is giving me a nickname completely platonic and professional?

I need to know.

The rest of the drive is quiet. I don't try to fill it, knowing Dean seems to be concentrating on nothing but the road. He sits up straight in the driver's seat, his eyes scanning the road meticulously as he drives us into town. The only sound is that of the rain pelting the truck.

Finally, we make it to the heart of the town. Dean parks in front of a dark green building with a sign that reads Sutten Mountain Treasures. We haven't even been inside yet, and I already love it. I've been to a lot of thrift stores. Thrifting is one of my favorite things to do. It's rewarding to give things that have been discarded and given away a new life. You can tell a lot about a thrift store just by the outside of it, and I have a good feeling about this one.

I pick my purse up from the floor and place it in my lap, looking over at Dean.

He stares ahead of him, his jaw tight, making small muscles feather along his cheekbones.

"Dean?" I ask cautiously, wondering why he looks so tense. He has one hand still on the steering wheel—his knuckles still white as can be—while his other one rests against his thigh. His fingertips dance along the worn denim of his jeans, something I've learned he does when he's nervous.

"Dean," I repeat, leaning over the center console to try and get his attention. He stares blankly ahead.

I let the silence hang between us for a moment before he finally looks at me. When he does, I see sadness and worry etched into the handsome features of his face. "She died because of the rain," he croaks, his words taking me by surprise.

"What?" The word comes out of my mouth before I can even think through an appropriate response. If the rain wasn't smashing the windshield, he'd be able to hear the intense beat of my heart at his words.

"The other car was driving recklessly in the rain. Going way too fast along the narrow mountain roads. They went into Selena's lane, but because of the wet asphalt, there was nothing they could do to stop the cars from colliding. He walked away with a broken arm...and Selena..." He takes a shaky breath in. I've never seen so much emotion on his face, and I don't know what to do. I don't know the right thing to say.

So I don't say anything. I reach across the center console and place my hand on his cheek. He leans into it, accepting the physical contact as comfort.

He stares at me for a few moments. It feels like so many things are said in this moment, and yet nothing is said at all. I've never felt more confused in my life. The way he stares at me, there's so much pain in his eyes, but there's also something else. Something I can't read, but it makes my heart beat so fast it might just beat right out of my chest.

"It wasn't even supposed to rain that day." I hate the sadness in his voice. It's so raw and broken that it breaks me right along with him.

If only I knew how to fix the hurt man staring back at me. *If only I didn't have feelings for him that I know will end up breaking me in the end.*

"You couldn't have known," I whisper. I wish I could make my voice stronger or find better ways to comfort him, but I don't think anything in the world can take this guilt and grief off his shoulders. All I can do is try and shoulder it with him—if he'll let me.

He sighs as his eyes shut for a moment. When he opens them again, the mask he puts in place to protect himself from the world is back. He doesn't remove my touch. He shocks me by placing his hand on top of mine and pressing my palm even harder into his cheek.

"I can't think about the what-ifs about that day. I've tried, and they slowly killed me over time. I'm trying not to do that anymore. But I just needed you to know why I couldn't let you drive today. I just needed to be in control of keeping you safe, okay?"

I nod, swallowing past the lump in my throat. His "okay" comes out hoarse and like a plea. I'd agree to anything just to hear the pain disappear from his voice.

His fingers squeeze my hand before he drops his hand to his lap. I take that as my cue to pull my hand away. He lets out a controlled breath as he pulls himself together. "Thank you. For listening. For being here. For understanding."

I scan his profile, trying to gauge how he's doing just by the small, little nuances of his demeanor. It's hard to tell—he's locked his emotions back up and put on a brave face.

I wish he knew he didn't have to always be brave with me. He can be hurt and broken and scared and vulnerable and anything he wants to be. It won't make me leave. It won't change my mind about him.

"Of course," I whisper, not knowing what else to say. Nothing I've said since he put the truck in park has probably been right, but I try not to second-guess my words. I know my feelings for him run deeper than they should, but despite that, he and I have an undeniable connection. On my side, it's feelings that surpass friendship and how one should feel about their boss, but for him, I'm sure it's just finally having someone in his life who can listen and sit with his grief without sharing in it.

The raindrops get a little lighter against the windshield as we sit in the quiet for a few moments. I don't say anything, letting him take as long as he needs to gather himself.

Finally, he looks back at me, and the rawness and vulnerability are gone from his features. I can't tell if the half-smile he gives me is real or fake. "Let's get inside and get you some winter clothes. And, most importantly, a damn coat."

Chapter 27
DEAN

"I CAN'T BELIEVE ALL OF THIS," LIV SAYS UNDER HER BREATH, grabbing another item of clothing from the clothing rack and adding it to the pile of clothes in my hands.

"Think some of these will work?" I ask her, curious to know her answer. If she adds much more to the stack in my hands, I'll have to drop them off in the dressing room before everything overflows.

Liv looks at me from over the rack. I love the brightness in her eyes. How wide her smile is as she nods. "Yes," she responds. She pulls another piece off the rack and inspects it. "I think so much of this will work. I can't believe they have so many items with tags still on in my size. It's like I've hit the jackpot."

Ms. Beth laughs from her stool at the register. I glare at her for a moment, hoping Liv doesn't notice, before looking back at her.

"Great," I respond, my voice a little tight.

"I never thought such a small town would have such great thrift shopping," she notes, placing yet another shirt in the pile in my hands. Her eyes meet mine before giving me an apologetic smile. "No offense."

I can't help but laugh. "None taken."

Her shoulders drop a little with her sigh of relief. "I just thought it'd be hard to find unworn clothes. I was ready to find some vintage, well-loved pieces. Never did I expect so much new."

"Really was your lucky day," Ms. Beth pipes up from her counter again. I shoot another look her way. Normally, Ms. Beth minds her own business. I don't know why she feels the need to make little comments.

Liv adds a pair of jeans and a jacket to my pile. "Okay, I think I'm ready to try some things on."

"Dressing room is right back there," Ms. Beth instructs, pointing to the small little area where a curtain hangs from a rod and can be pulled all the way around to create a makeshift dressing room.

I walk back there, carefully hanging the pieces Liv's picked out before stepping out. She really did find a lot of items that are much better options for the upcoming winter months.

"I'll wait out here while you try them on," I tell her, trying not to focus on her beautiful smile. She's radiant, and the joy on her face at something as simple as finding clothes at a thrift store gets to me. The longer I'm around her, and the more I earn the smile she's giving me right now, the more I realize that the way I care about her is not the way a boss cares about his employee.

And that realization is incredibly dangerous.

"Sounds good to me," Liv responds. She bounces on the balls of her feet a little as she begins to pull the curtain shut. "I'm so excited," she says, her face hidden by the drawn curtain. I don't have to see her face to know that smile is still on it.

I sigh, turning around and walking to rifle through a nearby rack of clothes to keep busy. I try to keep my thoughts from Liv, but that's becoming harder and harder with each passing day.

It took me over a year until after Selena passed to agree to a date with a woman. It was someone who was visiting for a work event, and it was exactly what I needed. Something casual with no strings attached. I've had plenty of one-night stands and brief relationships since then that never amounted to anything. I didn't want them to. I never wanted to care for someone again, but I was only human. I wanted to feel a connection with somebody else on a physical level.

I thought I was doing good at preventing myself from ever developing feelings. I believed I was doing a great job at keeping myself closed off and ensuring I'm never put in the place again to be hurt.

It turns out I just hadn't met the right person yet. Unfortunately, I'm still very capable of caring about another woman. My broken heart healed enough to develop feelings again, and of course, of all the people in the world I could care about more than I should, it's for my daughter's nanny.

The irony isn't lost on me. Of course I would get feelings for someone who's been very up-front from the beginning that she hadn't ever planned to stay in Sutten. She seems to have a past she doesn't want to talk about, which I won't force her to do. But fuck, with each passing day I spend with her, I think I want to be a part of her future.

"Did that shirt do something to you?" Ms. Beth calls from across the store.

I shake my head, realizing I've been staring at the same T-shirt this entire time. I was so lost in thought—or panic—at how much I'm starting to care about Liv that I hadn't realized I was glaring at the shirt like it offended me.

Ms. Beth whistles. "You could've fooled me."

I shake my head again and make my way to her. I don't know how long it'll take Liv to try on and decide what clothes she wants, so I go to chat with Ms. Beth. "I was just deep in thought," I explain, resting my forearm against the counter.

Ms. Beth looks at me over the top of her glasses. She smiles as if she could read my thoughts.

"So, are you going to explain to me why you overnighted a bunch of brand-new clothes to the store and told me to pretend that someone just happened to bring them in to donate?"

My eyes go wide as I look over my shoulder to check and make sure Liv hasn't heard.

I look back at Ms. Beth. "Keep your voice down," I demand. If Liv knew I was the one who made sure she had an abundance of brand-new clothes to choose from here at Sutten Mountain Treasures, she'd never bring them home. She wouldn't let me buy new clothes for her, but I wanted to make sure she got what she wanted.

I knew the selection of clothes would be lacking for the current season, so I had to get creative. She got the variety of weather-appropriate options like she deserves but doesn't have to spend too much of her hard-earned money to get them.

Ms. Beth waves the air dismissively. She's known me since I was in diapers and will not let me get away with bossing her around. "Please, Dean. She can't hear me."

I grunt, knowing she's probably telling the truth but not wanting to risk it. Liv was so excited when she'd discovered the clothes I'd had overnighted to the store. The last thing I want to do is dull that smile if she were to find out who was behind the donation. "Can never be too careful," I finally respond, crossing my arms over my chest.

"Mm-hm."

Luckily, Liv saves me from having to further explain myself to Ms. Beth by opening the curtain and peeking her head out.

"Dean?" My name comes out more like a question. The uneasy tone to her voice has me pushing off the front counter and closing the distance to her.

"Yes?" I ask, a little worried by the way she stares at me wide-eyed.

"Can I have a little help?" she asks nervously. Her top teeth dig into her bottom lip as she continues to stare at me anxiously through the little hole in the curtain.

I clear my throat, realizing she needs me in there with her to assist in whatever she needs help with. "Yeah," I respond, stepping into the makeshift dressing room.

Liv watches me cautiously. She gives me a timid smile as I try to figure out what she needs help with.

She looks down at the camel-colored sweater she wears. "I got this on just fine, but when I try to pull it off, it's making sounds that scare me. I'm worried if I try to force it off by myself, I'm going to tear a seam or damage the delicate fabric. It might be stuck on my bra."

My eyes travel over the sweater. It does appear to be cashmere or something similar that's incredibly soft. I don't notice any rips yet, but I can't tell if it's stuck to her bra or not.

"Think you can help?" she asks, her voice soft. We're so close, and the small confines of this dressing room don't help.

All I can do is nod. Even through the different scents that come with being inside a thrift store, the smell of her overpowers it all. She always smells like apple blossom and something else. Something fresh. Something that drives me wild every time she walks past me.

Now, I'm stuck in this room with her, with her wide, expectant, beautiful blue eyes staring up at me. I should be able to focus on helping her, but the proximity of our bodies goes to my head.

"I can see if maybe Ms. Beth will..." she offers, her words trailing off.

I shake my head, forcing myself to get it together. "No, I'll help."

I take a hesitant step forward. The tips of my boots almost kiss the toes of her own shoes. I can feel her breath against my chest as I look down, trying to figure out the best way to get the sweater off.

"I'm just going to lift slowly," I tell her, my voice rough. I've done so well pushing my attraction to her to the back of my mind, but with her so close to me, it's hard to remember why I wanted to fight it so badly.

She nods, her teeth still digging into her lip.

Fuck, I want to kiss her. I want to take her plump bottom lip between my own teeth and discover what she tastes like.

She about does me in when her tongue peeks out to wet the spot where her teeth just were.

"Go ahead." Her words cut through my thoughts of leaning forward and pressing my lips to hers.

My eyes meet hers, and there's a slight moment where I forget I'm supposed to be helping her get the sweater unsnagged, and I think her words were permission for me to kiss her.

Slowly, I reach down and place my hands on either side of her narrow waist. I gather the fabric in my hands, trying not to let my skin touch hers in the process.

My efforts are useless. The moment I start guiding the fabric up, my knuckles brush the soft skin of her abdomen.

Air hisses through my teeth at feeling her skin against mine. She sucks in a breath at the same time as me. I've barely moved the fabric up an inch, and all I want to do is rip it from her body and crash my lips against hers.

I lift another few inches, my knuckles trailing against her skin the entire time. She shivers, and I have to rip my eyes from hers before I do something incredibly unprofessional, like pin her against the dressing room mirror and kiss the hell out of her.

The room is silent. The only sound is that of our hurried breaths as I continue to carefully inch the fabric higher and higher. I need to just rip it and get the fuck out of here. Too much of her perfect pale skin is on display for me right now. It's taking every ounce of restraint I have to keep my eyes pinned over her shoulder.

A few more inches and I know if I looked down, I'd be able to see the swell of her breasts. I've almost got the sweater lifted enough to see where it's snagged. I hadn't thought about what happens when we're alone in here without her in a top.

"Almost got it," I get out through gritted teeth. My jaw is locked so tight it hurts. It's my way of trying to keep myself from doing something stupid. She doesn't want me to kiss her. She just wants help not ruining the sweater.

I risk a glance down to see how close I am to being able to lift it all the way off. It's a mistake. Her breasts threaten to spill over the top of her black lace bra.

Fuck fuck fuck.

In one fluid motion, I yank the sweater off her, not caring how rough I am to get it unstuck. I don't know if it rips. I can't hear over the crashing sound of blood rushing through my ears. The sweater drops to the ground as I tear through the closed curtains and rush to the store door.

I can't meet Ms. Beth's eyes as I press my fingers to the glass. "Have to take a work call," I lie. "I'll wait for Liv outside. Tell her to take as long as she needs." I try to keep my voice composed, but I probably fail at it. I don't have the mental capacity to come up with any further excuses or lies.

I shove the door open and welcome the feel of the rain against my skin. It can cleanse me of all the inappropriate thoughts I have about kissing my daughter's nanny.

Chapter 28
LIV

MY HEART RACES AS MS. BETH RINGS UP ALL OF THE CLOTHES I picked out. I found way more than I thought I would. So many items that still had tags on them were in my size. It's the best thrift haul I've ever had, and I can't even focus on my excitement, thanks to the encounter I just had with Dean.

Something was different in that dressing room. I know the way he looked at me hungrily and like a man possessed wasn't all in my head. I think he wanted to kiss me, and I was more than ready to let him before he stormed out of the dressing room.

It'd taken me a full minute just to get myself together after that. I'd been so desperate for him to kiss me. I've thought about his lips more times than I'd care to admit. It turns out you can daydream a lot about the different ways someone can kiss you in two weeks. And I've thought of every possibility in the recent days.

Ms. Beth finishes folding the last item of clothing and places it in the bag for me. I'm coming out with four huge bags filled to the brim.

I shake my head in disbelief. "I still can't believe I got so lucky."

Ms. Beth laughs as she presses the buttons of her card reader.

"We had a great donation early this morning. Someone was feeling very generous."

I nod in agreement. "I'm so happy I chose today to come in, then. I was worried I wouldn't be able to find everything I needed, but now I'm coming out with way more."

"Your total will be twenty-nine dollars even."

I frown. "Are you sure you rang everything up? That seems low."

She smiles at me. It's one of those smiles that makes me feel like she knows something I don't, with the slight raise of her eyebrow and a mischievous tilt of her lips. "That's right. We were running a special today. Everything in the store was half off."

I bite my lip anxiously. "I don't feel right only paying twenty-nine dollars for all of this stuff. I got two new coats, multiple pairs of jeans, sweaters, and many other things I'm forgetting about. I got a whole new wardrobe. Please let me pay more than twenty-nine dollars."

Ms. Beth gives me a warm smile. It's refreshing how kind every single person in this town is. I have yet to come across anyone rude or even remotely close to it. "Darling, that's the price of the pieces. Everything was donated."

"Do you take monetary donations?"

She narrows her eyes at me. "You're really not going to take the clothes for that price, are you?"

I shrug as I give her a smile. "It just doesn't feel right to pay only that for brand-new clothes. Let me at least donate to the store? I don't have any items to donate, but I do have some cash I planned on using today."

"Yes, we take donations. Every month, we donate clothing and household items to different families in need. The money helps fund that."

I smile, loving that I can feel a little bit better about leaving with a whole new wardrobe for such a low price. "Great." I take the hundred-dollar bill I'd budgeted for clothes today and lay it on the counter. "Then here's this, and keep the change. Thank you for today and having so many amazing pieces. I'll absolutely be back."

Ms. Beth laughs under her breath as she takes the money and begins to hand my bags over to me. "I'm not sure it's me you should be thanking."

Before I can ask her what she means by that, I risk a glance out the front window and find Dean standing in front of his truck. He stares right at me with his arms crossed over his chest and his typical scowl on his face.

"He's all bark and no bite," Ms. Beth mutters from my side.

I blink a few times and look back at her. I want to ask her what she was talking about, but I keep my questions to myself. Dean's waiting in the rain, and I don't want to keep him waiting any longer. The rain and distance make it so I can't make out all of his features, but by the angry way he ran out of the dressing room, I don't think making him wait is in my best interest.

"I better get out there," I tell her, taking two bags in each hand. I'm already excited to get home and put it all away. I've never had a fall and winter wardrobe like this. I've also never had this many new clothes. I turn my head to look at Ms. Beth. I smile, hoping she understands how grateful I am to have found her store. "Thank you again. I'll see you again soon."

"Nice to meet you. I've got to go take some inventory in the back. Do you need a hand with the bags?"

I shake my head. "No, I've got it."

She watches me carefully for a minute before coming around the counter and walking toward the back door. "Goodbye now," she calls.

I turn and walk to the door, suddenly nervous to see Dean again.

Is he upset with me? Was I staring at his lips too much? Did he notice the way I couldn't breathe when his knuckles brushed up against my skin? God, I wanted to feel even more of his touch. I wanted to feel his callused fingers against my tender skin. I wanted to feel his lips press against mine and wipe away his scowl with my mouth.

There were so many things I wanted to do with him right there in that dressing room. I can't help but wonder if he somehow could read my thoughts, and those are what drove him to run out of the store like I'd offended him.

I take a deep breath as I use my back to push the door open. I'm scared to look at Dean, so I stare at my feet, wondering if all of these winter clothes will be necessary.

If he decides to fire me after making things unprofessional in that dressing room, then I won't have a need for warmer clothes. I'll have to disappear from this town—and maybe even this state —due to embarrassment.

The tips of two cowboy boots I'd recognize anywhere appear in my line of sight. I pull my eyes up, finding Dean's intense gaze aimed right at me. Without saying a word, he reaches out to take the bags from me.

"I've got them," I protest, tightening my grip on the handles.

His sigh can be heard over the rain hitting the pavement. "Let me."

Yeah. He's mad. This isn't grumpy Dean. This is more.

"They're my clothes. I can carry them." I should just hand them over to him, but we're close to the truck anyway. If he hadn't decided to stop me, I'd already have them loaded in the truck, and we'd be on our way out.

Dean lets out an aggravated growl. He reaches forward and grabs the bags from my hands. Before I can even argue, he's turned around and stomping to his truck.

I stand there, watching him angrily walk back to his car. My heart pounds as I try to figure out if I want to address what just happened in the dressing room. I think I have to. I know it could all be in my head, but I swear we had a moment back there. And if he's going to be upset with me anyway, I might as well bring it up so I can know once and for all if the tension is one-sided or if he feels it, too.

"Did I do something wrong?" I yell over the sound of the rain. It's gotten heavier than when we first walked into the store. It beats against my face, making my hair stick to my cheeks. I don't care. I barely feel the drops of rain as I focus all of my attention on Dean.

His spine straightens the moment I get the words out. He stops what he's doing, the door to the truck still hanging open as he turns to face me.

"Did I?" I shout, hating the pathetic shake to my voice. I know I should just sweep this all under the rug and pretend I don't have feelings for him, but I can't.

I'd bet everything I had—which isn't a lot—that we had a moment back there. Whatever this is, he's got to feel it, too. I'm sure of it.

And if he doesn't, then I'll pay whatever price I have to for bringing it up. At least then I'll know the truth.

"You didn't do anything," he answers. His voice is void of any emotion as he puts my bags in the back seat.

"Then what happened back there?" I press.

"It's raining, and you're already soaked. Get in the car, Liv."

I shake my head. My clothes cling to my skin because of the rain, but I don't care. I'm too focused on finding out if Dean wants to kiss me as badly as I want to kiss him. "Not until you answer me."

He slams the door shut. The intimidating way he looks at me from where he stands should scare me. It doesn't. If anything, the hard set of his jaw and his hooded lids make my heart race even more.

"Get in the fucking truck." His voice leaves no room for inter-pretation.

Hearing him say *fucking* sends chills down my spine. "Tell me what happened back there, Dean. Why'd you run out so fast?"

His shoulders rise and fall with a deep sigh. One moment, he's standing against his truck with his angry eyes pinned on me; the next, his eyes are just as angry—maybe even angrier—but he's standing right in front of me.

"You don't want me to answer that," he growls.

I let out a frustrated sigh as I throw my hands up in defeat. "Yes, I do."

He stares at me, and I stare right back. His nostrils flare, and my chest heaves up and down with the intensity of my breathing. His hair looks jet-black, thanks to the rain. Stray pieces stick to his face as he glares right at me.

"Fine," he says through gritted teeth. "You want to know what happened in there?"

I nod. "Yes," I get out breathlessly.

"I left because if I'd allowed myself even a second longer in there, I was going to do something I have no business doing."

At what point does a pulse get too high? Mine has to be getting close. It spikes in eagerness at his words. "And what's that?" It feels like my words come out as barely a whisper, but he hears me anyway.

His eyes drop to my lips, and I know what he's going to say before he even says it. "Like kiss you as if you were mine to claim."

I suck in a breath. I can't help but smile, feeling the biggest wave of relief wash over me that the tension between us isn't all in my head. I know I shouldn't say my next words, but I say them anyway. "Then what are you waiting for?"

Chapter 29
DEAN

"Liv." Her name comes out like a warning—or maybe it's more like a plea. I'm desperate to do what she's asking. I desperately want to kiss her. It's the only thing I've thought about since the moment I left the dressing room.

But I shouldn't for a multitude of reasons.

She's my daughter's nanny. I'm her boss. She could leave any minute. She's also more than ten years younger than me. If we kiss, things are bound to get complicated. I can't afford complicated. More importantly, Clara can't afford complicated. She needs stability in her life, and kissing her nanny isn't the way of providing that. We can't risk losing someone else important in our lives.

I recognize every single reason I shouldn't kiss her. But it doesn't stop me from wanting to do it regardless.

"Stop overthinking it." Her voice breaks at the end. Like she's so desperate for my kiss that she can't even get her words out fully.

"I have to overthink it," I respond hoarsely.

She takes a step closer to me, and I let her. My resolve can only last so long. If she keeps pushing me, she's bound to make it snap, no matter the consequences.

"Don't. You want to kiss me. *I* want you to kiss me— desperately."

She carefully places her hands on my chest. I still don't stop her. Feeling the warmth of her palm through the wet fabric of my shirt makes my breaths still in anticipation. "You're Clara's nanny."

"And I'll still be her nanny even after we kiss." Her fingers tighten around the fabric of my shirt as she pulls my body against hers. "I'll quit right now if you keep looking at me like that without kissing me, Dean Livingston."

I can't hold back any longer. My hands find either side of her face as I soak in the feeling of getting to hold her just like this. I can feel the erratic beat of her pulse beneath my fingertips. It dances as wildly as my own.

I look into her blue eyes for a few moments, needing to know she hasn't changed her mind, that she wants this just as badly as I want her. Her eyelashes stick together from the rain as she stares up at me expectantly. There's not an ounce of hesitation in the way she stares at me defiantly and eagerly, like she's just ready for me to finally give in.

Her lips part, and she licks them, yanking on the fabric of my shirt to pull our bodies even more flush. Lightning illuminates her face seconds before my resolve finally snaps. My lips crash against hers at the same moment thunder cracks around us. The thunder shakes the ground beneath our feet as the feeling of her lips against mine rattles me right down to my bones.

The kiss is a lot like the storm raging around us, our mouths fusing together like the rain to our skin. My tongue swipes against the seam of her mouth, and she parts for me instantly as her needy moan vibrates against me.

Fuck. Our first kiss isn't even over, and I know it'll consume my thoughts for days, weeks, hell, even months to come.

My fingers tangle in the wet strands of her hair as I try to fuse our mouths together. If this is when I finally get to ravish her mouth the way I've been fantasizing about, I'm going to do it right.

Liv hungrily kisses me back, as if she's getting everything she wants out of the kiss as well.

I'm not gentle, and she isn't either. My fingertips press into her scalp as I move her head to the side, allowing me to deepen the kiss even more. She grabs at my clothes furiously as if she can't get enough. She pulls and tears like she can't bring our bodies close enough.

Rain pelts our skin, but it does nothing to stop me from drawing this out for as long as possible. I can't fucking stop. It's like the only air I need is the breaths I'm getting from her.

Her tongue caresses mine. With one swipe, it's gentle, and the next firm and demanding, as if she's trying to memorize every single way our tongues can meet. I'm not gentle with her. I can't be. Not when I've been desperate to kiss her for days— maybe even longer, if I'm honest with myself.

"Dean." Liv pants the moment our mouths part for a second, just long enough for us to get air.

Now that I've tasted her, I can't get enough. My lips trail along her neck like a crazed man. I want to taste every single inch of skin she has on display—even the skin she doesn't. I nip right at the spot where her neck meets her collarbone, my tongue immediately poking out to soothe the sting. Her skin tastes like the falling rain and apples. I could taste it all damn day and never grow tired of it.

I could kiss *her* all day long, and it'd never be enough.

I guide my lips all the way back up her neck, leaving a trail of nips and licks until my lips hover over hers once again. Our chests rise and fall in perfect sync as we just stare into each other's eyes.

It was fucking stupid of me to think this one kiss will stop me from fantasizing about her. I know it, she probably does, too, but that's a problem for a different day. The only problem I see right now is the fact that I'm not tasting her at this very moment.

Our lips are centimeters apart, but I don't close the distance. Not yet. The first press of our lips was hurried and untamed like the spontaneous storm around us. This next one will be slower, more methodic. Like the clouds that slowly roll in before the rain.

"I need to kiss you one more time to memorize every detail about it," I tell her, my lips barely brushing against hers with my words.

She lets out a small moan. The sound rattles me as I feel it everywhere. "Kiss me anytime you want."

A satisfied growl comes from deep in my chest. "Don't fucking tempt me." I don't give her time to respond. I press my lips to hers for a second time, knowing that if I do the right thing, this will be the last time I get to do it.

I'm slower this time, making sure I take my time with it. I brush my lips against hers softly, a featherlight promise of what's to come. The storm gets even more vengeful as the wind picks up, blowing her hair around and pelting raindrops onto her skin.

I deliberately move my tongue along the seam of her mouth. This time, I coax her mouth open with my tongue. The kiss starts out slow. We aren't as desperate. We give it the time it deserves to build and intensify before our lips are moving violently against one another's again.

I move my hands to cradle her face, my thumbs swiping over her cheekbones as I keep her mouth pressed to mine. We get lost in that kiss for so long three more crashes of thunder erupt around us before I finally break it.

The two of us gasp for air as we try to gather our bearings. My head spins with the intensity of how incredible that kiss was. I stare at her red, swollen lips, wondering how the hell I'm going to sleep in the same house as her and not obsessively kiss her the way I know I'll want to.

I already want to kiss her again.

A shiver runs through her body, and I don't know if it's from the aftermath of the kiss or because her clothes are soaked all the way through because of the rain and she's cold. Either way, I open up either side of my jacket and tuck it around her, keeping our bodies pressed together.

I take a deep breath, trying to slow my hurried breathing. "You're really doing something to me," I admit.

Her eyes track my face for answers. "Doing what?"

I don't want to hide from her. Not right now. Not even though I know I shouldn't be honest with her and further complicate this. "Making me want things I shouldn't, sunshine."

"I don't see any sunshine right now."

I press my forehead to hers, making sure she can't see anything else but me with my next words. "I do."

Chapter 30
LIV

I press my fingers to my lips as Dean guides his truck into his long driveway. We haven't said a word the entire drive back from shopping, but we don't have to. The silence is comfortable even though the air between us feels thicker than ever after what just happened.

We finally kissed. And it was, tragically, far better than I could've ever imagined.

I'm already thinking about doing it again. I'm desperate to feel him claim my lips with his again. I trail my fingertips along my swollen bottom lip. The skin around my mouth feels chafed from his stubble.

I love it.

Dean pulls into the garage and puts the truck in park. It stays quiet between us as we both stare ahead. I don't know what to say or how to break the silence. I want to know if he has regrets or if his thoughts are trailing into dangerous territory like mine are.

He clears his throat. "We should get inside and get some dry clothes on."

I nod, wondering if we're going to address what just happened.

If we are, it isn't happening yet because Dean opens his door and steps out of the truck. I keep my eyes pinned forward, my fingers still trailing my lips as I wish it was his lips I was feeling right now. My door opens, and Dean steps in front of me. Our eyes finally meet, and it's like a bolt of lightning through my veins.

I'm never going to be able to look at him again and not think about how perfect his lips felt against mine.

"Let me help you down," he demands. His voice is gruff and thick. Is he still feeling the same tension I am? God, being alone with him right now, all I want to do is throw my body against his and kiss him all over again.

I want to do more than kiss him.

"Okay," I respond quietly. I expect him to offer his hand, but instead, he leans into the small opening and grabs me at the small of my waist.

My breath hitches at feeling his touch again. The wet fabric of my clothes clings to my body. I can feel every inch of where he touches me. His fingertips are a warm, welcome feeling through the coldness of my clothes.

Neither one of us moves for a moment. He keeps his hand resting on the narrow of my hips as I get lost in his eyes. We should probably talk about what happened outside the store, but I don't want to talk about it. Not right now. All I want is a repeat and maybe even to take it further.

Before I can tell him what I want, his grip tightens a little as he lifts me from the passenger seat and places me on the ground.

"We need to get you inside and get you dry clothes before going back out to get Clara." There's little room for interpretation in his tone. It isn't cold. It's just matter-of-fact.

I nod, still so entranced by kissing him that I'll do anything he asks me to.

He surprises me by reaching out and taking my hand in his. I like that he confidently takes it without a second thought about whether he should or not. The only sound is that of our footsteps as he leads me into the house.

We make it to the laundry room when I pause. "I should

probably get my new clothes from the truck." My voice comes out just above a whisper. Everything feels so quiet in the house without Clara or Honey here. Even the storm has slowed, the thunder no longer crashing in the distance. The only sounds of the storm come from the raindrops hitting the roof.

Dean's fingers tighten around mine as he thinks through my comment. I watch in fascination as he swallows slowly. His eyes travel to the laundry baskets with neatly folded clothes inside before focusing on me once again. "You can have something of mine in here. We need to get you out of your wet clothes. Now."

A shiver runs through my body at the commanding way he says *now*.

I don't want to let go, but I run my thumb along the inside of his palm once before dropping his hand. We stand there, staring into each other's eyes as our sopping wet clothes drip onto the tile floor of the laundry room. I kick off one shoe and then the other before pulling my socks off and discarding them to the side.

My pulse begins to climb as my fingers find the button of my jeans. I can't look away from his heated brown eyes as I pop the button open and slide the zipper down.

"Liv." He says my name desperately. I just don't know what kind of desperation. Is he desperate for me to stop or keep going?

"You can turn around if you want to." My voice comes out breathier than I intended it to, but I can't help it. My body feels on fire at the thought of undressing in front of him.

Dean clears his throat, his eyes traveling up and down my body. My body breaks out in goose bumps at the intensity of his gaze. If he could undress me with a single swipe of his eyes from head to toe, I'd be standing in front of him naked.

When his eyes meet mine, I can barely see the whiskey color of his irises. His pupils are dilated with pure want. "I can't," he responds, his voice thick with lust.

His answer makes me smile with relief. We already crossed a

line we can't come back from with the kiss. I want to do it again but cross it even further this time. I need his touch—his lips—everywhere. I'm ready to give in to the physical connection between us and take it as far as he's willing.

The wet denim sticks to my hips and thighs, making it hard to remove. I shimmy a little to lower it. My eyes stay on his as I slowly drag the jeans down my legs. He watches every single one of my moves carefully.

Even as I bend at the hips to get the jeans fully off, I keep my gaze on him. I want to focus on every single one of his reactions.

His body stills as I toss the wet jeans to the side. They make a loud plop as they land somewhere neither one of us looks. We're too busy staring at each other to care.

I stand back up and allow the heaviness of the moment to sink in between us. He seems to fight it for a few seconds before he breaks eye contact and instead looks at my half-naked body.

"Fuck." He groans, and it's the sexiest sound in the universe. I'd picked up some new underwear while at the Chic Peak the other day, and I've never been so thankful for a simple pair of black lace panties.

He stares at me as if I'm standing in front of him in lingerie and not a soaking wet shirt and panties. His tongue peeks out to wet his lips, making me fight the urge to close the distance between us and let my tongue caress the same spot his just was.

"Your turn," I tell him, feeling bolder than I've ever felt before. The desperate look in his eyes fuels me. We can worry about how this complicates things later. Right now, it feels like the least complicated thing to do is make out and explore each other's bodies the way we're both desperate for.

The smirk he gives me makes heat rush through my body. I have to squeeze my thighs together as my core throbs with need for him. He shrugs one arm out of his jacket, then the other, before it falls to the ground at our feet.

"Done," he gets out, his voice thick with lust.

I gasp. "That doesn't count."

"Your turn," he responds, not even acknowledging my protest.

I smile, even though it seems a little unfair how many more layers he wears. It doesn't really matter. I want to shred every single piece of clothing on my body and memorize the heated way he looks at every inch of me.

My breaths get quicker as I grab the bottom of my shirt and begin to pull it up. Fire courses through my veins at the memory of the dressing room. How it felt to have his knuckles brush against my skin as he helped me pull off the sweater. I wish he was helping me rid myself of the shirt right now, but I keep the thought to myself. Having him watch me so intently as I pull the fabric off, his eyes hooded with lust, is just as good as him doing it himself.

It might be even hotter to have him watch me.

He shifts his weight between his feet. It's quick, but I don't miss the way he has to palm the tented fabric of his jeans. I lick my lips at the thick outline of his length through the wet denim. The proof that he wants this just as badly as I do almost stops me from teasing him. I'm able to hold on to just enough control to keep my feet planted as I toss aside yet another piece of clothing.

His gaze is hot as it roams my body. He isn't touching me, but it feels like he is. I swear I can feel every brush of his eyes. My nipples harden under his intense inspection.

It should feel weird for me to stand in nothing but a bra and panties in front of him while he's fully dressed, but it doesn't. Nothing can feel weird when he stares at me like a man starved.

"You're killing me," Dean announces. His voice comes out strained. Everything about him seems tense. His posture is stiff, and he keeps his jaw clenched. Even his fists stay in balls at his side until he grabs the hem of his wet shirt and pulls it off in one fluid movement. He doesn't tease me when removing his shirt. One moment, it's on; the next, it's discarded somewhere behind him. I don't bother to look where. I'm too caught up in seeing him without a shirt on for the first time.

It's the most beautiful sight. He's made of muscle, something I'd expected with how expertly his tailored clothes fit him. But this is even better than I could've ever imagined.

Dean Livingston is a lot of things. He's kind underneath his tough exterior. He's the best father. A surprisingly excellent cook. Apparently, an excellent businessman who is even more attractive by the way he doesn't flaunt the excess of money everyone says he has. He's charming and witty when you least expect it. And he's got a body that deserves to be on TV screens.

"Oh my god," I mutter under my breath. I don't know where to look. His biceps are thick but not in an overbearing way. He's got a set of abs that I already want to trace with my fingertips. And there are two perfect muscles on his hips that lead into the waistband of his jeans I desperately want to explore.

"You licking your lips while you stare greedily at the outline of my cock is making me want to do very dirty things to you, sunshine."

My eyes snap to his as I purposefully lick my bottom lip. "Like what?"

A low growl comes from his throat before he closes the distance between us. "Like this."

Chapter 31
DEAN

LIV YELPS AS MY HANDS ROUGHLY FIND THE SMALL OF HER WAIST and lift her off the ground. Without any direction, she wraps her legs around my middle as our lips crash against one another's once again.

We're straight passion as our tongues collide. We kiss each other like we've been starved of the other, even though the car ride back from the shop wasn't long at all.

I'm in big trouble. I could get addicted to kissing this woman, and there are so many reasons why I shouldn't, but I don't give a fuck about any of them at the moment. Not when her hips are grinding against me, and the only thing that keeps her warm cunt from me is a pathetic excuse for fabric.

I slide my hands down from her hips and cup her ass. She moans as my fingertips dig into the curve of it. In response, she digs her fingernails into the base of my neck, deepening the kiss.

She moans. Or maybe it's me. At this point, I don't know. All I know is that I need more of this. More of her.

I walk forward, keeping my grip on her firm as I find the nearest surface. It happens to be the counter over the washing machine. I set her down at the very edge, giving myself room to stand between her thighs.

"Dean." She moans my name against my lips, and it's the sexiest sound in the world. My name has never been hotter.

I pull my mouth from hers and place my hands on the insides of her thighs. I push them open, wishing her panties were gone so I could have a perfect view of her. "You sound sexy as hell moaning my name. Bet you'd sound even better screaming it."

Her head falls back when I lay a chaste kiss to her shoulder, and my fingertips dig into her thighs to feel even more of a connection.

"We shouldn't be doing this," I tell her, trailing my lips along her collarbone.

"I don't care," she announces. There's no hesitation in her voice. I'm sure she knows just as much as I do that giving in to the sexual tension between us can only complicate things, but it's clear she doesn't care enough to stop it.

And honestly, I don't either.

"I'll be so pissed at myself if you leave us because I couldn't resist you," I admit. I playfully nip at the tender skin at the base of her throat before letting my tongue drift over it to soothe the pain.

"I'll be so pissed at *you* if you don't just accept that us doing this right here was inevitable. We'll figure the rest out later. I just need more of you, Dean."

I come undone at the way she says my name. It's full of passion and desperation, her tone dripping with lust. It mirrors exactly how I feel about her and just how badly I need her. "What do you need from me?" I ask, slipping a finger underneath her bra strap. I slowly pull it down, my pulse thumping in anticipation of freeing her breast. I'd been so achingly close to seeing it in the dressing room. I need to see her nipples, to take the peaks into my mouth and find out how reactive she is to my touch.

"Whatever you'll give me," she instantly responds. Her voice is breathy and hurried. She arches her back as I run my thumb along her nipple, which is still hiding behind the fabric of her bra.

I laugh at her response. "So very needy for me, aren't you,

sunshine?" I run my thumb over her nipple again, loving the soft moans that fall from her mouth at just a simple touch.

"Dean." Fuck, I could never get tired of hearing my name on her lips. She desperately says it, like a plea.

"Your perfect tits need me, don't they?" I ask, reaching behind her back and unclasping her bra as she nods her head and lets out another moan. I don't take my time removing it. The moment it's undone, I'm helping her coax her arms from it and tossing it to the side.

I place my hands on either side of her hips as I grip the edges of the washer and take in the sight of her fully bare to me from the waist up.

"God, you're perfect," I mutter. My cock strains in my jeans, desperate to get some kind of attention. It fights against the wet denim, needing to be touched to relieve the ache of wanting her so intensely.

I appreciate the view for one more moment. I was so frantic to kiss her earlier that I didn't take my time. With tasting other parts of her, I want to savor it as much as possible. She's so beautiful just like this, her eyes wide as she watches my every move.

It's dim in the laundry room, the thick rain clouds preventing the sun from illuminating the space around us. Despite the clouds, I can still make out every perfect inch of her. I plan on placing my lips to every inch of her soft, delicate skin.

With every hurried breath in, her tits bounce ever so slightly, teasing me. Unable to resist her for a second longer, I hover over her and take her full breast in my hand. I test the weight of it in my palm, letting out an uncontrolled groan at finally being able to touch her like this. I'd been so fucking close in the dressing room it'd driven me absolutely fucking mad.

But I'm glad I was able to keep a hold of myself—kind of—at the store. Because now, I can take her perfect peaked nipple in my mouth and not have to worry about being quiet.

I lean in, blowing hot air on her nipple to test her reaction. She jumps, her hips lifting from the machine for just a moment.

Goose bumps break out all over her skin as I inch even closer. All I'd have to do is barely poke my tongue out, and I'd have her nipple against it.

I lift her breast and finally bring her nipple into my mouth. My tongue circles it, making her eyes flutter shut with pleasure. I relish in the sound she makes as I continue to circle the peaked bud. I pull my mouth off, smirking when she lets out a mewl of protest.

Before she can let out any more sounds of protest, I'm circling her other nipple with my tongue and pulling it into my mouth. Both need ample attention, and at the moment, I can't deny her a thing.

Her hips rock back and forth as she searches for some kind of reprieve. I smile while taking her nipple between my teeth. I pinch her other nipple between my fingers before letting my hand drift down her stomach. Her breathing stills as my hand snakes lower and lower. I dip my fingers into the waistband of her panties and stand up straight for a moment to meet her eyes.

"Is this okay?" I ask, keeping my fingers right where they are until she tells me it is.

She nods her head up and down. Wet strands of her hair fall into her face with the movement. "Yes. Please," she adds, her tone begging.

I smile, inching my fingers down a little more. "Such a good girl saying please. Is this what you need?" I keep going. My fingertips brush against her clit for just a moment. "You need me to touch you right here?" I circle her clit slowly. She's so wet my fingertips effortlessly glide over her.

"Yes." She pants, moving her hips for more friction. She's greedy, trying to take more than what I'm giving her right now, and it's sexy as hell.

"Let me get the panties off," I demand. "I want to see all of you."

She nods, and that's all I need. I pull my hand free from touching her just long enough to pull the black fabric down her legs and throw it to the side. My hand is on her again immediately. At the same moment I run my fingers through her wetness, I lean in to kiss her.

Our lips meet again in a frenzy of pure want and need. I taste her moan as I slide one finger inside her. She's so fucking wet, and even with only one finger inside her, she's tight around me.

"Fuck." I groan, beginning to rock my finger in and out of her as my thumb circles her clit. "You're so fucking wet."

"For you," she responds. She pulls my bottom lip between her teeth, making my cock jump with arousal. I need her so fucking bad, but I want to take my time with this. I want to focus on making her come before freeing myself and worrying about my own release.

"So fucking bad of you to want your boss like this, sunshine. This isn't professional." I coax a second finger inside her, wanting to feel her stretch around me.

"I don't care." She moans. "This feels too right to ever be bad."

My forehead falls against hers for a moment as her words crash through me. I wish I could disagree with her, that I could regret letting this happen between us. But the tension between us has been too much, the attraction too strong, for me to feel bad about it.

At least right now. All I can do is take her at her word that no matter what happens right now, it won't affect anything with Clara.

"Do you want me?" Liv asks, pulling me from my thoughts. She wiggles her hips, making me realize my fingers had stilled inside her.

"Yes," I answer immediately, pressing a kiss to her lips to prove it.

"Then have me. We'll figure out the rest later."

I nod, deciding to enjoy the moment with her. I've tortured myself for days over wanting her. I've listed every single reason this shouldn't be happening countless times, but none of it worked. I couldn't resist her, and I still can't right now.

I hook my fingers inside her, reveling in every pant and moan that falls from her lips. She's right. Nothing about this could ever be bad, not when it feels so fucking perfect with her.

"Do you need my fingers or my tongue?"

Chapter 32
LIV

DEAN'S WORDS MAKE ME STILL. I DON'T KNOW HOW I NEED HIM other than I just need him. Desperately.

My eyes meet his as I suck in a nervous breath. "I've never...I mean, no one's ever..." My words trail off as I try to think of a way to tell him that no one's ever gone down on me.

Dean's eyes darken as he looks at me. His fingers still for a moment, but he doesn't pull them out. His thumb still slowly circles my clit as his eyes search my face.

"No one's ever what?" he asks, his voice serious and rough.

I stifle a moan. I didn't think I'd be having this conversation with him, but then again, I didn't expect his resolve to snap between us either. I hadn't expected any of this to happen before we left to go shopping this morning. I didn't think about how I'd tell him my sexual experience equates to a few backroom hookups with one of my coworkers just because I wanted to get being a virgin over with. There was never time for anything else.

"Liv," Dean gets out, his voice strained. "Answer me, please." The please is said desperately. It's hot, knowing that he's feeling as depraved for me as I am for him.

"I've never had anyone go down on me," I rush to get out, my cheeks feeling hot with the admission.

I wish he wasn't so good at keeping a straight face. His features don't budge with what I've just told him, and I'm desperate to know if the knowledge of knowing no one's ever done that to me turns him off.

"Are you a virgin?" he asks, his voice tight.

I shake my head. "No."

He nods. Much to my dismay, he pulls his fingers from me. I look down, unable to look him in the eyes a second longer.

Does my inexperience make him want to stop? He did stop, so maybe that's all the answer I need.

I begin to close my legs, not wanting to be on full display a second longer, when his large hands stop me from doing so. His fingertips press into my inner thighs, preventing me from closing them any further.

"Don't," he demands, the word coming out strangled.

"You weren't saying anything. I just thought—"

He stops my words by leaning forward and pressing a kiss to my inner thigh. His breath is hot against the sensitive skin, sending a bolt of arousal through my entire body. My toes curl at the sensation of having him so close but still not close enough.

I can feel his deep breath against my core. He looks up at me, and I make a point to memorize the look of him in this moment. His head between my legs, so close to my core his breath tickles my clit, his hands possessively on my thighs as he holds me open and on full display for him.

His eyes are hooded with lust, but they're trained right on me. The way he stares at me is something I could never forget. It feels like tasting me is the only thing he could ever need in this moment.

"I was just thinking about how fucking lucky I am to be the first."

My breath hitches at his words. He places another kiss to the inside of my thigh, this time even closer to where I want him.

For some reason, I feel the need to fill the silence and give him one last out from being the first man to ever go down on me. "You don't have to if you don't want to." My words are rushed as another wave of heat washes over me. I don't know why I say it. The man is staring at my pussy like he's starved. I know he wants to—maybe I just need to hear him say the words.

"I want to." He lets out a low growl of appreciation as he stares at me. If it were anyone else, I'd feel embarrassed by being on such display, but it's Dean. Everything's different with him. Instead of feeling embarrassed, I feel even hornier at having him stare at me like I'm his last meal.

His lips move to my hip bone, where he presses another chaste kiss. "I'm going to give you a warning, though, sunshine."

"What is it?" I all but pant. He's so freaking close to being where I need him. My clit aches for him. I'd take even his touch there again if it wasn't his mouth. I just need *something*.

"After I'm done eating this pretty pussy, you will be ruined for anyone else but me." His tongue peeks out for one quick lick against my clit before he stops, continuing to torture me with anticipation. "Mmm…" he notes, wrapping his arms underneath my thighs and coming over the top to pin me in place. His fingertips sear into my skin like a brand as he keeps me wide open. "After one taste, I'm already ruined for anyone but you."

He doesn't even give me time to obsess over his words and decide what they mean before his tongue flattens against me and he begins to eat.

"Oh my god." I moan, my head falling backward and hitting the shelf behind me. Something falls to the ground with the movement, but neither one of us pays it any attention.

He licks up and down, giving every part of me attention as his tongue makes my toes curl with pleasure. It feels too good. It's too much. My hands slap against the top of the washer as I try to search for something to hold on to. I eventually find his head, and my fingers tangle in the strands at the top of his head that are just long enough for me to get a good grip on.

One of Dean's hands leaves my inner thigh, allowing my hips to move a little more as he uses that hand to now inch inside me. The combination of his tongue and finger is lethal. I try to keep my eyes on him to watch every single one of his movements, but I can't do it. The pleasure is just too much, and they flutter shut from the overwhelming amount of sensations.

"I'm close," I pant. I didn't think he'd be able to make me come, let alone come this fast. The only time I've been able to come is if I was the one in control of making it happen. Leave it to Dean to figure out a way to do it quickly and, from the way it begins to build, powerfully as well.

He sticks a second finger inside me and spreads his fingers. The movement stretches me in such a delicious way that when he pulls my clit into his mouth again, I'm sent over the edge.

"Dean." His name comes out so loud that it echoes off the walls of the room. My moans are loud and untamed as my entire body feels like it's on fire from the orgasm.

It lasts way longer than I expect it to. Dean makes sure I savor every second of it; his tongue and fingers don't relent until I've experienced every last second of the orgasm.

My eyes flutter open and find Dean already staring at me. He pulls back and gives me a wide grin. I don't know what's sexier, the fact that he's smiling so freely at me when I know how hard it is to earn a smile like that from him or the fact that his lips and all around his mouth are covered in me. I love seeing the proof of the effect he has on me all over his face.

"Can't decide which one I like better," Dean cockily says, feathering kisses all the way up my body.

"What?" I ask, a little breathless from the intensity of the orgasm.

Another smirk graces his face, and all I can think about is how I want to make him do it again. "Can't decide if I like it better when you moan my name or scream it. Both are sexy as hell."

A blush creeps over my cheeks. I don't know what I was expecting, but I certainly didn't expect for him to have such a dirty mouth. His words alone send a shiver down my spine.

I bite my lip, my eyes focusing on his mouth. He's still wet from me. "You're making me blush," I admit.

He laughs a deep, throaty laugh that sends my heart racing. "I also find it sexy as hell that you're blushing after I've made you come so hard you screamed my name."

My face flushes even more. His eyes move from mine and focus on where I bite my lip. He reaches up and pulls my lip from between my teeth.

"I really want to kiss you right now," he admits.

I smile, letting my hand snake out and mess with the waistband of his jeans. They're still wet from the rain. "Then do it," I respond, popping open his button. I want to feel his length, to make him feel good the way he's done for me.

"Good. I want to show you how good you taste." He leans in and presses his mouth to mine as one of his hands reaches up to cradle my jaw. His tongue finds mine, and another rush of lust runs through me at the taste of me on him.

This kiss is slower than the others. It's as if he's just now realizing that he doesn't have to rush to kiss me, that he can take his time. I slip my hand in the waistband of his jeans as my pulse spikes.

I want to touch him desperately and see how he reacts. He's always so quiet, but he was much more vocal as he went down on me. Will he stay that vocal as I stroke up and down his length? I'm dying to find out.

My fingers find the tip of him, and he gasps against my lips at the slight touch. I haven't fully felt him yet or even seen him, but I know from the thick outline against his jeans that he's big.

We continue to kiss as I let my hand drift even lower into his pants. I gently wrap my fingers around the base of him, wanting to test the feel of him in my hand.

"Fuck." A low growl comes from deep in his chest.

"I think you'd be much more comfortable if we got rid of the jeans," I tell him, already pulling at the sides.

I want to see him. All of him.

Dean nods. My hand falls to my side as he takes a step back. I love how he doesn't look anywhere but at me as he hooks his hands on either side of his jeans. He doesn't waste any time pulling them down and kicking them aside.

The moment I see his dick, I lick my lips, desperate to take him in my mouth. There's no way I'll be able to take all of it. He's thick and long. His length stands at attention, just beckoning me to come closer.

I slide off the top of the washer and drop to my knees in front of him.

Air hisses through his teeth when I wrap my fingers around him once again. Just as I begin to pump up and down on his length, the sound of a door hitting the wall fills the silence.

"Daddy!" Clara yells, making both of us scramble, realizing we're no longer alone.

Chapter 33
DEAN

Liv and I have barely pulled on random clothes from the laundry baskets when Clara comes barreling into the laundry room.

"Daddy! Livvy!" she excitedly calls, looking between Liv and me with a wide grin. "Found you."

I laugh nervously, risking a glance over at Liv to, thankfully, find her fully clothed, albeit a little red in the face. "Found us," I respond tightly and high-pitched. I shift my weight. Clara yelling my name while Liv was moments away from putting her mouth on my cock was like having a bucket of cold water tossed on me.

Before I can ask Clara why she's home early, my mother and father pop into the laundry room.

"Hi," my mom says slowly, looking between both Liv and me. "Clara knew you didn't like storms, so she wanted to come home. We tried calling but figured you might be waiting the storm out, so we decided we'd just meet you here to ease her worries."

I look to my daughter, my heart feeling like it could swell inside my chest at her thoughtfulness. "You don't have to worry about me, Clara."

She smiles up at me. "You okay, Daddy?"

I nod before crouching down and pulling my daughter into

my arms. I've always tried not to show her how much storms still bother me years after the accident. I've gotten better about being out in them and trusting others being out in them as well, but deep down, I know the fear that comes with storms and driving will never truly go away. "I'm perfect. Thank you for checking on me."

"And Livvy," Clara adds, resting her chin over my shoulder and looking over it. "Why are you in here?" she asks after a few seconds. She pushes against my chest and takes a few steps back, her little eyes assessing the both of us.

I stand back up, awkwardly meeting the eyes of my parents, who both stare at me expectantly. My mom's eyebrows are raised as she waits for an answer.

She's absolutely onto us.

"I was helping your daddy with some laundry," Liv explains, her voice more high-pitched than normal.

Dad lets out a nervous bark of a cough.

Mom nods her head with her lips tilted up in a smug smile. "Mm-hm," she responds, not buying it for a second.

I run my hand over my mouth as I feel like a teenager again at almost being caught doing the deed by my parents. "We got wet from the rain leaving Sutten Mountain Treasures, so we decided to come back here and get some warm clothes," I explain. I don't know why I even waste my breath. It's clear as day neither one of my parents believes me.

At least Clara does.

"Why don't you wear rain boots like me?" She lifts a foot to show off her bright pink rain boots she insisted on having.

"Livvy and I just didn't plan as well as you did, sweetie," I tell her, playfully tickling the back of her neck. She howls and runs away from me. She runs right into Liv, throwing her body against hers and pulling her into a tight hug.

I love the way that even though it's only been two weeks, Clara's effortlessly accepted Liv into her life. It's obvious she trusts Liv and really loves her. A pang of guilt courses through me when I wonder if I jeopardized that by involving myself with Liv when I know I shouldn't have.

"Maybe we'll go play in the living room with Honey and wait for Daddy and Livvy to meet us in there?" Mom offers, a teasing tone to her voice.

I let my eyes roam to Liv for a moment, wondering if our appearance makes it obvious what we were just doing. Her cheeks are very pink, and her already large, beautiful blue eyes are wider than normal as she hugs an old T-shirt of mine to her body.

"Sounds great," I tell my mom, continuing to look at Liv. My ears feel hot with embarrassment at what my parents and daughter just about walked into. What a sight they would've walked in on if Clara hadn't announced their arrival so loudly.

They all leave and close the door behind them.

I blink as the vision of Liv on her knees in front of me floods my mind. Fuck. I was so close to feeling her lips wrap around me. Even the feeling of her fingers around me about did me in. I lick my lips at the memory, which does nothing to satiate the hunger I feel for her now because I can still taste her on my lips.

With a loud sigh, I rub my eyes with the heel of my hands to try and rid myself of the memories. My daughter was moments away from walking in on me doing some very unprofessional things with her nanny. The last thing I need to be doing is replaying those unprofessional things in my mind when I'm supposed to be getting my shit together enough to go spend time with my daughter.

Liv watches me carefully. She's probably waiting for me to say something; I just don't know exactly what to say.

I take a step closer to her. After what just happened, I feel the need to be close to her. To have some kind of contact. I choose to keep it somewhat safe by reaching out and tucking a piece of hair behind her ear.

"That was close," I tell her, my thumb brushing over her cheekbone. "You okay?"

She nods, her eyes roaming my face. "Yeah."

I allow myself to feel my skin against hers for a few moments longer before my hand drops to my side. I take a step back and let out a controlled breath. "We'll, uh...talk more about this later?" I offer, not knowing where to begin about what's transpired between us.

I want her. Still. I want to finish what we started and feel her wrap around me. But having Clara almost walk in on us was a wake-up call of sorts for me. Liv belongs here with us as Clara's nanny. I'm confident in that. And I don't know if having a physical relationship with her is a good idea. I can't complicate things when it comes to her. Clara can't lose her.

I can't lose her.

My breath is a little shaky as I let out a sad sigh. "You can go upstairs and get changed into your actual clothing if you want. I can even bring up the bags from the truck."

Liv nods. "I can get the bags later. I've got clothes in there I can wear for now."

We stare at each other for a few moments. There's so much I want to say, the biggest being that I don't regret what happened between us at all. The only thing I regret is the fact that Clara almost caught us. I keep my words to myself because I don't know what to say in this moment.

Allowing myself to give in to my attraction to her is a very dangerous, slippery slope. I can lie to myself and say it's purely physical, but it isn't. I've only known her for two weeks, and there's something about her that's just different.

I've let her in, and I know I'll continue to let her in.

But I don't know if I'm strong enough to let another person all the way in and risk losing them. So I keep all my thoughts to myself and instead begin to back away from her and head toward the living room without saying another word to her, even though I know she deserves so much more from me.

Chapter 34
LIV

A COOL BREEZE RUFFLES THE PAGES OF THE BOOK IN MY LAP. HONEY lets out a little snore at my feet as I rock back and forth on the porch swing. It's chillier outside than I was expecting, but I couldn't pass up the opportunity to just sit in the fresh air tonight. I needed a way to clear my head after the events of today with Dean, and coming out here has done just the trick. At least a little. Even as I try to get lost in the pages of my story, my mind still wanders to Dean.

No matter how many times I try to push away the memory of his lips on me, I can't. It's like I can still feel them against my own. Against the swell of my breast. My hip. On my inner thigh. And then...against my pussy.

Despite the cold, my cheeks warm as my mind drifts to places it shouldn't. It was the first time a man has ever gone down on me like that, but I know it can't be normal for it to feel *that* good. To feel so perfect. It's like every time he pressed a kiss to my skin, he was branding the memory of him—of us—in my mind forever.

I'm remembering the crazed look in his eyes moments before he gave in and finally kissed me when the man himself opens the front door.

"Hi," he says, his voice low as he waits in the open doorway.

He stands there, as if he's wanting permission to step out here and join me.

I adjust the thick blanket on my lap and scoot over to make room for him. "Hey," I respond, giving him a soft smile.

My heart does a little leap in my chest when he pulls the door shut behind him and sits down next to me. The swing creaks under his weight. Almost instantly, he takes over being the one to push the swing back and forth.

"At this point, I should start checking out here to find you before ever looking in your room."

I smile at his words as I shut the book in my lap. "It's so peaceful out here. There's no bugs, and it isn't humid. I'd spend all night out here if I could."

The smallest of frowns appears on his lips. "It's too cold for that," he mutters, his thick, gravelly voice sending shivers down my spine. I could listen to the deep tenor of his voice all day long. Even hearing him talk turns me on and gives me butterflies, something I fully recognize shouldn't be the case, but it is anyway.

"Clara asleep?" I ask, changing the subject. From the moment his parents and Clara caught us in the laundry room, we've been nothing but professional with each other. It's been friendly, at least, as we all spent time together into the evening. I was scared he would fully pull away like how he was with me when I first started, but he didn't do that this afternoon. He just didn't act like he'd had his face between my thighs earlier as we went about our day.

"Yeah, she fell asleep while I was reading her fifth book of the night."

I let out a little laugh. Somehow, she's talking us into reading more and more books to her before nap and bedtime. She's incredibly hard to say no to, so her requesting Dean read her a fifth book could be partially my fault. "I'm sure she was tired after running around and chasing Honey."

Dean leans forward and looks at the sleeping puppy at my feet. "Seems like it wore Honey Bear out, too."

His use of her nickname makes me smile. I like that he's using the one I came up with. "She's not used to that much exercise. I think we managed to pick out the laziest puppy ever."

"I still can't believe you two talked me into her," Dean mutters, shaking his head. He leans back on the swing, outstretching his arms so far that one of them goes behind my back.

"I still can't believe you said yes." I pull my feet up onto the swing with me and cross them. If Dean's going to rock the swing for us, I might as well get comfortable.

I look up from adjusting my position to find Dean staring at me. He wears a blank expression, but not one of indifference. This one makes it seem that he's thinking hard about something. I'd give anything to get in his head and figure out what.

Is he regretting kissing me? Regretting letting it progress the way that it did? With our proximity, is he thinking about finishing what we started as much as I am? Just having his smell surround me makes me want to close the distance between us and continue where we left off earlier.

The tightness in his shoulders loosens as he lets out a deep breath. "We should probably talk about earlier," he offers. I wish I could get a read on his demeanor and tone. It doesn't sound like there's regret, but he does seem a little sad.

My smile wavers a little at his words. "Probably," I respond softly. My stomach drops a little with nerves and anticipation.

"You don't have any regrets about us kissing, right?" he asks, his voice tight and unsure. He scratches his chin as he watches me carefully. "Or regrets about the laundry room?" he adds, his voice a little quieter this time.

"I don't. Do you?"

My muscles relax a little when he shakes his head. "Not at all. Part of me wishes I could. It'd be a lot easier to do the right thing if I did have regrets. But I don't." His voice gets husky as he swallows, his eyes dropping to my lips for a moment before returning to my eyes. "I'm glad I kissed you, sunshine."

My heart leaps at the nickname. He called me his sunshine on a cloudy day, and it's something I could never forget. I'd do anything to be a positive light for both him and Clara. His use of the nickname makes me feel like maybe I am. "I'm glad you kissed me, too, Dean."

He reaches across the space between us and cups my cheek with his hand. His callused fingers run over the tender skin of my cheek. Just by the look in his eyes, I know what he's going to say before he says it.

"But we can't kiss again." His voice is sad, and his words break at the end. It makes me sad for him. For us. For the situation we're in. I understand why he's saying it, but it doesn't make it hurt any less.

"I know," I respond, my voice barely above a whisper.

"You scare me," he admits. Of all the things I thought he'd say back to me, it wasn't that.

I lean into his touch, my eyes curiously roaming over him in an attempt to get a read on him. "How?"

"Because the way I care about you, it doesn't feel like we only met two weeks ago. I've let you in when I don't typically let people in. Clara's let you in. She loves you, and because of that, I can't kiss you again...no matter how badly I want to."

I nod as I try to gather my thoughts. He keeps his hand pressed to my cheek, his thumb caressing my cheekbone, as he gives me all the time I need to think of a response. I want to tell him that no matter what happens between us, I'd never let it get in the way of being Clara's nanny. I want to be in her life for as long as possible.

I've fallen in love with the little girl in the two weeks we've spent together, and the last thing I could ever do is hurt her. But I keep all of that to myself because I understand why Dean's worried. I would be, too, if I were in his position.

"Say something." He slides his hand to the back of my neck. I wish I didn't find so much comfort in his touch. I wish he wasn't my boss. I wish he could allow himself to open up more, to go after what he wants.

"I understand," I tell him, knowing that's what he needs to hear. "I don't blame you. I want you in a way I've never wanted someone else. The attraction…" I let out a sigh as I try not to think about how close he is and how easy it'd be to close the distance between us. "The attraction is there. I've never had that kind of physical connection with someone. But I also…" My words trail off as I try to think about what else I want to say and how I want to say it.

"Feel more than just the physical?" Dean offers.

I nod as I look into his whiskey-colored eyes. "Yes."

"That's the part that scares me," he whispers. "I've known you for a short time, but things just feel right. But you're not meant to stay in Sutten forever. And I'm a broken man who can't give you anything, even if you had plans of being here long-term. I can't get hurt again. I can't hurt Clara."

I know I shouldn't, but I can't help it. I wrap my arms around his neck and crawl into his lap. He instantly wraps his arms around my waist and pulls me against his body. I nestle my face into the crook of his neck and savor being in his embrace. I know it won't happen again.

"I won't hurt you, Dean." My lips move against his neck. "I won't hurt Clara."

I can feel his intense sigh of relief. His entire body slackens against mine. It makes me sad. This man is so terrified of losing people that he chooses to close himself off from them instead. I push off his chest a little so I can look him in the eyes with my next words.

He doesn't move me from his lap, and I don't move, choosing to make this moment last for as long as possible. "I can't imagine leaving anytime soon. I'm here. And I understand we should stop the kissing and the…other stuff." A blush creeps onto my cheeks at the mention of what else we've done, what else we were going to do had we not been interrupted. "But please don't shut down on me. I still want to be the person you open up to. I want to keep these late-night porch swing talks and the coffee together in the morning and all of it."

His fingers twitch against my lower back as he keeps my body pinned to his. "I want to keep those, too. And I'll try not to. I'm not used to..." He pauses as he tries to think about what else to say.

"I know," I finish for him, not needing him to say anything else. I don't want to force him into thinking he has to share his every thought with me. I just need him to know that the unlikely friendship we've built in the last two weeks is something I want to hold on to. Even if I still think about kissing him as well.

Dean leans forward and rests his forehead against mine. Our breaths fall in sync, and I don't know how long we sit there, forehead to forehead, enjoying the comfort of each other's touch for the last time. "Thank you," he whispers. "For understanding."

I nod before climbing out of his lap. I miss feeling his touch the moment I'm gone, but if things need to go back to being somewhat professional between us, I should probably start by not sitting in his lap.

I plaster on a smile as I get comfortable on my side of the swing a safe distance away from him. I take a deep breath. I can do this. I can be the friend he so clearly needs. "So tell me what your Halloween costume is going to be on Monday."

Chapter 35
LIV

"LIVVY! HURRY UP!" CLARA DEMANDS, WAITING AT THE DOOR OF Wake and Bake for me.

I smile at her, making sure to lock the car before joining her on the sidewalk. I've now officially been her nanny for just over a month, and sometimes her bossiness still takes me by surprise.

"I'm coming," I tell her, pulling the door open and ushering her inside.

I knew November in Colorado would be cold; I just didn't realize how cold it can feel when the wind is blowing like it is today. Clara runs inside Wake and Bake, forgetting all about me at the door.

"Clara!" Lexi yells from where she places pastries in the display case. "I've been looking forward to you visiting me all day."

Clara runs behind the counter as if she owns the place and wraps her arms around Lexi in a big hug.

Just when I'm about to say something to Lexi, Pippa walks out of the back room with her fiancé, Camden. They seem deep in conversation about something, but Pippa's face lights up the moment she spots us.

"There's my favorite Clara and my favorite nanny of hers!" Pippa says, looking over at me and winking.

Clara shakes her head before running over and giving Pippa

a hug, just like the one she gave Lexi. "Livvy's my only nanny right now, Pippa. Daddy tells me Livvy's his favorite, too. And that he wants her to stay."

My cheeks heat a little as Pippa looks at me with a smug grin. Her arms cross over her chest proudly. "Oh, does he?" she accuses jokingly.

I look at my feet, trying not to react to Pippa's obvious attempt to goad me for information. She's been hounding me about spilling if there's something going on between me and Dean since the pumpkin festival. If only she knew about what happened between us two weeks ago. I haven't told a soul about what happened between me and Dean, even though there have been chances. I could've told Pippa, Lexi, or even Marigold who I've learned everyone really calls Mare that I've been able to get to know in the last two weeks in Clara's and my daily trips to Wake and Bake.

I pick at a nonexistent piece of lint in an attempt to avoid Pippa's knowing stare. I've never had friends I've had to keep secrets from. Because of that, I think I'm a terrible liar and probably have the world's worst poker face.

"Is the cake ready for us?" I ask, returning my gaze to Pippa's when I feel like my face is maybe a little less red than it was.

Pippa thankfully lets me change the subject. "Yes. And it's ready to be decorated." Her eyes move to Clara. "Will you help me decorate it?"

Clara jumps up and down as she claps her small hands together. "Yes!" She twirls in the dress she was insistent on wearing this morning, letting out a gleeful laugh when the skirt of the dress lifts with the spinning.

"She's adorable," Camden notes. He looks over to his fiancée with a smirk. "I can't wait to have five babies with you."

Pippa rolls her eyes at him like that comment is something he says in passing all the time. She places her hand on his chest and gives it a playful pat. "You're a little ahead of yourself there, babe. First, we have to finish wedding planning. Second, I have to get my honeymoon in Paris. Then you can talk about getting me pregnant with all the babies."

He leans down and kisses her, not caring about an audience. "I can't wait," he mutters against her lips.

"Ew!" Clara calls, looking at me as if she can't believe Pippa and Camden are kissing right now. She sticks her tongue out dramatically like it's the most disgusting thing in the world.

All I can think is how close she was to catching me and her father doing something much worse. We've been nothing but professional since…kind of. There are still lingering stares and touches that make me want more again, but we've both held back.

I was scared Dean would pull away after what happened between us, but instead, I feel like I've learned so much about him in the last two weeks. He's continued to let me in despite us slipping and giving in to the attraction. The only problem is the more I learn about Dean, the more I want him.

I thought I'd leave Florida and find a new place to live and never once talk about my past. But the more he opens up to me, the more I want to open up to him and maybe share about the life I left behind.

A loud laugh from Clara pulls me from my thoughts. I find Pippa leading her to the back room as Camden leans down and whispers something to Clara that makes her continue to break out in a fit of laughter.

I smile at the interaction. It's sweet to see firsthand how much everyone in this town loves Clara. Dean's mentioned multiple times how he couldn't have survived his wife's death if it weren't for this community, and it's touching to see even three years later how much they all still step in.

Pippa leads us to the back kitchen. The first time she took me back here, I was shocked by just how good it smelled. There's always something baking in the oven that makes my mouth water.

"I'm going to go take some calls at home." Camden kisses

Pippa on the cheek, tells us goodbye, and is off. Pippa watches him go with so much love in her eyes. I can't help but wonder what it feels like to find your person the way they have.

Clara pushes a chair close to the island and crawls up on it so she's tall enough to help. She bounces up and down on the chair with excitement to finally decorate the cake she's been asking about all morning.

Pippa grabs a tall box from a back counter and walks it to the island. "I went ahead and did the crumb coat for the cake. That way, it was ready for us to decorate when you got here."

I smile, having no idea what a crumb coat means. "Thank you. And thank you for offering to make the cake and letting us help decorate it. I love to cook, but baking isn't my thing."

Pippa sets the box down and reveals the cake before dismissively waving her hand in the air. "Are you kidding? I'm honored you asked me to help." She reaches across the island and gives my wrist a gentle squeeze. "I think it's really thoughtful of you to do this in the first place."

I let out a hesitant breath of air. I have no idea if Dean will like this or not. It could go either way, but one thing he's been vocal about is wanting to celebrate Selena's life more instead of focusing on her death. Celebrating her birthday today I hope is a step toward that. And everyone needs a birthday cake for their birthday.

"I hope Dean thinks the same," I admit to Pippa. Clara's already busy looking at the different bags of icing Pippa's prepared to decide what she wants to use.

"He will." Pippa seems confident, which makes me a little less nervous. She's known Dean through all the ups and downs, and if she thinks he'll appreciate the gesture, then I'm just going to trust her.

"What color of icing should we do?" I ask Clara, resting my elbows against the island. Pippa's gone a little overboard preparing colors for us.

Clara stares at the cake with her little lips pursed. Her eyes meet mine, and there's a little bit of panic in them. "I don't know my mama's favorite color."

My heart breaks a little at the distraught look in her eyes. I reach out and rub my hand over her hair to comfort her. "I bet your favorite color and her favorite color are the same."

Clara's eyes light up as a little gasp falls from her lips. "Really?"

Both Pippa and I nod. "Yes."

Clara picks up a light pink bag of icing. "I want this one," she announces proudly. You'd never know that only moments ago, she was so sad at not knowing her mother's favorite color.

"Pink's my favorite color, too," Pippa tells her. She twists the top of the bag and squeezes it until icing comes out of the tip. "So what we're going to do is put this pink down first. You'll squeeze real tight and put it all over. Then we'll spread it. Sound good?"

Clara nods, already reaching to grab the bag from Pippa. "I can do it," she tells us, beginning to squeeze the bag and emptying almost half of it on top of the cake.

"Whoa!" Pippa laughs. "Maybe just a little slower."

The look Clara gives Pippa is hilarious. "I know how to do it, Pippa." Her tone makes her seem sixteen and not three.

Pippa and I share a look before breaking out in laughter. We let Clara do the rest of the decorating for the cake in fear of getting another scathing look from a three-year-old.

Chapter 36
DEAN

Today's been a shit day. I sit in my parked car in the garage, enjoying a moment of quiet before heading inside.

Everything that could've gone wrong today did. A huge commercial deal I've been working on to bring a lot of jobs and tourism to Sutten might not happen because of drama outside of my control. The town was very excited about this complex possibly coming into town, which means I was excited, too. It's hard navigating the happiness of the locals here and making them feel like Sutten stays the small town we love, but also bringing in more opportunities for the town to grow the right way.

This was supposed to be it.

And it might not happen, and I can't do anything about it.

Add in the fact that Tonya was out sick today and I had to manage more than I normally do.

It was rough.

Not to mention, it's Selena's birthday. She absolutely adored birthdays, and today hits harder than others. I know she would've loved celebrating with Clara. She would've made a big deal out of today and the entire week, milking her birthday for everything. I pretended to give her shit about making it a birthday month or week instead of a day, but deep down, I loved it.

I've been so happy recently with things going so well with Clara and Liv that I almost feel guilty. Am I supposed to be happy even though I lost the woman I loved? I was ready to celebrate every single birthday with her until the day that I passed.

I always kind of assumed it'd be me who went first. I never thought it'd be her. I grieved her for so long and shut myself out to the world, but now I'm finding a balance between missing her and also learning to live with the grief.

Learning to allow myself to be happy despite what's happened. And sometimes the guilt for that hits hard, like today on her birthday.

I sigh, raking a hand over my mouth as I question if I'm a shit father for not having an elaborate day planned to celebrate her mother. I'd planned on taking her into town this weekend and picking out some flowers to visit Selena's grave. Liv had inspired me to tell Clara more about her mother, and I wanted to do that with maybe a picnic or something at her grave.

But now, I'm wondering if I should've had more planned for the actual day.

I lean back, letting my head fall to the headrest. I can't help but wonder if there will ever be a time where I don't second-guess every single one of my decisions as a father. They never seem right, and I can't even talk them through with Selena because she isn't here to help me make them.

I close my eyes and allow myself a few more moments of grief before heading inside. Despite the shit day, the sadness that comes with the date, and the fears I have about how I'm doing as a father, I'm excited to see my daughter. Everything feels right when I get to wrap my arms around her and remind myself that even with all the pain, she's the best thing to ever happen to me.

I'm also excited to see Liv. I can't deny that a big factor in my happiness recently is because of her. And I can't shake the guilt —and unease—I feel at allowing someone who isn't my daughter into my life enough to affect my happiness.

With a sigh, I push the truck door open and head inside. It smells delicious. One of my favorite parts of the day has easily become getting home from work. It's the way that Honey comes running to me every time, her tongue lolling out of her mouth as she immediately rolls over at my feet for belly rubs.

She does that right now. I've barely got the door to the garage shut before the puppy is begging for pets. I crouch down for a moment and give her what she wants, unable to resist the dog, even though I swore I didn't want her. She's grown on me more than I thought she would. But I guess that's the story of my life recently.

I'm more open to letting things in than I thought.

The sound of faint laughter coming from deeper inside the house has me giving Honey one last belly rub before standing back up. The biggest reason coming home from work is one of my favorite times of the day is because I love coming home and seeing what Liv and Clara are up to. I can almost always count on them laughing and goofing around when I walk through the door. Sometimes, they're in the kitchen cooking together; other times, they're dancing in the kitchen and belting out lyrics to songs I don't know as Liv cleans up.

But they're always happy. Clara's always happy. And fuck, seeing Clara happy and seeing Liv's smile...well, it makes me happy, too.

I walk toward the kitchen, wondering what Liv made for dinner because it smells incredible. My stomach growls in anticipation.

"Hi!" I call out, wondering why Clara hasn't already run up to greet me. Most nights, the moment Honey comes running to me, Clara will closely follow.

"In here," Liv responds from what sounds like the kitchen.

I round the corner and stop in my tracks at the sight before me.

Clara and Liv are in birthday hats with a birthday banner strung up behind them.

"Surprise!" Clara yells, holding her hands out wide. The birthday hat goes a little lopsided with the movement, but she doesn't care to fix it.

I can't move as my eyes roam the space in front of me. There's a birthday cake sitting in front of the girls with candles carefully placed all around the top. There's a wrapped present sitting next to it.

A flash of movement catches my attention. Clara runs to me, her arms wrapping around my legs as she gives me a big squeeze. "It's my mama's birthday today, Daddy. Livvy said we should celebrate."

My throat feels tight as I take a step back in shock.

She'd planned a birthday celebration for Selena.

I open my mouth to say something, but no words come out. Emotion clogs my throat at the sheer thoughtfulness of the sight in front of me.

"Daddy?" Clara says, pulling her head back so she can look up at me. "Do you like it? We decorated, and we made cake!" She jumps up and down at the word "cake."

My eyes lock with Liv's, and so many things run through my head. The biggest being I have no idea what I did right in my life to deserve her. She never met Selena. I didn't even know she was aware when Selena's birthday was. Yet, here she is, making sure that I'm doing what I told her I wanted to do—celebrate Selena's life instead of focusing on her death.

"I love it," I finally manage to get out as Clara grabs my hand in hers. My words come out gritty and nowhere near as composed as they should be, but I don't care. I hope that Liv can hear the emotion in my words.

Clara pulls me all the way to the counter, where a messily decorated birthday cake sits that reads "Happy birthday Mama." My eyes burn as I take it all in.

"I decorated the cake myself," Clara announces proudly. "Up," she demands. Liv takes the cue and lifts her onto the counter so she can get a closer look at the cake. Clara's brown eyes focus right on me as the most adorable grin spreads across her cheeks. "You like it? I didn't know Mama's favorite color, so I did mine."

I laugh a little, taking in the lopsided dollops of icing all over the cake. "This is…" My words die because I have no idea what to say.

I look at Liv again, finding her watching me carefully. She's got her hands over her mouth as her eyes cautiously scan my face. "Is it okay?" she asks quietly, her nerves evident with the shakiness of her question.

A wave of emotion I haven't felt in years washes over me at the tenderness and cautiousness in her voice. The fact she would even question if this was okay or not really speaks to how caring she is about others. "Of course," I answer, my voice gritty. "It's more than okay. I can't believe you…" It seems like I can't even finish sentences. I'm in such shock by what she's planned.

I sigh as I blink a few times. My eyes burn with unshed emotion. I open them again and meet Liv's caring blue gaze. "Thank you," I croak. "Just thank you."

She rubs her lips together as she tries to fight a smile. It's clear she's not great at just accepting my gratitude. If only she knew how much this gesture meant to me. I was so concerned about how to properly celebrate Selena today when all along, Liv knew just what to do.

"Pippa baked the cake because I'm a terrible baker. Hattie told me Selena's favorite was chocolate, so that's what we went with. And then, well, Clara beautifully did the decorating, as you can tell."

I stare at her. I should look at the cake, but I can't look away from her. It isn't lost on me how much planning she must've done to do this. Asking Hattie Selena's favorite flavor, recruiting Pippa for help, she went above and beyond for today, and I don't even know how to begin to thank her.

"We also got Mama a present!" Clara declares, lifting the present from the counter and pushing it into my chest.

I look down at the neatly wrapped gift. It's got a bow on the top and simple yellow wrapping paper.

My eyes move from Clara to Liv, unsure if I'm supposed to open it or not. Luckily, my daughter decides for me. She grabs a corner of the wrapping paper and pulls, revealing part of what's inside. It looks to be a large book of some sort.

"We worked really hard on this, Daddy," Clara tells me, her voice totally serious.

"Did you?" I ask, still trying to get my emotions together enough for whatever's inside. My mind still reels from how thoughtful it was for Liv to do this. I can't move past it. I can't move past how incredibly lucky I feel to have her in my life. To have her with me navigating the hard moments of life. Especially the ones like today, where I had no idea how to honor the amazing woman Selena was with the beautiful daughter we created and not make it too sad.

"Everyone helped. Mimi, Papa, Aunt Hattie, *everyone*." Clara emphasizes the last one to really let me know how many people were involved.

I carefully pull the rest of the wrapping paper off until I'm left with a large book.

"It's a rapbook," Clara announces proudly, leaning over the book to get a better look.

Liv laughs. "Scrapbook," she corrects, her tone gentle.

Clara looks at Liv for a moment. "Yeah. Scrapbook. Just like I said."

Liv and I share a smile. That's definitely not what she said to begin with, but we let her believe it is.

I run my fingers over the front cover. It's plain leather with nothing on the front. I'm not sure how it's a gift for Selena yet, but I open it to find out.

My hands still.

The very first page is a picture of Selena holding a newborn Clara.

"Mimi said that's me!" Clara points to the picture of her. She leans even closer to inspect it. There are stickers all over the page, some even covering the picture. There are also butterflies that were clearly drawn by Clara.

I hope Liv doesn't notice the way my hands shake as I take in the picture. I remember the day so vividly. Selena had mentioned she thought she was having contractions all day. Finally, after dinner, I convinced her we should go to the hospital. This picture was taken two hours later.

"That bow's bigger than me, Daddy," Clara whispers, still inspecting the picture. I laugh, remembering how I'd said almost the same exact thing to Selena. She hadn't cared. She loved the huge, obnoxious bow on Clara, so I did, too.

"You remember that day?" Clara asks me.

I nod, my eyes misting over the memory. "I do, sweetie," I croak. It was the best day of my life, and somehow, when I look at this picture of Selena holding our newborn daughter, I don't feel sad. Not the way I used to. Instead, I'm catapulted to that very moment and the rush of happiness I felt welcoming our daughter into the world.

Clara turns the page for me, this time showing off a collage of photos from high school and college with Hattie and Selena. There are neatly printed descriptions below each picture from, I assume, Hattie, explaining what's happening in each photo.

I continue to turn through the pages of the scrapbook as my eyes burn even more. Eventually, a tear I can't stop runs down my cheek.

Clara sees it immediately. "Oh no, Daddy, don't cry. Livvy said we were supposed to be happy when we look at these pictures of Mama. They're good memories," she informs me.

I close my eyes, knowing more tears are bound to fall after her statement.

Just when I thought Liv couldn't get any more thoughtful, she does something like this.

"I'm not sad," I manage to get out through the thickness in my throat. I rub a hand over my heart, not used to the constricting feeling in my chest. "I'm just—this was really nice of you and Livvy."

I look at Liv, taking in the moment with her. She wears a party hat with little tiny dogs with balloons all over it. Her eyes watch me carefully. A whisper of a smile is on her lips as she bashfully looks at the counter for a moment before looking at me again. "I got as many pictures as I could from everyone in town. I figured it'd be nice to have a memory book of Selena on days like today. Or any day," she adds last minute, her tone getting softer with the addition.

I swallow. The book is open in front of me, but for the moment, I just want to look at her. I hope she can read the emotions on my face and understand I'm terrible at words but that what she did today for me, for Clara, well, it means the world to me.

She's beginning to mean the world to me, and it's something I don't think I can run from.

"This is the best gift anyone's ever given me," I tell her. My voice is barely above a whisper. That's all I can get out through the stray tears that fall down my cheeks and the emotion clogging my voice.

She smiles so wide that I feel it all the way to my bones. Maybe even deeper—I feel it in my soul. I can fight it all I want, but this woman is imprinting herself on every fiber of my being, and I can't stop it.

She's my sunshine on a cloudy day, and I hadn't realized how much I missed the sunshine. How much I really needed it... until her.

Chapter 37
LIV

A TEAR RUNS DOWN DEAN'S CHEEK AS HE STARES AT ME. He doesn't look away despite the tears that have freely fallen.

I savor it, knowing how hard it is for him to show emotion. This moment feels big. Like it's proof that he's let me in, that he feels comfortable enough with me to show me this vulnerable side of him.

Clara continues to flip through the pages as if this is the first time she's seen the scrapbook. It isn't. She's helped me decorate the pages for the past week and make it personalized, but I love how excited she is to look at it.

"I don't know how to thank you," Dean gets out. His voice is deep and thick with emotion. I love this side of him, the one that doesn't hide from me.

I shake my head. "You don't have to thank me."

He looks down for a moment before meeting my eyes again. "I want to. You doing this…it means everything to me."

I tuck a piece of my hair behind my ear, hoping that he doesn't see the blush spreading over my cheeks. I didn't plan any of this for recognition. I just wanted to do my best to share happy memories of Selena.

I thought it'd be great to have something here for Clara to look at when she had questions about who her mother was. I guessed today would be hard for Dean, and my hope with planning the birthday celebration was that I could do my best to make today even a little less sad. I loved that his family and the rest of the town wanted to help, too. I'd tried to reach out to the number Shirley gave me of Selena's mother, but I didn't hear anything back. Shirley told me they don't hear from them a lot, which makes me sad for Clara.

"Daddy, look, it's you. And you're a prince!" Clara's words catch my attention. I look down and find the picture of Dean and Selena from their high school prom. Shirley told me all about how Dean and Selena won prom king and queen their senior year.

"That seems like so long ago," Dean mutters. He seems to say it more for himself than anyone else. No more tears have fallen down his cheek, but the wistful look of what I hope is happiness is still apparent in his eyes. They seem softer as he looks at the picture in front of him. Even his jaw seems to be relaxed for once.

It allows me to take my own sigh of relief. He isn't the same grumpy man I first met. The warnings I got from those in this town were right. He's closed off, but behind all the walls he puts up is a man deserving of so much happiness.

I force myself to pull my eyes from him. When he smiles at me with his guard down, I almost feel like I can't breathe. I thought the knowledge that we can't ever kiss again would stop me from crushing on him, but it hasn't. I've developed real, raw feelings for Dean, and it's terrifying because he's made it very clear that nothing can ever happen between us.

I understand his reasoning; my heart apparently just doesn't care.

Clara still stares at the picture of her parents at their high school prom. She's decorated this page by tearing little pieces of paper and gluing them everywhere. There are also a few star stickers and a random leaf she found outside that she insisted had to go in the book. I stare at the photo, too, wondering what it was like to know a Dean who hadn't endured tragedy yet.

"She's beautiful," I whisper, admiring the stunning woman Selena was. She had brown hair that was about shoulder length in the photos. It's thick and curly, making me wonder if that's where Clara gets her little curls from. Her smile reminds me a lot of Clara's.

"Yeah." Dean nods his head, his fingers running over the photo. He lets out a little laugh as he continues to stare at the two of them captured in time. "I remember she had her makeup professionally done that day. She hated it so much that she wiped it all off during the limo ride to the event and used whatever she had in her purse to do her makeup the way she liked."

The story makes me smile. I like hearing about her personality. She seemed to be fiery and carefree, just like Clara. It's fun to put together the pieces and discover what quirks of Clara's might be from Dean and what might be from Selena.

"Clara looks so much like her," I whisper, reaching across the island and playing with the end of Clara's braid.

Clara smiles at me, completely entranced at looking at the photo of her mom. "Mama very pretty, and I'm very pretty."

Dean and I both laugh. "Yes. Absolutely, sweetie," Dean speaks up, looking at his daughter with so much love that it makes my heart feel like it could burst.

"I wish I could've met her," I admit, looking back at the photo of Selena and Dean. The moment the words leave my mouth, I wonder if they were better left unsaid.

Dean's wide eyes immediately find mine. Time seems to slow in the moment as he stares at me with an unreadable look in his eyes. My heart begins to race, and my stomach sinks as I wonder if I shouldn't have said that.

The corners of his mouth begin to turn up ever so slowly until a smile graces his full lips. "She would've loved you."

I swallow as I let his words sink in. I can't explain why, but they mean so much to me. The little pieces I've learned about Selena over the last month tell me how great of a person she was.

I know I would've loved her, and for Dean to think we would've gotten along, it means more than I can even put into words.

"Can we have cake now?" Clara blurts.

Dean continues to look at me for a few more seconds before he gently shuts the book and focuses on his daughter. "Have you had dinner yet?"

Clara grins at him as she lifts her shoulder in a small shrug. "I had a snack," she counters.

Dean looks at me with a raised eyebrow. "I guess it is a special occasion. Maybe just this once, we can do cake before dinner..."

"Really?" Clara almost falls off the island as she waves her hands in the air with glee. Dean reaches out and places his hand on her back to steady her, a wide smile on his face the entire time.

Happy looks so freaking good on Dean. When his entire face is lit up with pure joy, it's hard not to develop strong feelings for him. Feelings I know I shouldn't have but ones I have regardless.

"What do you say, sunshine," Dean begins, his warm brown eyes aimed right at me. The smile on his face sends my pulse racing. "Should we have some cake before dinner?"

"That's the best idea you've ever had."

Chapter 38
DEAN

It's beautiful tonight for November, so when I walk downstairs after putting Clara to bed, I'm not shocked to find Liv outside with Honey. I bought an outdoor space heater last week and put it on the porch because Liv has been so insistent on sitting outside every night despite some nights being colder than others.

I don't think twice about joining her outside. It's become our tradition. Honey's tail thumps against the wood porch, but she doesn't bother moving. She's too comfortable lying in front of the heater.

"Mind if I join you?" I ask, holding up the bottle of wine.

Liv smiles because of course she does. It's her. She lifts her blanket and pats the spot next to her. "Of course not."

I close the distance and take a seat next to her. When she places the blanket on my lap and her thigh brushes ever so slightly against mine, I don't scoot away from the small bit of contact between our bodies.

I can't deny that I miss her, even when she's sitting right next to me. I barely found out what it was like to freely touch her, kiss her, be inside her, but it was enough to ruin me. The memory of her is burned so vividly in my mind that even the smallest brush of our bodies makes me desperate for more.

I let out a loud sigh as I try to push the thoughts from my

mind. I didn't come out here to be reminded of what happened between us. Today was just a hard day, and I'm finding that I want to spend the hard days with her. Even if it's just sitting on a porch swing with her as she reads her book. Just being in her presence calms me. It's something I've come to accept instead of fighting.

Liv begins to close her book, but I reach across us and stop her. "You don't have to stop reading. We don't have to talk."

She watches me carefully for a moment. The wind picks up a little and rustles her hair, blowing pieces of it into her face. My fingers twitch in my lap to reach up and tuck them behind her ear, but she beats me to it.

"I don't mind. I was at a good stopping point."

"You sure? I can sit here quietly. I just didn't want to be alone." It's a half-truth. It wasn't that I didn't want to be alone; I just wanted to be with her. Even sitting next to her in silence soothes something deep inside me.

She nods, carefully leaning over and placing the book on the porch.

She adjusts her position on the swing so that her back is against the armrest and her body faces mine. The way she keeps her legs tucked into her chest so she doesn't encroach on my space doesn't seem comfortable.

I know it probably isn't the best idea, but I can't bring myself to care enough to stop. Reaching forward, I grab her feet and place them in my lap. I adjust the blanket over us, making sure she stays covered with our new position.

We sit in silence for a bit. I don't remember when, but at some point, my thumb begins running circles along the bottom of her sock-clad foot. Her toes stick out from underneath the blanket, showing off her socks that have flowers with smiley faces all over them. They fit her perfectly.

I smile, continuing to rub the bottom of her foot. When I look her way, I find her eyes already on me.

"Thank you for today," I say, keeping my voice quiet and

controlled. I wish I knew a better way to tell her just how much it meant to me that she went to such great lengths to celebrate Clara's mother.

"I was so nervous you wouldn't like it. Or you'd feel like I overstepped." Her voice is timid and unsure. I wish it wasn't like that. I wish I'd been able to be more open with her from the beginning so she didn't feel like she had to walk on eggshells around me.

I watch her for a few moments as I try to think of the right thing to say to her. I want her to know that in the month she's been here with us, she's become part of our family. If you have good intentions, you can't overstep when it comes to family. Not really. "You could never overstep, Liv."

She gives me that radiant smile of hers that chips away at the stone around my heart. It's so effortless to care for her...to feel stronger about her than I should.

I sigh, letting my head fall backward against the swing. "What am I going to do with you, sunshine?"

"What do you mean?"

"I mean, you're just too good. For me. For this world. I don't deserve you, but I also can't give you up."

"You deserve all the good things, Dean."

I roll my head to the side and really look at her. There's a feeling that washes over me that if she stays another month or two—which I hope she does—that I won't be able to keep things professional. Not that having her feet in my lap and feeling an intense need to be around her at all times is professional to begin with.

But I know that I can only keep pretending that I don't have feelings for her for so long before I have to accept them. I never thought my heart would crave the company of someone else again, yet here I am, wondering if it's possible for a cold, dark heart to come back to life.

"Tell me what you're thinking about," she whispers. She pulls her sweatshirt—well, actually mine—up closer to her face and folds her hand by her cheek to get comfortable against the back of the swing. She looks so relaxed and peaceful, the same way she makes me feel.

You. These days, it seems to always be you.

I keep that answer to myself for both of our sakes. I'm not ready to admit that to her. Not yet, at least.

So I go with something that has been on my mind a lot recently. "I was thinking about how I don't know much about you. It seems like you know so much about me, but I know nothing about you."

Sometimes I lie awake at night and wonder what she's running from. I know it has to be something. There are clues here and there that tell me that she left Florida behind for a reason. I'll never forget the fear in her eyes when she asked me not to tell her references where she was applying for a job.

I never called the references at all. They spoke so highly of her in the letters it didn't seem necessary. Or maybe it was the fact I couldn't get the desperate plea of her tone out of my head. I didn't want to risk calling them and alerting whatever or whoever she's running from as to where she's ended up.

Liv's eyes flutter shut for a moment as she mulls over my request. I won't push her. If she says she doesn't want to tell me about the life she knew before Sutten, I'll let her brush it aside. I know firsthand how frustrating it is for people to demand you talk about something you're not ready to discuss.

But fuck, I want her to trust me enough to tell me about her past. I opened up to her faster than I ever thought I could. I just want to be someone she's comfortable enough with to do the same.

It stays quiet between us for a while. I don't try to fill it, instead hoping if I give her enough time to think that she'll decide to trust me.

"I don't know where to start," she finally confesses. "I'm not that interesting."

I shake my head. "Anything about you is interesting to me."

She tries to fight a smile by pulling her lip between her teeth, but it doesn't work for long. Her lips spread into a soft smile as her perfect, deep dimples make an appearance. "I just don't want you to feel bad for me. I grew up in not the best of circumstances, but I'm okay. I'm *more* than okay right now." Her voice gets softer with the last sentence, but even though her tone is soft, it packs a punch to my heart.

I hope she means she's more than okay right now because she's here safe with Clara and me. That maybe things didn't used to be great for her, but she feels differently now.

All in all, I just hope she feels happy. Happy enough to stay here with us. Maybe even forever if we're lucky. I try not to think about what that actually means for me to want something like that. It's not something I'm ready to face, not tonight.

"I know what it's like to have people pity you, sunshine. I know you're too strong to be pitied. I can already tell you that I'll never pity you. Whatever you've had to endure, I care enough about you to want to protect you from ever having to face it again."

Her mouth parts as a small little gasp falls from her lips. She blinks a few times, as if she's completely stunned by my words. I repeat them in my head, wondering if I said too much. "Why are you looking at me like that?" My eyes scan her face as my heart picks up speed. Hopefully, I didn't say the wrong thing. I was just letting myself be honest with her and not hold back with her for once.

"You said you care about me." Her voice is hesitant, as if she's also unsure if she should be saying it out loud or not.

I frown a little. "Of course I care about you. I thought that was obvious."

She lifts her eyebrows. "Is anything obvious with you, Dean Livingston?"

I grunt as I narrow my eyes at her a little. She has a fair point. It does make me annoyed with myself a little that I have her questioning if I care about her or not. The problem has never been if I cared about her. It's been that I care about her too much, and it happened quicker than I ever expected.

"You don't have to tell me everything about your past and what it looked like. Just tell me something. Anything."

She nods her head as she shifts her position on the swing. She doesn't pull her feet from my lap. If anything, she nestles them against my stomach as if she's trying to warm them up with my body heat. "There's not that much to it, I promise. Mom left me as a newborn with my father and never came back. The man she left me with was not prepared—or fit—to be a father. He was a drug addict, had a mean temper, and ran with bad people. I was in and out of his care as a child. Saved for years to be able to leave home when I finally turned eighteen. Found out a week before my birthday my father had found my stash and spent it all on drugs. Secretly saved again for years to get away, and here I am."

I stare at her in disbelief. I have so many more questions, but I don't want to bombard her with them. One stands out more than the others. I swallow, rage already seeping into my veins at her story without even knowing the answer to my next question. "Did he ever hurt you?"

The sad smile she gives me tells me everything I need to know. I clench my jaw as the rage inside me builds.

"I'm okay, Dean. Promise. I got out."

A strangled noise comes from deep in my throat as I want to fire off a million questions at once. The biggest being what her father's name is and how do I find him. He deserves hell after what he put her through, and I know she hasn't even told me all of it.

As a single father to a daughter, I can't imagine ever putting my daughter in harm's way. My entire existence revolves around Clara. I'm constantly wondering about how to keep her safe. I go to bed every night worrying if she felt loved. I can't imagine how Liv must've felt in her own home. She was let down by the two people who were supposed to love her the most in this world.

How could her father live with himself after treating her this way? He doesn't even deserve to be related to someone as beautiful and incredible as Liv.

Liv leans forward so that our faces are only inches apart. She rests her forearms on her knees as her eyes briefly look at my lips before looking me in the eyes again. "Whatever you're thinking right now, stop," she whispers. "He's not worth any more of your thoughts."

"Will he come looking for you?" Panic starts to build as I imagine him coming to Sutten to find her. She's made it sound like she's been careful enough that there's no way he'd know where she is, but it doesn't stop me from worrying.

Liv shakes her head, giving me the smallest bit of relief. "No. He won't waste his time on that."

My chest still feels tight, but I have to accept her answer. She sounds confident, and that gives me the smallest piece of mind. "Okay," I respond.

"Now, let's not talk about him. He doesn't deserve it."

I nod, and before I think better of it, I'm reaching out and cupping her cheek. "Tell me something else then. If you could be anywhere in the world, do anything in the world, what would it be?"

She smiles, and I love that she nuzzles deeper into my touch. I crave a physical connection with her. Just the simple press of our skin lights something deep inside me. "That's a hard question. I love it here in Sutten. It's everything I imagined a small town to be and more."

"Okay, so if you could do anything here in Sutten, what would it be?"

"I love being Clara's nanny. It feels like I have a family again between you two, your family, Pippa, Lexi. Everyone in this small town has accepted me this last month. I'm happy being a nanny."

Her words comfort me. There's nothing I want more than for her to want to stay here. But I also wonder if she's ever allowed herself to dream big, to want more for herself. "Think bigger." My words come out pleading, and I'm not sure why. She's given me the answer I should want. I should want her to want to be Clara's nanny forever. But Clara won't always need a nanny, and for some reason, I want Liv to envision herself doing something different in Sutten when that time comes. Maybe then she won't leave.

Even in the dim lights of the porch, I can see the blush that creeps up her cheeks. "I think it'd be fun to work at a bookstore. Maybe Bluebird Books will have an opening for me when the time comes."

I smile wide, my fingers twitching against her skin at her answer. Her answer makes my shoulders relax a little as my heart perks up as well. I like the way she talks, as if she sees a future here. I'm afraid of how much I want her to make Sutten her permanent home.

Tonight, I find comfort in her presence and the knowledge that she doesn't plan on leaving anytime soon. Tonight, that's all I need.

Chapter 39
LIV

I'M CLIMBING THE STAIRS FROM THE BASEMENT TO THE MAIN FLOOR when a sound comes from the hallway that leads to Dean's room. I pause for a moment at the top of the stairs, wondering if I'm just hearing things. It's now been just over two months since I started as Clara's nanny, but it's only been a couple of weeks since it got too cold outside for me to sit on the porch, even with the space heater. We've been getting light dustings of snow, so now my new reading spot is in the basement.

Typically, Dean comes down there with me and works from his laptop, but he'd had an early morning and a day filled with meetings. Christmas is in a few weeks, and he's been busy trying to get things done before the new year, so when he'd said he was going to go to bed early, I understood.

But as another sound comes from his room, I can't help but wonder if he's okay. A strangled cry comes from down the hall, making me take a step in that direction.

It's been over a month since we kissed, and we haven't done it again, even though it's obvious we both want to. Although we haven't given in to the temptation, I still feel closer to him than ever. Because of this, I continue down the hallway to Dean's room just to listen and make sure he's okay.

I've never been in his room. I haven't needed to be. There's nothing really down this hall except his bedroom, so I haven't been down this way. I stop in front of his door and listen. Just when I'm confident that everything's okay and I was just overreacting, another cry comes from his room.

My heart pounds with not knowing what to do. In the late nights Dean and I have spent getting to know one another, he's admitted that he'll still get nightmares occasionally. Although, they aren't as frequent as they used to be. He even confided that sometimes they'll be so loud that they'll wake Clara up.

I press my hand against the door and grab the doorknob with my other. Clara's having a sleepover with her cousins, but I still don't want Dean to have to suffer through the nightmare if I can stop it.

I softly push the door open and take a hesitant step into his room. It's dark. The only light in the room is the moonlight that filters through the opening of his curtains. He lets out another strangled cry as I carefully shut his bedroom door. I stand in place for a moment, trying to decide if this is a good idea or not.

He lies in the middle of his large bed. He's pushed all of the blankets off him, leaving him in nothing but a pair of gray sweatpants that I've never seen before. Even with only a small amount of moonlight illuminating the room, I can see a sheen of sweat across his bare back.

Dean faces the opposite direction, so I can't get a clear look at him, but I don't have to see his face to know that he's having a nightmare. Even in his sleep, his body is stiff, and the muscles on his back are bunched together.

I walk closer to the bed. My heart pounds, and I don't know why I'm so nervous. If I was having a bad dream and he woke me up from it, I'd appreciate him. But he's been in my room. He's sat on the edge of my bed at the end of a long day, after putting Clara to bed, as we just talked about the most random of things.

I haven't ever been in here. Something feels different about being in his room.

I push my worries about upsetting him by intruding on his

personal space from my mind. If he gets upset, he gets upset. At least he won't have to suffer through the nightmare longer than necessary.

As quietly and gently as possible, I press my knee into the corner of his mattress. I repeat the motion until I'm on the bed with him. I didn't think this through. How do I wake him up? Do I whisper his name? Pull his body into mine?

I hadn't come up with a plan. All I knew was I heard him having a nightmare, and I needed to stop it. His breaths are heavy as he hugs his pillow tighter, his body reacting to whatever's happening in his dream.

Carefully, I reach out and place my hand on his back. I begin to rub circles along his back in an effort to comfort him.

"Dean," I whisper, trying to get his attention but not startle him.

It doesn't help. His body thrashes against the mattress as he mutters what I think is the word *no* against his pillow.

My hand travels up his back until I'm able to cup the back of his head.

"Dean," I repeat, this time a little louder. "Wake up." My heart hammers inside my chest. His hair is damp from the cold sweats of his dream.

"Please wake up," I plead, hating the way his body shakes with whatever's going on in his dream.

He startles as he abruptly pushes himself off the mattress while letting out a loud gasp.

His eyes immediately find mine, and all I can see in them is panic.

"Sunshine," he croaks. His eyes frantically scan my face as if he's trying to figure out if I'm real or a dream.

"I'm here," I tell him, placing my palm to his cheek. "I'm right here."

His chest rises and falls in rapid succession as he tries to catch his breath. As if he doesn't believe that I'm actually here, he reaches up and grabs both sides of my face. His fingers tangle in my hair as he roughly pulls my forehead against his.

"You're here," he repeats. He says it over and over again, as if he's trying to convince himself of the statement. "You're okay," he adds, his voice breaking.

My heart breaks at the sound. I don't know what was happening in his dream, but whatever it was still infiltrates his mind as he tries to regain his bearings.

I nod my head, placing my other hand on his cheek until we're both holding each other's heads.

He closes his eyes for a moment as he takes a few deep breaths. I feel every long exhale against my cheek. "You and Clara were in the car, and I couldn't stop it," he gets out, his words strangled with emotion. "I couldn't stop it. You were—"

I slip my fingers underneath his chin and force him to look at me. "I'm right here. I'm okay. Clara's okay. It was just a dream."

He lets out a shaky breath before nodding. A tremor runs through his entire body, and it kills me. I sit back and pull his head into my chest. My arms wrap around him tightly as I hold him right against my racing heart to prove to him I'm okay and that I'm right here with him.

I don't know how long we sit with his head cradled to my chest and his arms wrapped around my middle. I know it's long enough for his breaths to slow and even out. When he speaks, I can feel the vibrations against my body.

"Fuck, Liv, did I wake you up?"

I shake my head. I run my fingers through his hair, trying to comfort him. "No. I was coming upstairs from the basement when I heard you. I didn't know if you'd be okay with me waking you up or not, but your cries got worse, and I—"

"I'm happy you came," he interrupts. He presses his large hand into the mattress to prop himself up and line his eyes up with mine. "Thank you."

My body relaxes with a sigh of relief. He isn't mad that I barged in and woke him up.

He lifts his free hand and moves the long braid I'd put my hair in from my shoulder to behind my back. A small shiver runs down my spine when he traces a callused finger along my collarbone. "I was so fucking scared. You were just...gone in my dream." He looks from where he touches my skin and brings his whiskey-colored eyes to meet my gaze. "I thought I'd lost you." His voice is barely above a whisper, but it feels like he yelled it with the way I feel it throughout my entire body.

"Never," I respond, my voice thick with emotion.

His eyes trace over my face for a moment. "Stay with me tonight?" he asks, the vulnerability obvious in his tone.

My breaths still with his request. I've never slept in the same bed as a man, but I can't imagine leaving him alone in here after the fear in his eyes and voice.

I nod, even though I know lying next to him will just fuel the desire I have for him. It doesn't matter. I can't say no to him. I'd do anything he asked me to.

His entire body relaxes with a small nod of my head. Slowly, he lets his hand drop to the mattress. I watch him closely as he grabs the blankets from the end of his bed and pulls them up. He lies down facing me, sliding one hand underneath his pillow and lifting the other one to let me in.

"Can I just hold you tonight?" he asks quietly.

Without a second thought, I lay down next to him. He wraps his arm around me and, with one simple movement, pulls my body flush to his. He tucks his chin over my head and places his fingers to my neck as if he needs to feel my pulse against his fingertips to assure himself I'm here.

I don't know how long I lie awake, but I know it's long enough for his breaths to slow enough that I know he's asleep. Eventually, sleep pulls me under right with him.

Chapter 40
DEAN

I WAKE UP TO A WARM BODY PRESSED TO MINE. MY HAND SPLAYS across Liv's stomach, keeping her pinned against me. I don't think we moved our position all night. The night may have started with me having a nightmare, but after she agreed to stay in here with me, I slept better than I had in years.

No woman has ever slept in this bed next to me. After Selena passed, I couldn't keep the bedroom furniture she'd picked out. I donated all of it, unable to keep the same bed she'd slept in after her scent disappeared from the sheets. After that, I thought I'd never sleep next to another woman again, but that all changed with Liv.

I should be scared at the knowledge things are so different with her, but I'm not. I haven't been at peace in the morning in a very long time, yet this morning, that's exactly how I feel.

She still sleeps soundly, allowing me the freedom to just stare at her without being caught. Slowly, I prop myself up on my elbow so I can get a better look at her. I gently push pieces of hair from her face. She had it neatly braided back last night, but now, pieces around her face have fallen out and splay out in different directions on her pillow.

Her long, blonde eyelashes kiss her high cheekbones. Even in her sleep, she has the softest of smiles gracing her lips.

I want to lean in and kiss it, to feel her lips turn up into that stunning smile of hers. I want to pepper kisses all along her body until her eyes pop open. And then I want to feel her tongue against mine before thanking her for saving me from my own mind last night.

My heartbeat accelerates at all the things I want to do. I've tried to keep my distance from her, to look at her as just a friend and as Clara's nanny. It isn't working. We're like two magnets, being drawn together despite our best efforts.

What happens when you try to do the right thing and it doesn't work? Can I kiss her like I've been dreaming about ever since the moment I tasted her? Can I tell her that I'm terrified of the feelings I've developed for her? Can I tell her that I thought my heart would never want anyone else, yet here it is, desperately needing her?

I let my thumb drift to her bottom lip. Memories flash through my mind of when I had it between my teeth. She moaned when I bit and then licked the very same spot.

I close my eyes for a moment, letting the pad of my thumb rest against her lip as I try to get my thoughts under control.

Her body stirs against mine, making my eyes pop open. She squirms a little, rubbing her ass against my cock. It's rock hard. Partly from it being morning but mostly because I'd woken up next to her.

Her eyelids flutter open, her bright blue eyes landing on me immediately.

"Good morning," she whispers, her voice still groggy from sleep.

I smile at the same moment my heart lurches in my chest.

She's so fucking perfect. I have no right to want her to be mine, but that's exactly what I want. I want to kiss her whenever I want—which is always. I want to wake up with her in my arms every damn morning. I want to hold her hand in public. I want a lot of things when it comes to her.

"Morning," I respond as my thumb caresses her cheek.

It's scary wanting things again. I never thought I would. And now that I do, I'm terrified of her not wanting the same things as me.

"You sleep okay?" She arches her back a little in a stretch, her ass rubbing against me again in the process. I pull my hips away as fast as I can, a struggling sound coming from my lips at the small tease of the connection of our bodies.

I nod my head as she rolls to her back. Her eyes roam over me, and I feel nervous under her gaze. No one makes me feel nervous anymore. No one but her. I want to crawl inside her mind and figure out what she's thinking.

Does she regret sleeping in here with me? Does she think about me as much as I think about her? Does she feel the connection between us and realize it's so much more than just physical?

"I can't tell you the last time I slept that good," I admit, anxious to see her reaction to my confession.

Her eyes go wide for a moment before they crinkle at the sides with her growing smile. "Same."

An overwhelming sense of happiness washes over me at her words. It feels so right to wake up next to her, to see the way the sunlight reflects off her blonde hair in the morning and see her sleepy smile.

I want to beg her to sleep in this bed with me again tonight—and tomorrow. And the night after that—and ask her to never sleep upstairs again.

"Can I make you breakfast?" I ask, knowing I need to get out of this bed because I'm seconds away from kissing her and confessing how stupid I was to ever think we could prevent the inevitable between us.

If my question takes her by surprise, she doesn't show it. "I'd love that."

It's my turn to smile. Unable to help myself, I lean in and press a kiss to her forehead. "You stay right here in bed while I go make breakfast."

I don't know why I want her to stay in bed so badly instead of coming to the kitchen with me while I prepare food, but I do.

Something about the vision of her in my bed does something to me. I don't know if I'll have the nerve to ask her to stay in here with me again tonight. Because of that, I want to keep her in my bed as long as possible today. Clara isn't supposed to return until this evening. Liv and I have never had a day alone together like this. I wouldn't be opposed to keeping her in my bed for every second of it.

"Can I at least shower?" Liv teases as I climb out of bed.

I pause, thinking about her question for a moment. "Yes. If it's short. I'm bringing you breakfast in bed."

She bites her lip in an attempt to hide her smile. Her eyes travel across my naked torso. I revel in the feeling of her heated gaze on the muscles I work hard to maintain as I age.

"I'll be here," she responds, her voice breaking a little. She clears her throat as she pulls her gaze from my abs and to my eyes.

I smirk, wanting to call her out for checking me out. I keep the teasing to myself. She can do it all she wants. I was planning on grabbing a shirt from my closet but decide against it.

A grin stays on my face as I back out of my room. I pause in the doorway, wanting to remember this very moment forever. Her messy hair, the timid smile, the flush to her cheeks.

The happiness consuming me just because of her.

It's something I never want to forget.

"You have twenty minutes before I'm back with food. You better be in my bed when I get back, sunshine."

"There's nowhere else I'd rather be," she responds.

I wonder if she has any idea that even with an answer as simple as that, she makes it incredibly easy to fall for her.

Chapter 41
LIV

My heart feels like it could beat right out of my chest as I hear Dean's footsteps down the hallway. I don't think I've ever taken such a fast shower in my life. He seemed so insistent to find me in his bed when he came back with food. I wanted to do exactly as he asked. It feels like we woke up in some kind of bubble where we aren't fighting the attraction between us, at least not completely.

There was a moment when I was just waking up that I swore he'd kiss me, but he didn't.

Even without feeling his lips against mine, he seems more... free this morning. Maybe it's because he slept well, or maybe it's something else. Either way, I'm going to do whatever I can to stay locked in this moment with him for as long as possible.

His footsteps get closer, and my heart speeds up. I have no idea why my body feels like it's on fire when he hasn't even walked through the door. All he's doing is bringing breakfast. But it's breakfast in bed, and some dirty fantasies come to my mind at the thought of being in his bed. They all stem from seeing him in a pair of gray sweatpants that sit low on his hips. Of course dirty things come to mind when that's the first thing I see in the morning.

Dean walks through the door, holding a tray of food. He smiles the moment he sees me. How can he expect me not to catch feelings for him when he gives his smiles so freely now? I've had to earn getting him to grin at me like that, and now that I have, it's hard to picture my life without seeing him look at me just like he is right now every day.

"You listened," Dean notes, setting the food down on the nightstand on this side of the bed.

I smile, moving my wet hair off my shoulder. "I did. Although, I hope you don't mind, I used your shower and stole your clothes. I didn't know if I was allowed to run upstairs for my own."

His eyes darken as I move the comforter from my lap and show him that I'm wearing a T-shirt of his I found.

He swallows, his body seemingly frozen in time except for that small movement of his Adam's apple along his throat.

It's quiet for so long I wonder if I shouldn't have raided his closet. I didn't think he'd mind. He seems to love to see me in his Livingston Real Estate hoodie; I thought he wouldn't care about the T-shirt either.

"If I wasn't supposed to, I can go grab my own—"

"How hungry are you?" Dean interrupts, his words quick and to the point.

I frown for a moment, wondering why he's changing the subject. Is he that upset?

"What?" I ask, pulling the comforter back over my lap to hide as much of me in his shirt as possible.

"How hungry are you?" he repeats, his words slower this time. His question doesn't match the heat in his eyes.

"Umm…" I don't know how to answer him.

He runs a hand through his disheveled hair. The movement makes his muscles ripple, making me throb between my legs. "Please tell me you aren't too hungry."

"Why?"

"Because at the sight of you in my shirt in my bed, the only thing I want to eat right now is your pussy."

I gasp, having to blink a few times as I try to think through if

I heard him correctly. I have to squeeze my thighs together at what I think he said. I didn't have any clean underwear in his room, obviously, and his shirt was long enough on me I didn't think he'd ever know. I'm regretting the decision because wetness pools between my thighs, and I have no way of hiding it.

My breaths get heavy as Dean crawls onto the bed. His eyes don't leave mine, and mine don't leave his. I keep replaying his words in my head, wondering if there was any way I could've misheard them.

I know I didn't. Not with the way he's looking at me right now.

"Dean." His name comes out like a plea. I don't know if I can handle having him touch me again, tasting him again, and him pulling away. I've done my best to not let the prolonged stares and unexpected touches go to my head, but if he kisses me again, I'll have no choice but to fall for him.

He yanks the comforter from my body, making me suck in a breath when the cold air hits my thighs. I squeeze them together as hard as I can, trying my best to hide my arousal from him.

"I'm tired of fighting this, sunshine." His words come out like a growl. Like he despises the fact he was fighting this between us in the first place.

"Fighting what?" I ask, trying to keep my breathing calm, even as he presses his muscular thigh between my knees, forcing me to spread my legs open.

Luckily, he keeps his eyes on me, at least for the moment. He hasn't figured out yet that the only thing I'm wearing is his T-shirt. "Fighting how much I fucking want you. Every part of you."

His mouth hovers over mine as his large hands hold on to the headboard above my head. He cages me in with his strong arms as his thigh moves a little higher up, forcing my legs even wider. It's clear he isn't trying to hide his desire from me. His hard dick presses against my thigh with the position he's put us in.

His eyes frantically search mine. I can barely see the color of his eyes with how dilated his pupils are. When he lets out a long sigh before talking, I can feel it against my lips. "I'm tired of fighting how bad I want to see your smile first thing in the morning, and I want to hear your moans late into the night. I'm tired of not coming clean on how much I think about you and how much I fight the urge to ask you to stay in Sutten forever. The biggest thing I'm tired of is fighting how bad I want you. That won't change, and fuck, sunshine, I'm tired of fighting how much I need you."

I don't know what it's like to fall for someone. I've never done it, but I have to imagine it's something close to this. Although I know it's impossible, it feels like my heart bursts with an overwhelming sense of love for the man staring at me. I know it could be a terrible idea to willingly hand my heart over, but I can't help it. His confession left me with no other option.

"What are you waiting for?" I ask breathlessly.

A tiny little crease appears between his eyebrows. "What?"

I smile, my teeth raking against my lip with how much I want him. "If you need me so badly, then what are you waiting for? I'm right here. Do whatever you want with me, Dean."

I barely get the words out before his lips are against mine. I moan, relishing in being able to taste him again. It's all I've wanted since the last time he kissed me. I didn't know a kiss could be so depraved, that we could be so starved for each other, but we're proof of how desperate two people can be for one another.

Our mouths crash together. We're teeth and tongues and desperate moans. His fingers twist in my wet hair, already creating tangles that I'd just brushed out.

Dean's hand snakes up my inner thigh. A small whimper escapes his lips when his fingers are met with my wetness instead of fabric. "You're killing me," he groans, his finger circling my clit.

"Dean." I pant against his mouth when he doesn't even wait

to inch that finger inside me. I love how rushed and desperate he is because I feel exactly the same. I want him in every way possible, and I don't want to wait for it.

Dean's hips rock against my thigh as he attempts to get friction against his erection. I moan at the feeling, wanting to feel it inside me.

"Did you put my shirt on with nothing underneath on purpose, sunshine? Did you know it'd drive me fucking wild to see you like that? I bet you did. Naughty fucking girl."

I moan, my eyes squeezing shut at his words. He's so fucking dirty, and I love it. For a man of not many words outside of the bedroom, he knows how to use them in it. My pussy tightens around his finger.

Maybe I *had* done it on purpose, I don't really know. All I know is I'm glad I did because seeing him snap like this, the desperation for me taking control of him, is the sexiest thing I've ever seen.

"I want it off," Dean demands, pulling his finger out of me and grabbing the hem of the shirt.

In one effortless tug, he pulls the fabric off my body and tosses it to the side. Once again, I'm laid out naked in front of him, and somehow, he seems even hungrier for me than the last time.

He pulls back, his eyes raking over my body for so long I want to protest. He doesn't touch or kiss me; he just lets his eyes travel every inch of my body as if he has all the time in the world.

This time, he does. But I don't want him to take his time. I need him. His tongue, his fingers, his cock, anything more than only the heated gaze he gives me now.

A low growl comes from his throat as he continues to sweep his eyes over every inch of my body. "You're so fucking sexy."

I moan, my hips bucking in search of some kind of friction. I didn't know it was possible to want someone else this desperately. If he doesn't touch me soon, I might combust with need for him right here on this bed.

"Fuck, sunshine, I think you just got even wetter for me," he notes, his eyes between my legs.

"I need you," I plead, not caring about the begging tone to my voice.

A delicious grin spreads across his lips. "Yeah, you do, don't you, baby?"

I nod, moving my hips some more to try and get some sort of relief. "Yes," I moan.

"You know what I need?"

I let out a small cry of disappointment when, instead of touching me, he lies down right next to me. Before I can voice my displeasure, he licks his lips and looks at me with pure lust in his eyes.

"I need you to ride my face, sunshine. Now."

Chapter 42
DEAN

Liv stares at me, her chest rising and falling with quick breaths as she thinks through my question. She blinks as if she's trying to figure out if she heard me correctly or not.

"I-I-I can't." She fumbles with her words, her eyes wide and her cheeks pink as she stares back at me.

I let out a low growl, reaching out and grabbing her waist to pull her closer to me. "You can, and you will," I demand, desperate for her. I've been starved for her for over a month. Now that I have the chance to taste her again, I want her taste to consume me. "Please," I add, not above begging.

"Dean, I'll smother you," she responds nervously.

I smile. "That's the point, sunshine."

She gives me a timid smile as she grabs onto the top of my headboard and swings one leg over me. Before she overthinks it, I grab her hips and line up her perfect pussy with my mouth.

I run my tongue along her, reveling in the way she moans unabashedly at the first swipe of my tongue. I lick again, circling her clit. It must feel good because she allows herself to relax a little, lowering herself against my face even more.

It's heaven, tasting her, being able to breathe nothing but her. I keep a tight grip on her outer thighs as I keep her in place right above me. It's been torture the last month knowing how she tasted and not being able to do it again. The wait just might've been worth it to have her again, but just like this.

Her moans get louder and louder. At first, she let me be in control, even though she was on top. But with every swipe of my tongue and suck of her clit, her hips move more and more as she chases her release.

I want to tell her how fucking good she's being, that I love her riding my face, but I'm too busy making her feel good to stop long enough to say anything.

She grinds against my tongue, her moans getting louder and closer together. My name falls from her lips over and over, her voice getting more high-pitched by the second.

"Dean!" she screams, her hips moving against me in rapid succession. She pulses against my tongue, her breathy moans echoing off the walls as she finds her release. I don't stop until her hips still and she lifts herself from me. My grip around her thighs loosens, and I pull my body up so we're face-to-face once again.

Her wet pussy lines up perfectly with my cock. If I wasn't still wearing my sweatpants, I'd be able to slide into her with ease.

Liv's breathing is fast as she still rides out the aftermath of her orgasm. "That was…" She doesn't even finish her sentence. There's a dreamy look in her eyes as she tries to calm her breathing.

"Incredible? Perfect? Fuck, sunshine. You did so good riding my tongue. I want to start every morning with you riding my face."

Her cheeks turn pink. She pulls her eyes from mine for a moment as she bites back a smile. She reaches up and wipes my chin. "Oh my god, is that *me* on your chin?"

I didn't think it was possible, but she gets even more red. Even her chest turns red as she attempts to wipe her cum from my face. I gently grab her by the wrist to stop her. My eyes stay locked on hers as I stick my tongue out to lick all around my mouth. "It sure is, sunshine. The messier, the better."

She shakes her head. I love how easy it is to make her blush. Even when her skin is turning the prettiest shade of pink from my words, it's obvious that she loves the filthy things I say to her. She bites her lip and begins to move her hips against my cock, already wanting more.

Achingly slow, she grinds her pussy against me. My head falls against the headboard as air hisses through my teeth. Licking her until I felt her come against my tongue was incredible, but I still need more. This time, I want to feel her pussy hug me as she comes and screams my name.

"Liv." Her name comes out strangled and desperate as she continues to tease me.

"I want you," she responds, the sexiest, sultry tone to her voice. She circles her hips, and a low groan comes from my lips at how badly I want her.

"Whatever you want from me is yours," I respond tightly. She's dry humping me, and I could come any minute from it like a damn teenager. I don't even have it in me to be embarrassed by it. My desperation to come with her wrapped around me outweighs anything else.

Liv must like my answer because she gives me a wide smile. Without saying anything, she moves her body from mine. She sits herself between my legs and hooks her fingers into the waistband of my pants.

"Sorry," she mutters, looking at the wet spot on my gray sweatpants.

A low growl comes from deep in my chest at the sight of it. "That's fucking sexy," I tell her, loving the proof of her arousal on me.

She doesn't respond. Instead, she pulls on the waistband of my pants and begins to pull the fabric down my thighs. She sucks in a deep breath when my cock springs free. Her eyes don't move from me while she pulls my pants all the way down and tosses them aside.

"Dean." She lets out a shaky moan just looking at my length. "That isn't going to fit."

I wrap my hand around my cock and pump up and down, needing some sort of relief. She watches me carefully with parted lips. "It'll fit, baby," I assure her. "I'll be nice and gentle for you. I need you so fucking bad. We'll make it fit."

She nods as she leans forward. The strands of her wet hair tickle the tops of my thighs as she leans in close to my cock.

"Can I?" she whispers. "I've never...but I want..." She's so fucking eager to touch my cock and take me in her mouth that she can't even finish her thought.

My eyes flutter shut for a moment as her words settle in. "Yes, baby," I croak, unable to get out anything more than that.

She reaches out to touch me. Her fingers wrap around my length as I let out a strangled sound. Fuck, her touch feels phenomenal. I only got the briefest tease of it before we were interrupted last time. I'm fucking ready for more. To savor having her touch me and wrap me in her mouth before I bury myself inside her like I've been dreaming of.

"Like this?" she asks timidly, pumping up and down so slow it's like a taunt.

All I can do is nod. I thought just her touch would be enough, no matter what pace she sets. But I need fucking more. I place my hand over hers and guide it up and down my shaft, showing how to rub from the base all the way to the tip. She lets me guide her and speed up the pace until our joined hands work me fast.

"I'm probably not any good, but I want you in my mouth." Liv groans, as if she's as desperate to suck my cock as I am for her to do it.

"You're perfect, baby," I tell her, my voice coming out husky.

Liv's eyes shine bright with eagerness as she leans in and licks a bead of precum from the tip of my cock. I hiss at the whisper of her tongue against me.

My hand drops from hers and tangles in her hair. I keep it

there, letting her have full control but needing more contact with her. Her tongue flattens against my shaft as she begins to take me in her mouth. Liv doesn't waste time trying to take all of me, her throat gagging as I hit the back of it the first time she makes it all the way down.

"Fuck." I whimper at her actions. All of my focus is centered on how good it feels to be inside her mouth—to be the first one she's ever taken this way.

She goes up and down a few more times before letting go with a pop. Her eyes watch me carefully. "Am I doing it right?"

My fingers tighten in her hair. The sight before me is one of the best fucking sights in the world. Her on all fours, propping herself up by her elbows between my legs with her mouth inches away from my cock. "There's no way you could ever do it wrong," I manage to get out.

This makes her smile. She tucks her hair behind her ear before she leans in and takes me in her mouth once again. I allow her to go up and down for about another minute before it's too much.

I pull my cock free from her and sit up. My hands find her hips, and I spin us in one quick move so her back presses into the mattress and I hover above her.

"Don't take this the wrong way, baby. You were doing so fucking good." I can't help it—I run the tip of my cock through her wetness, loving the way her hips jolt at the contact. "But when I come, it's going to be inside your pussy. That okay with you?"

Her smile and fervent nod are the only answers I need.

Chapter 43
LIV

D EAN TEASES ME BY RUNNING THE TIP OF HIM AGAINST ME A FEW times. I moan, my back arching from how good it feels.

Dean stills and lets out an irritable growl. "Fuck, I have to find a condom."

"Please don't," I beg, lifting my hips to get contact between us again. My eyes find his. "I'm on the pill and just got checked."

He teases us both by inching himself inside me, just barely. "You sure, sunshine? I've been checked and cleared, too, but I'm fine using protection if that's what you're more comfortable with."

I shake my head. "I want to feel all of you," I explain, my voice a bit desperate. "It's been so long, and I've never been with someone I cared about. Please, I don't want anything between us."

It seems like my words are all he needs. He quickly presses our bodies together and brings his mouth close to mine. His eyes search mine for a moment. "Just tell me if it's too much."

I roll my hips a little, trying to force him a little deeper inside me. Now that I'm so close to finally feeling him in me, I don't want to waste another second. He doesn't want to either because at the same moment, his lips press to mine in a kiss that can only be described as passionate and slow. The way he kisses me makes it seem like he plans on doing it for the rest of his life.

Like he knows he has all the time in the world to run his tongue along mine and memorize the feel of our mouths together.

I focus on the feel of his lips against mine as he inches himself inside me. He goes slow, giving me time to adjust to how thick he is. It hurts, but I don't care. I want it to hurt, to feel him even after this stops as a reminder this finally happened between us. I melt underneath his touch and the way he wraps his fingers behind my neck and keeps my lips pressed to his in a kiss. The other times we've kissed have been intense but rushed. We were throwing weeks of pent-up tension between us into them.

It might be my mind playing tricks on me, but I hope it's true that we have all the time in the world to do just this for the rest of our lives. He seats himself all the way inside me, our moans mingling together. He stills, his lips moving from my mouth and down my neck as he gives me a moment to adjust to all of him.

"You feel so fucking good," he tells me, his lips moving against the sensitive skin of my neck. "Your pussy is hugging me so tight, like it's greedy for more."

I throw my head back on the pillow and arch my back, allowing him even deeper.

"More," I pant, my fingernails digging into his back as he bites right below my ear.

Dean listens and begins to rock his hips back and forth in a delicious rhythm.

His lips find mine again, and I get lost in the kiss. I already knew I was falling for him. It was something completely out of my control, but now, feeling him move inside me, having him kiss me like this, I know I'm not falling.

I've fallen.

All I can hope for is that I continue to break down his walls enough for him to really let me in, and maybe after that, with enough time, he could fall for me, too.

I'm about to ask Dean to go faster, to give me more, but as if he can read my mind, he does it without me saying anything. He picks up pace, his hips thrusting in and out of me in a rhythm so perfect another orgasm begins to build.

"Dean." I moan his name, feeling too many things at once as the building pressure gets even more intense.

"I know," he responds before taking my nipple in his mouth. "I'm close, too, baby. Let me feel you come around me."

His demand is all I need. The feeling of his fingers in my hair, his mouth around my nipple, and his dick moving in and out of me at a punishing pace sends me over the edge.

My eyes squeeze shut as my entire body feels like it combusts. I can't open my eyes as the most intense orgasm ricochets through my body, making my toes curl and my back lift from the mattress.

"Fuck," Dean growls before pushing himself as deep as he can and emptying himself. His entire body shakes as his body rocks against mine. Our lips meet again as we both ride the waves of the orgasm.

He makes sure that I feel every last bit of the orgasm. Only after my body stills does he pull himself out.

Before our bodies ever joined, I knew I was falling for him without him knowing. It happened slowly instead of all at once. It's because of the way he let his guard down for me or gave me that smile of his that is so hard to earn. The times I get to see how incredible of a father he is and how he gives Clara the world. Little by little, I was falling for him. It was impossible not to. Now, the way he leans down and kisses me chastely and slowly, even after what we just did, just solidifies my heart is his.

We're both quiet for a moment as we try to collect our breaths. I've never felt something so intense. Everything about what just happened was utterly perfect, and I can only hope we can do it again...and again...and again. I don't think I could ever get enough of him.

"Sunshine." He says it so quietly that the only reason I hear it is because the only sound in the room is that of our heavy breathing.

"Yes?" I whisper, my heart racing.

The look in his eyes gives me hope. He looks at me the way I imagine I'm looking at him in this very moment. I stare at him the way you do when you're in love with someone. When every part of you is theirs to do with as they choose. To cherish, to break, anything.

I've never been in love before, but I'd bet everything I am that he looks at me like he's falling right along with me.

He swallows, the silence between us as I wait for him to answer sending my heart into overdrive. "I want you to be happy. It's all I fucking want. But please tell me happiness is right here in Sutten. Right here with me and Clara."

I smile, letting myself release a slow, labored breath. It isn't a love confession, but I know Dean enough to know how hard it has to be for him to ask me to stay. He doesn't ask anything of anyone and hates being vulnerable, so his insistence on me staying is all I need to know that I'm not the only one with feelings involved here.

All I've ever wanted is to have a family. To feel like I belong. I've found that here. I've found even more. I never expected Dean and Clara to become my family, but they have. Family doesn't have to be blood. It can be the people you choose...the people who choose you. I choose them, and I know Dean's desperate plea for me to stay in Sutten is him choosing me. That's all I've ever wanted or needed. I couldn't be happier to know he wants me here with him and Clara as much as I want to be with them.

I grab either side of his face, making sure to meet his eyes so he knows how much I mean my next words. "There's nowhere else I'd rather be, Dean Livingston. You and Clara make me the happiest I've ever been. I'm here as long as you want me."

He playfully bites at my lip. "How's forever sound?"

I laugh, letting him pick me up and carry me to the shower. I don't know if he actually means forever, but I hope he does.

I can't imagine a better forever than one with Dean and Clara.

Chapter 44
DEAN

"DADDY, WHERE DO BABIES COME FROM?" CLARA ASKS, nonchalantly stabbing a piece of steak and popping it into her mouth.

My eyes go wide as I try not to spit out the drink of water I'd just taken. The rest of my family smiles at Clara's question as we enjoy a Saturday night dinner at my parents' house. My dad coughs as Mom hits his back to help him clear his throat.

I set my cup down, my eyes moving to Liv's for a moment, who sits directly across from me. Her lips turn up in a radiant grin at the topic Clara's chosen to ask at family dinner. The question isn't totally random since Finn and Ashton just announced they're expecting their fourth child—a baby girl.

I'd suspected Ashton was pregnant just by how often Finn had been out of the office recently. Ashton's always been really sick with her pregnancies in the beginning, and Finn helps out more with the boys when that happens.

"You going to answer your daughter?" Mom asks, attempting to hide her smile by wiping her face with a napkin.

"Yeah, Daddy. You going to answer me?"

My lips twitch with the hint of a smile despite not knowing how to answer her. I thought I'd have another year or two before she'd ever question where babies came from.

"I've heard some stories on how," Max says to his brother.

Reed snorts from Liv's side.

Ashton's eyes go wide as she looks from Finn to her son. "And what have you heard exactly?" she asks, her voice a little tight and unsure.

Miles leans in and asks Hattie something. So many side conversations begin and smiles get wider just because of one simple question asked by my daughter.

"Daddy..." Clara pushes, her tone very dramatic. "Do they just pop up in bellies?"

Reed lets out another snort and shakes his head. "Not quite, Clare Bear," he mutters.

I kick him underneath the table, making him yelp like a child.

I ignore my youngest brother's complaints of pain and focus back on Clara. "You're exactly right, sweetie. They just pop up into bellies."

Clara narrows her eyes on me. "Livvy tells me lying is bad, Daddy."

My eyes shoot to Liv. She throws her hands up defensively, that smile I've completely fallen for on her lips. "Lying is bad, Clare Bear. But your dad isn't lying."

Clara folds her arms over her chest and lets her eyes roam over the entire table. Everyone continues to laugh at my expense as she tries to figure out if we're lying to her or not.

"Look what you started." I jokingly roll my eyes at Finn.

He shrugs, looking over at Ashton and putting his hand over her stomach. "Sorry, Dean, that our excitement about our baby girl has caused you so much duress."

I laugh. "You know I'm very excited about the baby you put in Ashton's belly."

Clara gasps. "So Uncle Finn put the baby in Aunt Ashton's belly? How?"

"Oh my god," I say, pinching the bridge of my nose and settling back in my chair. I already know Clara's not going to let this go.

"Oh my *goodness*," my mom corrects, pointing her fork at me.

"Sorry, Mom," I mutter. I look over at Clara and find her still staring at me. Just by the look in her eyes, I can tell her little brain is working overtime trying to figure out the answer.

"Anyway!" Reed says, popping a piece of garlic bread in his mouth and looking over at Liv. "What are your plans tomorrow after we eat? I think it's time we decide if you're going to board or ski and get you fitted for your preference."

I sit forward in my chair as a low growl comes from my chest. Liv and I haven't fully talked about what happened between us this morning or defined anything yet. I want to, but we spent the morning and afternoon just enjoying being with one another. Defining the relationship and talking about how we explain things to Clara will happen; it just hasn't yet. She told me all I needed to know the moment she reassured me she had no intentions of leaving Sutten.

I'm about to open my mouth to tell Reed to back off when Liv speaks before I can. "Actually, I have plans tomorrow evening."

My eyes swing to hers. "You do?" I ask, my voice coming out a little gruff.

She bites her lip in an attempt to hide her smile. "I do."

"And what are those exactly?" I press, fully aware everyone around the table is probably staring at us.

Liv doesn't back down from my intense line of questioning. She pushes her shoulders back and stares right back at me with a slight smile on her face. "Well, that's a surprise. For you. For your birthday, which you just so happened to forget to tell me about."

Clara excitedly claps her hands next to me. "Yes! Daddy told me he's going to be thirty," she explains to Miles, who sits on her other side.

I laugh, remembering how I may have told a little white lie about how old I'll be turning. She doesn't need to know my thirtieth birthday was years ago. "I don't need you to go get me a gift," I tell Liv, trying not to notice the way Reed stares at me with raised eyebrows.

I don't know if he's pestering Liv about spending alone time together because he's trying to get me to admit that I have feelings for her or because he's actually interested in her. Either way, I'm going to have to find a way to tell him to back off.

She's mine.

"It's already planned. You can't tell me no."

Reed lets out a low whistle. He leans over to talk to Jace, who sits on his other side. "Are you seeing what I'm seeing?" he whispers, but it's a terrible excuse of a whisper.

Jace laughs before taking a drink of his water. "Yes, Reed, I sure am."

"Honey, would you pass me the salad?" Mom interrupts, the request probably louder than it should be.

Dad gives her a puzzled look. He looks at the salad bowl, which is closer to her than it is to him. "This one?"

Mom widens her eyes while keeping the smile plastered on her face. "Yes. That one."

He hands it over to her without any further questions. I smile, going back to eating my dinner, knowing my mom was absolutely trying to help me out by changing the subject. It works—small little conversations break out around us.

I find Liv's foot underneath the table. I run the tip of my boot along her foot, making sure I have her attention. Her eyes find mine.

"Why don't Clara and I go with you to pick up my gift?" I ask, keeping my voice lower as my family continues to chat around us.

"Because I want it to be a surprise." I love that her cheeks get a little pink as I play footsie with her. Seeing her react so quickly to the little things that I do drives me wild. I'm already ready to get her alone tonight and kiss her. She put on some sort of lip gloss before coming to dinner, and it's been driving me wild all night. I can't wait to find out what it tastes like.

"I promise not to look," I counter. I don't know why I'm so persistent about going with her. We don't have to spend every moment together, but I'd like to. Work next week will be busy, and I selfishly want to soak in every moment I can with her this weekend.

"I'll only be gone an hour or two. The weather's supposed to be nice, just cold," she adds at the end. Her words send a tinge of admiration through my heart. She's so thoughtful, thinking I'm scared of her driving alone. We're supposed to get snow, but not until late tomorrow night. She should be perfectly safe driving to wherever she needs to for my gift. So it's not that I'm scared of her driving—although I'd prefer to be the one doing it—it really just comes down to me wanting to be with her.

Now that I've accepted there's no way I can fight falling for her any longer, I want to spend as much time with her as possible. I pull my eyes away from her long enough to see that my family aims curious looks in our direction.

I sigh, sitting back in my chair. I still want to try and convince her to just let me and Clara tag along, but I'll try again later. Right now, my family's being nosy, and I've probably already given them enough indication that something's up between me and her.

"We can talk more about this later."

Chapter 45
LIV

"LET ME DRIVE YOU," DEAN DEMANDS, SITTING ON THE END OF MY bed as I rifle through my closet to find clothes to change into. We've had a busy day of church and spending time at his family's house before he had to bring me back here to grab my things and get my car.

I shake my head, pulling out one of the sweaters I'd thrifted. "I'm very excited about what I got you, and I want to go pick it up. You need to go back to your family's house and spend time with them and not be my unneeded taxi driver."

A corner of his lip turns up in a smirk. "I can be a very sexy taxi driver, though."

I roll my eyes at him before pulling off the dress I'd put on earlier in the day. My body heats under his stare. It was only yesterday morning that we first had sex, and since then, we can't get enough of each other. The moment he put Clara to bed last night, he carried me from the basement to his room, where we stayed up way too late, lost in each other. "Can you not just let someone surprise you with something?" I tease, pulling on the sweater, even though I'm tempted to close the distance and let him undress me the rest of the way.

Dean shakes his head. "It's all your fault. If you weren't so perfect, maybe I wouldn't be desperate to spend every second with you."

I let his words sink in for a moment. A smile spreads across my face before I close the distance between us. I still need to put on a pair of pants, but it can wait. First, I just have to kiss him for saying something so sweet.

His arms instantly wrap around my waist as I climb into his lap. I lean in, softly pressing my lips to his. He lets me, his hands strong against my back as he presses our bodies together. We lazily kiss for a moment before I pull away just enough to be able to talk and look him in the eyes. "Have you ever heard of absence makes the heart grow fonder?" I tease.

He lets out a low, disapproving groan. "That's a myth. Let me drive you."

Before I can respond, he kisses me again, but this time, he deepens it. His hands drift lower until they're cupping my butt. His fingertips press into my skin as he kneads the muscle.

I have time, so I savor the moment with him. I've thought about kissing him so many times it almost feels like an out-of-body experience to actually do it.

Eventually, the kiss ends, and our foreheads fall against one another's. "I'm going to run a town over and pick up your gift. You're going to spend time with your family. And then I'll give you your gift on your birthday, and you'll love it."

He lets out a dramatic gasp. "On my birthday? You mean I have to wait until the weekend to get it? But you're picking it up today."

I shake my head at him and playfully swat at his chest. As much as I'd love to push him into the mattress and get tangled in the sheets with him, I'm supposed to pick up the gift in just over an hour, and I don't want to be late. "Maybe if you're good, you can have it sooner."

Dean chuckles as I walk back to my closet to grab a pair of jeans. "Oh, I can be a very good boy for you, sunshine." When I look back at him as I pull on my jeans, I find him standing in the doorway of my closet, looking far too hot. He holds the molding above the door. The position makes his defined biceps stand out.

A rush of heat washes over me as I remember what it feels like to be caged in between his arms as he rocks into me. Or maybe it's the tone he uses with his words. Either way, I need to get going before I make myself late and jump his bones.

"Dean," I whine, knowing he's teasing me with dirty innuendos on purpose.

He playfully holds his hands up, trying to pin his features into a look of innocence. "What?"

I grab a pair of boots from my closet and pull them on. Dean's smile turns into a frown when he realizes that I'm serious about leaving without him.

"I think you're going to love the gifts I got you," I say, biting back a smile. Before I even knew it was his birthday soon, I wanted to have these made for him. Shirley spilling the beans that it's his birthday just gave me the perfect excuse to hurry up and order them.

"Gifts, you say? Tell me more." Dean walks up to me and grabs either side of my face. I love how in the last day, he can't stop touching me. Even when we've been with his family, he's snuck in little touches every now and then.

It's as if he has to reach out and feel my skin against his to make sure I'm still here.

"I'm not telling you anything more," I finally respond, wrapping my arms around his neck.

He lets out one of his famous growls that I love so much. He can pretend to be grumpy all he wants. Now that he's let me in, I know underneath the charade how sweet he actually is. "I'm going to miss you." His voice loses the playful tone and instead turns serious.

My lips twitch as I fight a smile. I'm trying not to think too far into the future about what happens next between us and instead soak in having him look at me just the way he is right now, but it's hard to not want so much more when he says things like that.

"We're going to be away from each other for a few hours,

tops. What are you going to do tomorrow when you'll have to be at work all day?"

He leans in and presses a kiss to my neck. "I'm going to miss you tomorrow, too."

I laugh, my fingers playing with the hair at the nape of his neck. "I don't know if I'm going to get used to hearing you say things like that."

He continues to pepper kisses along my neck and jaw, sending shivers down my spine with how good it feels. "Oh, I've been missing you for a while now. I just finally accepted there was no use in pretending anymore."

His words make me smile. Logically, I know his feelings for me didn't just appear yesterday, but it still feels good to hear him voice that they've been there longer. It didn't take long after I became Clara's nanny for me to realize I was attracted to him, both physically and emotionally.

His gaze meets mine. I sigh, my eyes searching his face. It's on the tip of my tongue to tell him that I love him. I don't need him to say it back, not yet. I just really want him to know that he's loved. My heart races. This might be the dumbest idea I've ever had. I just got him to finally stop fighting the connection between us, and I'm going to push things by admitting how I really feel.

But I can't help it. There's something about the look in his eyes that convinces me now is the perfect time to tell him how I feel.

"If I tell you something, you promise to not freak out?" I ask, my words hurried. Standing in my closet minutes before I have to leave probably isn't the best way to tell someone I love them for the first time, but I also don't want to keep it in any longer.

Dean cocks his head to the side. "Should I be worried?" he asks, his voice hesitant.

My heart beats so fast I wonder if it's loud enough for him to hear. "That depends," I respond, my voice a little shaky.

"Okay..." His thumb traces my cheekbone as his eyes search mine for any clues about what's going through my mind.

"I know things have always been a little complicated between us, and we just stopped fighting our attraction for one another, but it's more than that for me, Dean. Yesterday when you asked me to stay forever, I meant it when I said this is the happiest I've ever been. I truly can't imagine my life anywhere else—*with* anyone else. I wanted to tell you that I'd do anything you wanted because I..."

I take a deep breath, fully aware of how rushed my words are and how shaky my voice is. "Well, because I've fallen in love with you. And with Clara. And I know it's fast, and I don't expect you to say it back. But I had to say it. For myself."

He holds my face even tighter but says nothing at first. All he does is stare back at me, his eyes a little wide and his lips slightly parted. He doesn't run or push me away or really react at all.

He just stands there, and I can't decide if it's a good or bad thing. I give him a hesitant smile, not regretting getting the words out there despite his silence.

"Sunshine," he begins, the nickname he gave me coming out a bit strangled.

I press my fingers against his lips. "You don't have to say anything, and it doesn't change anything for me. I can love you enough for the both of us until you're ready to love again."

I don't know what I expect him to do or say, but he takes me by surprise by leaning in and kissing me. The kiss makes my toes curl inside my boots with how much heat and passion he puts into it.

I have no idea how long we stand there in the closet kissing, but it somehow feels like forever and still nowhere near long enough. Eventually, I pull away and look up at him with a smile. "I really have to go now."

He frowns, making it obvious he still doesn't approve of me going without him. "I'll miss you," Dean says, his voice quiet.

"Good thing you won't have to miss me for long." I press one more kiss to his lips before backing away. I'm scared if I stay any longer, I really will miss my pickup time for Dean's gift. I leave him standing in my closet as I grab my purse from my dresser and walk to the doorway, feeling happier than ever to have the confession off my chest.

I knew he wouldn't say it back, but even the desperate way in which he just kissed me tells me everything I need to know.

If I give him enough time, he'll get there. Luckily, I have all the time in the world.

Chapter 46
DEAN

MOM'S SHOULDER BUMPING AGAINST MINE PULLS ME FROM thoughts of Liv and what she'd told me in her closet.

"You seem awfully deep in thought," Mom notes, taking a seat next to me on the couch in Dad's study. Clara was in here sitting at Dad's desk, coloring a picture before she ran off somewhere with Miles and Jack. I meant to follow her out, but I got lost in my own head and forgot all about it.

I let out a heavy sigh. "Yeah. I guess I was."

Mom crosses her legs and adjusts her dress, pinning her gaze on me. "Want to talk about it?"

I look at my feet, unsure of what I'd even tell her. My guess is that after Liv's declaration of love, she wouldn't mind me telling my mother, but I also don't know that for sure. "I don't know," I answer honestly.

My mind goes back to Liv. To the happiness in her eyes. The hope in her smile. She seemed so confident telling me she loved me, and it terrified me.

Mom reaches across the couch cushions and grabs my hand. "Am I right to assume it's something to do with Liv?"

I lift my head to look at her. A sad laugh escapes from my lips. "Is it that obvious?"

"Only because you're my son and I know how to read you."

I nod, running my hands down my face as I try to decide if I can even voice my thoughts well enough to talk it over with her.

She squeezes my hand reassuringly. "You don't have to keep those thoughts of yours bottled up inside, dear. I know it's what you're used to, but it's okay to let them out...to let yourself feel."

I swallow slowly, trying not to remember what happened the last time I let myself feel. When I look at her, my face crumples.

"I promised myself to not feel again, Mom," I whisper, worried if I raise my voice any more my words will come out broken. "I can't feel again."

She nods in only the way a mom can. The one that tells you she's soaking in your words and really thinking them over. That she understands you and will love you no matter what you say. "But you do," she responds. It isn't a question. She can tell just by my reaction how much I've failed at keeping myself from getting hurt again.

I don't answer her. Instead, I look out the window as I take a steadying breath. "Liv told me she loved me today. That she was in love with me."

Mom's only response is a small hum. Her fingers squeeze mine as she thinks about what to say back. I can feel her gaze against my cheek even though I don't look over at her.

"I can't say I'm shocked," she finally responds. She keeps her voice cool and composed, the total opposite of what mine is when I do manage to get words out. "She looks at you with so much love it warms my heart as your mother. She looks at Clara that way, too."

"I know. She's perfect. It's just terrifying. What if she leaves? What if something happens to her? There were days I didn't think I'd survive Selena's death. And now I'm going to open myself up to that pain again? Open Clara up to the prospect of being hurt?"

She nods, her eyes roaming the room for a minute before she lets out a deep sigh and looks at me. "I think there are two things you can't control in life—we don't get to decide when we die, and we don't get to decide when we fall in love. Selena was taken far too soon. You'll miss her for the rest of your life. You'll love her for the rest of your life. But listen to my words carefully: You still have the rest of *your* life. You don't know how long that'll be, but you can't spend it being afraid of forces outside of your control. Selena would want you to be happy, Dean. She'd want you to fall in love again. I think we can both agree that you've already fallen in love with Liv. You just haven't accepted it—that is something you can control."

There's a heaviness in my chest as her words sink in. I never thought I'd have this conversation. No part of me ever thought I'd fall in love again. "I wasn't prepared to fall in love again, Mom. I don't know if I'm ready."

"How lucky are you, honey? To get two epic loves in your lifetime. Some people go their whole life without getting one. It's time to allow yourself to accept the love you're more than deserving of."

I swallow the lump in my throat, my eyes stinging with unshed tears.

If I were honest with myself, I'd admit that my mother's right. We can't control when we fall in love. I wasn't ready to fall for Liv, but I did. I love her despite all the pain of my past and all the fears that consume me. I love her so much it terrifies me.

I'm about to respond when Clara runs into the room with Honey hot on her heels. She doesn't look twice at my mom or me as she runs right to the window. She presses her face to the window and smiles. "Daddy, it's Mama!" she yells.

Mom and I share a look before I focus back on Clara. She hasn't moved. Her nose stays scrunched against the glass as the window fogs up in front of her mouth.

"What do you mean?" I ask, standing up to join Clara.

She presses her finger to the glass. "See, right there. It's Mama."

Mom and I both look at what she's pointing at. There's a

cardinal outside the window. It looks right at us as snow begins to fall.

I swallow, not knowing why Clara thinks the bird is her mom but not knowing what to say to her.

"Mama told me while I was sleeping she'd come visit me. I know that's her, Daddy."

My eyes get misty all over again at her words. I look at my mom, wondering what this means. Clara seems so confident. Tears stream down Mom's cheeks as she looks back to the cardinal still perched on a tree branch right in front of us. The snow begins to fall even harder, earlier than any of us were expecting, but the red feathers of the cardinal still stick out against the snow blowing around.

Clara turns and grabs my hand. She pulls on it a little, waiting for me to look down at her before speaking. I try to keep my composure as my eyes meet my daughter's. Clara smiles, and it looks so much like Selena's that it tugs at my heart. I miss Selena so much, but I feel so incredibly lucky that I get to keep this part of her. Clara tugs at my hand again, trying to pull me to her level. I follow her lead, crouching down so she and I are eye to eye.

Her small, warm hand finds my cheek as her smile grows. "Mama told me to tell you it's okay to be happy, Daddy."

Mom gasps behind me as my body goes still at Clara's words. Emotion washes over me. I rub the heel of my hand over my chest as a dull throbbing takes over. The world around me gets fuzzy, and I feel light-headed as I try to absorb what she's saying.

"She said that?" I ask, my voice breaking. I hate that I don't sound strong for her, that she's witnessing me fall apart in front of her eyes. But I can't help it. The timing of her words seems too perfect. I have to believe that, somehow, her words are true. That this can't be a coincidence.

That maybe Selena is giving me the sign I need to allow happiness in again. To love again.

Clara nods, her little thumb wiping over my cheekbone where I hadn't realized a tear had fallen. "Don't cry. She said everything will be okay. That she's here and that she wants you, Livvy, and me to be happy."

Hearing her say Liv's name makes me break. I pull my daughter into my arms and nestle my face into her hair. My emotions get the better of me, but she doesn't comment on the way my body shakes as I hold her. She hugs me back and somehow is the strong one between the two of us. Her little hand rubs on my back.

"Mimi, why are you crying, too?" Clara asks, her chin resting on my shoulder as she looks at my mom.

I stand up, bringing Clara with me as I lift her in my arms. When we turn to face my mom, her eyes are red, and her cheeks are wet.

"I'm okay, sweetie," Mom tells Clara, closing the distance between us and patting the top of her head. "It was just...really special to hear you say that."

Clara looks between Mom and me for a moment before she looks back out the window. The bird's still there, watching us through the downfall of snow. Clara reaches out to press her hand against the window. I mimic her gesture, something coming over me, making me feel like it's what I needed to do.

As if on cue, the bird takes flight. It flies right to the window, its wings flapping quickly as it keeps itself right in front of us before flying away.

We watch it disappear in silence. I'd like to believe that the bird was a sign from Selena somehow. That she found a way to ease my fears about letting myself fall in love again.

Mom lets out a shaky breath next to me. She puts her hand on my shoulder and leans her head against it. "I think that's all the sign you need. Time to let yourself be happy again."

Clara nods before her attention turns to Honey, who's trying to jump onto the couch to get comfortable. She laughs, and I set her down, taking one calming breath after another to try and process what just happened.

I meet my mom's eyes and let my face break out into a smile, tears still coating my cheeks. "I think it's time for us to head home. I want to make sure Liv made it back safely. There's something I've got to tell her."

Mom gives my shoulder a squeeze before pulling away and nodding. "About time."

I pull her in for a hug, hoping she understands how much I needed this talk with her. It was good to voice all of my fears and have her talk me through it. Clara's interruption was unexpected, but it was the final thing I needed to feel assured in my decision to tell Liv I've fallen for her.

It's absolutely terrifying to let myself love someone deeply again. I'm all too aware of the devastation that follows after losing someone you love. But my mother is right. I can't control what happens in life. Tomorrow isn't promised, and I don't want to lose one of the best things to ever happen to me just because I'm scared of what can happen.

I don't want to live in fear for the rest of my life.

The cardinal and Clara's words were a sign. Selena would want me to be happy. And somehow, I'm lucky enough to have found someone to brighten up my world again.

I can't lose that. I have to tell Liv that I love her and that I plan on loving her for the rest of my life. I'm quick at saying goodbye to the rest of my family and getting Clara into the truck, desperate to get home and tell Liv what I should've told her earlier in the day.

Now that I'm ready to give my heart to someone again, I don't want to waste another second. I don't want to wait. I'm ready for the rest of our lives to start right now.

All I have to do is get home to her sunshine smile and tell her that.

Chapter 47
LIV

A LOUD GASP FALLS FROM MY LIPS AS I TAKE IN THE THREE PIECES OF art in front of me. I don't know which one to look at—they're all perfect.

"You like?" Axel, the artist Camden connected me with, asks.

"These are stunning," I breathe, my hands coming up to my mouth as I smile at how great they turned out. "I can't believe you were able to get them done so fast."

He shifts next to me, crossing his arms over his chest as he stares at the pieces he painted last minute for me. "I work great under pressure. I love a time crunch."

I look over at him and give him a smile. "Well, thank you for fitting me into your busy schedule. Camden told me you've been working hard getting stuff ready for a gallery exhibit next year, so I really appreciate you squeezing me in."

He returns my smile, a piece of his long, shaggy hair falling in front of his eyes. He's got paint above his eyebrow, and I wonder if I should tell him about it or not. I choose not to. It's all over his overalls and up his arms, too, so I'm assuming he knows. "Like I said, I love a time crunch. These were fun to do. You have a beautiful family."

I swallow, my lips faltering a little at his words. Clara and Dean do feel like my family. They're the only family I've ever had. I just hope when Dean thinks of his family, I'm there, too. "They're both incredible," I tell him, not wanting to admit that things are a little unclear right now.

"Now that you've seen them and approve, is it okay for me to wrap them up and help you take them to your car? The snow seems to be coming down a little harder, and it's a bit of a drive back to Sutten."

My eyes get wide as I turn around to look out the window. There wasn't any hint of snow on my way here, but Axel's right. It has started to snow in the time I've been in here picking up the paintings.

"Yes, please," I answer, getting a little nervous to drive in the snow. I took my car instead of taking the SUV, since it had Clara's car seat. I didn't think it'd be a problem to take mine because the snow wasn't supposed to start until late tonight. Now I'm wondering if it was a bad idea to take my little sedan out. Hopefully, it does okay in the snow.

Luckily, Axel is quick at getting the paintings wrapped for me. I want them to be as protected as possible for the journey home. It's a bonus that you can't see the contents of them now because I want to try and keep them a surprise from Dean until his actual birthday.

It's dusted snow a few times since I moved to Sutten, but I've never seen it come down the way it does currently. It sticks to Axel's hair as he helps load the paintings into the small trunk of my car.

"Thank you again for this," I say, giving him a smile. My teeth chatter with how cold it is, despite having a winter coat and boots on. "I really think he'll love it," I add.

Axel smiles. "Of course." He doesn't shiver at all, even though he has no coat on, and the shirt underneath his overalls only goes right past his elbows. Maybe eventually, I'll get used to the cold in the mountains, but right now, I'm ready to get into the heat of my car and get home before the snow starts coming down any harder.

"If we're all good, I hope you don't think I'm rude by bolting out of here. I'm a Florida girl, so I'm a little nervous about driving in the snow."

He nods. I want to know if anything fazes this man because he's had the same even and happy demeanor from the moment I met him. Camden did warn me that Axel does his best work while high, so maybe he is right now. It would make sense why the smile hasn't been wiped from his face once.

"Drive safe out there. Remember to take it slow and not slam on the brakes. You'll be good if you do that."

I give him one final smile before climbing into my car and getting on the road.

At first, it doesn't seem so bad. The snowfall is pretty heavy, but my car seems to drive decently in it. But the moment I leave the town of Pinehurst and get on the back roads, I learn how much harder it is to drive on untreated roads.

My back is straight as a rod as I sit forward in my seat, trying to see through the dense layer of falling snow. Despite being in the thick of the trees, the wind is still heavy outside. It blows the fallen snow around, making it almost impossible to see anything.

I try to take calming breaths and just keep both hands on the wheel. Luckily, so far, I seem to be the only one with the bad idea of driving through the unexpected snowstorm. Only one vehicle has passed me in the twenty minutes I've been on this narrow back road, and that was a truck with a snowplow on the front that seemed far more equipped to travel in this weather than I am.

"You're doing great," I whisper to myself, trying to keep my heart calm. Every now and then, my car slides a little while taking a turn, and it feels like my soul leaves my body for a minute. I wish I could be enjoying the first major snowfall I've seen, but instead, I'm white-knuckling my steering wheel, hoping that the sign for Sutten Mountain will pop up soon.

I squint, trying to see through the snow. The sun's started

setting, and the way it disappears behind the tree line makes it even harder to navigate through the roads.

Feeling risky, I reach over to the passenger seat to see how far away I am from Dean's house. I grab my phone and tap the screen, but a pit forms in my stomach when I realize it's dead and my charger is in the SUV.

"Shit," I mutter, feeling incredibly irresponsible right now. I can't even call Dean and tell him that I'm on my way. Hopefully, he's still at his parents' house and has no idea I haven't made it home yet. I want to beat him to the house so he doesn't know I was out driving in this weather. Guilt crashes through me when I realize how panicked he might be if he gets home and I'm not there.

"You've got to be getting closer," I mutter. I left Axel's studio about forty minutes ago. And while the drive is a little over an hour with normal road conditions, I'm sure the slow, creeping pace I keep my car at now is adding even more time to the trip.

Hopefully, it isn't too much more.

I'm leaning forward in the seat when a deer runs out in front of me. It stops in the middle of the road, its eyes shining bright in my headlights as I panic. My foot slams against the brake as I yank the steering wheel to the right.

I know the moment I hit the brake that it was a bad idea. The tires of my car slip against the snow-covered, icy road, doing nothing to slow the speed of the car. My entire body tenses as I get closer and closer to colliding with the deer.

It runs away at the very last second, but it's too late. My car spins out of control no matter how hard I try to guide it back on track. It feels like I'm whipped in every direction. One moment, the road is in front of me; the next, my car spins off it. My buckled seat belt is the only thing that keeps my body in the seat as I collide with shrubs and tree branches and fall down a steep incline into a ditch.

I let out a terrified scream as I head right for a large tree. I close my eyes and try to brace for the impact, but nothing can prepare me for what it feels like to run right into a tree at the speed my car's going. My head flies forward, and the last thing I remember before slamming against the steering wheel is how worried Dean will be about me.

Chapter 48
DEAN

My heart pounds as I stare at the door. I haven't heard from Liv yet, and a sinking feeling settles deep in my bones as I do the math in my head.

She should've been home hours ago. I thought she'd be home by the time Clara and I got back from my parents' house, but she wasn't. I tried to keep it cool and assure myself it was fine. She was driving all the way to Pinehurst, so it'd take her some time to get there.

But now that I've put Clara to bed and it's gotten dark, I start to worry since she still isn't home.

I close my eyes, trying to settle my panicked breathing. My mind wants to go to the worst-case scenario, but I try to steer it from that. Maybe she's just lost or needed gas, or the most logical thing is maybe it took longer for her to pick up my gifts than she expected.

But why isn't she answering her phone?

I try her again, but it goes straight to voicemail. Just like the other twenty-seven times I've tried calling her.

"Fuck." I slam my phone down on the kitchen counter and try to figure out what to do. My brain fills with all the worst possible things that could've happened to her.

She's lost.

Her car broke down.

She's hurt.

She got in an accident.

I scrub my hand over my face, trying to rid myself of any intrusive thoughts. It doesn't work.

"No, no, no," I plead. "Not again." My voice breaks as my forearms find the corner of the counter. I place my head in my hands, trying to decide what to do next.

I don't want to overreact, but something deep in my gut is telling me something bad happened. I can't even go out to search for her because I can't leave Clara alone.

My hands shake as I pick my phone back up. I press my father's name in my phone and wait for it to ring.

He picks up on the third one. "Did you forget something here?" he asks, humor in his voice. I can picture him perfectly, sitting in his recliner as he pretends not to be invested in whatever reality TV show Mom's watching.

"Dad," I begin, my voice barely audible through the panic coursing through me.

"What is it?" His voice gets serious immediately.

"It's Liv," I manage to get out. I do everything I can to keep my voice calm enough so he can understand me. "She hasn't come home yet. I'm worried."

"We'll be right there."

I hang up before he can hear the strangled sound that comes from my throat. I begin to pace, feeling useless waiting for my parents to get here. My teeth dig into my bottom lip as I wonder if I should call the police. I have Sheriff Phillips's home phone number; I could call him and see if he thinks I'm overreacting or not. But I don't know if Liv is even in his jurisdiction.

I'll wait until my parents get here and see what they think. Maybe if I can just hit the road in search of her, I'll find her immediately and realize I'm just severely overreacting. I wish I'd known where exactly she was going in Pinehurst so I could call and see if she's still there.

Should I call the local hospital there and see if anyone matching her description has been brought in?

I shake my head as I continue to pace back and forth. I hate feeling helpless, and that's exactly how I feel right now. Maybe I could call around to see if Liv told anyone where she was going.

I try Pippa first. She and Liv have gotten close, and there's a chance Liv could've confided in her about where she was going to get my gift. I'm worried she isn't going to answer when, finally, her voice picks up on the other line.

"Dean?" My name comes out like a question. "Is Clara okay?"

"Clara's fine, but Liv's missing. She went out before the storm to get me a gift somewhere in Pinehurst, and she hasn't come back. It's been hours, and I'm worried." Somehow, I manage to keep my voice together enough for her to understand me, which is a shock because, internally, the panic gets worse each minute that passes by and she isn't here.

"Pinehurst?" Pippa questions. "I knew she was going out, but she didn't tell me where..." There are rustling sounds on the other end. "What?" she asks, seeming to talk to someone else instead of me. "Camden knows where she went. He's going to call, and we're going to head over to your place and think of a game plan. Maybe she's still there. He's calling right now, and we're on our way."

"Please keep me updated," I respond, my voice heavy.

"I will. We'll be there shortly, Dean." She hangs up the phone, and I'm once again left wondering what to do.

I try calling Liv again, but just like every other time, it goes straight to voicemail.

"C'mon, baby," I mutter, clicking her name again to put out another call, even though I know she won't answer. "Just pick up."

She doesn't.

I don't know how long I spend pacing my kitchen when, finally, the front door opens and my parents hurry in. They must've rushed to leave because my mom is still wearing her nightgown and robe, not having even bothered to change into normal clothes.

Immediately, her arms wrap around me as she pulls me into her chest. "It's going to be okay." Her hand runs circles along my back reassuringly.

"You don't know that." My voice is so low it's almost a whisper.

Mom squeezes me even tighter. I appreciate the comfort. She helps me hold on by a narrow thread as she attempts to ease the fear overtaking my mind. "I do. It's going to be okay. We have to believe."

Dad clears his throat from where he stands a few feet away. "I called the police department, and they're going to send out some patrol officers to search. They're also going to contact those at the Pinehurst station. Your brothers are on their way to help as well. She's probably just stuck in the snow somewhere and will be okay."

I pull away from Mom and rest against the countertop. I try and take a steady breath. My heart races so fast it feels like it might just beat right out of my chest with worry. "I'm going to go out and look for her, too. I can't just stay here doing nothing."

Mom's worried eyes find my father's. They share a look. "Why don't you wait for one of your brothers? You shouldn't be driving..." Mom's tone is soft, but it's clear that she isn't going to let me drive.

I don't blame her. I know I shouldn't be in control of a vehicle right now, but I hate the thought of waiting any longer to go out and search for her. I run my shaky fingers through my hair. "I hate that so many people are coming out in this weather for me."

Dad shakes his head. "They wanted to, son. We all love Liv and want her to be safe."

Before I can respond, the door opens again, revealing Pippa in a pajama set with strawberries all over them. "We're here, and we're ready to make a game plan," she announces, putting her hands on her hips. Camden, Cade, and Marigold walk in behind her.

"You guys didn't have to all come. I know it's late, and the weather is—"

Pippa holds her hand up to stop me. "We wanted to. Camden called Axel, who said that Liv left his studio right when it started to snow about four hours ago."

My heart sinks. A small part of me was still holding out hope that she was just caught up in picking up my gift and got held up. "So she got on the road?"

Pippa gives me a hesitant nod. "Yes. But the good news is that there's only so many ways to get to Pinehurst from here. We'll go out and drive the few different routes she could take, and we'll find her. She might've just pulled over to wait out the snow or something."

"Yeah," I rasp, running my hand over my face. "Maybe."

Cade steps forward. He adjusts the hat on his head as his eyes look me over. "How about you ride with me, and we'll start looking down the main route we think she would've taken?"

Dad joins the half circle. "Your brothers should be arriving any minute, and we'll map out alternate routes she could be on and go out looking."

"I'll ride with one of them," Camden interjects.

Pippa nods, soaking in the conversation before she looks at Marigold. "We'll stay here and call around. Maybe someone's been out on the roads and saw her. We can also call the hospitals to see if anyone's been brought in with any minor injuries or anything like that."

All I can do is nod. I don't want to think about her sitting in an unknown hospital bed alone. But the thought of her stranded on the side of the road isn't any better. My eyes dart around the space. I try not to think of a scenario similar to the one I went through over three years ago. Everyone had gathered around me just like this, their faces solemn and filled with worry every time they looked at me.

I don't want to believe a scenario eerily similar to that is happening all over again.

Someone's hand comes to rest on my shoulder. I jolt, realizing I'd been staring off into space, letting my intrusive thoughts take hold of me.

My eyes meet Cade's. "Want to head out?"

I nod, terrified of what I'll find but desperate to find Liv safe and hopefully unharmed.

"We've got to find my girl, man," I tell him, my voice cracking. I refuse to acknowledge what would happen if we go out and she still doesn't show up.

Cade gives me a reassuring smile. "We will. Let's go."

I follow him out the door, hoping he's right and hoping that wherever she is, the woman I love is okay.

Chapter 49
LIV

A SMALL MOAN FALLS FROM MY LIPS AS I'M PULLED FROM A DEEP darkness. I rock my head from side to side, my head pounding with the movement. My eyelids flutter open as I take in my surroundings. I close my eyes from the pain overtaking me as I try to figure out where I'm at and what happened.

I didn't know it was possible to be this cold. My entire body aches right down to my bones. I slowly peel my eyes open and press my ice-cold fingers to my forehead, wondering why pain radiates from a spot above my eyebrow. When I pull my fingers away from my skin, I find them glistening with my own blood.

"Oh god." I hate blood, and the amount coating my fingers tells me that I need to get it checked out soon. I close my eyes for a minute, trying to figure out how I got here.

Memories of what happened crash through my mind. The snow. The deer. The ditch. The tree. It all hits me at once. I've been in an accident, and judging by the broken glass everywhere and the rough airbags scratching against my face, it was a pretty bad one.

I try to move, but it hurts everywhere, even just to lift my arm even slightly. I wince, fighting through the pain as I reach for my phone, which sits in the passenger seat. It takes a couple of tries, but I finally manage to grab it despite the sharp pain shooting up my arm from the movement.

A cry of frustration leaves my lips as I find the screen completely shattered. It's dead and now broken, and I have no way of calling for help or reaching anyone.

I need to reach out to Dean and let him know I'm okay. I know if he's made it home and not found me there, he's worried. The last thing I want is for him to be panicking.

I'm stranded in the freezing cold in the middle of nowhere, and I have no idea how long I'd been passed out after the accident.

I let out a loud groan as my eyes travel around my car. The only light that illuminates my surroundings is from my one headlight that's still working.

A shiver runs through my body as my mind races with what to do. I can barely feel my fingers as I attempt to get my seat belt unbuckled. A strong gust of wind blows snow in my face and makes my cheeks burn. It takes a few tries, but finally, I'm able to get the seat belt undone, even as I almost pass out from how much it hurts to move.

The moment I'm free, I suck in a deep breath. The strap had been so tight against my chest I felt like I could hardly breathe, but now that it's undone, it feels like I can bring slightly more air into my lungs.

God, it's so cold. I know I won't last long out here. I have to find a way to get to the road and, hopefully, flag someone down for help. The cold wind is getting more brutal by the second, and the broken windows and shattered windshield do nothing to shield me from it.

My achy muscles protest as I reach for the handle of my door. I push my shoulder into it, trying to force the door open, but it doesn't budge.

Can anything go my way right now?

I put my hands in front of my mouth and blow on them to try and warm up. It doesn't work well. They feel numb, making it hard to really move them at all. I try the handle a few more times before my hands drop to my sides. With one last failed attempt at opening the car door, I realize I'll have to come up with another way out of the car. I look around before realizing the only way out is through the broken car window.

I shut my eyes for a moment, trying to muster the courage to even move at all. All I want to do is stay in the car and wait for someone to find me.

But no one's going to find me here. My car flew off the road and down a steep embankment. There wasn't even a guardrail or anything my car broke through to indicate an accident even happened. Anyone driving the road would have no idea I'm down here. The snow falls so fast I'm sure even my tire tracks are covered at this point.

As much as it terrifies me to accept it, no one's coming to save me. I'm going to have to save myself. There's no other option. I have to get back to Dean and to Clara.

I let out a shaky breath as I talk myself into getting out of the car. It's going to hurt, and I didn't know it was possible to feel cold down to my bones, but I have no choice but to be brave right now.

I need to be brave for Dean. For Clara. They're my family, and they have to know I'm okay.

It feels like my body is on fire as I begin to crawl out. I try to keep my breaths steady, even as everything hurts. I don't know if it's from the crash or the intensity of the cold, but whatever it is makes me let out a cry of pain for no one to hear but me and the surrounding trees.

Slowly, I make my way out of the car before dropping to the ground next to it. The rapidly falling snow is making it hard to see, but at least it helps break my fall. I lie on the ground for a few moments to gather up the willpower to make it to the road in search of help.

"You can do this," I repeat to myself over and over. The biggest reason I get up despite the pain is because I need to get to Dean. I *need* him to know that I'm okay.

Every step I take is excruciating, but somehow, I manage to

walk to the bottom of the embankment with only a few stumbles and only one fall into the snow. A loud sob falls from my lips as I realize just how steep the ditch is and how hard it's going to be to climb up it.

"No," I groan, my eyes searching the snow-covered shrubs to figure out how to even begin to climb what's in front of me. Even if I hadn't just gotten in a car crash and wasn't freezing, making it up the steep incline would be challenging. So in my current state, it seems impossible.

I press my hand into a nearby tree trunk just to give myself a small break before setting out to climb out of the ditch. I know if I stand here too long, I'll talk myself out of doing it.

"I can do hard things," I mutter to myself, my voice completely raw from the cold. It's a line from one of Clara's books she has me read to her before every nap. It's a line we've adopted in saying every day when we're feeling sad or frustrated and want to give up. Little did I know how much it'd encourage me to keep moving forward when my muscles are begging me to just lie down in the soft snow and hope someone finds me.

A small rustling sound has me looking up. I squint through the darkness, trying to find out where it's coming from.

Has someone found me?

I shake my head, trying to rid myself of the fogginess around it. The sound is too soft and faint to be someone, but it's still a sound. It has to be something.

The sound gets closer, and only because of the small amount of moonlight that filters through the tops of the trees am I able to see a cardinal land just a few feet above me. It flaps its wings for a moment, getting comfortable on the tree branch closest to me.

I blink a few times, wondering if I'm just seeing things. I think I hit my head pretty hard, so maybe it's the injury making me hallucinate.

Do birds typically get this close?

I stare at it for a moment before focusing back on the steep hill in front of me. I'm disoriented and probably a little delirious, but for some reason, the company of the cardinal soothes me. I take one deep breath and decide it's time to start climbing.

My boots slip almost immediately, but I'm able to grab onto the thick base of a bush, keeping me from sliding down the ground and having to start over.

"I can do hard things," I chant to myself over and over as I grab onto different things to keep myself from slipping. Every time I fall, the wet snow seeps through my jeans and makes me even colder, but I don't give up. I keep going, despite the protests of my aching muscles and throbbing head.

The bird, which I'm positive might just be a figment of my imagination, stays with me the entire time. It lands on tree branches and bushes, keeping me company as I give it my all to climb the intense slope of the ditch.

Climbing up the final feet of the icy, steep incline of the ditch takes me a couple of tries, but I manage to finally get my footing enough to hoist myself onto level ground.

I fall to my knees as I let out a cry of relief.

I did it. I'm one step closer to finding help…to getting back to Dean.

My chest heaves up and down from the exertion of climbing up the ditch. I allow myself a few moments to gather myself as I look around. I can barely make out the road because of how dark it is, but my fears from earlier were correct. You'd never know I spun out and ran off the road. It's calm and peaceful right now, giving no indication of the accident that happened below. The moon tries to peek through the thickness of the trees, but it only provides the smallest amount of light.

It's completely silent. The only thing filling the quiet is the sound of my labored breaths and the beating wings of the cardinal as it lands on the road right in front of me.

"I've got to be imagining you," I whisper. The bright red of the bird sticks out against the white snow. The scene in front of me is almost void of all color. There's the darkness of the sky and the night around me and the bright white of the snow. The cardinal is the only color, probably just a figment of my imagination to get me through the situation I'm currently in.

It seems like forever that there's nothing but darkness. Not a single car drives by as my body gets more numb from the cold with each passing second. I'm about to give up hope when I finally catch a glimpse of headlights in the distance.

Hope blossoms deep in my chest as I hastily push myself from the ground and wait for the car to get closer. The bird flaps its wings next to me but doesn't take flight. I stare ahead at the car, praying it will see me waiting on the side of the road. Hoping it'll stop and give me aid. I stand far enough from the road to avoid getting hit but still try to keep myself visible for them to see me and slow down to help.

Luckily, the car goes slow enough down the icy, snowy road that they're about to spot me. I let out a deep sigh of relief when they do come to a stop. An older man with wire glasses steps out of the large SUV.

"Are you okay?" the man asks, his tone full of worry.

I look to where the bird just was, finding it gone. Maybe it really was something I just imagined so I didn't feel alone.

I press my fingers to my forehead. Through the struggle of trying to climb up the steep embankment and waiting for a car to come by, I'd forgotten about the cut on my forehead. At this point, everything hurts so bad I'd drowned out the pain from the specific spot. "I think," I answer.

"Should I call the police? Do you need an ambulance?"

"Would it take long for them to get out here?" I ask. I have no idea where I'm even at. There's a chance I could've taken a wrong turn, although I thought I'd been going in the right direction before the accident. Things are a little too fuzzy to tell.

The man mulls over my question for a minute. I try not to get nervous about being alone with him. I've never been trusting of men because of my father and the men he'd bring around, but I'm not left with a lot of options. The deep crease of worry across the man's forehead gives me hope that he's someone I don't have to be afraid of. "The weather's bad. We might be out in the cold for a while waiting. Where were you headed?" He looks over my shoulder, where you can see the dim light of my lone shining headlight down below.

"Sutten Mountain." I wobble on my feet a little.

He quickly reaches out to steady me. "I think you need a hospital. That cut looks deep."

I can't keep my body from shaking as I stare at the man in front of me. My brain is telling me not to get into a car with him. I have no idea who he is, and my injuries from the accident make me vulnerable.

But I have to get to Dean. I don't want to put him through the torture of thinking something happened to me one second longer than he needs to.

I could deny this man's help and wait the hour it would probably take for police to show up, or I could trust that this stranger has good intentions. If Sutten's taught me anything, it's that strangers can be kind. Not every man is like my father. Not every stranger is like the people he'd let hang around our house.

I let out a shaky breath. "I might need the hospital. But I need my boyfriend to know I'm okay." The word *boyfriend* slips out effortlessly.

I don't have time to overthink it. It's cold, and I just need to get inside.

"Who's your boyfriend?" he asks, his voice gentle.

I look over his shoulder for a moment when a flash of red catches my attention. It's the bird. It hadn't left. It's been here the whole time. My mind tricks me into thinking maybe it was just waiting to make sure I was going to be okay, that I was going to get help.

"Miss? Let's get you to the hospital. Tell me who your boyfriend is, and maybe I can find a way to contact him."

I watch the red bird fly away, thankful to have not been alone while I waited for this stranger to help me. I meet his eyes. "Dean. Dean Livingston."

He sucks in a deep breath. "I know the Livingstons well. Once we get closer to town, I'll have service, and I can tell them I'm taking you to the hospital. We'll get the word to him, I promise."

My teeth chatter, but my body relaxes slightly. "Thank you," I manage to get out.

"Let me help you." He wraps my arm around his neck and helps keep me upright as he walks me to his car.

It feels like heaven the moment he opens the passenger door and hot air hits me. The warmth feels amazing against my cheeks. I know this isn't the best idea I've ever had, but I don't have a lot of options.

This man seems nice. He wears nerdy, wire-rimmed glasses and looks old enough to be my grandfather. That has to mean he's nice, right? He seems to be telling the truth about knowing Dean's family. I don't have a lot of options but to trust him.

He presses his fingers to my head. "We need to get you to the hospital. I'll see if they can meet you there."

I shake my head. I don't know Dean's number. I don't want to go anywhere without going home first to tell him I'm okay. After that, he can take me wherever I need to go if I need a doctor. "No. I need to get home first to show Dean I'm okay. Will you take me there?

The man lets out a long sigh. "I'd feel much better if you got checked out first. You're unsteady on your feet, and that gash has to need stitches. I'll call Marshall to tell him where you are. He'll tell his son."

I shake my head again. I really wish I knew Dean's number, but I don't. "If you could just take me home."

He doesn't say anything else before he gently shuts the door. I try to stay awake to make sure he takes me to Dean's and not to the hospital, but it's hard. The darkness of sleep keeps pulling me under, despite how hard I fight it. As I drift off, all I can think about is Dean. I hope he isn't home yet. I hope he hasn't been worrying. I feel terrible. I should've listened and let him drive me to pick up the gifts. I didn't know it'd snow, but I still can't help but feel guilty.

Thoughts of Dean swarm my brain, but I'm pulled too completely into unconsciousness to be able to repeat that to the stranger.

Chapter 50
DEAN

My leg bounces up and down in place as Cade turns into the hospital parking lot. We were out driving back roads in search of Liv about an hour ago when we got the call that one of my father's friends had found Liv and taken her to the hospital.

She apparently was pretty banged up. I try to steady my breathing after imagining what's happened to her and what injuries she might have. Mom couldn't give me many details about how hurt she was. Eric, Dad's friend who found her, had just mentioned that she appeared to have a pretty bad head wound and maybe some other minor injuries they wanted to get checked out.

But she's alive. That's all that matters.

Cade pulls up to the front doors, and I don't even wait for the car to be fully in park before I jump out and race toward the entrance. My boots slip against the freshly fallen snow on my way there, but I don't let it slow me down. Now that I'm so close to her, the time it takes to get into the hospital seems to take forever. This entire night seems to have gone by achingly slow as I thought of every terrible thing that could've happened to the woman I love.

The moment the automatic doors open, I'm running inside, my eyes searching the busy hospital floor. I run to the front desk, my hands slapping against the counter as I try to get the attention of the receptionist.

"Excuse me?" My voice comes out rough and frantic.

The woman holds up one finger as she says something into the phone she holds to her ear. A frazzled cry comes from my throat.

"My girlfriend's here," I explain, my voice breaking. "I need to find her."

The receptionist gives me an apologetic smile as she continues to hold a conversation with someone else on the phone.

My hands find my head as I consider how crazy it'd be if I just started searching every room for Liv. Maybe that'll be quicker than waiting for this woman to get off the phone and help me.

I'm seconds away from doing just that when I hear my name.

"Dean." Mare steps forward with a soft smile. She holds a coffee cup in her hands, along with a bag of chips.

I let out a relieved breath as I close the distance to her. "Where is she?"

"Let me take you to her."

I nod, trying to keep my emotions at bay. "Is she okay?" I ask, my tone hesitant.

Mare nods as she walks to the elevators. "Yes. She's okay. She's asking for you."

My vision gets blurry as I stare at Mare. "Really?"

Her smile is reassuring as we step into the elevator. It takes forever for it to climb each floor, but each floor higher means I'm one step closer to the woman I love. The moment the doors open, I'm racing out of them. I find my loved ones in the waiting room, and as much as I want to talk to them, I have to get to Liv first.

"Which room?"

"Third room on the left," Pippa answers as she stands up.

She might say more, but I don't hear any of it. I race down

the hallway, my boots tracking snow everywhere as I hurry to her. I get a few odd glances from hospital staff as I make my way to Liv's room, but I don't care. They can look at me like I'm crazy. I have to get to Liv.

I get to the room Pippa directed me to, stopping in the open doorway and finding her propped up in a hospital bed, staring out the window.

It feels like everything in my life falls into place when Liv turns her head to look at me. Her hair is pulled back into a bun, bringing attention to a bandage wrapped around the top of her head. There's scratches and red marks all over her face. There's exhaustion in her eyes, but they light up as they travel my body.

No matter her injuries, I focus on the fact she's alive.

"Dean." My name comes out like a whisper.

A sob crashes through me as I close the distance to her. I carefully climb into the hospital bed with her, making sure I don't hurt her. I want to take her in my arms and never let her go, but I know she must be sore. I keep my shaking hands at my sides, even though every part of me wants to touch her to know she's really here with me.

She pushes herself off the mattress a little, a smile on her face despite the absolute hell she's been through. Her eyes track my face. "I'm so sorr—"

"I love you," I interrupt, unable to hold on to the words for a second longer.

Her eyes go wide. My fingers tremble as I reach out to run them along her cheek. I need to touch her, to make sure she's actually here in front of me. It feels like I can finally relax enough to take a deep breath, knowing that the worst didn't happen to her. That she's right here in front of me so I can finally tell her how much she owns my heart.

"I was so fucking worried I wouldn't be able to tell you that," I croak. "I hated myself for not saying it back to you the moment you told me. But I love you, sunshine. I love you so fucking much that the thought of something happening to you tonight, fuck, it tore me up inside."

"I'm sorry," she whispers, her eyes fluttering shut as I gently caress her cheek with my thumb. She's got what looks like burns against her cheeks, but I try not to focus on them. I don't want her hurt at all, but I have to remind myself that she's alive and she'll heal. She's in the right place to make sure whatever injuries she endured will be taken care of.

A sad laugh escapes me. "I just told you I love you, and you're saying you're sorry? What could you possibly be sorry for, baby?"

She grabs my coat and brings me closer to her until my body is flush with hers in the bed. I try not to focus on the way she flinches with the connection of our bodies. I don't know if they've been able to run scans on her to make sure she's okay, but she doesn't seem to want me to leave her side. If anything, she keeps a firm grip on my coat to keep me close to her. "I'm sorry for going out in that weather. For scaring you. With everything you've been through, I feel so stupid that I—"

I gently press my fingers to her chapped lips. It kills me inside that she thinks she needs to apologize to me. "You couldn't have known." I press my forehead to hers. I want to kiss her so bad, to pull her into my arms and never let go. "It isn't your fault. None of that matters anymore, anyway. You're here. You're safe."

"I'm right here," she confirms, pressing her forehead to mine.

"Did you hear me say I love you?" I ask, my heart racing.

I never imagined myself falling in love again. Quite frankly, I thought it was impossible. But it was only impossible because I hadn't met Liv yet. I should've known the moment she first aimed those beautiful blue eyes in my direction and gave me her perfect smile that she'd be the one to breathe life back into me.

That she'd be the one to make me want to feel again.

Her dimples appear with her radiant smile. "I think I might need to hear you say it again."

I gently cup her face in my hands. "I love you. Loving you might be the scariest thing I ever do, but I wouldn't change it. You came into my life and made me realize I was living in the gray. You make every single day brighter, and I want to cherish every day I'm given with you because it's a gift to love you and be loved by you."

When a tear runs down Liv's face, I lean in to kiss it. She slides her hands underneath my jacket to feel my skin, to get us even closer. I love how much love reflects in her eyes with the way she stares back at me.

"I love you so much, Dean Livingston. My entire life flashed before my eyes tonight, and all I could think about was how much I wanted a life with you and Clara here in Sutten. How I wanted more time with you two. I wanted forever. Forever and always, however long that'll be."

"That's all I want," I tell her, letting my eyes close and soak in the feel of her skin against mine. Her familiar scent surrounds me as we just breathe each other in for a few moments. "I didn't know I needed you. I fought it so hard because I didn't want to love someone again. But it was inevitable. My love for you, it grew over time. It blossomed into something that bled right into my soul, sunshine. Nothing excites me more than the life I have ahead of me with you and Clara by my side."

A happy sob erupts from her. She squeezes me tight and buries her face against my chest.

"Not so tight, baby. I don't want you to hurt yourself."

She shakes her head against me. "I don't care. It hurts me more not to feel your touch. I wondered if I'd ever feel it again. I need this, Dean. I'm fine, I promise."

I let my body relax a little and risk softly wrapping my arms around her. I keep my touch featherlight, trying not to inflict any pain onto her sore and tender muscles. But I need to feel her against me just as much as she needs it.

"I love you, and I'm so fucking grateful you're okay." I cradle the back of her head against my chest, savoring the feeling of having her in my arms. She might get sick of how much I'll want to hold her in the coming days after being faced with the thought of losing her tonight.

"My car is totaled, and I didn't even get a chance to see if your gifts were harmed in the crash."

As gently as I can, I tilt her chin up so our eyes can meet. "I already have the best gifts. You and Clara."

Her bottom lip trembles a little bit as her lips spread into a smile. "Well, if I wasn't already in love with you, that would've done it."

I smile, leaning in so our lips barely brush against one another. "Keep falling in love with me, sunshine. I know I plan on doing the same."

She smiles and closes the distance between us until our lips meet. The kiss is slow and soft, just what she needs after what she's been through tonight. It's perfect. It's a kiss that promises we have all the time in the world to do exactly this.

I savor in feeling her lips against mine. With each second that passes by, I can feel the worry leave my body. I'd been so fucking worried tonight, terrified I'd never see her again. Terrified I'd never be able to tell her how much I loved her and how she saved me.

Someone clearing their throat makes us break apart. I don't go far, still needing to feel her touch to remind myself she's okay as we turn and find a doctor standing in the doorway.

She looks at me with a friendly smile. "I'm Dr. Harold, and I'm in charge of Liv's care tonight."

I nod. "Is she okay?" The worry is evident in my voice.

Dr. Harold smiles. She looks from me to Liv. "You have quite the crew of family members that are worried about you. I was just stopped while looking over your chart at my desk by a very persistent blonde wanting to know if anything was broken."

Liv and I share a knowing look. "My money's on Pippa," I tease, trying to lighten the mood a little. My hope is that the casual tone of Liv's doctor indicates there isn't anything majorly concerning that showed up in her scans.

The pit doesn't fully leave my stomach as I wait for the doctor to confirm it. "It seems like you really had a guardian angel watching over you tonight," she begins, her eyes roaming over the clipboard she holds. "With the accident you had, I thought we'd see more injuries on your scans. But luckily, there's no sign of broken bones or internal bleeding. You do have a concussion that we need to monitor and a few stitches for the wound on your forehead, but other than that, you should be able to go home rather soon."

My shoulders shake as I let out a breath. Seeing her alive brought so much relief, but to know she walked away from the accident about as clear as one could seems more like a miracle. "That's incredible," I whisper, wondering how that even happened.

The doctor nods. "It really is a miracle. We'll monitor the concussion, and you'll be free to go home within the next twenty-four hours."

"Thank you," Liv says, smiling at Dr. Harold before she leaves to attend to other patients.

With the doctor gone, I grab Liv's face in my hands as I let it settle in that she's going to be okay.

She's safe. She's here. She's mine.

"Are you going to be okay?" a voice frantically asks from the open doorway. We both turn to find Pippa standing in the doorway. Mare stands with her, along with Cade, Camden, my dad and brothers. They all look concerned as they stare expectantly at both Liv and me.

"I'm all good," Liv answers. "The doctor said I even get to go home tomorrow."

Pippa places a hand to her chest as she lets out a relieved sigh. "I was so worried. I may have accidentally bullied every doctor and nurse out there to give me details on if you'd be okay."

We all let out a laugh as our loved ones begin to filter into the small hospital room.

Dad waits in the open doorway as he pulls his phone from his pocket. "Your mom stayed home with Clara in case she were to wake up, but I'm going to give her a call to let her know Liv's okay."

I nod, unable to fight a smile as everyone piles around the hospital bed to speak with Liv. I hope this makes her realize how many people care about her here in Sutten. I know she's said she didn't grow up with a family, but hopefully, this proves to her that family doesn't have to be blood. It can be an unlikely group of people who care about you, who drop everything to search for you in the middle of the night.

I hope she feels the love in the room. It's not just me that loves her. It's everyone.

She's found a home and a family. She belongs here with all of us. And I'm so fucking thankful that the events from tonight didn't take her from us.

Chapter 51
LIV

I ANXIOUSLY ROLL MY BOTTOM LIP BETWEEN MY TEETH AS I STARE AT Dean, trying to read his reaction as he stares at the art pieces I commissioned for his birthday. It's been a little over two weeks since my accident and exactly two weeks since his birthday, but it's better late than never to give him the gifts. Because of the accident, we waited to celebrate fully until I'd had time to recover. Plus, it took longer than expected to get them back from the tow company. He didn't even begin to track them down until a week after the accident; his focus was too much on making sure I was recovering from the crash, even though I kept telling him I was fine.

Dean runs a hand over his mouth, his eyes staring at the three pieces in front of him. I try not to focus on how good he looks. He wears a pair of dark jeans that fit him perfectly and a long-sleeved shirt that hugs his biceps like a glove. We're waiting for Shirley to come pick up Clara for a sleepover before Dean and I go out to celebrate his birthday with friends, hence why he's dressed up for a Saturday night. I wanted to make sure to give him his gift with Clara around so she could see them, too.

Clara and I have had a special relationship since the moment I met her. From the very beginning, we had a connection. But in the weeks since the accident, we've grown even closer. Dean insisted I rest as much as possible, and Clara took it upon herself to keep me company. She'd barely let me out of her sight in the hours she was awake. We've watched countless movies in bed together, and I don't know how many butterflies I've drawn for her. But the time with her while taking it easy has been incredibly special, making me even more excited for her to see the gifts I had commissioned for her dad.

"Do you like them?" I ask Dean, my pulse spiking with nerves. He's so quiet as he looks at them that I can't get a good read on him.

When his eyes meet mine, they're misted over. "I *love* them."

Clara comes running down the stairs with a pink backpack on. She skips to us, stopping when she sees the three paintings. "That's me!" she yells excitedly, pointing to the picture of her Axel had painted. I'd given him three photos I'd taken of Dean and Clara and asked him to paint them on large canvases. My vision was for Dean to hang them in the living room and bring a few more personal touches to the house.

"That *is* you," I tell her, fixing the braid I'd given her a few hours ago. I look at Dean, finding him already watching me with a slight smile playing on his lips.

"I didn't want to overstep, but I felt like the house could use a little more personality. I thought these would be perfect to hang here in the living room."

Dean's eyes stay on me, the slight smile not faltering. "You could never overstep. This is your home, too, sunshine."

Clara yanks on my arm, pulling my attention from Dean for a moment. "Livvy, where's your picture?" she asks, her eyes bouncing over each piece. There's a painting recreating a photo I'd taken of Clara while on a walk with Honey, one of Dean and Clara on the porch swing, and one of Clara holding Honey in front of the fireplace.

"Oh, I don't need one." A slight blush creeps up my cheeks. I'm not sure we even have a photo of the three of us, not that I was expecting to have a photo of me hung anyway. I commissioned these pieces before things between Dean and I evolved into how we are now.

It's crazy to think how much has changed for us in a short amount of time. It doesn't seem like that long ago I was just starting out as Clara's nanny. I'd quickly developed a crush on Dean and daydreamed about what it'd be like to kiss him. Now, I get to kiss the man I'm in love with—and the man who loves me back—anytime I want.

"But Daddy told me last night he loves you. That you're family, too, now. You need a picture."

My chest hitches as my eyes find Dean's. We'd been slowly easing into telling Clara that things had progressed between him and me. But he'd asked me last night if I was okay with him telling her that I'll be sticking around for a long time and that I'm now his girlfriend. I'd told him I was happy with whatever he was comfortable with; I just hadn't known when exactly he'd talk to her.

I'm not sure I'd expected him to tell her that he loves me.

Dean closes the distance between us and lifts Clara into his arms. He looks from his daughter to me. "I think you're right. We need to get Livvy a picture on our wall soon. Maybe even with all of us, our family."

This makes Clara smile. Her eyes are bright as she looks at me. "You be in our family, Livvy?"

"Yes, Clara. I'd love that." I can't fight the tears that stream down my cheeks. All I wanted to do was gift Dean some art pieces to hang on the wall and bring more life to the house. I didn't realize it would turn into him and Clara making my heart burst with joy.

I attempt to wipe underneath my eyes without messing up the makeup I'd carefully applied. I'd tried curling my hair and letting it fall over my forehead where my stitches were just removed, but the scar is still noticeable. My goal was to put a little more makeup on than normal to distract from the evidence of my accident.

In Florida, I didn't have friends to even go out with, so I'm extra excited about tonight. We're planning on telling everyone we're officially together. Although we both agree that with his concern about the accident, and his reaction in the weeks after, no one in his family or any of our friends will be shocked.

"Clara, should we show Livvy the surprise we got her?" Dean asks, kissing the top of his daughter's head.

Clara excitedly claps in his arms. "Yes!"

I pull my eyebrows in on my forehead. "A gift? For *me*? We're celebrating your birthday, not mine," I say, looking at Dean.

"I couldn't resist." He shrugs, already backing up toward the front door with Clara in his arms. Honey excitedly joins, circling his feet as he continues to back toward the door.

My feet stay planted for a moment as I wonder what he could've possibly gotten me, but curiosity gets the best of me, and I follow them out. My muscles are still a bit sore from the accident, but not as bad as I expected. Probably because from the moment I returned the other night, he's pampered me. I can't tell you how many warm baths I've taken and how many massages I've had. He even hired a team of professionals to come to the house yesterday and spoil me to help me feel better. I've told him countless times I feel fine, but he won't listen.

I let him dote on me, knowing he needs to feel helpful and in control.

When I walk out the front door, I'm shocked to find a massive SUV parked in the driveway with a big red bow on top of it.

"Surprise!" Dean and Clara yell together, the two of them standing in front of the hood.

I stop on the front porch, my arms crossing my chest as I try to keep warm in my sweater without a coat. "What is this?" I ask slowly.

Clara laughs as if I just asked the most absurd question ever. "It's your new car, Livvy. Daddy said this one is *extra* safe."

Dean nods. "Your old car was totaled, and the accident made

me realize you need the safest SUV out there money can buy."
He pats the black hood of the vehicle. "So here it is, sunshine."

I shake my head in disbelief as I take a few steps closer to
them. I know absolutely nothing about cars. I don't know what
the model is or who even makes it, but I do know the thing is
massive and has tires that look like they could drive through just
about anything. "You didn't need to get me a new car. I was fine
driving your extra."

Dean shakes his head, his cheeks turning pink from the cold.
"I wanted the safest option and wasn't going to settle for
anything less. If you're going to drive, it'll be this. I'm happy to
be your taxi driver anytime you want, though." He winks at me,
and despite the chill in the December air, my cheeks heat.

I stop in front of him, lifting on my tiptoes to plant a kiss to
his lips. "Thank you. This wasn't needed at all and feels very
overprotective."

He steals an extra kiss from me before pulling the door open
and gesturing for me to get in to look at it. "Nothing's overprotective when it comes to the woman I'm madly in love with."

I smile as I shake my head at him. I know even if I tell him
the gift is too much and not necessary, he won't listen. He's stub-
born. It's one of the things I love most about him, so instead of
arguing and telling him the gift is too much, I slide into the
passenger seat and let him show me every unique feature the
SUV has to offer.

After Shirley shows up to pick up Clara for their sleepover,
he insists on taking the new vehicle to Slopes for his birthday
celebration. We end up being fifteen minutes late because we
can't stop making out in the comfortable front seats.

Chapter 52
DEAN

My friends and family are gathered around the large table we'd reserved for the night at Slopes when I clear my throat and sit up straight in my chair. "Liv and I have something we want to tell all of you," I begin, waiting to get their attention.

The table goes quiet as all eyes look at us. I suddenly feel nervous, having everyone's attention on me. After Liv's accident, I hadn't wanted to celebrate my birthday at all. I'd just wanted to spend the day in bed with her, nursing her back to health. She had other plans and conspired with Hattie and Ashton to still give me a birthday celebration, even if it was two weeks late. I'd protested at first, but now, as the people I care about most sit around the table and wait for me to speak, I realize how nice it is to have a night out with them.

I look at Liv for a moment, fully aware everyone is waiting for me to speak. It seems like I went over many different things in my head that I could say to tell them about Liv and me, but I've forgotten everything.

"If you're about to tell us that the two of you are banging, we already know," Reed shouts from the opposite end of the table.

Pippa lets out a snort.

Jace high-fives Reed.

Hattie and Ashton share a knowing look.

Cade tries to hide his laugh by coughing into his arm.

Liv's entire face turns pink.

And I stare at my brother in disbelief, not knowing how to even respond to him. "Excuse me?" I ask.

Reed laughs. "It's obvious, Dean, and we're very happy for you. It took you long enough to finally admit you were crazy about her. I could tell the first time I saw you two together. It's why I nudged it along a little." He winks across the table at Finn.

I can't help but laugh. I already suspected Reed was trying to make me jealous with his insistence on getting Liv alone and asking her on dates. I shake my head at him, looking to my side at a beaming Liv. I wrap my arm around her and pull her body to mine, planting a kiss on her lips in front of everyone.

"Well, even though it was already apparently so obvious, I just wanted to tell you that this beautiful, incredible woman is my girlfriend. And I love her, and somehow, I'm lucky enough that she loves me, too."

Pippa's chair crashes to the ground as she stands up and claps dramatically. Mare joins her until the entire table stands up and is clapping for us.

Liv buries her face in the crook of my neck, her body shaking with laughter. "Oh my god, they're making this a bigger deal than I thought," she mutters for only me to hear.

"Let them." I kiss her temple, pure happiness radiating through me at the way everyone celebrates us.

Almost everyone here tonight saw me in my darkest hours. They sat there with me, letting me have all the time I needed to mourn the life I thought I'd have with Selena. They encouraged me to go on and were there for me despite the shell of a man I became after Selena's death.

To have them here with me tonight, to get to tell them that I made it out and somehow got lucky enough to find love again, it means everything to me. I want to cherish this moment with them.

"I knew it!" Pippa gloats, taking a seat again. She begins to pull one bottle of beer after the next out of the buckets that line our table until everyone has one in their hand. She points the top of her bottle at Liv and me with a wide grin on her face. "Lexi and I are matchmakers."

Liv reaches out her hand and waits for Pippa to take it. "It really is because of you, Pippa. Thank you."

Camden lets out a low, amused groan as Liv pulls her hand back. "Giving her the credit is really going to go to her head."

Pippa places a kiss on his cheek. "Hell yes it is, Hunter. Deal with it."

I shake my head at them before looking back to the people here to celebrate my birthday. "No matter who we're giving credit to, I really just have to give credit to the woman right next to me." I look at Liv, reaching up to cup her cheek. "I'm so happy you took that nanny job and that you didn't let my grumpiness deter you for a second. I love you and I'm excited for the world to know it."

Liv leans forward and kisses me. There's a wild smile on her mouth when she pulls away. "I like the grumpiness. Don't ever change."

This makes everyone break out into laughter.

"To the happy couple!" Hattie calls, holding up her beer to cheers. "To Liv's quick recovery. And I guess Dean's birthday."

Everyone picks up their beers and joins in on the cheers before taking a drink. We settle into an easy conversation between all of us. Since Selena passed, I hadn't celebrated my birthday. It didn't feel right to celebrate getting another year older when she'd never have another birthday again.

Now, I'm in a better mindset where I can accept that Selena would want me to celebrate every single birthday I'm given. She wouldn't want me to live in a state of darkness and grief forever. I don't know if that's something I wouldn't have realized if not for Liv.

I grab the corner of Liv's chair and pull her closer to me, wanting her as close as possible as I put my arm around the back of her chair.

"Liv! Are you going to ride the bull?" Pippa asks, wagging her eyebrows in excitement.

Liv's eyes go wide before she shakes her head. "I don't think I wore the right clothes for that. I think I'd rip my jeans."

I laugh. "I'll buy you another pair again. Ride the bull if you want."

Liv's head whips in my direction. "What do you mean *again*? I bought these at Sutten Mountain Treasures."

I clear my throat. "Yeah. You did." It turns out I'm a terrible liar because she raises her eyebrows and playfully swats at my stomach.

"That's why Ms. Beth was acting so weird!" She lowers her voice a little as Pippa gets distracted by another conversation, leaving no one paying attention to us for the moment. "I didn't just get lucky, did I? All those new clothes there that happened to be my size were all because of you, weren't they?"

My eyes roam her face as I try to figure out if she's upset or not. It was something I was never going to tell her. It seemed important for her to buy her own clothes; I just wanted to make sure she had options. But the smile on her face tells me that maybe she isn't upset at all. "Okay, I admit it was me, but baby, I only did it because I wanted you to have new clo—"

She interrupts me by kissing me. The kiss is a little heated, considering we have a table full of people bearing witness to it, but maybe they're all too distracted with their own conversations to even notice. It doesn't really matter even if they are watching. They can watch me kiss my girl for all I care.

Eventually, she pulls away. "If it wasn't so thoughtful, maybe I'd be mad at you, but that's one of the sweetest things anyone's ever done for me. Thank you."

I smile, pressing a kiss to the tip of her nose before leaning back in my chair. "I can't wait to do even sweeter things for you, sunshine. You deserve the world, and I'm going to give it to you."

She smiles, her dimples making an appearance. "I can't wait.

Now, let's get back to celebrating *you*. It is your birthday, after all. And I want us to have the best night ever before I get you home and give you the rest of your gift." She winks at me, and it makes my blood heat.

I lift an eyebrow. "The rest of my gift?"

She bites her lip playfully and nods. "I can't tell you about it here, but something tells me you'll really love it."

I smile, knowing *whatever* she has planned, I'll love. I'm already excited to get her alone to find out exactly what she means.

I'm quiet as she insists we order another round of beers before she even thinks about riding the famous bull at Slopes. I enjoy watching her interact with my loved ones, feeling incredibly grateful that of all the towns she could've ended up in, she ended up in mine.

Falling in love with Liv was unexpected. Little by little, she chipped away at the defense I'd put in place until she became my entire world. It didn't take long for her to become a part of every future I imagined for Clara and me.

I'll make sure I wake up every morning grateful that I'll get to know three great loves in my lifetime. First Selena's, then Clara's, and now…Liv's.

My sunshine on a cloudy day. The person who showed me you can find love even at your lowest point. I don't know what I did to ever deserve her, but now that I have her, I'm never letting go. She and Clara are my family, one I hope to add on to one day, if that's something Liv wants. My future looks brighter because of her.

I've spent years running away from the pain of loving someone. Liv made me want to stop running. For the first time in my life, I didn't want to run. I wanted to chase. A forever with her and Clara is everything I want. I'm so excited for a future with her by my side.

I can't wait to chase our forever.

Epilogue
LIV *two years later*

"Merry Christmas!" Clara yells as I walk into the living room. I stifle a yawn, somehow still tired even though Dean let me sleep in. Maybe it's because he kept me up into the early hours of the morning, giving me an early Christmas gift in the form of his face between my thighs.

Clara's body runs into mine as she wraps me up tightly in a hug. I lift her from the ground and wrap my arms around her, smiling at the candy cane pajamas she's wearing. They match the same ones Dean and I have on. "Merry Christmas, Clare Bear. Did you get any sleep, or were you too excited?"

Clara grins at me. "I think I closed my eyes for a couple of minutes."

This makes me laugh as I carry her to the Christmas tree. Dean's in the kitchen making us some coffee while Clara and I take a seat in front of the tree.

"We should open presents!" Clara declares, moving from my side and picking up one of her gifts from under the tree. She shakes it slightly, trying to figure out what's inside. I laugh, letting her shake it. There's no way she'll figure out what's in there.

"Let's wait for your dad, and then we can get to opening the gifts," I tell her, my eyes finding Dean in the kitchen. Even in the cheesy candy cane PJs, he looks incredibly good this morning.

There are some times I look at him and wonder how he's all mine.

His eyes catch mine as he puts a dollop of whipped cream on top of my coffee, just how I like it. "Clara, are you trying to open gifts without me?" Dean calls, his tone teasing as he walks to the living room.

Honey bounds after him, a stuffed Santa hat toy in her mouth. It appears Honey gave her perfect puppy dog face to either Dean or Clara and got one of her gifts early.

"No, Daddy. You're just taking forever."

I try not to laugh at her comment, but it doesn't work. At five, she's sassier than ever. She's growing up so fast that it makes me a little sad. It seems like it was just yesterday that she was confidently climbing into my lap at Wake and Bake and insisting I do her hair.

Now, two years later, I'm having to beg her to sit still long enough to do her hair.

Dean stops in front of me, holding out the mug of coffee. "Here you go, my wife," he says sweetly, dragging out the last word.

I smile, taking the coffee from him. "Thank you, husband."

We got married two months ago, surrounded by those we loved most. It was the most perfect fall day where there wasn't a cloud in the sky, and the trees at our venue showed off by creating a beautiful backdrop of reds, yellows, and oranges.

Having Clara walk me down the aisle to marry Dean was one of the best days of my life. Something tells me that today might be up there as another one of my favorite days because of a gift I've been excitedly waiting to give to Dean.

Dean leans in to give me a chaste kiss on the lips before he takes a seat next to me on the couch. Clara bounces on the balls of her feet in front of us in anticipation.

"Is it time?" she asks, her eyes ping-ponging between me and Dean.

"Go ahead and open one," Dean says, placing his coffee mug

on the coffee table and pulling out his phone to snap a few photos to send to his family. We've got a big Christmas Day dinner with them this afternoon where there will be even more gifts, but it's nice to have a quiet morning with just us before getting together with everyone.

Clara opening one gift turns into her opening all of hers. This is my third Christmas here in Sutten, and with each new one, I get more over-the-top with gifts. I can't help it. I didn't have anyone to spoil with gifts growing up, so now that I have people in my life who I care about and who care about me, I like to go a little overboard.

Now that Clara's in kindergarten, my free time is spent working at Bluebird Books. Ty, the owner, pays me more than what I'm qualified for, but he refuses to listen every time I tell him that. Dean is very insistent on me using whatever I make at Bluebird for fun, so I use it to spoil those I love most.

Dean's breath tickles my neck as he leans in. "I don't know if you picked out enough art supplies for her."

I give him a smile. "She's a budding artist. She deserves all the art supplies."

This makes him laugh as he looks back to Clara. She's already spread out all of the different art supplies she received on the floor so she can get a better look at them all. "How long until she starts requesting for Pippa and Camden to display her work at the gallery portion of Wake and Bake?"

I take a drink of my coffee before responding. "Oh, she's already talked them into it. She also talked Margo into giving her lessons when they come out for the new year."

Dean shakes his head. Margo is one of Camden's best artists. She's always doing different showcases at his gallery in Manhattan. When she and her family and friends first came to visit Sutten and Clara learned she was an artist, she became obsessed with peppering Margo with questions. Margo was sweet enough to even send me some beginner kits she thought would be great for Clara.

I set my coffee down and turn toward Dean. My heart races with anticipation as I think about his gift and what he'll think about it.

Before I can say anything, he gets up and grabs my stocking from the mantle. "Time to open your gift, my beautiful wife."

I blush. There's no way I'll ever tire of hearing him call me that. "What if I wanted you to open your gift first?"

He smirks, carefully placing the stocking in my lap. "I beat you to it. Plus, I'm too anxious to wait another second. This has been a hard secret to keep, and I need you to open it now."

I pick up the stocking, trying to feel for the contents inside to see if I can figure out what the gift is. I can't help but smile as I look at him with a lifted eyebrow. "That's funny. *I've* been anxious to give you *your* gift. It's also been very hard to keep it a surprise."

"I guess we'll find out which secret was harder to keep, then," he quips, gesturing for me to reach into the stocking.

Something tells me the gift I got for him was much harder to keep a secret, but I don't tell him that. Instead, I reach inside and pull out a small box. I give him a questioning look, wondering what's inside. I give it a little shake, the contents rattling with the movement.

"What is this?" I ask, glancing over at Clara. She's too busy playing with her new art kit to pay us any attention.

"Open it to find out, baby."

I pull on the red lid of the box, revealing a set of keys with a little book stack keychain. I lift the keys and dangle them in the air between us, looking at Dean with a questioning stare.

"What are these keys to?" I ask, keeping my voice low. I feel bad because I haven't really given him a reaction to the gift yet because I still don't know if I understand what the gift is.

"To Bluebird Books."

My head cocks to the side. "Okay...why are you gifting me the keys to Bluebird Books?"

Dean smiles, his teeth raking against his bottom lip. I fall in love with him more each time he smiles at me, even after having countless ones aimed my way over the last two years. "Because you're the new owner," he answers casually.

My heart skips in my chest as I fly off the couch. "What?" I ask, incredibly confused.

Dean leans forward, that handsome smile of his still on full display. "Ty was ready to retire. You've worked so hard there that he and I decided that you should be the new owner."

I shake my head. "You can't just give a bookstore as a Christmas gift, Dean. Books? Yes. Bookstores? No."

He lifts a shoulder. "Too late. I already bought it. It's yours, sunshine."

I stand in front of him, unable to look anywhere else but into his eyes as emotion washes through me. Books have always been the one thing that kept me company in my loneliest of times. Even working at the bookstore was a dream come true. But owning one? I can't even process that what he's saying is true.

"I can't accept that as a gift," I whisper, my emotions getting the better of me.

He stands up and closes the distance between us. His hands cup my cheeks as he tilts my face to look up at him. "Yes, you can. You will, baby. No one deserves it more. Bluebird Books is all yours."

Tears stream down my face. "I can't believe this." I stand up on my tiptoes and plant a kiss to his lips, knowing there aren't enough words to be able to thank him for the gift.

When we finally pull away, I still shake my head in disbelief. "I can't believe this. Thank you. I love you. I can't believe I own a bookstore."

Dean smiles, his thumb tracing over my cheek. "I love you, too, sunshine. You're the hottest bookstore owner out there."

I give him a smile. "Can I give you your gift now?"

He nods, and my heart races as I break the connection between us long enough to grab his stocking. I feel like I can hear my blood pumping through my body as I walk over to him and hand over the stocking. I have no idea what his reaction will be to the gift, but I'm more than ready to finally give it to him.

Dean gives me a cautious smile as he peeks into the stocking. "Why do you look so nervous all of a sudden?"

I give him what I hope is an encouraging smile. "Just open it," I whisper.

He does as he's told, pulling out a book. "It's a scrapbook," he notes, his lips pulling up into a whisper of a smile. I feel like I barely hear him over the sound of my racing heart.

I nod, waiting for him to open it. I want to tell him to do just that, but it seems like I'm suddenly too nervous to even speak. Luckily, he knows what to do and opens it to the first page.

My stomach jumps when his eyes meet the first page. "Liv," he whispers, his eyes finding mine instantly. "Is this...?"

I smile, tears falling down my cheeks as I nod. "I'm pregnant," I manage to get out.

The book drops to the ground as he pulls me into his arms. "You're pregnant?" he asks, his voice full of excitement.

I nod. "Yes. Eight weeks tomorrow."

Tears freely fall down his face as he lifts me from the ground and hugs me to his chest. His hand cradles the back of my head as we both cry in excitement. We'd started trying a couple of months ago, but I hadn't expected it to happen so soon. Keeping the secret until Christmas has been so hard but something I really wanted to give him, knowing how badly we both wanted it to happen. "I'm so fucking happy I don't even know what to say," he croaks, his lips moving against my ear.

I laugh through my tears of joy. "Did you hear that, Clara? You're going to be a big sister!"

Clara looks up from her art supplies with the biggest smile. "What?" she yells, pushing off the ground and running to us. Dean gently sets me down so he can pull both Clara and me in for a hug. "I'm going to be a big sister?" Clara repeats, as if she's trying to confirm she heard me correctly.

Dean and I both nod.

"Yes," I answer, running a hand over my stomach. "We're having a baby."

"Finally!" Clara yells excitedly, pressing her lips to my stomach. "Hi, baby. I'm your sister."

Both Dean and I laugh at her trying to talk to the baby. Clara's been begging for a baby sibling for a long time now. I can't believe it's actually happening.

Clara wraps her arms around my waist and gives me the biggest squeeze. "This is the best Christmas gift ever!" she yells.

Dean walks up behind her, wrapping his arms around me as well so we're in a group hug. "That really is the best gift ever, sunshine."

I smile at him. "You. Clara. This baby. You're the best gifts I've ever been given."

"I love you," he says with the biggest smile on his face.

"I love you, Dean Livingston," I respond. I turn my cheek a little, my eyes focusing on the window of the living room to the snow-covered mountains. Snowflakes fall peacefully, making it a beautiful white Christmas. Right when I'm about to look away, a cardinal lands on the tree right by the window. It gives the window a few pecks as if just to say hi for the morning before it spreads its wings and flies away.

Happiness washes over me as the three—well, kind of four— of us stand there in an embrace. Before I ever stumbled upon Sutten Mountain, I had no idea what true happiness felt like. I didn't know what I was doing with my life, and I didn't feel like I had a purpose. All I'd ever known was doing life on my own.

Then, I met Dean and Clara. It didn't take long for me to fall in love with the grumpy single dad and his sassy toddler. The two of them became the family I'd been missing my entire life. A happy sob runs through me as I think about just how grateful I am for the life I've been given with them.

I never knew a happiness like this existed until I found Sutten Mountain.

WANT MORE
Sutten Mountain?

Want more Dean and Liv? Subscribe to my newsletter to get an extended epilogue for their story.

SIGN UP HERE: www.authorkatsingleton.com

Make sure to check out the other books in the series!

Rewrite Our Story: https://amzn.to/3KNni8W
Tempt Our Fate: https://amzn.to/3W0K2XW
Chase Our Forever: https://amzn.to/3PIj85V

Acknowledgments

I can't believe this is the end for another series of mine. Sutten Mountain will forever have a special place in my heart. This series was a passion project of mine and it's very hard to say goodbye to this fictional town and the people in it. There's many people I need to thank at the conclusion of another series.

First, to *you*, the reader. You guys loved this series and cheered me on when I decided I wanted to write a small town series. You fell in love with characters as much as I did and supported me with each new love story. This book was written for every single one of you who begged for Daddy Dean to have another chance at love. Your endless support means the world to me. It is *you* who is the lifeblood of this community. It is you that keeps me going even on the hard days. You're the reason I get to wake up every single day and work my dream job, and for that, I'm so freaking grateful. Thank you for choosing my words to read. Thank you for supporting me. You've given me the greatest gift by choosing *my* books to read. I love you so much.

To my husband, AKA Kat Singleton's husband. We had so many things going on during the process of writing this book and you were the reason things still went off without a hitch behind the scenes. I love you forever.

Kelsey, you run my life and I'm forever grateful for it. I would be a hot mess without you and appreciate you always making sure everything Kat Singleton is running according to plan. Thank you for putting up with me even when I don't make things easy. Your friendship means to the world to me. I love you and everything you do for Team Kat.

Ashlee, thank you for creating the most stunning covers for the entire series. This is my favorite cover we've ever done together and I'm sad to leave this aesthetic behind. I value your friendship so much and can't wait to begin another series together!

To Chas and Lauren, thank you for getting the most raw and rough version of this story and loving it anyway. Dean and Liv's story wouldn't be what it is if it weren't for the two of you. You truly held my hand throughout the entire process of writing this book and I appreciate it beyond words. You're both stuck with me for life. I love you endlessly.

To Salma, Sandra, Holly, and Alexandra. This book was SO hard for me to write but you held my hand throughout it all. Your feedback is so important to me and I'm so grateful to work with the both of you. Thank you for helping making *Chase Our Forever* ready to be released to readers.

To all of my author friends who cheered me on while writing this book. I'm forever grateful to know such amazing women who encourage and support me. I love you forever.

To the content creators and people in this community that share my books. I'm so eternally grateful for you. I've connected with so many amazing people since I started this author adventure and it means the world to me to have all of you to connect with. I'm appreciative of the fact that you take the time to talk about my stories on your platform. I notice every single one of your posts, videos, pictures, etc. It means the world to me that you share about my characters and stories. You make this community such a special place. Thank you for everything you do.

To Valentine and everyone with VPR. Thank you for everything you do to keep me in check. It's not a secret that I'm a constant hot mess, and all of you are the reason I'm able to function. Thank you for making all things Kat Singleton run smoothly and amazing. I'm so thankful to call VPR home and for your help in getting *Chase Our Forever* out into the world.

To the amazing humans on my own personal content team, thank you for making every release amazing. You babes are forever blowing my mind with the unique content you create based on my words and I'm so grateful to have all of you on this journey with me.

I have the privilege of having a growing group of people I can run to on Facebook for anything—Kat Singleton's Sweethearts. The members there are always there for me, and I'm so fortunate to have them in my corner. I owe all of them so much gratitude for being there on the hard days and on the good days. Sweethearts, y'all are my people.

ABOUT THE
author

Kat Singleton is an Amazon top 5 bestselling author best known for writing *Black Ties and White Lies*. She specializes in writing elite banter and angst mixed with a heavy dose of spice. Kat strives to write an authentically raw love story for her characters and feels that no book is complete without some emotional turmoil before a happily ever after.

She lives in Kansas with her husband, her two kids, and her two doodles. In her spare time, you can find her surviving off iced coffee and sneaking in a few pages of her current read.

- facebook.com/authorkatsingleton
- x.com/authorkatsingle
- instagram.com/authorkatsingleton
- bookbub.com/profile/kat-singleton
- goodreads.com/authorkatsingleton
- tiktok.com/authorkatsingleton

ALSO BY

Kat Singleton

BLACK TIE BILLIONAIRES:
Black Ties and White Lies: https://amzn.to/40POdqu
Pretty Rings and Broken Things: https://amzn.to/3Ponrlc
Bright Lights and Summer Nights : https://amzn.to/48d9Kgg

PEMBROKE HILLS
In Good Company (Releasing Spring 2025): https://geni.us/
InGoodCompany

SUTTEN MOUNTAIN SERIES
Rewrite Our Story: https://amzn.to/3KNni8W
Tempt Our Fate: https://amzn.to/3W0K2XW
Chase Our Forever: https://amzn.to/3PIj85V

THE MIXTAPE SERIES
Founded on Goodbye
https://amzn.to/3nkbovl
Founded on Temptation
https://amzn.to/3HpSudl
Founded on Deception
https://amzn.to/3nbppvs
Founded on Rejection
https://amzn.to/44cYVKz

THE AFTERSHOCK SERIES
The Consequence of Loving Me
https://amzn.to/44d4jgK
The Road to Finding Us
https://amzn.to/44eIs8E

WANT MORE
Kat Singleton?

Sign up for Kat's newsletter and receive a bonus epilogue for *Chase Our Forever.*

SUBSCRIBE HERE: www.authorkatsingleton.com

CHAPTER 1 - MARIGOLD

What is it about airplanes that make people forget about all semblance of personal space?

We've only just landed on the tarmac when every person next to me stands up, despite the fact we're at the back of the plane. We won't deplane for another ten minutes at the very least, yet I've got all three passengers from the row behind me leaning over my seat and breathing on me as if huffing and puffing down some stranger's neck will help everyone else move faster.

I'd had to book the flight in the middle of the night after my best friend, Pippa, called me sobbing. There weren't many choices of seats for a flight at seven the very next morning. I'd had the wonderful luxury of sitting in a middle seat between two strangers; neither adhered to the armrest rules—AKA the person in the middle gets at least one armrest. It's just human decency in my own little humble opinion.

The phone vibrating in my lap snaps me from my thoughts. I look down at it, holding it close to me so the hoverer in the window seat next to me doesn't read my texts.

PIPPA

I checked the app and saw you just landed. I can't wait to see you!

MARE

I'll text you as soon as I'm through baggage claim. You know how it is here. I'll probably be awhile.

PIPPA

Sounds good. Love you, Mare. Thank you for coming.

MARE

I wouldn't be anywhere else.

My chest constricts as I recall the reason I'm here. Pippa's mom, Linda, suddenly passed away two days ago, taking everybody by surprise. She'd been in perfect health—or so we'd thought. Turns out, her heart wasn't in good condition. The night before last she went to bed and just never woke up.

Pippa had been in shambles when she'd called me with the news. I was in the midst of a writing retreat when I received the call. I'd been desperately trying to finish the book that was due to my publisher but I dropped everything to be here. I hadn't been lying to Pippa when I'd said I couldn't imagine myself being anywhere else. Even though I left the small town of Sutten Mountain for college, it'd always be my home. Linda was a mother to me. She picked up where my own mother left off when she passed away, and she filled the void in my heart effortlessly.

Linda Jennings was a ray of sunshine in my often dark life. Dad was never the same after Mom passed. He did what he could, but he was mourning the love of his life. He didn't have it in him to realize how much I was grieving not having a mom. That's where Linda stepped in. For years, she was my rock—my mother figure. She never let me forget my own mother, though.

Linda made sure she passed the memories she shared with my mom down to me. She always said she admired how I was as sweet as honey with a little bit of tang and sass.

As the man with the window seat next to me attempts to squeeze between my knees and the back of the seat in front of me, that sass comes out. I push my knees farther in front of me, preventing the man from inching his way even more into my personal space.

The guy glares down at me. "Excuse me." He coughs, making me grimace because that may have just been his spit that landed on my cheek.

I plaster on a fake smile. "Sorry sir, I just don't think it's our turn yet." My eyes flick to the rows of people in front of us that are still waiting to grab their bags from the overhead compartments.

The man on the other side of me snickers. Even though he's an armrest thief and stood up entirely too early, he seems to be on my side in this case. "Are you trying to catch a connecting flight?" he pipes up, looking over my head at the window guy.

Window guy furrows his eyebrows. "Yes. I've got a flight in two hours to catch."

I try my best to fight the smile on my lips. This guy has more than enough time to cross the small airport before his next flight begins boarding.

Aisle guy clears his throat. "I think you'll make it."

I don't continue a conversation with either of the men. As soon as it's actually our turn to leave our seats, I grab my bag from the overhead bin and anxiously deplane.

The pit in my stomach gets bigger as I wait at baggage claim and prepare for what's to come. Linda was the glue that held the Jennings family together. Her husband, Jasper, is probably beside himself. They had been together since middle school. She loved to tell the story of how he stole her pencil and she instantly fell in love with him.

And then there's Linda's pride and joy—her kids. I'm all too familiar with the pain that comes from losing a mother. Cade and Pippa have to be absolutely devastated. The pit in my stomach sours with a feeling of regret. I should've come back home more after I left for college. Linda had asked me to come home around every holiday and every birthday. She was always encouraging me to come back to the Jennings Family's Ranch and see them. I always found some excuse to avoid going back to the place that held so many happy—and so many terrible—memories.

The truth is, I never really intended to return home. Not really. At least not until my broken heart had mended. I'd loved Cade for so long, and when I finally came to the catastrophic realization that he'd never loved me in the way I wanted him to, I was gutted.

The sight of my dented black suitcase looping around the luggage carousel brings me back to the present. A few unlady-like grunting noises leave my body as I try to heave the suitcase off the lip of the conveyor belt. With a few more tugs, the suit-case falls to the ground with a loud *thump*. Taking a deep breath, I push the blonde curls out of my face and grab the handles of both my bags.

Pippa had only asked me to stay until after the funeral, but I knew my best friend would need me longer than that. It's the reason I told Rudy, my agent, that I'll be finishing up the book in Sutten. It isn't ideal, and he didn't seem thrilled about the sudden change of plans, but there isn't much I can do. We both know how behind I am on this book. I had so many people supporting me when I wrote my debut novel—the first book in this duet—and I don't want to let the people who took a chance on me down with the conclusion to this couple's love story.

Before leaving baggage claim, I text Pippa that I'm heading out and slide my phone back in my pocket so I can have use of both my hands. My phone vibrates in my back pocket as I wheel my suitcases toward the exit. I'm guessing it's Pippa texting me back, but I don't have a free hand to check it. If she's texting me that she's here, I'll find out soon enough when I see her truck outside.

The sun coming up over the mountains is blinding, and I have to squint to search for Pippa. I frown, not seeing her anywhere. I'm seconds away from pulling my phone out when I hear a familiar voice.

"Goldie." My stomach plummets from the way the nickname sounds coming out of *his* mouth. The two syllables coming from his lips still make my stomach twist, even years later. It used to be in anticipation. Only now it's in distress. Maybe it has something to do with the menacing way he pronounces the name he's called me for as long as I can remember.

I stare at my feet, afraid to look him in the eye. I knew I'd have to come face to face with Cade again. It's just that…I thought I'd have time to prepare myself. I thought I had the two hours it took from the airport to the ranch to get my shit together and to goad Pippa for information on how Cade is doing—on what I could expect from him.

A pair of cowboy boots come into view. I don't have to look up to know who they belong to. Just like Cade always felt me when I'd shown up at his bedroom door late at night, I can feel him. In any room, any place, I can feel him. Just like right now.

Taking a deep breath, I look up and into the eyes of the boy who broke my heart. Except, it's no longer a boy that looks back at me. It's a man, and he looks better than I could've ever imagined.

Links

SPOTIFY PLAYLIST:
https://geni.us/COFplaylist

PINTEREST BOARD:
https://geni.us/COFpinterest

Made in the USA
Middletown, DE
20 October 2024